# Inseperable

# Inseperable

## Unbreakable Love Series Vol. 2

The love series continues from Vol. 1

Lance J. Kendrick

**To order additional copies of this book, contact:**
Xlibris
1-888-795-4274
www.Xlibris.com
Orders@Xlibris.com
780734

# DEDICATION

This work is dedicated to my Lord and Savior who gives me the strength and inspiration to use the gift he has planted deep within my soul. I want to thank those friends that stood side by side with me listening to my ramblings on and on. Thank you for your support and words of encouragement. If I start naming names it would take another page.

Peace, Blessing and Love. Be well.

# Chapter 109

Shawn was standing at the door with Chameleon when this big, huge guy looked at them. Shawn looked at him and said, "Have a VIP for Cook." The bouncer looked at Shawn for a few seconds.

Chameleon mumbled, "Again with the eyes. Yo, what is up with this Dracula thing?"

Shawn ignored Chameleon, still looking at the huge bouncer in front of him. Shawn smiled; the man with muscles on top of muscles said, "You see something humorous, pretty boy?"

Chameleon quickly looked around and responded, "Wow, a big word, wasted a lot of brain cells on that one. Be careful, don't want you to veg out right here."

The giant responded to Chameleon, "What!"

Chameleon took a step toward the giant. Shawn casually smiled and held out his arm, preventing Chameleon from proceeding toward the giant. The giant looked at Chameleon and smiled with a smirk on his face. Shawn said, "Sir, can you please check VIP Cook . . . please." The man eyed Chameleon. "You need to check your friend."

Chameleon sarcastically responded, "Wow, how original."

The bouncer responded, "What!"

Shawn said, "Sir, he didn't mean anything by it. He has a condition, sir. We are on a time scheduled."

The giant bouncer was looking when he allowed three guys in. Chameleon decided not to say another word. He heard the three guys talking; one of them said, "Yo, that bitch went inside here."

Chameleon wanted to say something but didn't. The bouncer handed Shawn a phone; he said, "Dial this number." Shawn nodded; he dialed the number.

The phone rang a few times before it was picked up. "What took you so long, Mr. Cook?"

Shawn responded, "Traffic."

The stranger responded, "Hmmm, really? Anyway, I hope you're not late. There are three men that will be in the place—"

Shawn interrupted him, saying, "Three men at a club—are you serious?"

The stranger said, "As serious as you wanting Serenity back. Now how serious is that?" The stranger gave that sick little laugh.

Shawn sneered and blew out a harsh breath. He listened and hung up. He handed the phone back to the bouncer. Shawn shook his head. "I don't understand." Chameleon asked what was going on. Shawn replied, "This is going to be like looking for a needle in a haystack."

Chameleon replied, "Come on, fill me in. What the hell was that about?"

Shawn looked at him and said in frustration, "How are we supposed to find three dudes in a place like this looking for a woman about 5'7" with caramel complexion? She may be wearing shades, or she may not be, coupled with the possibility of being high. What the hell? How can we first of all find three guys and also a mysterious freakin' woman?"

Chameleon sarcastically chuckled and said, "Yo, that dude we're dealing with is one sick dude, man."

The bouncer intruded on their conversation. "You punks are going in or staying out? Come on, bitches, make up your minds. If you're not going in, move the hell over so that folks could get in. Let's go." Shawn and Chameleon turned around to see what the big deal was in regard to this huge crowd this mammoth jerk was talking about.

Chameleon looked back at the bouncer and said, "There is no one behind us. What crowd?"

The bouncer waved his hand for them to move to the side. "You heard what I said. Move your asses over or move in. Keep the line flowing, bitches."

Chameleon wanted to confront the jerk. Shawn once again held him back and said, "In time. I really need you to stay focus."

Chameleon said in frustration, grinding his teeth, "I am. I'm so focused on kicking this big jerk's ass." Shawn looked at him, Chameleon raised his hands in a surrender gesture. "Okay, okay, I'm freakin' good. Go ahead. What were you saying?"

Shawn shook his head. "This is crazy. The only clue this nutjob told me that one of the three men would say something like, 'There goes or something about that bitch is . . .'"

Chameleon looked at him. "Hold up, Wall Street. Shit, about a few minutes ago, three dudes walked in. And one said something about he thought that bitch went in here . . . something like—"

Shawn cut him off. "Are you sure? Are you sure you heard that?"

Chameleon kissed his hand and held it up, looking at Shawn. "Yo, why would I make up something like—"

Shawn was excited and asked, "Do you remember what they looked like? Can you point them out if you saw them again?"

Chameleon nodded his head. "Hell yeah, even in the dark . . . yeah, three punks."

Shawn responded, "Come on, we need to get in there."

They walked toward the entrance.

"Hold up." That was the bouncer; he continued, "Let the others go first. You guys had your turn. Back up."

Shawn was anxious; he looked around as he raised his voice. "What people? Come on, dude, we need to get in there. I'm asking you kindly with respect, please."

The bouncer laughed. "I love this job. Ask me 'please' again, and I'll think about it, asswipes."

Chameleon blew out a harsh breath, turned, took a few steps away from the bouncer, and came back. Shawn had about enough; he was ready to release his beast from the east. He gave Chameleon a nod. Chameleon walked up to the bouncer, who stood at least three inches taller and weighed at least twenty to twenty-five pounds more. Chameleon, at this point, didn't care. Shawn knew size only played a part when you knew how to use it; this guy was all size and no skills whatsoever, he could tell.

Chameleon stood in front of him, looked slightly up in his face, and said, "Look, we've been overly nice. We've put up with your bullying and bullshit. Enough, Frankenstein."

The bouncer said, "What?" Then he moved toward Chameleon; he telegraphed a reach to grab Chameleon, who knocked it away. The big guy went to grab him again and this time was met with a barrage of blows that started at the midsection and worked its way up to the man's face. The big guy was too slow to block any of the blows, but he stood his ground to the point Chameleon was amazed and surprised. Chameleon was ready to work the barrage of blows back down when Shawn walked up to the bouncer and gave him a quick thrust to his throat. The bouncer grabbed his throat. Shawn grabbed the bouncer by his shoulders, pulled him down to him, and drove a vicious knee into the big guy's stomach. He made an awful sound of pain as he dropped to his knees. Shawn lifted high his right leg in the air and held it with his hand as he put all his force into a power heel kick to the shoulder. The blow caused a loud cracking and snapping sound like wood breaking. Shawn knew he just dislocated the man's shoulder. The bouncer fell like a tree in the forest; he was done.

Shawn looked at Chameleon. "Now stop playing games and let's go."

Chameleon looked perplexed. "I wasn't play . . . Forget it."

As Then they both quickly hurried into the club. The few people there applauded Shawn's skills.

# CHAPTER 110

Shawn looked around; he looked at Chameleon. Chameleon looked around and said, "Damn, I can't see anything."

Shawn, looking disgusted, said, "I thought you said you could pick these guys out in the dark."

Chameleon sucked his teeth and said, "That was just a phrase, that's all. Don't take it . . ." Chameleon stopped. "Right there, Shawn. That's them."

Shawn followed Chameleon's eyes; he saw them at the bar, but he had only one question. Chameleon asked, "Where's the girl? I don't see the girl."

Shawn responded, "The sunglasses is a red flag, a dead giveaway. Look around. How many women are wearing sunglasses in this place?" Chameleon did not respond. Shawn interjected, "Exactly."

# Chapter 111

The music was booming; the bass of the music was like a heart defibrillator and heart stopper. Chameleon shook his head. Shawn tapped Chameleon on the shoulder and pointed to the back door. Chameleon looked. Shawn said, "That's her. That has to be her."

Chameleon made a face. "Why?"

Shawn got closer to Chameleon's ear. "Instinct, my instinct never failed me. That's the one. Two, she just had on sunglasses and just took them off. The stranger said she may have them on or off. She just had them on, and then she took them off. And now look, she has them back on."

Chameleon responded, "Yo, she's freakin' high."

Shawn looked at him. "How do you know?"

Chameleon said, "You have your instincts. I have my experience."

Shawn nodded his head. "Fair enough."

Chameleon said, "Damn, she's gorgeous, oh my G."

Shawn looked at him. "You need to focus."

Chameleon, smiling, responded, "I am, I am."

Shawn added, "On the right thing."

Chameleon nodded and, still smiling, said, "I thought I was, but cool, fair enough." Shawn nudged Chameleon; he turned, annoyed. "Wh—"

Shawn said, "Look, the Three Stooges are making their move."

Chameleon took a determined step in their direction. Shawn lightly grabbed his arm and, with a slight smile, said, "Appreciate the tiger intensity. Just relax . . ."

Chameleon protested, "But . . ." He still made a light move in that direction. Shawn placed a tighter grip on Chameleon's arm. Chameleon looked at the grip as if he wanted to curse Shawn out.

Shawn ignored Chameleon's response and was looking around, pretending as if everything was cool; he emphasized, "Just be cool. Just relax. If you make a move, we can blow this whole thing. Let them make a move first. Don't stir up the hornet's nest or frighten the bees."

Shawn and Chameleon watched the three walked right past the girl and headed toward the restroom. Shawn was baffled; maybe that wasn't the girl. He didn't want to second-guess himself. Chameleon added, "Maybe that's not the chick." Shawn looked at him. Chameleon corrected himself, "I meant to say 'woman,' the young woman."

Shawn, looking with intensity, said, "That's her. She fits the description, coupled with the fact you heard what they said, right?" Shawn was talking but looking in the direction the three guys went. "No, I'm absolutely sure it's her."

Shawn was still looking at the three young men as they turned the corner; he didn't hear Chameleon say, "One way to find out." Chameleon took off in the direction the three guys went.

He said to Chameleon, "Excuse me. What was that you—" Shawn quickly looked around and then saw Chameleon going in the same direction as the three guys. Shawn called him, but Chameleon couldn't hear either because of the loud music or because he was simply ignoring him.

# CHAPTER 112

Shawn took off after Chameleon. Chameleon said hi to the young lady with his best smile; she smiled back. He put up one finger and pointed to the bathroom; he mouthed that he would be right back. He gave her his best smile; she smiled and nodded her head. He took off.

Shawn A few seconds later, Shawn did the same thing; he smiled and pointed to the restroom. He took off, stopped, quickly came back, walked up to her, and whispered over the music, "Don't go anywhere. Let's blow this joint. They still say it like that, right?" She lightly laughed and smiled with a cute blush.

He took off. He trotted and caught up to Chameleon right before he got to the door of the restroom. He reached out and grabbed his arm. "What the hell are you doing?"

Chameleon looked at the grip and lightly shook it off. "I'm going in and have a talk with these guys, that's all. You want to come?" Chameleon was agitated; he said, "Yes, dammit, a talk that's it. Is that a crime?"

Shawn responded, "A talk is not a crime, but that attitude is. I don't like it."

Chameleon looked at him. "Really?"

Shawn pushed further. "Okay, what's wrong?"

Chameleon brushed it off. "I'll be okay." He turned to go in the restroom. Shawn grabbed his arm again. Chameleon blew out a frustrated breath.

Shawn said, "I'm not buying it. Nah, what is going on, man? I'm not going somewhere with you, and you look all bent out of shape, looking like you're ready to rip someone's head off. Now what's the problem?"

Chameleon looked at Shawn with a look of frustration and said, "I need to feed."

Shawn looked confused; he thought the man was hungry. "Okay, we'll get something to eat as soon . . ." Shawn stopped, and it hit him. *Damn, the man needs to score. He needs to get his hit.* Shawn nodded with a little nervousness. "Gotcha, okay. Hey, I got this. I can handle this. Why don't you sit this one . . ."

Chameleon gave Shawn a hard look and said, "I don't need your empathy, pity, understanding, or sympathy. I'll be fine. Let me work my way through this." There was slight pause as he continued, "Sorry about that. Let's do this, and I'll take care of that monkey that is kicking my ass when this is over."

Shawn still felt very uncomfortable. *I don't know the state Chameleon is in, what damage—temporary or permanent—he can do.* Shawn knew he had to keep an eye on him, or things could get real ugly. He said, "Okay, a plan—we need a plan."

Chameleon still seemed a bit agitated and responded, "I have one. Let's go."

Shawn shook his head with his hand out, preventing Chameleon from going in; he said, "Nah, you have a plan. What is it? I want to hear it."

Chameleon looked tense and said, "You don't trust me."

Shawn looked at him and said, "I trust you. I don't trust that monkey on your back."

Chameleon gave a satisfied look; he paused for a brief second and said, "The plan is very simple. We go in, and we . . . start kicking ass and asking questions later."

Shawn shook his head and said, "That's really ass-backwards. That monkey is really talking to you, huh?" He continued, "To give you a proper response, that's a negative. No, we go in as—"

Chameleon interrupted. "Vice squad, 'Against the wall, motherfu—'"

Shawn responded, "No, as NYPD. Yeah, that's it."

Chameleon slightly smiled and nodded his head. "Hmmm, sounds like a plan, but without the 'Against the wall, motherfu . . .'" Shawn looked at him before Chameleon can get the other word out. "Okay, cool, not a problem."

# CHAPTER 113

Shawn led the way. Chameleon placed a cleaning sign in front of the restroom. Shawn kicked the door open and announced, "NYPD!"

At the same time, Chameleon announced, "Vice squad . . . from NYPD. Against the wall!" Chameleon looked at Shawn and slightly smiled.

Shawn, looking serious, looked back at Chameleon and gave a quick nod and wink.

# CHAPTER 114

All three young men were against the wall. Chameleon spoke. "We've been tracking you guys for a while. You finally got caught." The young men were nervous. One of them was so nervous that he stuttered, saying, "T-targeting us, w-what did we do?"

Shawn looked at his watch; he had to speed up this process. He appeared frustrated. "Shut up! Don't say another word, ringleader."

The young man with the baby face looked at his friends with tears in his eyes. "Whoa! Ringleader? I'm no ringleader. I'm just a student."

Chameleon, who had a slight tremor in his hands, said, "Yeah, I bet . . ." He said to Shawn, who was very much concerned with what was going on with Chameleon, "We should call it in, let them all be taken to Central Booking. Have you guys ever been there?"

They all said together, "No."

The young man who looked like a football player from a professional team cried, "Yo, my mom's going to beat the black off me, and then my father is going to kick my ass man-to-man style. Ahh, man . . . Where's Teddy? He's never around."

The young man with the baby face was very upset and said, "I know, punk-ass bitch."

Chameleon stopped what he was doing and asked, "Who is this dude you're talking about . . . another one of your thug friends?"

The young man started crying. "Sir, we are not thugs." He looked at Shawn and said, "Please, mister—I mean, Officer. We're not thugs, straight up for real. We are honor roll students."

Shawn said, "Who were you referring to as bitch?"

The baby-faced young man was ready to respond when Chameleon stopped him. "Shut your face! I want this one to speak. Yeah, you." The young man's mouth was trembling.

Shawn felt something wasn't right; something was wrong. He could feel it. The young man was having difficulty getting the words out of his mouth. Shawn thought to himself, *What kind of thug is this?* Shawn said, "Who is the young lady you passed? Isn't she the target?"

The baby-faced young man's voice cracked. "What lady . . . what target, mister—I mean, Officer? Oh god, please, we are students, that's all."

Chameleon, frustrated, took out his cell. "Don't you lie to me. You understand, punk?"

They all said together, "Yes."

One of them said, "We are telling you the truth."

Shawn looked at them, shook his head, and said to Chameleon, "Yo, partner, go ahead. Make that call down to headquarters. Lying bastards."

They all yelled, protesting, "What! Ah, come on, please! We are telling you the truth, please!"

Shawn instructed them to take out their identifications. "Do it now." , without a moment of hesitation, dug into their pockets and pulled out billfolds and wallets. Shawn said, "Put them on the sinks now. Move it! We're not playing games. Now let's see what's going on here." He was studying the IDs.

Chameleon responded, "Who's the woman that you walked past, huh? She's the target, right?"

They all three looked at one another, confused.

Shaking, Chameleon was becoming worse. He saw his hands shaking; he had no control over it. He was trying to hide it; he was becoming angry. This was becoming a problem; he said with anger, "Don't bullshit me, punks! It was you three guys that walked into the club, and you!" Chameleon pointed to the big football player–looking one and said, "I heard you say something about that bitch being in here."

The big guy, who looked like a giant, was nothing more than a teddy bear; he said, "Yes, sir, I did. I was referring to our friend. He was supposed to wait for us, and the four of us was supposed to go in together and . . ."

Shawn stopped looking at their IDs; he asked, "Excuse me. What did you say?"

The big guy said, "The four of us was supposed to go in together to check out the—"

Chameleon looked at him. "What!"

Shawn continued with a slight panic in his voice. "These are not the guys . . . Shit, these are not . . ."

Chameleon looked at him, bewildered. "What . . . what the hell are you talking about?"

Shawn pulled Chameleon over to the side. "These are not the guys. For one, there are four. We're looking for only three. Second, these guys—every single one of them . . ." Shawn turned toward them, gave them a hard look, and turned back to Chameleon, saying, "Is underage."

Chameleon asked with surprised, "Are you serious? How much underage are you talking about?"

Shawn gave them another hard look as he glared at them. "Junior and senior high school age. They're young punks asking for trouble . . . Damn." Shawn rubbed his hand down his face. Chameleon looked at the wall and slammed his hand against it. Shawn looked at the young boys and said, "I catch you guys in here again, we will be taking a ride down to Central Booking. And if you think staying in a cell with twenty to twenty-five men until your case is called okay, do it."

The one with the baby face said, "Okay, okay, Officer, we won't do it again. We promise. Thank you, Officer." The others joined in showing their gratitude.

Shawn cut off their gratitude and told them to get out and go home as he swung at their heads, purposely getting close to hitting them but missing. They couldn't get out quick enough. Chameleon said, "Yo, Wall Street . . . sorry, man, I really thought we had a breakthrough, man."

Shawn waved him off; he stopped and thought out loud, "Hold up. If these cats weren't the ones . . ." Shawn thought some more and came to the gripping realization. "Oh shit . . ."

# CHAPTER 115

Chameleon was right with Shawn as the two quickly stormed out of the restroom. They quickly went down the corridor to the main area. Shawn stopped; he looked in the area where the woman was last seen. She wasn't there; she was gone. He quickly scanned the dance floor; she wasn't there. He was losing hope fast. He scanned the floor again. *Damn, nothing.* He looked at the exits—nothing. She was gone. He looked at the exit all the way on the other side . . . Nothing. *Wait!* He looked again; he saw a female. He couldn't make out her appearance; too many people were mingling and moving and dancing. Plus it was too dark to see. But there were three other people with her, and from their movements, they looked like guys. He couldn't say for certain, but it felt right. His instincts kicked in. It felt better when he noticed the way they were walking; it wasn't a "buddy to buddy, hanging out and having a great time" walk. There seemed to be some resistance; his instincts told him to go. He looked around quickly one more time to build his case, but he had nothing else to fall back on.

This was it; he knew he was putting all or nothing. Right now, he decided to put it all; he tapped Chameleon and pointed across the overcrowded dance floor. Chameleon looked surprised. "You think so?"

Shawn tapped his midsection and said, "Yeah."

The two took off across the dance floor as they threaded and skirted the way between and around the crowd. They didn't want to go back to the exit and then go around and try to cut them off. They wanted to see if the theory of A-to-B straight line stuff really worked. The crowd was like sardines; they made the phrase "standing room only" look like a joke.

Shawn was trying to see if he could still see them, but there were too many people; and since he fit the average height of the people on the floor, he couldn't see over their heads. In addition, the floor had very little light that it was almost like walking in the dark. They both turned and twisted, bumped and pushed, skirted this way and that way as they weaved, threaded, and dodged their way through the crowd. The music was extremely loud as they continued to step on toes and bump into elbows; it was unavoidable. Shove matches started happening on different parts of the floor; as long as it didn't turn into a Chris Brown brawl, everything was cool.

They finally made it to the other side of the club. The young woman with the three young men was gone. They couldn't have gotten too far; the door was still closing, which meant they had just walked out of the door.

# Chapter 116

Chameleon hurried to the door. Shawn pushed it open with such force that it caused the doorknob to slam into the brick wall. He looked around and cursed under his breath. They both heard some noise, a scuffle coming from the alleyway. Shawn reached into his pocket and pulled out some brass knuckles; he slipped them on both hands. Chameleon asked where his was. Shawn responded, "You already have." Chameleon smiled.

They got to the alley and saw two of the men holding the woman down on either side. Chameleon said, "Wow, time to put the dogs back in their cages." Shawn agreed. These punks were going to take turns with her—the gravy train, he called it. He thought, *Not on my watch.*

The man who had so-called first dibs was loosening his pants; he said, "Baby, I'm going to give you what I call the snake." He turned from her and said, "Let me put this happy hat on because who knows what your stink ass has." He slipped it on and said to his friends, "I should have gotten the King Kong size because King Kong has nothing on me." They all laughed. He continued, "Now let's see what this ho got."

The young lady was kicking, screaming, and pleading, trying to get free; it was useless. She was overpowered. The man walked up to her and kneeled; he looked at his partners. "Come on, spread those wings so I can do a crash landing." He laughed; they laughed.

His partners were encouraging him. "Do it, M."

The one they called M came closer; he fondled her and went to put it in when he felt a searing pain in his back. He howled, cursed in pain, and rolled off to the ground in tremendous pain. The other two looked on in confusion. One of them said, "What the hell?" They looked at Melvin and saw he had something protruding from his back.

One of them said in his country twang tone, "Hey, isn't that one of 'em Teenage Ninja Mutant Turtles thing?"

They let the girl go and went to attend to their friend Melvin. Melvin was still in pain, yelling and howling. One of friends went to pull the ninja star out. Melvin's eyes shot open as he screamed, "Don't take it out! Don't take it out! Ahh, damn, do not take it out!"

As he cried in pain, one of them said to the woman, "This is your fault, bitch."

The two men saw a figure walking toward them, saying, "Hey, where I'm from, no means no in any language, children."

One of the guys tapped the other on the shoulder. "Children?" He stood up. "Well, where I'm from, punk, butting your nose in grown folks' business deserves an ass whipping or worse."

Chameleon stepped into the light. "Well, I guess this eliminates you guys because I don't see grown folks. I see two little bad boys that need a spanking."

The other partner stood up. They stood the woman up, and he flung her to the side, where she fell and scraped her legs. One of them laughed, and the other one said, "Now we are gonna have to beat your ass like a child."

Chameleon looked around. "Really?" He walked toward them.

Shawn was looking ready to jump in if he needed to, but he figured Chameleon had a score to settle, especially with that monkey on his back. He'd let him take care of his business. The two guys stood in front of him, and then one began to move around him. Chameleon stood his ground. Shawn was impressed; he said to himself, *Good, stay calm. Show no fear.* Fear could make two against one seem like ten against one. Showing no fear keeps the playing field even, and with Chameleon's skills, he might have a slight edge.

They approached him. Chameleon could see that they were edgy; that was good, he thought. Chameleon turned to the side where he could see both of them from the corners of his eyes. They came charging together. Chameleon did a James Brown split as they swung and missed. He came with a hard backhand fist to their nuts; they both grunted and bent forward. Chameleon got up so fast as if somebody pulled him up. He held one of them and delivered a series of hard blows with the palm of his hand to the face and head. The other one was still in recovery on one knee, just to get a hard side kick to the midsection. He made a sound as if the wind was snatched out of him; he managed to stagger back and crashed to the ground. While he was still bent over in pain, Chameleon delivered a relentless series of blows to the man's body. Chameleon stood him up and gave him a hard thrust to the nose with the palm of his hand. Blood splattered everywhere as the man fell to the ground.

Chameleon went over to his partner, the one he kicked in the stomach. He had his hands up in surrender fashion. Chameleon said, "Now what was that you were saying?"

The man shook his head and said, "Nothing. Jay made me say those things." He pointed to Jay and continued, "He did." The man ratted out his partner.

Chameleon nodded his head. "Okay, we're making progress." He turned to Shawn and said, "Loyalty, does anyone have it anymore?"

Shawn made a face that read "Get on with it."

Chameleon said, "Okay, okay, apologize to the woman."

The man pointed his finger at himself. "Who? Me?"

Chameleon responded, "No, the brick wall behind you, idiot."

The other man who was referred to as Jay was still on the ground and in pain; he said, "Don't do it. You hear me, Gary? Don't do it. She's a slut, a whore. She got what she deserved."

Chameleon shook his head, shrugged his shoulders, and said, "Time-out, sidebar, a commercial, whatever." He pointed to the man. "Don't go anywhere." Chameleon walked over to the man called Jay, who was still on the ground and in pain, and said to him, "I had about enough of you, Jay. Get up."

The man cried out in pain. "My nose, you broke my nose, you son of a bitch! Have a heart."

Chameleon grabbed Jay by his shirt collar and yanked him up. "So many contradictions in that one sentence you just said, Jay. Have a what? You must be preaching to the air, my man." Chameleon paused and continued, "You really haven't learned a valuable lesson of learning to swallow your pride because you are still talking crap. I mean you called her a slut, a whore, and I'm an SOB. I mean I could blame it on the alcohol that reeks all over you, or I could just blame it on the fact that you are one hardheaded dumb ass." He tightened up on Jay's shirt and said, "You should have kept your trap shut, Jay. Now look at you, a bloody mess. You said she deserved what she got and, you deserve what you're about to get. Someone wants to meet you. No, not the man over there in the shadows. Say hi to Mr. Brick, you prick."

Chameleon took Jay by his arm and swung him hard. The man slammed into the wall, fell backward, and collapsed. Chameleon looked at him and said, "First name is Wall. Last name is Brick."

Chameleon turned and looked at the man Jay called Gary. As he was walking closer, Gary cried out to the woman so fast, "I'm so, so, so sorry, miss. I'm truly am so sorry. Please accept my apology, ma'am, please." Gary looked at Chameleon. "Oh god, please."

Chameleon looked at the woman for approval of the apology; she nervously nodded her head quickly. Chameleon smiled and took a bow. "At your service, ma'am."

Shawn came out of the shadows, shaking his head. "You're done, kid."

Chameleon smiled at her; she smiled back, then looked down, blushing. She looked back up at Chameleon and said, "Thank you."

Chameleon, with a Shakespearean voice, responded, "I would do it a million times over, milady."

Shawn stopped her. "You have the phone?"

She looked confused. Shawn sounded desperate. "Listen to me. Did someone give you a phone, huh?"

Shawn backed off slightly and took a careful step toward her. "I'm sorry to raise my voice."

She nervously shook her head. "No."

Shawn instructed Chameleon to check the man they called Jay, the one with the broken nose. "I'll check this one." Shawn looked at Gary. "You have the phone?"

Gary shook his head. "No no no, he has it."

Shawn looked at Chameleon, who walked over to Melvin, the one with the ninja star in his back. Chameleon held out his hand; the man was still in pain as he was trying to rub his back. He dug into his pocket for the phone. He handed the phone to Chameleon, who tossed the phone to Shawn. Chameleon looked back at Melvin and said, "So you had it all this time, and you knew we were looking for it."

The man tried to rub his back where the star was still embedded in his skin. "Yo, my back."

Chameleon asked, "Who gave you the phone?"

The man was caught off guard with the question. He was still in agonizing pain as he responded, "Huh?" Chameleon twisted the star slightly in the man's back. The man howled in agony. "Oh, man, damn! What is wrong with you?"

Chameleon responded, "Come on, I'm not playing games. You better talk because the next time isn't going to be pleasant. Talk."

The man had tears in his eyes from the excruciating pain; every slight movement caused the star to move in his back. Melvin said, "I can't tell you. They will kill me."

Chameleon responded, "If you don't talk, I'll get to you before they will. I will destroy your life . . . Talk."

Shawn was on the phone talking with the commissioner when he overheard Melvin tell Chameleon something that rocked him to the core.

# CHAPTER 117

Shawn's world almost came apart; he hung up on the commissioner without saying bye. He took a few determined steps toward Melvin and, without warning, grabbed him by the collar and swooped him up as if he were a weightless puppet. The man howled in pain from the jolt; he cried out, "Damn, oh sh—"

Shawn cut him off. "What did you just say?"

The man looked at Shawn as if he could bargain his way through this. Shawn didn't have the time as he drove the man's body hard against the concrete wall. The man made a sound. Shawn said, "Let me tell you this. This is my apprentice, my student. I'm his teacher, so if you think the student was bad, wait until you meet the teacher. That's me, punk. If you think he's bad, I'll be your worst nightmare." He continued, "So I'm going to ask you once. What did you say?"

The man was in excruciating pain; he said, "A man gave me the phone . . ."

Shawn pushed him hard against the wall, causing his head to slam up against the wall. The man went to grab his head. Shawn punched him hard in the stomach. Melvin grunted and doubled over. Shawn said, "Be slick and coy if you want, and I will end you right now, punk. NOW GIVE IT TO ME!"

Melvin had a look of panic on his face; he stuttered, saying, "The man's name, I think, is Evans. He gave me the phone and the instructions—"

Shawn interrupted him. "What did he look like?"

The man was in such pain that he shook his head with a look of agony on his face. Shawn pressed the star in his back further; the man yelled in pain, cursing. Shawn said, "I'll do it again. I'll go deeper next time until I get what I want."

Melvin pleaded and begged for Shawn to stop. "Please . . . Okay, okay. He was short with a strong upper-body build."

Shawn looked at the man. "Are you sure?"

Melvin nodded his head profusely. Shawn thought to himself that something was wrong; this was not the same description he received before. He looked perplexed. Chameleon looked at him; they heard sirens coming in their direction. Through all of this stuff, Shawn had forgotten to call the stranger. Chameleon heard the sirens get closer. "Yo, Wall Street, are we ghosts?"

Shawn shook his head. "Nah, I can't chase after these people while being chased by the police. We'll wait."

Chameleon gave him an astonished look, shrugged his shoulders, and leaned against a garbage can. Shawn called the stranger. The stranger responded, "My my my, you are amazing, Mr. Cook. You took out three dudes. Even though they were the scum of society, I picked them from the bottom of the so-called trash can. So in essence, you did me a favor and a service. We are partners."

Shawn sneered into the phone, "Like hell we are! We are like darkness and light. I guess you know which one I think you are."

The stranger was getting ready to speak when Shawn continued; he recoiled and blasted the stranger. "This wasn't a favor to you! You are no better than they are, just a step higher on the scumbag pole."

The stranger's anger came out forceful. "You will show me and give me more respect, Mr. Cook. Let me remind you, you are putting the beautiful Serenity in dangerous peril. And whatever happens to her would not be my fault, but yours."

Shawn responded, "The only thing I'm going to give you is your choice of a quick death or a long and agonizing one. That is the only choice you will have." The stranger laughed; his laugh continued. Shawn responded, "You think this is funny, huh?"

The stranger replied, "No, sir, not at all. As a matter of fact, it is so tragic, Mr. Cook. You can't help but to laugh at the irony."

Shawn looked confused. "You need help."

The stranger replied, "No, sir, you do. You let a life slip away from you, Mr. Cook. Tsk tsk tsk . . ."

Shawn was confused; he didn't know what the stranger was referring to. He said in frustration, "What the hell are you babbling about? What do you mean?"

The stranger responded, "Mr. Cook, you are running late, my friend-enemy. I told you when you have accomplished a task, sir, to call me. You are . . . let's see, twenty, twenty-five minutes late, sir." The stranger continued, "That word 'friend-enemy,' a funny word young folks came up with, isn't it? Such creative minds wasted, don't you think, sir?"

Shawn didn't have time for small talk as if he and this diabolical nemesis were in a philosophy class. Shawn said, "I don't have time to deal with this. Get to the point. What are you talking about? What life?"

The stranger said, "I don't know what took you so long, sir. I mean you saved one. But there were two, Mr. Cook, two poor, worthless souls. These are the rejects of society, Mr. Cook. They are worthless scum. They are like roaches. Why do they exist? What purpose do they have just to be smashed?" The stranger took a second to inhale and continued, "These folks are like roaches. I try not to question the Creator. But their purpose is senseless, useless, and I'm tired of spending my hard-earned taxes on them."

Shawn was fed up as he blew out a harsh breath and said, "Would you get to the damn point, you sick mother—"

The stranger cut him off. "Temper, temper, Mr. Cook. Be careful. I already warned you."

Shawn yelled, "What is the damn point?"

The stranger was silent as he continued, "Okay, to the point. There is a woman that is or was, excuse me, associated with the one you saved. But due to the fact you took so long getting back to me, you won't get there in time to stop her from shooting the heroin into her veins. She doesn't know it, but that shot she will take is a potent amount she thinks she can handle. But she will find out rather, hmmm, quickly she can't. Her heart will collapse or rather burst in her chest. But if you are able to get to her, Mr. Cook, you will be her hero. And you will save her."

Shawn cursed under his breath. "How much time do I have?"

The stranger said, "I don't think—"

Shawn raised his voice, saying, "How much time, dammit!"

The stranger chuckled. "It was ten minutes. But due to your mouth, you now have eight minutes to get back to the east side, Second Avenue in Thirty-Fourth Street. There is a park where these losers—"

Shawn cut him off. "I know where that is." He smiled; he said to himself, "That should be easy."

The stranger said, "True, but things don't always appear as they are, Mr. Cook. If you get to the east side and save this woman, you have saved a life. And you will be rewarded, which is to let this worthless piece of trash die another day. Or if you fail to reach her, she will die, and poor Serenity will have another strike against her. I believe the rules of baseball are three strikes, you're out. Well, the same thing applies here, Mr. Cook. You have eight minutes . . . Go . . ." The stranger continued, "Oh, I forgot to tell you, Mr. Cook. To get to where you are going will not be by car, sir."

Shawn responded, "How the hell would I get there?"

The stranger said, "In the corner, there are two bikes. You will be using the black bike, which is behind the blue bike, sir."

Shawn quickly ran over to the bikes and looked at them; the blue one was a professional bike, and the black one was old and looked as if it was going to fall apart. Shawn said, "What is this, some kind of joke? This thing can't make it across town."

The stranger said, "Like I said, things may not appear as they are, sir. Manage it somehow, Mr. Cook." The stranger added, "You better hurry. Time is running out and that bike." The stranger laughed and said, "Hurry, Mr. Cook."

The phone disconnected. Commissioner Moore and his men arrived. Shawn was walking past him. Moore held out his hand. "Hold up, Cook, one minute. What the hell is going on? We arrived. The bouncer has a broken leg, a dislocated hip, a broken collarbone. I come back here, and I find more destruction. Like I said, just follow the destruction path, and we'll somehow find you."

Shawn looked at him and said, "Listen, I'll explain later."

Moore shook his head and said, "Cook, what the hell is going on?"

Shawn replied, "I promise to explain later. You have my word. Right now, I need police escort to Third Avenue in Thirty-Fourth Street." Shawn looked at Chameleon. "Take Gordon."

Chameleon was excited. "Wall Street, are you serious?"

Shawn hopped on the bike. He looked at Chameleon. "Straight to the place, you understand?"

Chameleon nodded his head, smiling. "No problem."

Shawn sat on the bike, getting ready to go. He looked at Chameleon and said, "Straight to the place." Chameleon smiled.

Moore went up to Shawn and said, "Where are you going, Cook?"

Shawn shook his head. "I have to get there by this bike. This nut job gave me no other choice."

Moore looked at the bike and at Shawn and said, "What! On that thing? That thing can collapse on you while you're riding it. What type of shit is that?"

# CHAPTER 118

Shawn had two squad cars in front of him; their sirens were blaring. He had clicked the gears to 18. The gears were making all kinds of sounds, trying to switch. Shawn thought the bike was going to fall apart. An 18 speed will give him a faster and smoother ride. He looked at his watch as he pedaled as fast as he could; the handlebars were shaky. Shawn switched the gears again; he could feel the friction in the pedal as his legs were burning as if they were on fire. He moved his body low to break the force of the wind. His legs were cycling so fast; he was soon at Lexington Avenue.

The escort had everything working like clockwork: horns, lights, the siren blaring. One had to be unable to see, hear, or speak to know that something was wrong. Shawn looked up at all the red lights and how Commissioner Moore and his crew were paving the way for him.

He took a quick look at his watch; he cursed under his breath. "Shit." Time was running out. His legs were starting to cramp on him. "Damn." He smacked his legs. "Wake up, dammit. Not now, not now." He ignored the cramp as he pushed and pedaled as fast as he could go. He realized he had to make a left and go up two blocks. At the last minute, he made a wide left turn; the handlebars were shaking as he followed the escort. He was right behind them when the squad car in front of him had to put on the brakes. There was a loud skid sound as the squad car tried to avoid another car coming in the crosswalk. The squad car swerved right and left and just missed the car.

Shawn was traveling too close; he tried to adjust, but he was going too fast as he put on both the bike's brakes, hitting the car and flying off the bike as he tumbled forward and crashed hard on his back. There was a loud cracking sound of bones as he hit the pavement. His adrenaline was pumping; under normal circumstances, the average person would just lie there, but he jumped up. He was shaken up pretty bad.

On the loudspeaker, Moore asked Shawn if he was okay. Shawn, in pain, waved him off. He looked at the bike; it was done. He hobbled toward the destination, limping. Chameleon ran toward him. "Get in the car."

Shawn, in pain as he continued to hobble, shook his head. "I can't."

Chameleon shook his head. "Yo, this shit is crazy." He continued, "Well, this isn't against the rules." Then he put Shawn's arms around his neck; the commissioner ran on the other side and placed Shawn's arm around his shoulders. The so-called two and a half men ran toward the destination.

Shawn saw the woman; everything seemed to move in slow motion as he saw the syringe still in her arm as her arm fell limp to her side. She started convulsing as she collapsed when they got to her. Shawn immediately started administering CPR; she was already turning blue. Shawn prayed and begged God to save her as he frantically gave chest compressions while Chameleon counted. Chameleon continued to breathe into her mouth as he counted. Shawn would go back and give compressions.

Chameleon stopped as he and the commissioner knew she was gone; they watched Shawn painfully continued to give chest compressions, counting to himself as he stopped and told Chameleon to breathe. "Go, go ahead. Go ahead, go. Dammit, breathe into her mouth. Go, go." Tears came running down his cheeks as he looked desperately at Chameleon. "Why did you stop? Help me . . . help me . . . please." Shawn slumped over her as his shoulders heaved up and down as the cry of agony and exhaustion overtook him.

Chameleon got up as he wiped his eyes; he knew she was dead even before Shawn started the compressions, but he was hoping for a miracle or something. He had watched so many people in that hellhole where he used to fight overdose. He kicked at some rocks as he cursed at himself, thinking, *If it wasn't for the accident with the car, Wall Street probably would have made it.* Chameleon turned his back away from the situation; as he stood there with his hands on his hips, he dropped and shook his head. He looked up and yelled. Was it a painful cry or a war cry? It was hard to tell.

Moore was trying to help Shawn up; he looked over at his officer. "Get me that EMT worker over here now!" Shawn waved him off as he slowly got up from the lifeless body; he could tell she was a beautiful woman at one time. What the hell happened? Who the hell stopped that process?

Shawn raised his hand and said, "Please, I'll be okay."

The commissioner looked at him. "No, you won't. Cook, you are really messed up. You need medical attention. Look at you."

Shawn looked at Moore and shook his head; he was completely exhausted. Commissioner Moore called the EMT worker over and said, "Get this man to the hospital now."

Shawn protested but knew Moore was right; he needed medical attention, but he couldn't take a chance to waste time. He said in defiance, "I can't . . ."

Moore looked at him. "What do you mean you can't? Have you lost your mind while you were falling off that piece of crap they called a bike, huh? No. Even if I have to do it myself, your ass is going to the hospital."

Shawn looked at Moore. "It's complicated."

Moore responded, "Complicated or not, I don't give a rat's ass. You're going, and I'll do whatever it takes to get you there."

The young baby-faced EMT worker came over. Shawn looked at her and said, "Just give me some painkillers, and you have done your service."

The young lady slightly smiled and said, "Sir, I'm not authorized to give you any type of medication unless I know why I'm doing it."

Commissioner Moore nodded his head with a light laugh and said, "Good answer."

Shawn looked at the commissioner and said, "Look, Curt, I appreciate what you are trying to do. But you really don't understand what I'm dealing with . . . what I'm up against. You have no idea."

They all heard a cell phone chime; all three checked their phones. They looked at one another, saying it wasn't theirs. The cell chimed again. Shawn walked toward the direction he thought the chime was coming from. The more he walked, the louder the chime. He was standing over the dead girl's body. He quickly bent down and went through her pockets.

One officer yelled at Shawn, "Hey, what are you doing? That is a crime scene, sir!"

Shawn ignored the officer and kept on looking until he pulled out the phone. Moore looked at the officer and motioned for him to stand down. Shawn opened the phone. "Hello?"

The stranger said, "So you are human, Mr. Cook, and humans have a tendency to fail just like you have." There was a pause; then the stranger continued, "But don't feel too bad about it, Mr. Cook. She was worthless, a roach, a failure, and a loser."

Shawn sneered and said, "Who the hell are you to determine who has worth and who is worthless?" Shawn yelled into the phone, "YOU'RE NOT GOD!"

The stranger made a cocky sound and said, "Really? I warn you, Mr. Cook, you need to speak to me with respect. Now if you insist to continue to take this path and continue to piss me off, then continue to do what you are doing." There was a brief pause as the stranger continued in a calm but firm tone, "As I was saying, Mr. Cook, when a task is assigned to you, sir, from point A to point B, it must—and I can't stress this enough—must be impeccably followed, sir. I will not accept any excuses. I know you wouldn't."

Shawn's anger was at boiling point. "I'm not a monster like you. You sit where you sit, thinking you are some kind of deity. You can kiss my ass. Your day is coming. You are going to have to answer for this."

The stranger shouted back, "And so will you, Mr. Cook! Don't blame me. I gave you more than enough time to get to her, and you didn't! So don't blame me. This is your fault! What happened, Mr. Cook? You had an accident?" The stranger made a slight laugh.

That was it for Shawn; he gritted his teeth. "You son of a bitch. You set me up. You caused what happened to me. You arranged for this accident to happen. You knew I was going to save the girl. You are going to pay—"

The stranger cut Shawn off, saying, "Mr. Cook, you're starting to become paranoid. You're acting as if I had something to do with what happened—as if I'm, as you say, God." The stranger gave this haunting laugh. The laugh died down as the stranger became serious again. "One more task, Mr. Cook."

Shawn was exhausted, but he couldn't show it. "What!"

The stranger made an impressed sound. "Wow, Mr. Cook, your tenacity is amazing! I'm so impressed. Most men would have been broken by now, but you, you have this . . ." The stranger chuckled and continued, "But you, sir, are an amazing specimen, Mr. Cook. But let's see how much you can take. Let's see how much further you can go. Let's see which straw will break your back, sir. In the Bible, the man Job had his limits. Let's see where yours is."

Shawn blew out an air of frustration and irritation as he responded, "Would you get to the damn point?"

The stranger smiled. "Oh yes, you are so right. I get so easily distracted. Thank you, Mr. Cook, for helping me to stay focused. Okay, yes." The stranger cleared his throat. "Here we go, Mr. Cook. You have fifteen minutes to get to your next point of destination, sir. Mr. Cook, I don't know how else how to put this. But if you should fail this opportunity, this opportunity will not come up again, sir. Good luck, or rather, Godspeed. Fifteen minutes go."

Shawn sneered into the phone and said, "What do you mean go? Where the hell am I going?"

The stranger lightly laughed. "Hmmm, yes, that would be so helpful, wouldn't it? Let's see, you're going to the South Bronx, 176 in Jerome Avenue, a place of whores and dopeheads and, of course, the homeless." The stranger could hear Shawn letting out a frustrated breath as he continued, "There is a pay phone. I'm surprised they still have some of those around. Anyway, as I was saying, there is a pay phone there. Get there in time, and you would get your next assignment, sir. If you miss it, Mr. Cook, this will be your second strike."

Shawn countered, "And if I make the call in time, then what, huh?"

The stranger chuckled, very much amused at having people at his beck and call—how they jumped and moved whenever he told them to. He responded to the question, "Then you will put your so-called base runner at second, and two more saves of these society losers, and your precious and gorgeous Serenity will be all yours. Game over. I play fair. Plus if you will win, Mr. Cook, I would have to admit defeat and that destiny was in your favor. But I'm going to do my best to make sure that does not happen."

Shawn sarcastically made an arrogant sound. The stranger ignored him and said, "Okay, Mr. Cook, you need to get going. This is one phone call you don't want to miss."

# CHAPTER 119

Evans sat up on the side of his bed; he looked at the makeshift monitor he had secretly placed in Serenity's room. He wanted to tell her that he was spying on her to see what she was doing; he wanted to catch her doing something wrong, but so far, she had been better than a Girl Scout. He looked at his watch; he just got a call from Mr. X. Deep within, Evans was happy he was able to be open with Serenity, sharing his feelings and emotions; it had been very meaningful. Deep down, he was a little jealous and envious how attentive and very observant she was; her husband, he thought, was a very fortunate man.

He looked at the monitor and watched her; she was so beautiful and gorgeous and so sensitive. His thoughts slowly vanished as reality hit him; he knew he had to do what he had to do. He beat himself thinking; he couldn't wait until this thing was over. This was it for him. This last job made him realize it was time to walk away and not look back. He rationalized what he did; he killed only the bad people. He stopped and thought that made him no better than Mr. X, but this was it, and why not? He had enough money for him and maybe his family to move on—maybe his own island or his own land, acres of acres of his own land hidden somewhere where not even Mr. X could find them.

He looked at the monitor; he had to wake up Sleeping Beauty up. "Beauty" did not describe Serenity Cook. He said into the microphone, "Serenity, time to get up." She was decent. Before walking inside the room, he placed his ears on the door; he didn't hear anything. He lightly knocked on the door; there was no answer. He waited a few seconds. He slowly turned the doorknob and slowly pushed to go in. He stuck his head in first; he called her name again—still no response.

She was out cold. He went in and saw her lying there; she was so gorgeous and stunning. Her hair was flared out like feathers on a beautiful bird; it gave her such an erotic look, a look of rapture and ecstasy. He knew he was teething on the wrong turf; he knew he was about to cross the line. He knew if this continued, he would compromise the mission, which in turn meant he was placing everyone he knew in a serious deadly position that Mr. X would have someone carry out the hit. He looked at her as his manhood became hard; he knew that he was coming closer to the line he thought about. He closed his eyes to focus; he opened them with a new perspective. He called her name with a harsh and frustrated tone. "Serenity, get up! Let's go . . ." He felt like a heel having those feelings for Serenity and now coming down hard on her. He softened his tone and lightly touched her shoulder. "Serenity . . ." Damn, why did he touch her shoulder? He chastised himself.

Serenity stirred as her eyes fluttered; she was still in a sleep state. She slightly smiled. "Hey, baby, good morning. Mmm, do I smell coffee, baby?"

Evans wanted to run out of the room and put some water on for coffee. He smiled at the term of endearment; he didn't know she felt that way about him. He said in a soft tone, "Time to get up."

Serenity was stretching; she said, "Hon, I was dreamin' that we were making love and . . ." Evans was smiling. Serenity continued, "And, Shawn baby, it felt . . ." Her eyes shot open up as she quickly sat up. She covered her mouth. "Oh my god, Evans, I'm so sorry! I . . . please—"

He cut her off and said, "It's time to get up. We have to make a run. C'mon, let's go." Evans turned and was walking toward the door.

Serenity called him. "Evans, Evans, please!"

He took another step and turned to face her. He looked at her with such a serious look; she didn't know what to say as she put her head down. When Serenity raised her head and looked at him, she was biting on her bottom lip; she said in a low and sincere tone, "Evans . . . sorry."

He was looking at her, and then he looked around and back at her; he nodded. He seemed so uncomfortable. He briefly looked away from her, and then his eyes found hers again; he said in sober and serious tone, "Get dressed."

# CHAPTER 120

Shawn looked over at Chameleon and asked, "Are you okay?"

Chameleon shook his head and then nodded it and said, "Wow, does that answer your question?"

Shawn could tell his shotgun partner was weighing his options; he was fighting a relentless evil force, and he couldn't tell who was winning. He felt it was obvious—one good look, and you could tell who was getting their behind kicked. Shawn looked at his watch; he said to Gordon, "G, we need to get to that address I gave you. We need to get there in seven minutes. Can you make it happen?"

Gordon responded, "I will try, sir . . . Uh, according to my traveling guide, there are two main streets that are currently under construction."

Shawn asked, "Are those streets detoured?"

Gordon responded, "Yes, sir. But it wouldn't make much difference, sir. I'll just break the law like I've been doing. I'm sure one more is not going to make much difference."

Shawn just shook his head and said, "A smart-mouthed car."

Chameleon said under his breath, "Yo, I got to get one of these."

Shawn said out loud, thinking to himself, "The detours probably take you around the long way and taking us out of the way." He cursed under his breath. He continued, "Gordon, listen to me. I really need you to—"

Gordon cut him off. "Yes, sir, I am evaluating the street in the event I need to . . ." Gordon pause and continued, "Permission to go down this one-way street the wrong way, sir?"

Shawn looked at the GPS and tried to figure out why Gordon wanted to do that. "Gordon, your GPS does not indicate a street if you go down that way."

Gordon repeated, "I just need permission, sir."

Shawn's time was getting short; he thought for a second and said without hesitation, "Permission granted . . . go."

Gordon's system took over.

Chameleon looked on in amazement and said, "I have to get one of these when I land that *job*, son."

Gordon's system flashed and inquired, "Son? Is Mr. Chameleon your father, sir?"

Shawn shook his head. "No, I'll explain later." Shawn was still wondering what Gordon was doing; perhaps he made a mistake, a miscalculation.

Gordon turned up on alleyway that wasn't even a street, and that was the reason why it didn't show up on the GPS. Shawn smiled. "Wow, ingenious, Gordon! Amazing! You did it."

Gordon replied, "Thank you, sir. Breaking the law is never good, sir. But in some cases to serve the better good, breaking the law can be resourceful."

Gordon came out of the alleyway right on the street they were looking for. Shawn looked at his watch; they had about a minute and a half to go. He told Gordon to park across the street by the phone. Gordon did so.

Shawn and Chameleon got out of the car. Shawn looked at his watch—forty-five seconds. He made it with seconds to spare. He stood in front of the phone, waiting, anticipating for it to ring . . . Nothing. Thirty-five seconds to go. Shawn was becoming concerned; from concerned to anxious, he could feel himself starting to panic. He was by the phone; he was there. He knew it. He looked at his watch. Damn, twenty seconds. Shawn slammed his fist against the phone exterior.

Then they both heard a ring; they looked at each other. Shawn stepped closer to the phone; he heard the ring, but it wasn't coming from this phone. He picked it up. No, it wasn't. He slammed it back in its cradle. Shawn cursed. "Dammit, son of a bi—"

Chameleon tapped Shawn and pointed to the phone across the street. Shawn, frustrated, said, "The bastard purposely wanted me to fail. It'll be my second strike." He quickly checked his watch—fifteen seconds.

Then he and Chameleon took off running in the direction of the cars. Traffic was moving slow. Shawn and Chameleon were running between cars or any space they could find as they slid off the hoods of the cars, dipping and threading themselves between cars. Shawn glanced at his watch. Damn, the countdown. He gave it all he had; he was running on empty as the countdown continued. Ten, nine, eight, seven . . . He ran hard as drivers cursed and got out of their cars, gesturing with their fingers and fists at him and Chameleon. Shawn was almost at the phone. Six, five, four . . .

He was practically at the phone when he saw five or six young people goofing off, getting ready to pick up the phone. He and Chameleon dashed across the street, jumping in front of them. Shawn apologized as he stood there looking at the phone. One of them asked him if he was going to use the phone or not. Shawn nodded and said "Yeah" when the phone rang.

Shawn looked at the young group of kids, three guys and three girls. *How cute*, Shawn thought; they looked to be about anywhere from nineteen to twenty-two years of age. The guys were acting tough, showing off in front of their female friends; this was not the time for Shawn to show them some of his skills. No ass whipping tonight.

Shawn looked at Chameleon, who got the message. He looked at them; at this point, Chameleon looked terrible. He looked like the walking dead, but the look made him appear insane and dangerous, just waiting for the right buttons to be pressed. He looked at them, blinking like crazy and shrugging his shoulders repeatedly. He was asking the same question several times, looking like someone who escaped from a criminal insanity institution.

One of the women told one of the guys to forget it. "Come on, let's go. Forget about it."

Meanwhile, Chameleon was still asking the same question; as he continued to twitch and scratch, he started talking to himself as if he was reading the headlines in the paper. "Three young men killed after what appeared to be a sacrificial ritual. Meanwhile, the three women they were with were severely tortured and raped repeatedly . . ." He gave this scary laugh and continued, "This has been a special report. Now back to Dr. Phil." Chameleon looked at them and smiled. "Dr. Phil, I like him. He tried to help me and told the doctors there was nothing he could do for me. They locked me up and threw away the key. I was a done man. But look at me. I escaped. I can't wait until I find that Dr. Phil. He's dead." He looked at them and grinned.

The girls began to pull their men away, begging them to come. "Bobby, let's go . . . please. We'll find another phone. Come on."

The guys were scared as well, but they couldn't just punk out; after the girls pleaded with them, they knew they earned their respect. They were to fight or die, but deep down, they knew they were going to walk. They all left.

One of them had to tie his sneakers. His fingers were moving so fast; he called out nervously to the group, "Hey, wait up, guys!" He stood up; his legs were slightly shaking.

Chameleon got his attention. "Psst, psst."

The young man turned to Chameleon, who told him, "Hey, punk. You'll thank me later. Better to lie in a bed satisfied than in a grave unfulfilled."

The young man, Jones, asked nervously, "Is that Confucius?"

Chameleon, looking crazy, responded, "No. That's me, the Chameleon." Chameleon gave a haunting grin and laugh. The young man cursed and took off after his friends.

Then Chameleon came over to Shawn, who was on the phone; he had been on hold for a while. He looked at Chameleon and mouthed the words, "Thanks, good acting."

Chameleon did a slight bow and said, "Who said I was acting?" He looked at Shawn and said, "I hope that is good news . . ." He pointed to the phone and said to Shawn, "I'll be back. I must feed the need now."

Shawn shook his head. "Now? In this neighborhood? Yo, be careful! Here." He tossed Chameleon what looked like a big button.

Chameleon looked at it and said, "Yo, what's up? What is this?"

Shawn responded, "It's a tracker, just in case you get in trouble in the hood." He looked around with a wary look and said, "Call me on your cell."

Chameleon made a face; he was getting ready to toss it back to Shawn, who gave him a serious big brother look. Chameleon shrugged his shoulders and put the device in his pocket. Shawn took out what looked like a small pocket radio; he pressed a button and showed the dot on the screen. Shawn smiled. "That's you, that blue dot. Now I can track you. Go."

Chameleon looked at the dot and said, "Wow, my identity has dwindled down to a blue dot, wow." He gave Shawn a thumbs-up; his hands were slightly trembling.

Shawn waved for him to go; under regular circumstances, he would not approve or even endorse drugs, but he had consented to it now because it met the need. He went back to the phone. He had been on hold for a while; this stranger dude liked to play mind games. He wasn't in the mood to talk or listen to the stranger; he knew there was going to be some consequences just for the simple fact the stranger had the upper hand. Shawn gruffly and firmly spoke into the phone. "Hello!"

What he heard on the other end made his knees weak as they buckled; he held on to the phone stand as he was overcome by what he heard.

# Chapter 121

"Hi, baby."

Shawn's eyes became filled with water as he could feel the tear ducts of his heart and soul open up; he couldn't believe it. He had to make sure this wasn't one of the stranger's crazy schemes. "Serenity?"

She repeated those two words, that lovely phrase that captured his heart, soul, and mind so many times. "Hi, baby. It's me, Serenity. I love you." Shawn held the phone so tight as if he was holding Serenity; he wasn't going to let go. He wasn't going to lose her again.

"Oh my god, Lord, thank you. Are you okay, baby? Oh my god, are you all right?" Shawn had not realized he was crying as the tears came down his face like a flood. The pain of hearing her voice hurt as much as the pain of not hearing her voice; the tears continued to flow down his cheeks. He asked, "Thank you, Lord. Are you okay, baby?" He cried.

She cried also as she tried to comfort him and convince him that she was okay. "Baby, baby, my love, please don't cry. I'm okay, sweetie. Really, I am, babe. I love you so much. I miss you, my love."

Shawn tried to control himself; he took a deep breath. "Okay, okay, I'm okay. I'm sorry. This is just unbelievable. This is crazy." He held back the flooding of tears. He continued, "Babe, can you at least tell me where you are? A hint, an idea, a code, a signal."

Serenity looked around. Evans was too close; she couldn't take a chance and think he couldn't hear Shawn. She shook her head. "No, babe, I wish I could. But it's too risky."

Shawn nodded his head. "Okay, okay, I understand. Are you hurt? Were you tortured or beaten?"

Serenity smiled and said no to the questions.

Shawn's cell phone went off; he wasn't going to answer it, but he did. He told Serenity to hold on a second. Serenity looked at Evans, who gave her two minutes to end the conversation. She told Shawn, "Honey, I have to go soon, babe."

Shawn was speaking to Chameleon. Chameleon said, "Listen, I'll be there soon, Wall Street." Shawn thought Chameleon sounded a little better, a bit more relaxed. Chameleon went on, "Yo, Wall Street, how did the phone conversation go?"

Shawn smiled from ear to ear, and even that hurt; he said, "Great, it's Serenity, my wife. She's doing fine. I'm talking to her right now. Hold—"

Chameleon cut him off, saying, "Hey, that's great. Hold up. Seriously, don't hang up. I need a light . . . you know, a match."

Shawn was smiling, still elated that Serenity was still alive and sounding great. He was going to put Chameleon on hold and get back to Serenity; he knew his time was almost up. He could hear Chameleon asking people for a light. He could hear him asking someone for a match. Shawn shook his head. He could hear the person say, "No, sorry, I don't smoke." Shawn heard it, but it sounded as if it was coming through his cell phone and the pay phone as well; he heard Chameleon ask someone else. The person replied, "Nah, man, don't smoke."

Shawn realized that it wasn't coming from his phone or the pay phone . . . Chameleon was standing next to Serenity and her abductor.

# CHAPTER 122

Shawn's heart began to beat hard and fast; he could feel it. It felt as if his heart was coming out of his chest; the heartbeat shook him to his very core. He said in the pay phone, "Serenity, was the man who asked you for a match about 5'10", 5'11", 190 pounds, short crop hair, fair skin in complexion, decent shape?"

Serenity thought she was going to faint. Shawn asked Chameleon a similar question. "Chameleon, the woman you asked for a light, is she biting her bottom lip?"

Chameleon and Serenity looked at each other. Evans looked at both of them and told Serenity to hang up; he knew something was wrong.

Shawn said to Chameleon, "Chameleon, listen to me. Don't say a word. Play it off. Listen to me. The woman you're looking at is Serenity."

Chameleon's cigarette almost fell out of his mouth. "What! Are you serious? Yo, she's fine."

Shawn yelled at him, "Focus and listen to me!"

Shawn heard a man's voice, angry and upset, barking demands. "Serenity, hang up that damn phone now!"

There was a brief scuffle. Shawn heard Serenity yelping more in surprise. He could tell she was caught off guard. Shawn knew things were getting out of control; he asked Chameleon, "Where are you?"

Chameleon cursed under his breath. "Damn, what street is . . . ? In the block of 176th Street, right before you get to . . . shit . . ."

Shawn asked in a panicked tone, "What! What!"

Chameleon saw the man take the phone from the woman and let it drop. He then grabbed her by the arm firmly and led her toward the black car. Chameleon was walking toward them. He was approached by three guys. They stood in front of him. "Yo, C, what up? What's wrong?"

Chameleon motioned with his hands. "Yo, this cat needs to be stopped."

The leader nodded his head; he motioned for his two henchmen to flare out toward him. One of them asked, "How you want it?"

Chameleon responded, "Dirty, but alive."

Evans had just made it to the car; when he went for the handle, an arm grabbed him by the shoulder. "Yo, my man, you have a minute?"

Evans looked at the hand on his shoulder; the other guy had moved in a little closer toward Evans, mainly next to him. The third guy stood on the other side of him. Chameleon watched. Evans looked at Serenity. "Get in the car." She hesitated; he looked at her again. "Get in the damn car." She hesitated and got in.

He turned and looked at the three men that had surrounded him. "Gentlemen, this does not have to come to this."

Chameleon slightly smiled and said, "So true, but it has . . . Evans."

Evans looked at him as if to ask, "Do we know each other?"

Chameleon smiled as if to say that he knew enough about him; instead, he said, "Just give us the girl, and this ordeal would be no big deal."

Evans nodded with a smile and said, "And if I don't?"

Chameleon said, "This is going to get pretty ugly."

As fast a blink, Evans went to his waist and took out something similar to a blade. He drove it hard three times into the shoulder of the man who had his hand on his shoulders; the man howled in pain and fell. At the same time, he gave a straight power kick to the midsection of the man who had moved in front of him; he crashed hard into the car door. The other man on the other side of Evans took a hard haymaker swing at him. Evans stepped back and bent his body slightly back; the punch just missed. The man hit his hand against the roof of the car; he grabbed his hand. Evans came back with a hard-right palm into the man's temple. The man grabbed his head and became disoriented with his balance. Evans grabbed the man by the back of the neck and shoved his face hard into the car; he did this twice and then shoved him hard like a bag of laundry to the side away from the car.

Chameleon delivered a wicked blow to the side of Evans face, weakening Evans. He turned to face Chameleon, who smiled because he knew he hurt Evans; he came with a kick to the left of Evans's left knee. His left leg buckled, but he remained on his feet. Chameleon came at him with a variety of punches and kicks, roundhouses, straight kicks, and back kicks and punches. Evans moved like a dancer as he shifted this way and that way; he bent forward, bent backward, and quickly bent forward, making his body move as if it was like a rubber band.

Meanwhile, Shawn hopped in the car; he was in tremendous pain. He told Gordon to go straight three blocks, make a left, and go down two blocks; he barked the command, "Go, Gordon, go!" Gordon peeled out.

Back at the fight, Chameleon could not believe how good this guy was. Evans stood flat-footed in place as Chameleon threw a series of blows, which Evans dodged. Chameleon could see Evans's face; the man wasn't even breaking a sweat. Chameleon came back with a high kick. Evans blocked it and countered with quick jabs and chops to various parts of Chameleon's body, connecting and weakening Chameleon. Evans connected a hard body shot to Chameleon, came back up with three quick jabs, and finished Chameleon off with a quick elbow to his jaw. Chameleon stumbled backward. Evans said, "Your fighting skills are not bad. You are strong with good stamina. I wish this could go on, but I need to go. I'm sure you have backup coming, and I can't stand crowds."

Chameleon had a tense smile of pain on his face and said, "That's cool, but I need the chick."

Evans looked at him and said, "Chick, do you see a chick? No, my friend, this is a woman."

Chameleon came at Evans with a quick jab. Evans was so quick to lean back, causing the blow to miss. Evans saw an opportunity; as Chameleon was pulling back his jab, Evans grabbed Chameleon's arm and had him in a tight arm hold. The hold caused Chameleon to fall on his knees in pain. Evans had Chameleon in this submission hold, and Chameleon could do nothing about it. Evans was in complete control as he grabbed Chameleon by the throat; the move happened so quickly. As Evans began to squeeze, the air was slowly seeping out of Chameleon. Chameleon was trying to fight as he aimlessly swung, hoping to connect or something. Chameleon's blows were hard at first but slowly lost their power; it came down to nothing—light, harmless, with nothing behind it. Evans looked at Chameleon fighting to keep the little life he was slowly losing; he was almost done as life was hissing out of Chameleon's body.

Meanwhile, Gordon had turned the corner and came to a quick stop. The street was blockaded due to construction. Shawn cursed, saying, "Gordon, meet me on the other side."

Gordon responded, "What about you, sir?"

Shawn got out. "Two blocks I have to run . . . go."

# Chapter 123

Evans continued to squeeze. Chameleon was losing consciousness as he made an attempt to fight death away, but he soon realized it was a losing battle. Serenity got out of the car and begged Evans to stop. "You're going to kill him. Evans, stop, stop . . ." She grabbed his hand to break the grip, but it was like a vice.

He looked at her; she begged him to let go of Chameleon's throat. Evans looked at Chameleon as his body had gone limp; he shoved Chameleon to the ground. "Get in the car. Sorry, please get in the car."

Evans looked and saw Shawn running; he was at least a block away. Serenity had already gotten into the car and had not seen Shawn running toward them. Evans got in, started the car, and peeled out down the street. Serenity turned and saw Shawn; her breath got caught in her chest as she gasped. She looked at him; her heart longed to be with him. She could tell he was hurt. The tears began to fall down her face. Evans looked at her; he wanted to let her go to go to her husband, but he couldn't. This was his last job. He didn't want Mr. X to look for him for the rest of his life; he didn't want to constantly look over his shoulder to see if he was being followed or to become paranoid that he and his family would have to move from place to place just because he felt someone was after him.

Serenity was sniffing as she was holding back the tears. Evans was concentrating on the road even though he was very much concerned with what was going on with her. He knew why she wanted to cry; the woman was dedicated and totally committed to her husband. The thought put a sting in his heart; he had come to like her, maybe a little more than like. He looked over at her and back on the road; he said in a soft, compassionate tone, "Are you okay?"

She didn't respond immediately. He had to know that she was okay; he didn't want to hurt her in any way. He glanced at her again and back to the road. He admired her for so many reasons. She interrupted his thoughts. "You could have killed that man back there, Evans."

The sound of his name flowing from her mouth to his ears broke him down even further. He looked straight ahead. Her response surprised her; here he was thinking she was crying over her husband, but in reality, she was crying over the man he was fighting with. He knew she didn't care for him, not in that way, but she cared for him as one human being toward another human being. He was confused; he responded with a nod and said, "True, or he was going to kill me."

She nodded at the wisdom of his answer; he asked, "You know him?" She shook her head. He looked at her; she verbalized it. "No."

They drove a little farther; he had to know. "Why didn't you run? You had at least two or three chances."

She was still looking straight ahead; she said, "Actually four."

He looked at her; she was looking straight. Her profile was soft, yet there was strength in the look. She turned and looked at him. "I really don't know." She turned back and looked at the road. He nodded his head with respect and drove a little farther before he pulled over and told her to get out.

# CHAPTER 124

Shawn ran toward Chameleon. He stopped; he couldn't believe the bodies sprawled all over the ground. He walked around the injured, carefully visually inspecting their condition. They were all hurt, but nothing life-threatening. Police cars zoomed in as Shawn knelt down; he felt for a pulse in Chameleon's neck. He placed his hand on Chameleon's chest, trying to feel his heartbeat. He put his ear to his mouth to see if he was breathing. His mouth was very close to Chameleon's mouth when he heard. "What are you doing?"

Shawn leaned back and looked at Chameleon. Chameleon was in pain, but very much alive. Shawn slightly smiled. "Hey, you okay?" Chameleon struggled to sit up. Shawn helped him to sit up. "Easy." That was Shawn.

Chameleon shook his head; he looked around at the destruction and said, "Damn, that dude is one wrecking machine. I thought I was bad." Chameleon put his head down between his legs and slowly breathed; he said, "Damn, he had me, Shawn. I was about to cross over to the other side. I felt it, man . . ." Chameleon paused and continued, "Your woman saved me, man."

That got Shawn's full attention; he asked, "What do you mean?"

Chameleon slightly smiled. "She begged him to let go of his freakin' death grip on my damn throat. She saved me." Chameleon paused and finished, "He let go. I was still on this side of Jordan, man."

Commissioner Moore came. Moore looked around and blew out a whistle. "Whew, damn! What army hit here?"

Shawn looked at him. "A one-man army."

Moore looked at Shawn, bewildered. "What! One man did this? Get the freak out of here! One man?"

Shawn nodded and said, "One man."

The commissioner looked at Shawn and asked, "This is the man you're dealing with, Cook?"

Shawn shook his head. "No, this is the one that works for the man I'm dealing with."

Moore slowly shook his head in astonishment. "Wow."

Shawn nodded his head. "Yeah. It doesn't matter. I'm taking that son of a bitch down. It doesn't matter who he gets, the army, navy, marines, the air force, or Special Forces—it doesn't matter. I'm going to rip him apart."

The ambulance came and took the wounded to the nearest hospital. Shawn helped Chameleon up; he said to him, "Come on."

Chameleon looked at him. "What? Where are we going?"

Shawn shook his head. "No, not we, you. You are going to the hospital to get checked out. Let's go."

Chameleon stared at him with a look of surprise and said, "Look, Wall Street, I'm good, really. I don't need a hospital. I'll be all right. I've had worst."

Shawn looked at him. "What, a near-death experience?"

Chameleon lightened the tone. "Well, not quite." He continued, "Plus I have some pre-med knowledge. I'll be all right."

Shawn looked at him, baffled. "I didn't know you have a pre-med degree."

Chamelcon looked at Shawn and confessed, "Well, not exactly."

Shawn rolled his eyes. "Look, it's either you do or you don't."

Chameleon smiled. "Well, put it this way . . . I walked the halls of John Jay."

Shawn looked at him and said, "That's criminal and not medical."

Chameleon responded, "Well . . . yeah . . . Ahh, I kinda figured that if I got caught doing something I have no business doing, at least I'll understand the law to defend myself."

Shawn looked at him, shaking his head. Chameleon tried to laugh, but it was too painful as he grimaced and grabbed his side. Shawn said, "Come on, I'll go with you. You need to have some x-rays done, the works. You're beat up pretty bad."

Chameleon consented. "Okay, I'll go. And afterwards, we get back out there and try to catch this bastard." Shawn asked how. Chameleon took the tracer monitor from Shawn; he showed it to Shawn and said, "With this."

Shawn smiled. "Wow, I thought that thing was broken during the—"

Chameleon said, "During the kick-ass session." Chameleon tried to laugh again as he grabbed his ribs. He placed his hand on his waist and took in slow deep breaths; he continued, "I put it on him at some point. Anyway . . ." Chameleon took another deep breath. "Probably a couple of broken ribs."

Shawn agreed, "Maybe." He went over to Commissioner Moore and said, "Any leads at all?"

Moore shook his head. "Not yet. The woman is still not talking. She said she told enough. Her greatest fear is that this guy could find her and her husband and two adult children. Can't blame . . ." He stopped, looked down the street, and turned back to Shawn. "Look, we are doing everything possible to find this guy. I have other agencies giving up tips." He paused and said, "We will catch him, Shawn."

Shawn tossed him the monitor. Moore looked at it and said, "A tracker monitor? It's off or not working."

Shawn shrugged his shoulders and said, "When it picks up a signal, it'll come on."

As soon as he said that, there was beep, and the tracker lit up. Shawn heard something; he looked at Moore, and Moore in turned look at him. The commissioner responded, "You mean something like this?"

# CHAPTER 125

Serenity looked at Evans; his tone was hard when she heard him tell her to get out of the car. She wasn't sure why. She thought this was the end; the man had about enough, and enough was enough. He looked at her. "Sorry about the harsh tone. We have to move quickly."

Serenity crinkled her nose. Evans wanted to kiss her; she was so beautiful and looked so innocent and cute when she did that thing with her nose. He held up the small tracker device. She looked at it. "A tracker."

Evans was sort of surprised she knew what it was, yet again, it seemed as if her man walked by her side when it came down to what he did; he did not keep her in the dark like he did with his wife. Perhaps this was the reason why she left; she was sick and tired of the secrets.

From the way Serenity described him, he seemed like the type of person that didn't mind her being in every aspect, every corner, every part of his life. No wonder she was so madly in love with him. Evans wished he had that. He couldn't just share stuff with his wife and kids. His work was too final, too brutal, too nasty and bloody. Could you imagine coming home and being asked how your day was, and your response would be, "Okay. Had two kills. Took a father from his family, you know head shot, but not too bad. Oh yeah, I used this seven-inch blade on some loser. Just plunged it into the man's neck. That thing went all the way in. It was sensational. And how was your day, babe?"

Evans shook off the thought. He was a loser; he deserved it. He didn't think that was a good idea at the kitchen table while eating dinner.

Evans looked at Serenity; she seemed to have read his mind as she looked down and back up at him, biting on that nice-looking lower lip. She was gorgeous; he would leave everything like the disciples did when

Jesus asked them to follow Him. He would do the same thing for Serenity if she asked him to.

Serenity interrupted his thoughts. "A tracker . . ." She looked at it and shrugged her shoulders. "A cheap one, but . . ." He listened to her, enjoying her tone, her inflections, the pronunciation of her words, how her lips moved, and how that tongue darted in and out at certain words, especially the ones that ended with the *th* sound. He nodded, knowing what she meant; she asked, "So where are we going?"

He looked at her and said, "Car hunting."

# CHAPTER 126

Several police cars took off following Shawn. Shawn was going by the tracker signal that was starting to become stronger; he said to Gordon, "Gordon, I need for you to decipher the exact location of this beep. Can you do that, buddy?"

Chameleon smiled and shook his head. "Yo, Wall Street, Gordon is so cool. You speak to him as if he's human, and he responds as if he's human. Yo, my birthday is . . . well, it's coming back up again . . . soon. Or maybe you could hook up a brother with a prebirthday present."

Gordon responded to Chameleon, "Mr. Chameleon, my AI comes from one of the most brilliant minds in the world. This is why I have such intelligence, sir."

Chameleon responded, "Damn, see what I mean? You lost me somewhere, but yo, I got to"—his voice went up pitch higher—"get me one of these, yo."

Shawn shook his head. "Enough, Gordon."

Gordon responded, "Sorry, sure. Just hold the item toward my GPS, and I will be able to match signals."

Shawn did so. It took only a few seconds for Gordon's GPS to make a match. The street and the location showed up on Gordon's GPS. "Good job, G."

Shawn called Commissioner Moore. "Moore, we have a location." Moore asked where; he could probably alert the local authorities to send a team of state troopers up there. Shawn wasn't feeling that. "No, I don't want any mistakes or trigger-happy officers going up there blundering this thing up, Moore. Hell no, that's a negative."

Commissioner Moore slapped the dashboard. "Shawn, you are one stubborn son of a bitch. Cook, don't be so damn difficult on this. Let us handle this. I'll make sure that my orders will be just to assist, nothing more." Shawn took a few seconds to respond. Moore added, "Look, Shawn, we could have them at the site. You are creating a window of escape. Think, man."

he commissioner was right; the trail was still hot. But with every second wasted, the trail became cooler and cooler until it became cold; and in the end, Shawn would still be at square one, and Evans will still have Serenity. Shawn spoke into the radio. "Okay, okay, proceed. But I'm warning you—if anything goes wrong, Moore, I'm holding you responsible."

The commissioner nodded his head. "Yeah . . . got it. Trust me, Cook, you are making the right move."

For your sake, I hope so."

# CHAPTER 127

Evans broke the window of the car that was parked in a two-family house. He said, "The man has three cars. I'll just borrow one."

Serenity watched Evans; he was quick, efficient, and smooth. He quickly opened the driver's door and jumped down to the floor. He was doing something down there where the alarm system did two quick short beeps and then went silent. He pressed the button to unlock the doors. Serenity quickly jumped in; she couldn't believe she was in cahoots with stealing this man's car. If she got caught, she'd be on the 5:00 a.m., 12:00 p.m., 6:00 p.m., 11:00 p.m., and even *Night Life News*; and years later, they would still bring it back up again and again like they do Patty Hearst—even after all these years. She knew she had another opportunity to run, but she didn't; they were like a team—a Bonnie and Clyde type.

Evans watched her when she got in. Serenity looked over at him and wrinkled her nose, signifying the question of what the problem was; she asked him why he was looking at her like that. He shook his head and said, "No reason." He had already hot-wired the car; he backed out, put the car in drive, and took off.

They drove about forty-five minutes when Evans turned on the radio. He channel surfed until he came to some nice jazz; he left it there. He looked over at Serenity; she was knocked out, sleeping like a baby. She looked so peaceful; in spite of all the chaos and craziness, she was still able to stay in touch and in control. He thought she was an amazing woman; he admired that in her. She stirred a bit as if his thoughts woke her up. She finally woke up; she was somewhat disoriented. "Where . . . what . . . ?" She nodded her head. "Sorry, I . . ."

He continued to drive. The sun was starting to come up. *What a beautiful sunrise*, she thought. *So majestic.* She said a little prayer. He heard her say, "In Jesus's name. Amen."

He Evans continued to drive when he asked, "Why do you believe in God?"

Serenity looked over at him; the question surprised her. "Don't you?"

At first, he shook his head; then he shrugged his shoulders. "I'm not sure."

She nodded her head and said, "Okay, that's a fair assessment."

Evans responded, "What's fair?"

Serenity was still looking at him and said, "Your response."

He continued to drive. "I don't have to fake it or pretend. This is me, either you like it or not."

Serenity nodded. She couldn't argue with that; she thought he sounded like he was becoming defensive. She paused, hoping that he could see his own aggressive reaction; he didn't. She continued, "You've been through a lot, haven't you?"

Evans shrugged his shoulders. "Who hasn't . . . ?" He continued to focus on the road.

Serenity noticed how his hands became tighter on the steering wheel. There was silence between them as the jazz continued to play; she thought it sounded like Kenny G or Boney James. Whoever it was, it was nice. Evans broke the ice; he loved hearing her voice, so crisp and charming. He said, "I've seen death in so many ways. Being in the armed forces, special unit, I've seen a lot and been through a lot . . . like Moses, that old dude in the Bible. He had seen the promise land like the way I've seen death." He paused and continued, "I wonder if it's seen me. So many times, it's put out the red carpet. But somehow, for some strange reason, I somehow eluded it. Or a detour had been provided by the big man upstairs." Evans pointed up. He shrugged. "Yeah, I believe in God . . ." He shrugged as he proceeded, "Too many reasons not to . . ."

Evans continued to drive along the Sprain Brook Parkway. He read a sign that said Welcome to Westchester County with Open Arms.

# CHAPTER 128

When Commissioner Moore and Shawn arrived, there were at least six state police cars there. The commissioner got out. Shawn said, "Looks like everyone and their mothers are here, damn."

Moore was looking grim and baffled; he said, "You never can be too careful, especially with this guy. That sucker is a one-man army." The commissioner went up to the captain. "What the hell is going on here?"

Shawn turned and looked at the commissioner with a slight smile; the commissioner looked at Shawn, thinking Shawn agreed with their discussion before they came down here.

The captain responded, "Sir, we didn't want to make any mistakes, so—"

Moore finished the young man's statement, saying, "So you waited for us." The commissioner looked at Shawn and shrugged his shoulders. Moore looked at the captain and asked, "Okay, so what do we have?"

The captain stated, "Nothing. The car is empty, sir. We didn't inspect the vehicle. We waited until you got here, sir."

The commissioner glanced at Shawn, feeling a bit apprehensive; he nodded his head as if he was on the same page as the decision made by the captain. The commissioner still had that false look of confidence; he could tell that Shawn wasn't too happy with the decision as he stepped in. "Okay . . . okay . . ."

The captain, not liking the commissioner's response, continued, "Sir, we just went by what you have asked."

Shawn looked at the commissioner, who appeared flustered. The captain said something Moore didn't want Shawn to hear. The commissioner responded, "No . . . no, it's okay. Ah . . . send in the dogs. Make sure there aren't any bombs or traps."

The captain nodded his head as he called one of his men over and gave the same directive Moore had given him.

Meanwhile, Moore walked up to Shawn, who was already frustrated. Moore said, "Look, Cook, I wanted to stay on the side of caution, that's all."

Shawn looked at him and responded, "That's all? Really? Well, you could have informed me, Moore. What, I have to hear what is going on between you and your officer? I should have been aware of your so-called caution, fear, apprehension—whatever the hell you want to refer to it as." Shawn took a few steps away and turned back, pointing his finger at Moore. "You make it sound as if it's a walk in the park, but what you've done is given Evans more time to escape. You didn't make it a walk in the park—you made it a walk in the dark. If your men would have followed through when they found the car empty, they could have branched out. It would have made a difference, Curt."

Moore was about fed up with Shawn barking lectures and directives as he stood his ground, saying, "You can't say that, Cook. I can't take a chance limiting my men."

Shawn raised his voice, saying, "So sending out a bunch of K-9 mutts is supposed to catch a smell? Who the hell knows how long or how far Evans has traveled? Their scent is long gone, Curt. C'mon, Moore, who do you think you're talking to? Don't treat me as if I'm some kind of idiot, okay? You and I both know what the deal is. The scent is gone, and so is my wife!" There was a pause; then Shawn continued, "You gave me your word. I asked you not to freak this up." He stretched out his arms and said, "So what do you call this? And then you want to impress me? Sending in the dogs, the trackers, the search party—I'm not impressed at all." Shawn pointed to Moore. "If I have to hire a team to do what you and your men couldn't do, you're not going to like me, Moore."

Moore raised his voice. "Look, you want to play Monday morning quarterback and criticize and point out what we did wrong? Well, we're doing the best we can under the circumstances, Cook."

Shawn looked at Moore and said in a stern tone, "Well, you better do better."

Moore turned and walked away, barking orders at his men. Shawn walked up to Moore and calmly said, "Curt, look, I want to apologize for that display. This entire ordeal has been a pain in the ass. I don't know if I'm coming or going anymore. I'm barking at the folks that are trying to help. Listen, you did right to play it safe. This dude we are dealing with is good. Anyway, sorry."

The two shook hands. Curt Moore said, "Shawn, we are going to nail that son of a bitch. I promise you."

# CHAPTER 129

Shawn stood there with Moore and Chameleon, trying to put the pieces of this puzzle together. Who was this stranger, this Mr. X, this ghost like some of his men refer to him as? Shawn was frustrated; every time he felt he was gaining ground, something would pull him back. He cursed under his breath. Moore and Chameleon were also frustrated.

Damn, not one clue who this guy is. The FBI didn't have any idea. They don't have anything, not even an inkling of a clue to run in their database, nothing to grip their teeth on." He slammed his fist into his hand. "Damn." He continued, "The only one who had half of a story was the woman who was in the hospital. She worked for him for so many years, but she didn't want to leak any information about him in fear this madman would retaliate against her family, and she wasn't going to risk that. She wasn't going to take a chance of losing them."

The commissioner chimed in, saying, "Can we blame her? This woman is so fearful that this dude has her thinking that he has some kind of supernatural power. He knew things, plans as if God is whispering in his ear."

Chameleon was awestruck by all of this. Shawn had to quench that fire of fear; he said, "The man doesn't have any supernatural powers or a pipeline to God. No, what he has is a tight network of folks that work for him, good and bad folks. Those are the ones whispering in his ears. One thing's for sure—they are a tight network. They are very together, well organized, and very dangerously lethal. And most of these folks are street punks that are well paid. Let's see what happens when the cash flow stops." Shawn kicked at the pebbles on the ground and said, "The problem is, I don't expect that to happen anytime soon."

Chameleon walked up to him and said, "No clue on Evans and Chameleon."

Shawn shook his head. "No, wherever Evans went, he's long gone. We're always a freakin' step behind them."

Chameleon cursed and said, "Damn, I thought we had him. I didn't realize the man was that good."

Commissioner looked from Shawn to Chameleon and said, "Who the hell is this guy?"

Chameleon looked at Shawn and shrugged, saying, "I don't know."

Moore looked at Shawn. "Cook, listen, I'm trying to help. If you know who this guy is—"

Shawn cut the commissioner off, saying, "I can't, not right now."

Moore shook his head and said, "More secrets . . . Okay, Cook, have it your way."

At that moment, Shawn's cell phone chimed; the ringtone was all too familiar. The phone chimed again. Shawn looked agitated; the commissioner said, "That's him, right? Right? Come on, Cook, let us in."

Shawn walked a few steps from them; he heard the commissioner curse. Shawn touched his Bluetooth. "Yeah?" The voice on the other end sounded haunting. Shawn, who wasn't the type to become frightened too often, felt a cold chill running up and down his spine. On top of that, he felt as if every bone in his body ached.

The stranger spoke. "Mr. Cook, you've had a rough night, haven't you?"

Shawn wished his fist could go through the phone and clock this dude. He did not say a word; he wasn't going to entertain this madman. The stranger continued to ramble on. "You don't like talking today, huh? I understand. So therefore, I will do the talking, and you can listen. Oh, by the way, Mr. Cook, I read somewhere that it takes more energy to talk than it is to listen. Isn't that interesting? But now this is the interesting factor . . . Listening is a key to—"

Shawn had heard enough as he cut the stranger off, saying, "Okay, now you listen to me, asswipe."

The stranger immediately cut Shawn off. "Tsk tsk tsk, Mr. Cook, you have such foul language. And I'm not sure whether you are that brash or just that stupid in regard to how you insult me and how you refer to me. You have no respect, and for someone that is holding the dearest thing in the world to you, you are living on very thin ice because the only thing that you are accomplishing is exacerbating the conclusion of the one I hold . . .

your wife. Your mouth will bring those consequences quickly to an end. Whatever happens to the lovely Serenity would be your fault." The stranger paused and continued to speak as if he and Shawn were best friends. "Oh, by the way, how did it feel to speak to your gorgeous wife? She has such a nice, lovely voice."

Shawn's face was intense; his eyes were moving rapidly from side to side. He shook his head, trying to clear it. The stranger continued, "Are you there, Mr. Cook? You know I hate to be ignored. That started, believe it or not, with my father. I hate that man."

Shawn responded, "Like I hate you."

The stranger had a smile in his voice. "There you go. I knew something would get you to talk. Anyway, with two strikes against you, if I were you, I would listen intently to what I have to say because—"

Shawn interrupted him and said with clenched teeth, "I have one strike and not two."

The stranger chuckled, saying, "Well, you are paying attention. Good." The stranger was humming a song. "Okay, Mr. Cook, I concur with you. One strike. You are absolutely right." The stranger chuckled again. Shawn growled in the phone; he was about to explode. The stranger continued, "You have surprised me, Mr. Cook, to the fullest. To be completely honest with you, I really thought you would have given up, and poor Serenity forfeit her life. But I must say, you've been a very good competitor . . . And by the way, before I forget, how is my secretary, Mrs. Stewart, doing? Such a lovely and naïve woman. As I understand, her husband and her boys are doing very well. Don't worry about them. I'm keeping an eye on them . . . Right now, Mr. Cook, they are safe. And as far as she is concerned, that is all she cares about at this time." The stranger gave a low diabolical laugh.

The stranger cleared his throat as he continued, "Moving off this topic, I have to get back on your abilities. I just can't stop thinking about them. You have kept up with me. You have met every challenge with success . . . well, except for one . . . But you are an amazing man, Mr. Cook. If this situation wasn't in the way, I would have offered you a job to work for me or even be a partner. We would be awesome . . ."

Shawn gritted his teeth. "I don't think so, not in a million years. All I want from you is your life."

There was a pause; then the stranger responded, "Wow . . ." He cleared his throat as he continued, "Well, anyway, moving forward. I was just thinking that you have earned your stripes today with the bumps and bruises you have suffered up to this point. I don't know how you did it. Excellent."

Shawn responded, "Why don't you and I meet up, and I can show you how it's done. I would probably start with the choke hold."

The stranger laughed. "Maybe one day, sir, but not today." There was a brief few seconds of silence before the stranger continued, "Okay, back to business, Mr. Cook. Our game must be interrupted—"

Shawn cut him off with agitation in his voice. "You think this is all a game, huh? You seriously believe taking lives is a game? You're sick . . ."

The stranger came back just as hard with such fierce anger. "Damn right! You thought it was a game when you took the life of Phillip Keys. You didn't have a problem doing that, right? One, two, three, you snapped his neck. You had no guilt, no remorse, no shame! It was a freakin' pleasure, wasn't it, Mr. Cook? Right? That day, you got a chance to play God for a moment and . . ."

Shawn tried to interrupt him, and the conversation became one big confused babble of words. As both men tried to outspeak the other as their volume went up with intensity, higher and higher. Shawn had about enough as his voice towered over the stranger's like Ali stood Sonny Liston, claiming victory as he spoke in that high, loud, booming volume. "You're not getting this. You are not seeing the full picture. I didn't want to kill your brother, but he was out of control. HE WAS ABOUT TO KILL THOUSANDS OF PEOPLE FOR NO REASON. Those people never did not one thing to him, but he wanted to spew out his anger just because of a government system he didn't like. Anybody in their mind would never do such a thing, and anybody in their right mind would never sit back and allow such a senseless act to take place. Your brother was emotionally disturbed, mentally ill, and . . ."

The stranger heard enough; his volume had gone down. It went from loud to cold, ice-cold as if he had become detached from himself. "And so you decided to become his justice system and jury . . . bullshit!"

Shawn raised his voice, saying, "I HAD NO OTHER CHOICE. It was either him or me and countless of thousands of people. I couldn't allow that to happen. I tried to talk him out of it, but he was determined. His mind was fixed on destruction."

The stranger, still sounding cold and detached, responded, "You did have a choice, and you made it. My brother, just in case you didn't know, was a prominent chemist. He had won so many awards. If you had gone inside his house, his walls were filled with these awards. He had photographs of presidents and famous people. He was proud of his achievements. The government knew he was on his way to receiving the highest honor any humanitarian could receive . . . the Noble Peace Prize. He had achieved breakthrough after breakthrough."

There was a pause; the stranger continued with a sneer in his tone, "Then one day, the government pulled the rug from under him. All the years of hard work, blood, sweat and tears, they took it in a couple of days. They took all the credit for what he had achieved. All his work, all his success snatched, vanished, gone, Mr. Cook. He was a blue-blooded American through and through, and they took that. He had every right to feel the way he felt. He believed in this government, but they betrayed him. They set him up." There was another pause as the stranger's tone became more diabolical; the chills were still running up and down Shawn's spine as the stranger continued, "They took his work. You took his life. And now, Mr. Cook, I take back that day you made a decision. In four days, Mr. Cook, I will also make a decision concerning your wife—an eye for an eye . . ."

Shawn started shaking from the core of his soul as he heard the stranger continue, "A tooth for a tooth, a life for a life, Mr. Cook. You took mine. I take yours. Now depending on the outcome of our . . ." He paused as he continued, "Our game, I will either take hers and a few others, or you will save her and a few others. And if that's the case, Mr. Cook, I will disappear as if I've never existed, as if all of this was just a nightmare, Mr. Cook. Let God be the one to make that final decision. Good night. Ah, correction, rather good morning. You will be hearing from me . . ."

Shawn tried to get in a word and tried to reason with him, but the stranger wasn't hearing it; he had made up his mind as the phone went dead. Shawn desperately was calling the stranger. "Wait, hello . . . hello . . . HELLO! Damn it, the son of a bitch is crazy."

Chameleon and Moore stood next to Shawn, Chameleon, in frustration, said, "So what was cuckoo for Coco Pops saying? Damn, that was intense."

Shawn was in tremendous pain as he was slightly bent over; he tried to stand up straight, but his body wasn't having it. His face told the story as the pain ripped through his body like locusts on a field of crops. It seemed as if every bone in his body cried out. Both the commissioner and Chameleon rushed to his side, aiding him. Chameleon looked at him and said, "Yo, Wall Street, you look like crap, man."

Moore added in a sarcastic tone, "Hmmm, that's an upgrade from looking like shit. Talk to us, Cook. What the hell is going on? What did your nutjob say to you? He's got you in a crazy state, man."

Shawn shook his head as the pain shot through his body; he grimaced as he responded, "The man is not crazy, and neither was his brother. These are two intelligent guys that got caught up in hate and revenge. And with his brother, Phillip Keys, he couldn't see straight. He just wanted to bring revenge. He wanted to bring his own 9/11. He wasn't crazy. Hate consumed him like a disease. As for . . ." Shawn grimaced again as the pain shot through his body as he continued, "As for his brother, he's going down the same path of hate and destruction and revenge. Payback is the only thing that makes sense to him. I have four days . . ."

Both Moore and Chameleon had looks of surprise as they both responded, "Four days?"

Shawn continued as he raised his hand, "He's going to contact me in four days." He grimaced and looked at Moore. "With this short break, listen to me, I need to question his secretary, Mrs. Stewart, again. I'm sure she can provide us with more insight into what is going on in the next few days. I need to see her." Shawn made a face that reflected the pain in his body and said, "Curt, I need for you to set it up, please."

The commissioner nodded his head. "Okay, when?"

Shawn grimaced as the pain shot through his body; he waited for the pain to subside and said, "Today."

Both Moore and Chameleon protested; the commissioner said, "You got to be out of your mind, Cook! Look at you. You could hardly stand up . . . no way."

Shawn looked at him. "What do you mean 'no way'? Curt, listen to me. This is the window of opportunity we've been waiting for. While this nutjob is giving me a few days . . . this is critical, Commissioner. We may not get another opportunity like this again."

The commissioner looked at Shawn and then at Chameleon, who shrugged his shoulders and said, "I can't believe I'm saying this. This is crazy, but he's right. I hate to say it."

The commissioner nodded and said, "Thank you, no—"

Chameleon cut him off. "No, I think Wall Street is right. This is an opportunity. We need to jump at it."

Shawn nodded his head at Chameleon; he looked at Moore, who cursed under his breath. "Only on one condition." Shawn looked baffled at Moore. Moore said, "You go straight to the hospital after your talk with Mrs. Stewart and get a complete checkup."

Shawn grimaced with a slight smile as he shook Moore's hand and said, "Deal."

# CHAPTER 130

Evans picked up on the second ring. "Yes, sir?"

The voice spoke methodically and slowly. "Good morning, Mr. Evans. I understand from the news you had a busy morning, sir. I take it they're talking about you. Is that correct, sir?"

Evans hesitated. "Ah . . . yes, sir."

The voice continued, "No harm, no foul, sir. You did what you had to do." There was a pause; then the stranger continued, "Can anyone ID you?"

Evans told the stranger, "No."

The voice made a contemplative sound. "Very good, hmmm . . ." The voice continued, "And how is the lovely Serenity Cook?"

Evans hesitated perhaps a little longer than he should have been.

The stranger cocked his head to the side and said, "Mr. Evans, are you okay?"

Evans was getting back his composure. "Yes . . . yes . . . why?"

The stranger said, "Ah . . . you sound, hmmm . . . never mind, Mr. Evans."

Evans knew Mr. X's "never mind" meant he was fishing and hunting, and he was very persistent once he suspected something. The stranger continued, "I will be away for a few days, business before pleasure." The stranger laughed; he stopped as fast as it started and then said, "When I return, Mr. Evans, I would like to continue my game with Mr. Cook . . ." There was a pause, and then he continued, "The final phase. In the meantime, the house where you and Mrs. Cook were staying is no longer safe—"

Evans cut off the stranger. "Mr. X, the police doesn't have a clue that Serenity and I—"

The stranger interrupted him, saying, "So now it's Serenity? Hmmm . . . interesting, Mr. Evans. I warned you once. When fire burns, sir, don't get too close to it . . ."

There was another pause. Evans wanted to kick himself. He knew he had made such a fundamental error on his part, a totally foolish mistake.

The stranger continued, "Mr. Evans . . . has this mission been compromised, huh?"

Evans told the stranger, "No."

The stranger continued with a firm tone, "Have you sold out, sir, huh? Have you cashed it in? Have you turned in your chips, Mr. Evans?"

Evans said, "No."

The stranger made a contemplative sound and asked, "Have you become emotionally attached, sir?"

Evans responded, "Sir, you know—"

The stranger raised his voice. "Answer the damn question, Mr. Evans. Have you?"

Evans paused and shouted back, "No, sir! No, I have not!"

After a brief pause, the stranger replied, "Mr. Evans, you took a few seconds too long. I will ask you again. Are you still objective about the mission? Can you handle this mission without letting your heart think for your head, huh? Are you still focused, sir? I need to know."

Evans had worked for Mr. X for so many years; he'd been contracted for so many missions. They weren't friends; they were business associates. Evans knew what that meant; he responded, "Sir, I'm fine. My objectives are clear, and I have not compromised this mission, Mr. X."

Now it was the stranger's turn to hesitate. When he spoke, he sounded so detached and cold as if Evans was his enemy and not his business associate; he said, "Mr. Evans, go up to my summerhouse. You know where it's at. You've been there before." There was a pause. "Stay there until I could get word to you for the final phase, sir."

Evans didn't know what to say; all he could do was nod his head and say "yes" or "no" or "no problem." He knew something wasn't right; he had to stay a few feet in front of Mr. X. He knew Mr. X was all business, shrewd and diabolical; he knew he could not be trusted.

The stranger hung up and steepled his fingers together as he stared straight ahead and said, "No, sir. On the contrary, there is a problem, Mr. Evans, a serious problem."

He picked up his phone and dialed; the person answered. The stranger did not bother to give any form of salutation. He said in a haunting tone, "Time to collect. Be ready when I call."

The stranger didn't wait for a reply; he pressed the button on his Bluetooth and disconnected the call.

# Chapter 131

Shawn said to the commissioner as he and Chameleon walked toward Gordon, "When day breaks—"

Commissioner Moore interjected, "Which should be in the next couple of hours. I want your ass in that doctor's office, Cook. We understand one another, huh?"

Shawn kept walking, waving his hand. "Yeah, got ya." His cell phone chimed; the commissioner by now knew the ringtone was only a few feet from Shawn. Shawn thought it was him; he was more than certain.

Moore walked quickly toward Shawn, picked it up, and started trotting as he was saying to Shawn, "Cook, we got a deal. Let us deal with this guy."

Shawn looked at the commissioner hurrying toward him; he responded, "He said no police involvement, sorry."

The ringtone sounded again. Shawn held out his hand. Moore was telling Shawn to wait, but he couldn't risk missing the call; he answered, "What!"

Moore stopped, looking pissed off. "Dammit."

The stranger picked up the conversation as if this was the first time they spoke today, when a few minutes ago, they were ready to rip each other apart. The stranger continued, "I have another assignment for you, Mr. Cook, before we break for recess for a few days."

Shawn responded, "Business?"

The stranger slightly smiled and said, "Excuse me."

Shawn repeated the word, saying, "Is it business?"

The stranger chuckled. "Don't worry, Mr. Cook. Before this is all over, you will get to know me in every way. Please don't try to play me dumb, sir. Keep in mind, my skills and knowledge are not equal, but I would say slightly better than yours. So a word of caution as well as a word to the wise, sir—don't do that again, or I will have to change the rules of engagement . . . Is that clear, sir?"

Shawn did not respond. The stranger continued, his tone was elated as if he was having a rush; as if his previous warning never happened, he said, "Okay, back to business, shall we? Okay, Mr. Cook, you will be on the uptown side of the number 4 train at 125th Street. You will encounter four thugs, worthless punks of society. They are considered armed and dangerous by the public." The stranger paused and continued, "They are out this late to harass riders—one in particular, a whore, a prostitute who rides the same train to go home. They are out to harm, hurt, and harass her." The stranger took a deep breath in and blew it out as he continued, "Your job, Mr. Cook, is to disarm them and save that whore in the process. This is like Cracker Jacks. Remember that in every box, there was a prize? Well, Mr. Cook, if you find the right thug, he holds the prize—an address in his pocket. Now pay close attention to what I'm about to say, Mr. Cook—"

Shawn cut off the stranger. "What does this have to do with me?"

The stranger chuckled. "A whole lot, Mr. Cook. Plenty, Mr. Cook. You find the right thug who holds the prize, which is that address. That address, sir, is where the lovely and gorgeous Serenity Cook is."

Shawn's heart jumped. The stranger continued, "Got your attention, huh? You find the address in time, you will find your wife. If you don't, you will miss her and lose her. Strike two and strike three. Yeah, this is a big one. I'm adding two strikes for this one, Mr. Cook. This is so exciting."

Shawn was waiting for more information, but the stranger had hung up. Shawn yelled in the phone, "The jackass! He hung up on me without giving me the information, damn idiot!"

The phone chimed. Shawn quickly touched his Bluetooth. "You really think this is a joke?"

The stranger chuckled. "Were you nervous, Mr. Cook? You thought I would let you suffer like that, holding the carrot in front of you, but not letting you get to it?"

Shawn's anger was evident as he growled into the phone, "You will make that mistake, stranger, and I hope I'll be right there when you do!"

The stranger chuckled. "You thought you weren't going to get this carrot. This could be the highlight of this game. This may lead you to your wife. Well, I can say it is a major connection." The stranger laughed.

Shawn didn't crack a smile; he didn't think it was funny as he gritted his teeth and said, "Glad to see you're in a jolly sick mood."

said, "No, Mr. Cook, not sick—simply in control. Let me explain something to you, Mr. Cook. I'm a shaker and a mover, and I get what I want. Enough about me. Let me give you the rest of this information concerning your assignment. All I could say is you better be ready, or poor Serenity will be like dust . . . puff." The stranger lightly chuckled.

Shawn shook his head and responded, "Sick." The stranger chuckled, which turned into an uncontrollable crazy laughter as Shawn sneered and responded, "Sick son of a—"

The stranger disconnected the call. Shawn pressed his Bluetooth firmly as he paced back and forth, cursing and slamming his fist into the police vehicle. The commissioner asked, "What did he say?"

Shawn was still fuming and cursing. "When I catch up to this son of a bitch, the only way you will be able to recognize him is through dental records. He is a dead man."

Moore asked again, "What the hell did he say?" The commissioner continued, "We need to trace his call next time he calls."

Shawn firmly raised his voice, saying, "No involvement at all. This is my fight. You interfere, you would be putting Serenity in serious danger."

Chameleon asked, "What else?"

Shawn placed his hands on his waist; he was slightly bent over, appearing to be looking down at the ground. He blew out a long breath, then shook his head. "He has upped his game . . . He gave me another assignment . . ." Shawn kicked at the pavement. "Damn . . ." He yelled in frustration, "DAMN SON OF A BITCH! He wants to play games with me. This dude is demented."

Chameleon responded, "Okay, tell us something we don't know."

Shawn shook his head. "I have to locate three or four dudes on the number 2 train causing trouble. Anyway, they have been assigned to harass a particular individual. My job is to stop them."

Chameleon shrugged. "Okay, what's the problem? You can kick major ass. And once that is done, you are home free, partner. You get Serenity back. Butter boom, baby." Shawn looked at him. Chameleon looked baffled and said, "Uh, not that simple, I guess. There must be a stipulation, right?"

Shawn nodded his head. "Uh, yeah. Only one of these punks is carrying the location where Serenity is being held."

Chameleon was astonished. "What! Are you serious?"

Shawn nodded his head. "Yes, I am very serious. And on top of that, the sucker is timing me."

Chameleon looked at him. "What, get the freak out of here!"

Shawn looked at Chameleon and said, "Yeah, he's raising his game, and I need to raise mine."

The commissioner shook his head. "Therefore, with these four clowns, you have to pick the right one that has the information because if you don't, time will expire, and you . . ."

Shawn finished what Moore was saying. "I lose my wife—that is not going to happen."

# Chapter 132

Serenity looked over at Evans as he drove up the Spring Brook Parkway. She could tell he was in deep thought; driving might not be the wisest thing to do. She came to the conclusion that something was troubling him; ever since that phone call with that so-called Mr. X, his employer, his attitude has changed.

Serenity looked at the road; it was still early. The sun was starting to peek out from the morning fog. She opened up her window to let the musky air out and that wonderful cool summer air in. She was going to get as much of the air as she could before that nice cool air is replaced by the summer heat, where the car would feel like the contents of a cooking pot. She scooted herself against the door, leaning her back half on the door and half on the seat. Serenity leaned her head against the window as she felt that cool summer breeze; it was okay for now. She closed her eyes and began to drift off when she quickly felt the car jerk; she quickly opened her eyes with surprise. She was still recovering from the jerk as she looked around, wide-eyed. Evans calmly, with care and concern, asked if she was okay; she nodded yes. She gave another nod with an apology. "Sorry . . . I . . ."

He looked at her to make sure she was okay. "No need to apologize. My main concern is that you are okay."

Serenity blushed slightly, looking down as she nibbled on her bottom lip. "Yes, I'm okay. Thank you for your concern." He nodded.

Evans drove a little farther when she asked him a question that caught him off guard. She looked at his profile and asked, "Do you think I'll live?"

His eyes were straight on the road. Serenity was still looking at him, asking, "Huh, do you?"

He kept his eyes on the road; she knew he wasn't going to answer. She put her head down and asked the next difficult question. "Would you be the one to carry out the assignment? Can you put a bullet in my head . . . Evans?"

Evans took his eyes off the road and looked at Serenity. He pulled into a restaurant parking lot. If he was hungry, he knew she had to be hungry as well. She wiped a tear from the corner of her eyes. She was getting out of the car when she turned and looked at him and said, "You would do it, wouldn't you?"

Serenity was out by the car; he thought this was another opportunity for her to run or make a complete spectacle of herself just to draw attention. Evans was unclipping his safety belt. He said under his breath, "I'm a professional, not a monster." Then he got out and walked toward her. They walked side by side like a couple into the restaurant.

# CHAPTER 133

Shawn pulled out the bed for Chameleon, who looked at it. "Wow, that is sure nice of you, Wall Street, allowing me to sleep in the bedroom and you taking the couch bed. Thanks. Good looking out, man."

Shawn smiled and said, "Not a problem, but you're staying out here. The CB, the couch bed, is a wonderful sleep. I mean that's what I've been told."

Chameleon responded, "So why don't you sleep out here and let me—"

Shawn cut him off, saying, "Uh, no, I don't think so, slick." He slightly smiled.

Chameleon mimicked a sarcastic smile back. He looked at Shawn and said with a look of surprise and bewilderment, "Yo, hold up, Wall Street. You're telling me you never . . ."

Shawn was shaking his head before Chameleon could get finish. Chameleon mouthed the word "wow." Shawn smiled and said, "Isn't that something?"

Chameleon responded, "The only 'something' is one word, 'sad.'" He continued, "So let me get this straight. You're telling me that you and Serenity and your daughter live in this, what, four-bed—"

Shawn interrupted him. "Five and a half."

Chameleon continued, "This five-and-half-bedroom mansion with two bath—"

Shawn interrupted. "Three bathrooms."

Chameleon continued, "Damn. I won't guess on walk-in closets that were probably as big as rooms."

Shawn smiled. Chameleon shook his head, then continued, "So you're telling me the times you dropped the little one off with your parents, you and Serenity stayed in that one room to—"

Shawn cut him off, saying, "I said I haven't slept in the rooms. I never said if anything else ever took place in the rooms, okay?" He smiled.

Chameleon smiled and said, "Okay, that sounds so much better because if it was me . . ."

Shawn gave Chameleon a stern look. Chameleon's excitement deflated like air coming out of a balloon; clearing his throat, he said, "Okay, moving on to Mind Your Business Avenue."

Shawn nodded as he went over to the linen closet and pulled out some linen with a pillow and a pillowcase and a pair of pajamas. Chameleon looked at them and said, "You wouldn't have a Spider-Man or Hulk pajamas?"

Shawn just gave him that look. Chameleon was just babbling. "Your guests probably think very highly of you."

Shawn shrugged his shoulders. "I haven't received any complaints yet." He handed Chameleon the linen and the other items and smiled. He turned back toward the closet to close it and snapped his finger; he turned back toward Chameleon. "Would you like a blanket or a quilt, something?"

Chameleon stared at him with a weird look. "Wall Street, it's like eighty degrees, bro, in this mother, 4:00 a.m.—why would I want a freakin' blanket or a quilt? Wow, haven't heard that word in years. A quilt. Anyway, it feels like an oven in this joint." He stopped with his hands out. "Hold it. More importantly, do you have central air?"

Shawn gazed at him with a look of confusion and said, "Central air? Of course. All the air is centered in my bedroom . . ."

Chameleon lightly smacked his legs in dramatic style as if that was the most funniest thing he's ever heard; he quickly stopped with a serious look on his face and said, "Damn, I went from fighting in Hell's Kitchen to Hell's House. Yo, this is a death trap. Yo, I can't. Wall Street, I can't."

Shawn looked at him. "Pardon my French, but that's a dumb-ass question, Cee."

Chameleon responded, "No, it's not. It's a question of survival. I need to know. Yeah, it's a life-or-death question." Shawn chuckled. Chameleon looked dejected, saying, "You can be very nasty and mean sometimes, Wall Street."

Shawn barked out a laugh and looked at Chameleon, who appeared very serious. Shawn said, "Yo, hold up. I'm dealing with one of the toughest dudes in the hood. Please don't tell me I found a soft spot in that iron ship of yours. Are you going soft and dainty on me, bro? A man who fights in a death ring is now crying about his feelings being hurt because how something was said? Nah, you got to be kidding me!"

Chameleon was jokingly going to put his hands on his hips but stopped and said, "No, seriously, why did you say my question was a dumb-ass question? Seriously, Wall Street, all joking aside."

Shawn was looking down, shaking his head; he looked at Chameleon. "Okay, you want to get real? All joking aside, think about it. A man who drives a talking car, and if you think Gordon is something, wait until you meet Complex, baby." He laughed and continued, "Man oh man . . . Anyway, a man who has all the modern comforts as far as you can see . . . Wait until you see my gym and the swimming pool out back and that nice piece of land . . . Who owns a restaurant and a couple of martial arts gyms and is big in the community and . . . ?" Shawn went over to a switch and flipped it.

Chameleon looked at him, bewildered, and said, "What? What did you just do?"

Shawn held up one finger and said, "Wait for it . . . wait for it . . ."

Both of them stood there waiting for . . . Then Shawn said out loud, "BOOM, BABY!"

Chameleon smiled from the east side of his cheek to the west side of his cheek, saying, "Wow! Yo, Wall Street, oh my . . ."

Shawn continued, "Like I said, if a man is going to have all those things I mentioned, he better have all of the modern comforts that money can buy."

Chameleon gave Shawn a high five and said, "You're the man." He stopped, shaking a little. "Uh, Wall Street . . . Uh, can I have that blanket? Better yet, the quilt and the comforter and the blanket. Yo, this bad boy just took a nosedive into Antarctica. It went from eighty degrees to twenty degrees."

Shawn just smiled. "Not a problem."

# CHAPTER 134

Serenity sat across Evans. He sat facing the door; he wanted to see who came in and who was heading out. He ate with one hand; the other hand was under the table, clutching his semiautomatic. He didn't like the vibe he was feeling; it might not have been anything, but his training and his experience were telling him something different. His training taught him to be ready for the unexpected. It might not be anything, but the next thing you know, you're caught napping, blindsided because you became too comfortable, a life-or-death situation because you became too negligent and took for granted the idea that just because you're in a small town, it doesn't mean much to a hit man—even in this small town, where everyone knows everyone. And as nice of a picture that may be, that may also be a major problem. When people in these so-called small towns know everyone and when they see someone they don't know, the gossip mill starts kicking in, turning and moving like an express train through that town, the whats and the "Who is that?" and "He's handsome" or "She's pretty" or "She looks like a stuck-up bitch," calling this person or that person to come down to the pub, the bar, the social club, check him out, on and on. Eventually, the gossip gets into the wrong ears, which starts a spark. The spark starts a flame, and the flame turns into a four- or five-alarm out-of-control fire, which brings people from all over town and nearby towns to come and see. They may see more than what they thought they would.

Evans a question when the waitress, an attractive thirty-something with dirty blonde hair tied up in a bun, came over. She was just trying to earn a buck, which probably went along with her second job, trying to make ends meet. Her makeup was holding her together likes Elmer's glue holding paper; it was a hostile environment for those that wore makeup. Once that make up came off her face, Serenity knew under the mask was someone that looked completely different; but right now sister looked good, applying the little tricks that would keep the makeup on. She was of average built; she looked like a cheerleader. She had a nice shape for a thirtysomething woman;, as far as Serenity was concerned, it was all hers—ass and breasts, no implants and no weaves. Cute bangs subtracted a few more years from her real age. She had beautiful white teeth, which looked like all hers. Age, the thief of life and beauty, could not touch that . . . not yet anyway. On a scale of ten concerning beauty, she was a nine.

Serenity noticed how Evans was gawking at the waitress and how Angela—that's what her name tag said—was soaking it all up like a sponge. Serenity couldn't blame her; when a woman feels they are losing their beauty and everything that goes along with it and someone every now and then reminds them that they still have it, it builds up some serious points in the self-esteem and self-concept categories of confidence.

She smiled at Evans and looked at Serenity with a look of approval; only women have this wonderful gift—this ability to communicate without any form of verbalization. She gave Serenity a nod as if to say "Nothing wrong with a little jungle fever . . . You go, sister." Serenity downplayed it with a modest smile. "Are you two ready to order?" She said that with a clip-on smile.

Evans looked at Serenity; he knew she had something to say to him. He gave her another look and said to Angela, "Uh, umm . . . give us a few more . . ." He looked at Serenity and continued, "Uh, about—"

Angela cut him off. "Just call me when you are ready, sweetie. Not a problem."

Serenity gave a slight nod. Angela picked it up. The slightest command or directive she gave Evans and like a good boy, he listened. *You go, girl.* Angela thought to herself, *James Brown had it right all along. It's a man's world, where women rule.* She smiled at the thought and said, "Okay, no problem. How about something to drink?"

She looked at the one in charge because the one in charge was always the one in charge of the cash . . . she looked at Serenity. Serenity slightly smiled; she was aware of the game that had been going on for the last several minutes. She responded with a slight smile, "Sure, a small container of orange juice."

Angela looked at her. "In a glass, ma'am?"

Serenity gave Angela a patient smile. "No, just the container with a glass, if you don't mind. Thank you. I could pour it, but thank you anyway."

Angela smiled as she looked at Evans and said, "Okay, what would the gentleman like?"

Evans was impressed with Serenity; she was amazing and constantly surprising him. But now she was thinking with clarity of possible scenarios, thinking ahead, like a detective. He smiled at Angela. "The same for me, prepared the same way please. Thank you, Angela."

Angela looked at both of them in an odd way; she said, "Let me know when you're ready to order."

Serenity and Evans both nodded and smiled. "Thank you."

# CHAPTER 135

Serenity looked at him. "That's your type."

Evans looked perturbed and uneasy about the question, but he flowed with it and gave it back to her, which caught her off guard. "No, not really. My type looks something like you."

Now it was Serenity's turn to be uncomfortable as she squirmed a little in her seat. He looked at her as if to say "Two can easily play that game, baby." She didn't want to take it any further. She nervously smiled as she nibbled on her lower lip. She looked away; she looked every which way except at him. They were both silent; she nervously changed the subject. *Smart move*, Evans thought.

She was looking down at the table when Angela came back with a pitcher of water and two empty glasses with ice. Evans responded, "Thank you. But, Angela, if you don't mind, may we have a bottle of water unopened."

Angela looked at him and repeated the request, "A bottle of water . . . unopened."

Evans nodded his head. "Yes please, if it's not too much trouble."

She put on a phony smiled and said just as phony, "No, sure, not a problem. I'm kind of used to it." Angela walked off heading toward the kitchen to put the order of beverages in.

Back at the table, Serenity looked at Evans; he responded, "Sorry, call it what you like or want, but I don't trust my employer about now. He knows something . . ."

She asked what; he hesitated, shrugged, and said, "About me not doing my job. He believes I've compromised the mission. The man is very tactful and clever and insightful and can be very, very dangerous." Evans took a deep breath and let it out as he continued, "He knows how to get things accomplished no matter where you are. He can be in Texas and have someone snuffed out in another state. That earned him the name Ghost. I've seen his work. Even if he's in another country, he knows how to find you, track you down, hunt you down, drag you down, and . . . The ending is obvious. I'm dealing with a lethal man who has government big shots on his payroll."

Evans took a deep breath and blew it out. "From this point forward, Serenity, I may seem paranoid. I'm just being overly cautious. You just have to forgive me." She nodded her head; she knew she was the cause of what was happening to him. He looked at her. "I need for you to do what I say, no matter what." She looked at him questionably; he said, "No, not in that sense, but in regard to safety issues."

Serenity nodded her head. She looked around; she was starting to feel paranoid. "I think we should go."

He nodded, slightly smiling as if he was telling her a private joke. "After we eat. We must act normal. To get up and leave before our meal would look strange and odd. That would draw attention to anyone, you understand. So . . . just try to be cool and act normal." Evans looked at Serenity; he could see some anxiety and some tension; he comforted her with a smile. "Relax . . . relax." She took a deep breath and slowly let it out. He looked at her. "Good, much better."

Serenity slightly smiled as she blushed a bit. "Thank you." She looked at him. "So what are you going to do when this is over?"

He smiled; he had that rugged smile as if he was raised on a farm where he took care of horses and animals. He responded, "Well, if I live to see this over, I was thinking about living up in the mountains . . ." He chuckled and continued with bright eyes that had lost their innocence sometime in his life. "Or this farm I've been looking at for the last couple of years. It's very nice land. It reminds me something of a storybook fairy tale. I guess that's why I like it."

Serenity crinkled her nose, indicating she didn't understand. His heart melted when she did that. He smiled; she was curious, wondering why out of the clear blue he started smiling. She asked with a slight blush, "What's with the smile?" Evans shook his head and waved his hand in a dismissive way; she lightly laughed. She was now curious. "No, what? Tell me, Evans."

He thought and then said, "The way you crinkled your nose for better understanding of something."

Serenity smiled and blushed with a slight nod; she said, "A force of habit, I guess . . ."

Evans looked at her and said in a low tone, "I find it very endearing and very attractive."

She put her head down with a smile as she pushed her hair behind her ears. She nervously straightened out her blouse; nothing was wrong with it. She looked at him with a slight smile and said, "Please . . . don't do that." He looked at her and had a confused look on his face; she continued, "It just makes me uncomfortable. I mean I do enjoy the compliments. It's just that . . ."

Evans looked confused; he said, "It's just that what?"

Serenity looked at him and said, "It's just that my abductor who probably has thoughts of killing me wants to flirt with me and shows emotional feelings toward me . . . That's a little morbid to me, wouldn't you say?"

Evans put his head down and lifted it back up; looking at her, he said, "Serenity, I think—"

Angela came over with two unopened containers of orange juice and two unopened bottles of water. She placed them on the table. "Are you ready to order?"

Evans smiled and said, "Yes, we are."

Angela looked at Serenity, and she nodded with a smile. Evans looked at the menu and said, "I'll take the multi-omelet, clog stoppers." Evans laughed.

Serenity looked at Angela and smiled. "Always joking." Serenity looked at the menu. She was so hungry that she wanted everything on it. She knew she had to order something that was quick to make and equally quick to eat and get out; she said, "Mmm, your stack of hotcakes with bacon."

Angela smiled, collected both their menus, and walked off.

Serenity looked at Evans. "What was that phone call about?" He looked perplexed; she brought it closer. "That call that put you on edge."

Evans opened up his orange juice and poured it in the glass. Serenity opened up her bottle of water. He handed her a straw; he said, "I'm not certain what Mr. X is up to, but I do know he's starting to suspect something, and that's not good."

Serenity sipped on her water, but deep inside, she knew they were in trouble.

# Chapter 136

Shawn was glad his doctor made house calls; sitting up in a clinic with other sick folks wasn't his thing about right now. He wasn't better than those folks; he just knew time was of the essence and that every minute, every second counted. His doctor was cool; no matter what time of the day or night, if he called on his doctor, his doctor would be there or would send his team. Shawn was given instructions to rest a few days. He knew he didn't have a few days to play with; he was currently in a code red situation.

Dr. Mann gave him some painkillers to start with. He said, "Now this is not a cure-all Shawn. This is just a Band-Aid, a patch-up until you get done what you need to get done. And afterwards, come in so I can arrange for surgery."

Shawn blew out a frustrated breath. "Yeah, okay." Dr. Mann looked at him with a serious expression. Shawn gave him a Boy Scout's honor sign and said, "I promise."

Shawn sat at the edge of the bed when Chameleon knocked and walked in. Shawn stared at him with a parental look and said, "Where have you been?"

Chameleon smiled. "I didn't know I adopted you as my daddy. I went out."

Shawn ignored Chameleon's smart remark and continued with his investigation. "Okay, I got that part. Where did you go?"

Chameleon chuckled. "Seventeen again. By the way, good movie."

Shawn made an impatient face. "Chameleon—and by the way, I'll get back to that—but can you please tell me your real name if that is not too much to ask."

Chameleon placed his tongue in his cheek; he looked like a light-skinned Will Smith. He said, "I went out to feed."

Shawn said sarcastically, "Oh, that's all? okay. I hope this upscale neighborhood obliged your polite intrusion, Chameleon."

Shawn just shook his head, looking flustered. Chameleon stood there with his head down as if he was being punished. Shawn continued, "So was anyone willing to donate to the cause or embrace your habit . . . ?" Shawn sarcasm's disappeared, and he became serious.

Chameleon responded, "Jefferson Newhouse."

Shawn looked at him. "Excuse me, come again."

Chameleon shook his head. "Nah, you missed it the first time. Not my problem, brah man."

Shawn slightly smiled. "Serious?"

Chameleon repeated, "That's right, you missed—" Shawn cut him off.

"Jefferson . . . Newhouse . . . Did you get it this time?"

Shawn laughed, holding his side. "Get the hell . . ."

Chameleon responded, "See what I mean? I thought you didn't hear me."

Shawn chuckled. "I never said that."

Jefferson said, "Well, you gave . . . forget it. So what? So now you know . . . I prefer Chameleon."

Shawn looked at Jefferson. "What! Hey, I like it! It's better than Chameleon. Chameleon sounds like you can't be trusted, always changing with what is going on, blends in when you need the person to stand out. But Jefferson Newhouse . . . yo, that's the name. You sound like one mean, tough son of a bitch. That name makes you sound like one bad mother. I need to shut my mouth. I could dig it."

Jefferson slightly smiled. "Really? Tell me why you like the name."

Shawn said, "It's different. It's unique. It has a nice vibe, a great image, and image is where it's at, baby." He gave Jefferson a high five. Jefferson smiled. Shawn continued, "Yo, picture this. 'Yo, here comes Newhouse, Jefferson Newhouse.' It sounds exec, man." Shawn smiled. "I like it."

Jefferson nodded his head. "Okay, good." They stood there, smiling.

Shawn said, "I have to get some rest according to my doctor. Did you see him when you were coming in?"

Jefferson nodded. "Yeah, cool-looking dude with sunshades. Nice black leather outfit getting on his Harley, that's your doctor?"

Shawn nodded. "Yep, that's Dr. Mann, the man."

Jefferson smiled. "Cool car and now a cool doctor, you're just one bad mother . . ." Shawn looked at him when Jefferson laughed and said, "Shut my mouth." They both laughed.

Shawn continued, "I'll follow doctor's orders, but I'm going to see my daughter first."

Jefferson looked at Shawn. The sun was already beaming at eight thirty in the morning; it was going to be a hot one today. Jefferson said, "Yo, Wall Street, you have a kid?"

Shawn looked at him. "No, I have a child, not a kid."

Jefferson waved his hand at him. "Yo, you know what I mean."

Shawn lightly chuckled. "I know what you mean, relax." Shawn explained to Jefferson what had happened at the mall.

After Shawn was finished, Jefferson was pissed. "Yo, it's one thing to go after a man. But when you start jerking with my Eve and my child, I'm writing out your death notice, bro. No wonder you want this bitch-ass punk. Yo, I don't know him, but I want to tattoo the punk, seriously."

Shawn was happy Jefferson was on the same page. Shawn took out his cell and started dialing a number. He heard a cute little voice on the other end. "Hellow, hellow." The tears began to well up in Shawn's eyes. It was the voice of an angel.

Jefferson stood alongside Shawn as he put his arm around his shoulder and lightly squeezed them. Jefferson walked off, wiping the corners of his eyes. He was going to wait for Shawn in the backyard. He was thinking about going for a quick swim but changed his mind. Things were too much rockin' and poppin' right now. Plus he was feeling the effects of his feeding; right now, he felt mellow.

# Chapter 137

Shawn knew this wasn't going to be a walk in the park, so to speak, speaking with his daughter; neither was he thinking it would be this difficult. He started, "Hi, baby, how is my milk chocolate baby?"

Ashley replied, "Don't hi me. Daddy, where have you been?" Shawn pictured his little mom with her hand on her hips, looking more like Serenity and sounding more like Complex. Shawn thought with a smile, *Oh my goodness, what a combination.*

He smiled and responded, "Sorry, baby, Daddy's been really busy. But I'm—"

She cut him off, saying, "Can I speak to Mommy please?"

Shawn put his head down; he lifted it back up when the tears started. Ashley asked, "Is Mommy okay, Daddy? I can't get anything out of Grandma and Grandpa. They look at me as if I'm not talking English or something." Ashley went on and on and forgot that she asked the question. She said, "Daddy, I miss you and Mommy."

Shawn replied, "We miss you too . . ." He had to change the subject. "Honey, guess what! I'm coming over there to spend some time with you."

Ashley got excited. "Really?" She jumped around; she stopped and, with excitement, asked, "Mommy too?"

Shawn shook his head and then, with a look of determination on his face, said, "Yes, Mommy too, but later . . . I promise."

Shawn asked Ashley if he could speak to her grandfather. Shawn's father, Travis Cook, came on. "Hey, son. The little lady is fine. You should be asking if we're okay. This little girl is a fireball from the time she wakes up to the time she goes to bed." Travis Cook laughed and said, "But she's not a problem. She is a blessing, son." There was a pause; then his father changed his tune. "How you holding up, son? What's the latest with Serenity?"

There was a pause; then Shawn's mother, Roberta Cook, jumped in on the other line. Shawn thought, *Here we go, the tag team twins.* He smiled. Shawn's mother asked, "Baby, have you heard from her?"

Shawn nodded his head. "Yes, she sounded okay."

Shawn's parents both let out huge sighs relief, which sounded as if they've been bottled up for the longest time. His mother started crying. Mr. Cook said, "Roberta, stop that. Don't let Ashley see you crying. You know how she gets."

Roberta Cook replied, "I can't help it . . ."

Listen, I'm heading over to spend some time with Ashley and to see the greatest parents and grandparents in the world . . . Thanks, guys, really. I don't know what I would have done if you guys weren't around. Thanks."

Shawn's father responded, "Thanks? C'mon, son, no need for that. We would do it in a heartbeat. She is as cute as a button. I mean quick and smart. And her sidekick, Snuggles, the best thing a kid would want to have."

Roberta Cook, feeling better, said, "I guess she takes after her grandmother." She lightly laughed. Mr. Cook playfully moaned, "Here we go." They all laughed.

Shawn thought, *Well, at least their sense of humor is still intact.* He said, "I'm heading—"

Mrs. Cook cut him off. "We have a surprise for you, hurry."

Shawn slightly smiled and said, "Wow, a surprise." He thought to himself that his parents were the best of the best. He continued, "Mom, Pops, I'm bringing a friend with me, if that's okay."

His mother gasped. "Shawn Cook, I hope it's not—"

Shawn responded, "Nah, Mom, not even close. He's cool. His name is Jefferson Newhouse. He's been with me since this thing started. He's been a real friend. I don't know how things would have gone without him. Nah, he's cool, peeps."

Mrs. Cook was sounding concerned. "Shawn, just be careful. There are a lot of so-called chameleons out there, son."

Shawn smiled and said, "I know, tell me about it. But Jefferson is cool."

Travis Cook said, "Well, one thing, I like that name. And second, we trust your judgment, son." There was a brief pause when Mr. Cook said, "Honey, Shawn is a grown man, and—"

Mrs. Cook responded, "And . . . Travis Cook, you stay out of the conversation if you can't say anything to contribute. Yes, I know he's a grown man. But right now, my baby . . ."

Travis Cook repeated in a low tone, "A baby."

His wife heard him and responded, "That's right, my baby. And right now, Mr. Cook—not you, Shawn, that's Mr. Know-It-All—right now, he's going through a lot. He may not be able to think straight, and that can lead to bad decisions and poor judgment . . . I've read—"

Shawn interrupted. Travis Cook responded to Shawn interrupting, "Thank God, whew!"

Roberta Cook responded, "I heard that, Travis. I'll take care of you. Watch."

Shawn pushed his comment forward. "Hello, the subject that you are discussing is still here."

They both stopped and made sounds of disagreement. Shawn told them he'd be seeing them soon and quickly disconnected the call; the last thing he wanted to do was to get into another subject.

Shawn smiled to himself as he went out back looking for Jefferson; he saw him sitting on the deck of the patio, listening to some jazz. He called him, "Jefferson!"

He turned toward Shawn. "What's up?"

Shawn wasn't sure if the guys had planted any bugs that night when they came out to get him. He had swept through the place, but he wasn't sure, and Complex wasn't 100 percent sure at the time. Normally, Complex would have picked up on any bug no matter how sophisticated or not; she was good. Shawn waved for Jefferson to come over. Jefferson responded, "What, are we going or . . . ?"

Shawn frantically waved at him in an old-fashioned way for Jefferson not to say anything. Jefferson responded, "Yo, Wall Street, if we're not going to see—"

Shawn did the hand-across-the-neck sign, which meant for Jefferson to stop or cut it and not to say anything else. Jefferson caught on and said a little too loudly, "Ohh, oh, uh . . . What beautiful flowers you have. Uh, may I pick a few of them? They are so lovely."

Shawn gave Jefferson an annoyed look. He waved him over this time with a sneer. Jefferson got up and added to the overacting, "It's so beautiful. You must tell me the type of dirt, I mean, soil you use."

Jefferson came over. Shawn gripped his arm. "The kind I would love to bury you with. Can't you pick on signals or sense when something is wrong?"

Jefferson looked at him as he peeled Shawn's claws off his arm. "What the hell!" Shawn explained the whole deal except for the part Complex played. Jefferson said, "Wow, so your place or, rather, your backyard may have bugs."

Shawn shrugged his shoulders. "Maybe."

Jefferson inquired, "Okay, so how would you find out?"

Shawn shrugged. "I'm not sure. I mean I could bring in a team and go over the area from top to bottom, but that may be a waste of time. Or for the time being, I won't hold any serious pertinent information or conversations in this area."

Jefferson nodded his head. "Yeah, we can speak in codes. Not a bad idea."

Shawn thought about what Jefferson said and added, "True, but with codes, you have to make sure it sounds real. Saying stuff like '10-4' or anything that sounds like it's designed for code language can become suspicious. But you are right."

Jefferson smiled because he presented a good idea. Shawn said, "Listen, I'm going to go and see my daughter. She's staying with my folks."

Jefferson had a look of concern on his face; he looked at Shawn and said, "You think you're ready for that?"

Shawn looked at him and said, "We'll soon find out."

# Chapter 138

Evans was driving toward the house. Serenity had fallen asleep; she looked so peaceful. He hated the idea of having to wake her up. He knew this tiny fantasy would soon be coming to a close. He didn't want it to. Perhaps Mr. X was correct; perhaps he did cross the line, but he had to do what he had to do.

The place where the house was situated was deep in the suburbs, where one could get lost, get a new ID, a new everything. No one would find them. The bad part was something bad could happen, and no one would ever know. That was the drawback, but Evans loved it. Surrounded by the landscape of trees and green grass where your neighbor was miles away from you and the town was a little farther and with no one in your business—that was ideal for him. He'd been in cities across the United States; and the beauty of the landscape and nature is gone, nonexistent, replaced by tall buildings and asphalt and parking lots and business buildings. *So sad,* he thought. What happened to the nature trails and trees and grass and the sounds of the grasshoppers and the butterflies and the lightning bugs and the earthworms and the birds and the deer? They were pushed farther back into a nonexistent world. He shook his head; nature trails being replaced by jungle gyms—a perfect name for the city that was already considered a jungle.

Evans thought about that and laughed. His laughter stirred her awake. Serenity sat up and looked around with a slight blush. She turned her head slightly and wiped the corners of her mouth. "Sorry."

He nodded. "Not a problem."

Serenity looked around at the scenery as they passed it by, gorgeous home after home. She stared out of the window; she seemed to be transfixed. He continued to drive when he heard her sniffle. At first, he wasn't paying attention until he heard it again. Something was wrong, he thought; he ruled out allergies just based on the fact that he also suffered from allergies, and he wasn't being affected. Something else was wrong. Evans drove and looked at her a few times. Serenity was still transfixed on nothing in particular; it bothered him to see her this way. He had to inquire, "Serenity, what's wrong."

Evans looked over at her with concern as he focused on the road and, at the same time, on her. This was really bothering him; did he do something wrong? "What's wrong? Talk to me." Serenity shook her head; he continued to press, "Did I do something or say something wrong? Have I hurt you in any way?"

Serenity wiped her eyes and sniffed; she shook her head. "No, you've been so kind, a gentleman in every way. If anyone would ask me if I knew of a good kidnapper, I would tell them you're the best in the business." She lightly laughed, sniffed, and wiped her eyes and nose. He slightly smiled. They were both quiet.

Then he continued to press the issue, "What's wrong then?"

She wiped her tears; she was still looking out the window. She said, "This." Her hands with palms up motioned to what she was looking at. "This, all of this, I miss my home, all of this. I want my daughter. I miss her so bad it hurts. I feel the pain going through my bones. Oh god, my heart aches for my baby. I know she's wondering, 'Where is my mommy? When is Mommy coming home?' I know she's dreaming about me, her nightmares, and I'm not there to hold her and reassure her or comfort her it's going to be all right."

Serenity was on a roll. Evans opened the gate, and now she couldn't stop, but he listened with patience as she continued, "Her father is good. But there is nothing like a mother's love, a mother's touch, a mother's words, a mother . . . oh god . . ." As the floodgates opened up as, she sobbed and cried; he could see that her pain went very deep. She said, "I love her so much, and . . ." She stopped; she wanted to mention how much she missed her husband, which pulled back the thought. She really did miss him; he was her best friend. He was like the air she breathed, her designed mate, but she didn't express those thoughts. She didn't want to upset Evans; he'd been a class A act; she wasn't about to throw that in his face. He'd been right there for her. He had gone beyond the call of duty. For some strange reason, she cared about him in an odd and different way.

Evans knew she omitted the part about her husband; he appreciated that. He drove until he saw one of those convenient stores. He pulled in; she was glad because she knew she looked like a mess. Serenity was dabbing at the corners of her eyes. "You read my mind, thank you. I need to use the restroom. I know I look like crap."

He slightly smiled. "If you look like crap, you could crap on me anytime."

Serenity smiled. "You are sweet." He looked at her; she knew what he was thinking, so she said, "Listen, I won't do anything to draw attention. I promise, please . . ."

He nodded his head. "Okay, I trust you."

She looked at him and knew she shouldn't have, but she did—she lightly airbrushed his cheeks with a light kiss and told him, "Thank you."

# CHAPTER 139

Ten minutes later, she came out looking like a brand-new woman. That wasn't the same woman that went in. It's amazing what some women can do with a brush, makeup, and a positive attitude. Evans was stunned; he couldn't take his eyes off her. She was beautiful. She was gorgeous. She was stunning. She walked up to him; he was getting ready to open up a Pepsi. She smiled as she walked past him. "Ready." She walked with such finesse and poise, topped with some sex appeal.

Evans just nodded his head, said yes, and opened the Pepsi, which blasted all over his shirt. He hadn't realized he was shaking the can while he was looking and goggling and ogling at Serenity. He didn't realize the opening of the can was facing him; he looked down at his shirt. "Damn." He looked at her; she was biting her lower lip. He made a weak attempt to brush off the excess soda. He thought to himself, *Great.* That gorgeous innocent look on her face didn't make things any better as he cursed to himself, "Dammit."

Serenity quickly went to get some tissues and handed some of them to him. He dabbed here and there and said, "Okay, that's the best I can do. What a mess."

She looked at him and smiled. "It's okay."

Evans told her to come with him; she walked over to him. They walked over to the gate that separated a deep drop. She was worried and concerned. *What does he want with me?* she thought as fear gripped her. Was this the end for her? She looked over the landscape that was separated by a low fence. Serenity looked at him; everything was quiet and isolated. She wanted to run, but how far could she get? Evans was so athletic, a physical guru. What choice did she have as she stood her ground? If he pushed her over the edge, she was going to make certain she wasn't going by herself; she had determined that in her mind.

Evans looked at her. He reached into his inside pocket; her mind told her to run, but Serenity planted her feet firmly. His hand came out of his pocket, holding something black. Her breath got caught in her throat. He pointed it at her; she froze for a second or two. She looked down at his hand and noticed he was holding a black cell phone. She looked at him; he said, "Here, call your daughter."

She was astonished and surprised. "What?"

Evans looked at her as he handed the phone toward her again. "Here, before I change my mind."

Serenity looked at him, still taken back. "But they could . . ."

He shook his head. "Nah, it's a track phone. There is no GPS, no tracking. Use it and then trash it. Here, call your daughter." He handed her the phone.

She hesitated and eventually took it. She looked at him; she knew he was taking a huge risk. Serenity wiped a tear or two from her eyes and hugged him. She whispered in his ear, "Thank you, thank you."

# CHAPTER 140

Shawn and Jefferson stood at his parents' door. Shawn felt a sense of emptiness; he was so used to standing at his parents' door with Serenity and Ashley. Ashley was so happy she couldn't contain the joy and excitement bottled up in her; she was always ready to explode. She could hear her grandparents on the other side of the door playing and asking her who was at the door. She would laugh, jump up and down, and respond, "It's me, Grandpa."

His father, the practical joker of the family, would pretend he didn't hear her and repeat the question, "Who is it?"

Ashley would jump up and down, squeal and laugh, and scream, saying it was her at the door. "Me, Grandpa!" she would say.

He would push the joke to the next level and say, "Who's me, me, me? Who?" He would pause to think of another way to get him to open the door.

The light bulb of a thought would go off in her head. Ah, an idea, and then a smile would come on Ashley's face, and she would say, "Me, Grandpa! Ashley." She knew she had him cornered; she knew there was no way he could squeeze out of this one.

Her grandfather would say, "Ashley? That pretty girl?"

Ashley would start jumping up and down again; she was getting closer to having the door open. She would burst out giggling. "Yes, Grandpa, open the door."

He would continue his investigating inquiry. "The one with the cute bangs?"

Ashley would jump and down with excitement; she knew she was just inches from her Grandpa opening the door. She would burst out, "Yes!"

He would continue, "The one with the cute ponytail?"

She knew she had him; she would finally crack the case and say, "Yes, Grandpa, open up."

Her grandpa would say, "Oh, that little cute girl with the bangs and ponytail that jumps up and down when she gets excited, which I bet she's doing now?"

Ashley would giggle and laugh and squeal and say yes.

Her grandfather would say, "Hmmm, I haven't seen her." This would get Ashley excited. Finally, he would say, "Is this Ashley, my pretty and cute princess?" She would say yes, and he would say, "Oh, why didn't you say so?"

ed as she was jumping up and down with excitement. He would open the door with his arms stretched out wide; she would laugh, squeal, and giggle as her grandfather swooped her up in his arms. Shawn stood there at the door, thinking about those moments that occurred every time they came over to see his parents. He and Serenity would get a kick out of the fun. Snuggles would get excited just seeing Ashley get excited.

Jefferson put a hand on Shawn's shoulder and asked him if he was okay. Shawn nodded his head. "Yeah, just memories . . ." His voice cracked as he cleared his throat. "Just good times." Jefferson stared at him. "Hey, stop with the staring. I'm okay." Shawn looked at Jefferson. "Listen, about my parents—"

Jefferson responded, "What, they are old-fashioned, right? I got this, bro. I've dealt with old folks before."

Shawn slightly smiled and said, "Nah, man, they are the opposite. Just be cool. My parents are really cool. They are trapped in the 1960s, man. They like to be treated as if they are at Woodstock, man." Jefferson looked at him with an odd expression. Shawn continued, "Yeah, man, really. I mean young, you know, using some of that urban slang." He gave Jefferson two thumbs-up as he continued, "My mom loves to cook. She loves when you just go into the kitchen without asking if you can taste what's in the pot. She likes when you just go into the pot without asking, man. Just drop that bad boy into that pot with a double dip, man."

Jefferson responded, "Get out of here with the double dip."

Shawn nodded his head. "Double dip, man. Boom, bang, dip, and taste twice." He snapped his fingers. "Oh yeah, put the icing on the cake, very important. Brag about how good it is. That gives her a lift."

Jefferson stood next to Shawn, smiling and nodding his head. "Cool tips, thanks."

Shawn, facing the door, turned his head slightly from Jefferson and, with a slight smile, said, "Not a problem."

Jefferson added, "Yeah, man, really, thanks. This gives me a leg up, you know, an advantage. I need to know this, dude. So okay, use slang . . . ah, urban street talk, and make sure to taste her food fresh out of the pot."

Shawn said with a look of caution on his face, "Yes, but don't forget to double dip, bam, boom."

Jefferson snapped his fingers. "That's right, the double dip, bam and boom."

Shawn thought, *Yes, there is going to be a bam and a boom.* He nodded his head. "Got it."

They both heard the locks being unlocked. Shawn cut his eyes at Jefferson, who was ready to go into his best Oscar performance; he was going to stop him, but he changed his mind. He needed something to lift his spirits. The door flung wide open. Shawn's mother, Roberta Cook, had such a wide smile on her face. She saw Shawn and covered her mouth with such joy, saying a prayer of thanks, "Jesus, Lord, have mercy. Thank You, Lord. Thank You, Jesus." She called her husband, "Travis, Travis, come here, come! Travis . . ." She slightly turned her head inside the house while keeping the corners of her vision on her son. "Travis . . ."

She continued looking at Shawn. "Baby, my poor baby . . ." She covered her mouth in shock as she continued, "What have they done to you, baby?" She looked Shawn up and down, touching different parts of his body; at the parts that hurt, Shawn flinched in pain. His mother noticed and covered her mouth again. "Oh my god, Jesus . . ." Tears welled up in her eyes. "Baby, you're hurt, my lord . . . Travis, get in here! Hurry up."

They could hear Travis Cook going as fast as he could; that sprint ability was gone. His mother wiped her eyes as she tried to hold back the tears. "I can't let the baby see me in such a mess . . . What have they done to you, son?"

Shawn put a smile on his face. "Mom, I'm fine, just a few—rather, a couple of scratches and a bruise here and there."

His mother huffed and said, "Don't downplay it, Shawn. I'm looking right at you. Over the phone is one thing, but now I see you and . . ." The tears started flowing again.

Shawn tried to calm her down. "Mom, stop. I'm fine. Don't let the munchkin see you like this."

Jefferson added, "Yo, Mama Dukes, your son will be fine. He could take a licking and keep on ticking."

Roberta Cook looked at Jefferson and said, "Young man, you call me—"

Shawn cut her off, saying, "Mom, I'm okay. Fix yourself up before Ashley comes, and don't mind Jefferson . . ." He came closer to his mom and said, "He has a few issues . . ."

She shot back, "A few?"

Shawn slightly smiled. His mother quickly nodded and agreed, "Okay, you're right. I'll stop for now and save the rest of the tears for later. I'm not finished yet." She looked over at Jefferson and back at Shawn and whispered, "Where did you find him?" She shook her head. She nodded and smiled, which made Shawn smile. She said, "That man is slower than slow." She was referring to her husband.

Shawn slightly smiled and said, "Uh, Mom, can we come in?"

he "we" caused her to move her eyes over to Jefferson. She thought he didn't look much better in appearance; he also must have gone to the same slap-'em-up factory because he had bruises as well. Jefferson remembered what Shawn said about the slang. Shawn wanted to stop him, but Jefferson was already going for it. Shawn turned away slightly from his mother and Jefferson and smiled a bit, covering his mouth. He thought to himself, *Here we go. Admission is free.*

Jefferson started, "Yo, what's up, Mama Dukes? Put it here." Jefferson had his hand out for a handshake. Roberta Cook thought about putting her hand somewhere—right across his face.

She looked at him and was getting ready to tear into him when Travis Cook and Ashley came down the stairs. Travis, looking nervous, said, "What, hon? What's wrong? Are you . . . ?" Travis Cook took one look at his son, and his knees buckled as he almost fell down the few more steps he had left to go; he said in surprise, "What the f . . ."

That's when he almost fell down the stairs, dropping the famous f-bomb, but it was drowned out by Ashley's joyous scream and excitement. "Daddy, Daddy! Grandpa, Grandma, it's my daddy!"

, and Shawn knew it was coming; he braced himself for the impact of the little tank. Ashley might have appeared small, but she was compact and solid as she jumped and stretched her arms and legs out, looking like Spider-Girl as she crashed solid into him. Bam . . .

Shawn's parents cringed. Roberta Cook said nervously, "Honey, be careful with your father. He's fragile."

Ashley repeated the word as she continued to bounce in Shawn's arms, "Fragile."

Her grandpa nodded. "Yes, hon, it means tender, easy to break."

Ashley's button eyes looked at her grandfather. "No, Papa, I don't want my daddy to break. I don't have any more glue to fix him." She leaned back in Shawn's arms, putting more pressure on his back, and wagged her finger at him. "Daddy, don't break, okay?"

Shawn nodded his head as he grimaced with a smile. "I'll try not to, okay, baby? But get some glue just in case."

They all laughed. Shawn was still holding her. Ashley kissed him on the cheek and said, "Okay, Daddy, I will. Grandma and Grandpa, somebody needs to take me to the store so I could buy some glue to fix my daddy just in case he gets a boo-boo."

Her grandmother dabbed at a tear from the corner of her eye and said, "Yes, dear, we will go later, okay?" Ashley nodded her head with excitement. Her grandma nodded as she dabbed at another tear from the corner of her eyes. "Yes, baby, Grandpa and Grandma will take care of your daddy, okay?"

Ashley nodded her head as she looked up at Jefferson. Snuggles was doing his own investigation of Jefferson, who said, "Yo, I feel like I'm on display." He looked down at Snuggles.

His attention was drawn away when Ashley asked, "Are you my daddy's friend?"

Jefferson looked down at Ashley and said, "Yeah, most of the time."

She looked right in his eyes. "Most of the time?" Jefferson nodded. Ashley continued, "Why?"

Jefferson made a sarcastic laugh and said, "You are full of questions, aren't you? With Snoop Doggy Dogg still checking me out."

Shawn's mother said, "He just wants to make sure whether you're clean or dirty."

Jefferson slightly smiled, which meant he was slowly losing patience; he said, "I'm as clean as a whistle."

Travis Cook responded, "Before or after it's used?"

Jefferson replied, "Wow, the entire family."

Shawn smiled as he looked at his daughter; he loved her so much. He thought about the day of the mall bombing; if Ashley was with Serenity, he wouldn't have neither one. He called her over, "Ashley honey, come here." She reluctantly came as she took one more look at Jefferson. Shawn responded, "Mr. Jefferson is tired and hungry."

Jefferson was a little too loud. "Two things we can't do without, you know what I mean, Papa Dukes." Jefferson held out his hand for Travis Cook to slap him five. Travis looked at the hand and backed up from Jefferson, who got the point and said, "Yo, Joe, I'm in a hostile environment."

Roberta Cook responded, "You think this is hostile? Young man, you are already walking a thin line, be careful." Jefferson looked confused.

Shawn picked up Ashley. His father knew that had to hurt. Ashley wasn't lightweight anymore; he intervened. "Ashley, you want to help Grandpa outside in the garden?"

She got excited; she enjoyed helping out her grandparents, but now she was torn. She looked at her father, and in a grown way, she said, "Daddy, I'll be right back. Why don't you and Mr. Jefferson watch some television?" Shawn nodded with a look of surprise on his face.

His mother shook her head. "That's the other woman of the house." They all lightly laughed.

Jefferson walked up to Roberta Cook and said, "That may be the case, little mama, big mama. I heard, Mrs. Cook, you know how to get down in the kitchen. Yo, you are ruthless." Jefferson growled at Mrs. Cook.

Mrs. Cook moved slightly back, looked at Jefferson, and said, "Boy, you better behave yourself. Now go over by Shawn and behave yourself."

He walked past Shawn's father. "Yo, the alpha male! Yo, Pops, you got a good thing going. You are the man, daddy-o."

Travis looked at Jefferson and at Shawn and said in a warning tone, "Shawn, you better."

Shawn nodded and felt this was a good time to break the ice. "Okay, okay, Jay, come with me in the kitchen. We need to talk."

Travis nodded in agreement. "You sure do. Fix that issue we talked about, son."

Jefferson said, "Fix what? I probably can help."

Travis nodded his head with enthusiasm, saying, "I'm sure you can."

Shawn nervously smiled and said to Jefferson, "Here, come here. I want to show you something."

Jefferson walked into the kitchen. "Yo, Wall Street, this kitchen is huge. Wow."

Shawn nodded and said, "I know. Cool, right?"

Jefferson nodded. "This place is bigger than one of the places I rented in that hellhole." He nodded and said, "Hey, how am I doing so far?"

Shawn wanted to laugh. "So far so good. Keep it up."

Jefferson had a look of slight doubt on his face; he said, "Are you sure? Because it looks like your parents are getting a little annoyed. I hope not. they are cool people."

Shawn waved a dismissive hand. "What, are you serious? They love you! You're about to win an Oscar."

Jefferson smiled. "Cool." He patted his stomach. "Wall Street, I'm starving, dude."

Shawn looked at him. "How are you doing with the . . . ? You know . . . the . . ."

Jefferson filled in the blanks. "Hey, it is what it is. Until then, I have to live and deal with it . . . But at this moment—this exact and precise moment—my name is Marvin, and I am starving. Feed me, Seymour."

Shawn said, "Seymour, Marvin, Jay—whatever. You have the pot of gold in front of you . . . Need I say more?"

Jefferson smiled, looked at Shawn, and said, "Say no more, my good man."

Shawn smiled, patted Jefferson on his back, and said, "Well, like I said, remember my mom likes that double-dip action. Remember to taste the food and dip it again."

Jefferson moved as if he was in a church service. "Double dip." He looked at Shawn and asked, "Are you serious? Because I'm a double dipper, baby."

Shawn smiled. "Yes, go ahead, taste test and double dip that bad boy."

Jefferson smiled. "Your mom is so cool. How about your pops? He seemed a little agitated with me out there."

Shawn nodded his head and smiled. "Pops is cool to the max, seriously."

Jefferson smiled and nodded his head as he walked over to the stove as he did a double dip as he was saying the words, "Time to double dip, baby." He was standing up, laughing. He nodded his head. "Everything smells so good. Yo, Wall Street, your mom should open a restaurant."

Shawn replied, "I agree. Right now, she's happy and content."

Jefferson said, "Me too."

Shawn encouraged him to sample the food. He heard his mother coming. "Yo, Jay, come out front when you're done."

Jefferson looked around. "Wall Street, wait for me. Yo, Wall Street."

Shawn kept on going as if he did not hear Jefferson. He met his mother right at the swing door of the kitchen right before she stepped into the kitchen. The doorbell rang. Shawn said, "I got it." He was happy somebody was ringing the front doorbell.

In the meantime, he heard his mother in the kitchen gasp out loud and said in her tough motherly tone, "Young man, what are you doing?"

Jefferson said with a smile in his voice, "Can't you see I'm double—"

The only sound Shawn heard was Jefferson trying to explain and a hard-cracking sound of flesh connecting with flesh and Jefferson reacting with an, "Ouch! Mama Dukes, Shawn told—" *Wham . . . crack . . .* "Ouch, my head!"

Shawn's mother said in that stern voice, "Didn't I tell you not to call me no Mama Dukes, huh?" *Whack.*

"Ouch my hand!"

Shawn, from the corner of his eye, watched Jefferson come flying out of the kitchen, grabbing his hand and then his head; he didn't know which one he should hold first as he grimaced in pain. Jefferson looked at Shawn, perplexed.

Shawn's father said, "I bet he tried to get slick and go into the pot."

Shawn was laughing as he nodded his head to his father's question as he headed toward the door, laughing; he looked back at Jefferson and said, "Jefferson, are you okay?" Jefferson didn't think it was funny. Shawn looked at him and said, "Seriously, are you okay?"

Jefferson looked at Shawn and said, "You set me up. That was wrong. Payback is a—"

Roberta Cook looked at him and said, "Say it and see if this spoon comes toward you like a javelin. You watch your mouth when you come into this domain. You understand?"

Jefferson was still rubbing the injured parts on his body. "Yes." He looked over at Shawn and made a face as if to say "This isn't over."

Shawn chuckled as he opened the door and could not believe who was on the other side.

# Chapter 141

Shawn was so excited that he grabbed and hugged both Marcus and Sandra like they were in a small huddle. Shawn was so thrilled. "Oh my god, thank you!" They held on to the little huddle they were in. little Ashley was in the middle of them as Shawn's parents looked on with tears and Jefferson was still mending to his head and hand. They broke the embrace, and all three were overwhelmed by the joyous and surprised occasion. They were all wiping their eyes as Shawn's mother was handing out tissue.

Shawn gave Marcus a nice and solid shoulder tap. Marcus said, "Man, C-4, so much is going on, so much, man. Our prayers are with you, bro." Another hard shoulder tap was given as they stayed in that position for a few seconds.

They broke the embrace. Shawn told him, "Thank you." Then he went over to Sandra and gave her a hug and a kiss. Sandra, with much love, could feel Shawn's pain; he smiled. He knew she knew the pain he had been going through—the emptiness, the waking up discovering night after night that Serenity was gone. He dismissed his feelings and focused on her, typical Shawn. He said, "Sandra, how are you?"

Sandra nodded when the floodgates opened; she cried with a deep cry. "I miss my sister, oh god." The tears kept on coming. Marcus held on to her, comforting her. Sandra carefully broke the embrace from her husband; as she smiled up at him, she dabbed the tears from her eyes, saying, "Thank you, baby. Thank you, everyone. I have moments like those where I feel the pain deep inside. My doctor tells me it's normal. Things will get better, but those nightmares are not as easy to . . ." She stopped and shook her head as the tears slowly started up again.

Sandra looked down at Ashley, who looked like she wanted to cry as well. Sandra looked at Shawn, put her head down, and shook her head as the tears continued to flow. She said to Shawn, "I miss my sister."

Ashley looked up at her. "Auntie, where is your sister? You can use my phone to call her, okay? Or maybe you can go and visit her. Don't cry."

Mrs. Cook came rushing into the living room, where everybody was. Jefferson covered up and said, "I didn't do it. I've been right here all the time." She ran past Jefferson; he blew out a breath of relief.

"Shawn, Shawn, oh my god, Shawn . . ."

Shawn looked at her mother; he became nervous as he watched the color drain from her face. He looked at her and, with a slight panic in his voice, said, "Mom, you okay? What's wrong?" He looked at his father. "Dad."

Shawn's father quickly went over to his wife's side. "Honey, what's wrong?"

Mrs. Cook seemed to have trouble breathing; they all gathered around her, trying to figure out what was going on. Roberta Cook was trying to speak, but she was still having problems breathing. Shawn said to his father, "Dad, call 911." Mrs. Roberta Cook's

breathing was still erratic as she held out her hand for everybody to stop as she shook her head. "No, don't call 911." She held out her hand, took a deep breath, and said as her voice cracked, "Shawn . . . it's . . . Serenity." Roberta Cook looked at Shawn and smiled as she handed the phone to him.

# Chapter 142

Shawn's knees buckled as Jefferson and Marcus held him up. Shawn recovered as he spoke into the phone. "Baby, is it you?"

Serenity had tears in her eyes as her voice cracked. "Yes, it's me. Listen, I can't talk long. I'm okay."

The speaker phone was on. They all heard her voice and got excited, cheering and clapping. Shawn heard Serenity saying something, but the noise from the happy moment was very loud; he motioned for them to bring it down. "I can't hear her. Bring it down, bring it down." He shushed them. "I can't . . ." The noise level dropped.

Shawn said, "Sorry, baby. Everyone is so happy that you are doing okay."

Serenity responded, "Yes, I am. Let me speak to my baby."

Shawn motioned for them to bring Ashley. Marcus picked her up and quickly brought her over to Shawn; he said, "Okay, baby, here she is." He gave the phone to Ashley, leaving the speakerphone on. Shawn said to her, "Honey, listen, Mommy doesn't have much time. You have to speak up, baby."

Ashley smiled with tears building up in her eyes. "Mommy, where are you?"

Serenity closed her eyes at the sound of her daughter's sweet angelic voice; she responded, "Baby, the main thing is I'm fine, and I hope to see you soon. You make sure you pray to God that I'll come home soon, okay, baby?"

Ashley was listening; she said, "Mommy, I will pray as soon as I get off the phone. This is important, right?"

Serenity's tears came streaming down her cheek. "Yes, baby, very important."

Ashley continued, "When I go to bed tonight, I'll pray again just in case God was too busy the first time I prayed. I'll have Grandma and Grandpa pray also. Even Snuggles, he prays. I saw him with his hands—sorry, his paws covering his eyes the other day. He was praying. I didn't want to disturb him, so I left the room."

They all lightly laughed. Serenity lightly laughed and said, "Baby, Mommy loves you so much."

Ashley rubbed her eyes. Sandra picked her up and held her in her arms. Ashley continued, "Mommy, why did you leave? Did you have a fight with Daddy?" Ashley looked at Shawn and said, "Daddy, were you mean to Mommy?"

Serenity looked up toward the sky and smiled; she lightly laughed and said, "Ashley honey, no, Daddy wasn't mean to me. I had to leave to do a few things, that's all." Serenity's voiced cracked toward the end of that sentence. Everyone was wiping their eyes.

Ashley started crying. "Mommy, I miss you. Come home right now. Daddy and Complex will pick you up, okay?"

Serenity responded, "I know he will if I ask him to, baby. But Mommy has to do a few other things, okay? Then Daddy and Complex and you and Snuggles—"

Ashley added, "Grandma and Grandpa, Uncle Marcus and Aunt Sandra . . ."

Serenity laughed and said, "You guys could rent a bus to pick me up." They all laughed.

Ashley cried; she tried to be a big girl as she nodded her head, saying, "Okay, Mommy. I love you."

Serenity asked Ashley to put her father back on the phone. Serenity had about thirty seconds left. Evans had been so kind to her. Ashley handed the phone to Shawn; he kept Serenity on speakerphone. He wanted everyone to hear her; he said, "Go ahead, baby. We're all here, including Marcus and Sandra."

Sandra shouted, "Hi, sister! Don't worry, God is good, girl. He will bring you home. Don't give up hope, baby."

Serenity was so happy to hear her best friend's voice; the tears continued to flow down her cheeks; she said, "Listen, I have to go. Everybody, pray for me."

Someone said to Serenity that her time was up. Serenity responded with an "okay," thanked the person, and hung up.

Jefferson was in deep thought; he thought about the voice he just heard. "Time's up." He said to Shawn, "Wall Street, that's the same dude, man."

Shawn looked at him questionably. Jefferson said, "Yo, I'm telling you that's him. The only difference is he sounds much more relaxed, but I'm telling you, that's him."

Mr. Cook looked at Shawn and said, "Shawn, what is he talking about?"

Shawn looked at his father and at the others; he instructed his mother to take Ashley outside. "Mom, take Ashley out to the swings. Dad will fill you in on everything later . . . please . . . Thank you."

Roberta Cook told Ashley to come outside so the grown-ups could talk. Ashley was happily ready. "Okay, we can play work. I'm the boss."

Her grandmother nodded and said, "Okay, come on . . ."

Shawn and the others went into the living room. Jefferson and Shawn told the others everything.

Marcus paced the floor. "So this is one sick army of one sick mother."

Mr. Cook said, "I don't understand why the law can't trace and find this nut. He needs to be put away."

Marcus added, "Let it be one of us, and they will find us even if they have to go to the ends of the earth. They won't do it to this guy because he has clout and money and he's white. But let it be one of us. They'll find us and locate us and bring us in, dead or alive. If they had to go to Africa, they would. This is crazy."

Shawn countered, "Hold up, we are not turning this into a racial thing. This man, Mr. X, is dangerous and calculating. He's not concerned about the color of the skin. He wants revenge, which means he wants me. He's coming after me through Serenity."

Marcus added, "There must be a way to get this guy. How did you get his brother?"

Shawn responded, "His hate and anger consumed him. It interfered with his plan, his intelligence." There was a pause; then Shawn continued, "But understand this—this man is five times smarter than his brother. He knows how to dot his i's. He knows how to cross his t's. The man is very complex and perplexing. He's hard to track. As long as he keeps me tripping and falling, this gives him more power and more confidence. The more tests I pass, the longer it keeps Serenity alive. The longer she is kept alive, then I have a chance of finding her because my man is going to make a mistake, and I'm going to be all over his ass."

Shawn's father looked at him and said, "Whatever I can do, let me know."

Marcus and Sandra agreed. They looked at Jefferson, who said, "Yo, Wall Street knows I have his back." He continued, "The man is smart, with lots of dough—that's not a good combination for those chasing after him."

Shawn continued, "Damn, it's like fighting a ghost." He shook his head. "In the meantime, stay alert and on your toes. And just keep in mind, this is my fight, not yours. You got it?" They all reluctantly agreed. Shawn continued, "Jefferson and I will hit the streets and find out what we can."

Jefferson added, "I still have some connections that may be able to help."

Mr. Cook said, "Fine, but are they loyal and reliable sources? We don't want things to go south. You wave a nickel bag to some folks, and you find out where their loyalty lies. Sellouts."

Jefferson felt a little stab as he cleared his throat. Shawn caught what was said and said, "Not in all cases, Pop. I have friends that are in recovery, and they are loyal to me." He gave Jefferson a shoulder squeeze. Jefferson just nodded his head as if to say thanks.

Mr. Cook caught the subtle message and corrected his mistake. "Yes, you are right. In some cases, loyalty is most respected and highly honored." Mr. Cook was looking at Jefferson, who felt he had passed the first test.

Marcus raised his hand and said, "Yo, hold up, C-4. what do you mean you and Jefferson? What kind of crap is that? Before the new kid came on the block, yo, it was just you, me, and Frank. You remember that?"

Shawn nodded his head. "Of course."

Marcus continued, "We did some serious rock and roll back in the day, and now you're telling me you and Jefferson." He was upset. "I'm not feeling that broth, not one bit." He looked at Jefferson and said, "Yo, my man, no disrespect or beef with you. But C-4 and I go way back, and I don't like the idea of being overlooked. I'm a key player in all of this crap, man. Trouble comes to our doorstep, and I'm overlooked? Freak that." Marcus shook his head and walked over to the other side of the room. Sandra was right by his side, rubbing his back and calming him down.

Mr. Cook raised his arms toward Marcus. "Marcus, you need to relax, okay? Why don't you listen to what Shawn has to say before you fly off the handle. Just relax." Mr. Cook paused and continued, "I'm sure he has a logical explanation, don't you, son?"

Shawn slightly smiled and nodded his head. "Yeah, sure. Marcus, this does not have to deal with what we used to do in the past. It has nothing to do with your status with me. You will always be my number one homeboy." He took a deep breath and continued, "Listen, the folks we are dealing with are dangerous and deadly, okay? If they find out who you are, they will come after you and whoever is associated with you . . . including Sandra. I can't and I won't put you in that situation."

Marcus tried to say something, but Shawn cut him off. "Listen to me. The man who has Serenity is a killing machine. I've witnessed the damage this man has caused. Don't believe me? Ask Jefferson. He was given his ass back to him and—"

Jefferson cut him off, saying, "That's an overexaggeration, Shawn, don't you think?"

Shawn folded his arms in front of him and looked at Jefferson. "Jeff—"

Jefferson responded, "Please don't call me that." Jefferson had all eyes on him; he slightly smiled, put his head down, and brought it back up. "Okay, I put up a good fight, so I thought." Shawn looked at him. Jefferson looked at Shawn and said, "Well, I did . . . well, sort of . . . in a way. All I can say is that the man is extremely good." Shawn nodded his head.

Marcus asked, "Wait a second, you actually ran into this guy? Really? How?"

Shawn looked at his watch and said, "Okay, I'll give you the *Reader's Digest* version." He told the complete story, the showdown between Jefferson and this dude Evans. Shawn said, "I'll let Jefferson talk to you about the fight."

Everyone was shocked and surprised. Mr. Cook said, "So you actually saw Serenity?"

Jefferson nodded his head. "Yes, I did."

Marcus asked, "How did she look? Did she look as if she was in danger or hurt or . . ."

Jefferson thought about the question and responded, "No, she looked concerned and worried."

Marcus asked, "For himself?"

Jefferson was looking straight. "No, for the ones that he was going after. It was as if he was like a freakin' machine gone haywire. He looked completely out of control. When he and I threw down, his skills were amazing, his speed was phenomenal, his strength was crazy. But I was on a mission to get Wall Street's woman back." He shook his head. "It was wrong from the start. A couple of moves and the man had me. Wall Street—rather, Shawn had it right—the man is lethal. I mean I've seen this guy in action. He's no doubt military trained, Navy SEAL, something."

Mr. Cook asked, "So what happened when you two fought? What, nothing?"

Jefferson said, "I was at a complete disadvantage. I knew I was in trouble when he had me in this crazy choke hold. He was slowly killing me, and he knew it." He looked down at the floor and back up at the others; he said, "If it wasn't for Serenity, I would have been at the gates begging Peter to let me in."

Mr. Cook was amazed at the story, but he wanted to know what part Serenity played. "What did she do?"

Jefferson paused, swallowed, and said, "She gently persuaded him to let me go."

Marcus asked, "And he did?"

Jefferson nodded his head and said, "Yeah . . . yeah. They took off. The next thing I remember was Shawn standing over me, reviving me." He looked at Marcus and said, "My brother, I play around. I joke, that helps me with my own issues in life. But I tell you this in all seriousness, I don't know anything about this clown who is running the show. But the one who works for him, Evans, is deadly and lethal. And by Shawn keeping you out of this fight, he's doing you a favor—trust me on that one."

# CHAPTER 143

Shawn was holding Ashley in his arms; she was still going strong, the energized bunny—she just kept ticking. He spent about two hours of nonstop playing, from house to pretend food shopping to preparing a meal to, of course, medical doctor and hide-and-go-seek. He was exhausted. He was ready to fall out; he was ready to crash. He was thinking that Ashley could be his new workout coach; she was tougher than his workout sparring partner. He held her up in his arms like a puppet.

Sandra kissed her on her cheek a bunch of times. Ashley was just taking it all in. She smiled brightly at the attention. Sandra hugged Shawn, kissed him lightly on the cheek, and told him he was an amazing man. Marcus gave him a dap and a brief shoulder tap; he said, "Hey, I'm here if you need me. And thank you for looking out for me, man."

Shawn nodded and said, "No doubt, my brother."

Marcus shook Jefferson's hand. Jefferson grabbed him and jokingly said, "I love you, man." They all chuckled at that.

Marcus said, "Yo, Jefferson, when this is over, bring that sick son of a bitch in . . ."

Shawn cleared his throat, and Marcus looked at him. Shawn looked down at Ashley, who looked exhausted. *Finally*, Shawn thought. Shawn said, "Easy, the child."

Marcus said, "Yo, C-4, I know the rules. Right, pumpkin?"

Ashley, being exhausted, did not have the energy to protest and said, "That's right, Uncle Marcus. Any bad word is punished by either giving cash or a gift of equal value to the Ashley Fund. Right, Daddy?"

Shawn kissed her and said, "Yep, baby."

Ashley said, "No, Daddy, not 'yep.' 'Yes,' okay?"

Shawn nodded and said yes. They all laughed.

Mrs. Cook came over and said, "Okay, young lady. Yes, you, the little grown one. Yes, you. Give Dad a kiss and get ready for bed."

Ashley pouted and made a face. "Please, Grandma, I haven't seen my daddy in a long time, please."

Roberta Cook looked at Ashley. "Honey, we went through this, haven't we? And what did you say? Do you remember?" Ashley whispered something again. Roberta Cook responded, "Huh?"

Ashley responded reluctantly, "The rules are the rules. Laws are broken, but rules are to be followed." Mrs. Cook nodded her head. Ashley was looking sad.

Shawn looked at his mother; he knew better than to get involved and override his mother.

He continued to look at his mother.

Mrs. Cook said, "In this case, because it's a special night, you may stay up for an additional thirty minutes. And, little lady, when time is up, that's it. If you in any way or shape or form cry, moan, pout, or whine, I'm going to get my leather belt special and tear that little grown behind up. You hear me, Ashley?"

Ashley jumped up and down with excitement. "Daddy, c'mon, I have thirty minutes. C'mon, Daddy, let's go outside." Shawn was being pulled by Ashley. Shawn wasn't in the mood, but for Ashley, he'd do anything; if he had a chance to bring the moon with some stars to her, he would. He couldn't understand where this little girl got her energy from; all he knew he had to slow her down. Ashley was still pulling her father toward the door to go outside. "C'mon, daddy, we don't have a lot of time."

Shawn resisted just enough to slow the little tank down; he said with as much excitement as he could, which was very little, "Listen, pumpkin, I have an idea. Let's go up to your room and watch a DVD, okay?" Ashley looked sad. Shawn knew he messed up.

Then her eyes lit up as her breath got caught in her chest from the thought she was thinking. She said, bubbling like a soda about to explode, "Daddy, that's a good idea! I have the perfect DVD." Shawn looked at her; his eyes were now almost bloodshot from exhaustion. Ashley continued, "I've been holding it for us to see together."

Shawn said, "How do you know it's good?"

Ashley said, "Daddy, I watched it about three times. And take my word, it's good, Daddy."

Shawn smiled and said, "Your word?"

Ashley nodded with her cute cartoon-looking smile. "Yes, Daddy, come on." She started pulling him now in the other direction, toward the stairs.

Shawn, while being pulled, said, "But you've been holding it for us, right?"

Ashley's little mind didn't realize she was being pulled into her father's web. She blew out a breath and said, "Yes, Daddy, for us to see, just you and I." Ashley continued to pull when she stopped, looked at her grandmother, and said, "Grandma, may we have some snacks please? I would like a Suzy Q with something sweet to drink." The others just watched and listened to this young girl with an old soul; they lightly laughed.

Mrs. Cook looked at her and said, "Okay, to wish and dream is okay. But this is one wish and dream that won't be coming true, my dear." Ashley's grandmother put her hands on her hips and said, "No way, I don't think so. You're not going to be bouncing off these walls when your father and Jefferson leave, leaving me with your grandfather peeling you off the ceiling, trying to slow you down like the Road Runner. I don't think so. I don't have the energy for that. That's not going to happen." Ashley pouted; her grandmother gave her a warning call, "Ashley! We can shut this thing down. Do you want that?"

Ashley quickly smiled. "Just playing, Grandma. See?" Mrs. Cook looked and saw Ashley with a big, wide smile showing her teeth; there were a couple of teeth not accounted for, but she was still so cute. Mrs. Cook looked at her; she shook her head, slightly smiled, and said, "I'll give you a little bit of ice cream and a little"—Mrs. Cook made a sign of "a little"—"slice of my homemade pound cake."

Ashley jumped up and down, ran over to her grandmother, and hugged her around her waist. Jefferson said, "Wow, Mrs. C, you bake also?"

Mrs. Cook slightly smiled. "Sure do, but in this case, this cake comes from my church. We had a cake sale. I have to admit, this was some good cake. Would you like to try a slice?"

Jefferson said, "Sure."

Mrs. Cook said, "Let me serve Ashley and Shawn, and then I'll be back to slice you a piece of cake."

Mrs. Cook came back down the stairs. She smiled at the idea her son was home; it may not be the ideal situation, and perhaps for a short time, it didn't matter to her—the main thing was he was here. Roberta Cook missed her daughter; she didn't believe in this daughter-in-law stuff. Serenity was her daughter, and she was her mother. The end. This daughter-in-law stuff in Serenity's eyes was complete nonsense, garbage. She walked over to get ice cream and cake; she said to Jefferson, "Okay, Mr. Jefferson, what do you want, small, medium, or large? Don't be shy."

; it had been a while since he came into anything like this—fun and family. His eyes gleamed with excitement. The goose bumps on his arms hit him; he loved this moment. He asked for a large slice and a lot of ice cream. As she was cutting, he said, "I change my mind."

She looked at him with curiosity and asked, "What's wrong?"

He shook his head, looked down and back up, and said, "Can you make that extralarge piece of cake please?"

Roberta Cook lightly laughed and smiled; she nodded and smiled. "Not a problem, sweetheart." She asked, "Ice cream?" It was more of a question of request rather than a question of inquiry.

Jefferson nodded his head with these bright childlike eyes; he said, "Yes please."

His eyes started to get glassy; one more thing could bring the waterfall down, but he promised to hold it together. He wanted to call her Mother; her smile was so genuine. His mother went to be with the Lord about a few years ago. Jefferson was so close to her; but the loss of his best friend, which was his father, really crushed him. His mother left him, and a short time later, his father left.

Roberta Cook came back with a huge plate filled with ice cream and cake. "Here you go." He took the huge bowl with a smile; she heard him whisper, "Wow." She laughed to herself with a smile.

She sat down by Jefferson at the table. She watched him eat as if he hadn't eaten before. She knew this was the right time to find out some things. Certain foods were happy foods in which the person eats and relaxes; the meal mellowed them out, took the edge off things, and caused the person to open up in conversation—some called these foods the "confess canal," and ice cream and cake were like that. Mrs. Cook knew she might not have this opportunity again, so better get what she could while Jefferson was under her food spell. She calmly asked, "So, Jefferson, or would you mind if I call you Jay?"

Jefferson stopped eating and thought; he shrugged his shoulders. "Either one is fine."

Mrs. Cook smiled. "Okay. So, Jay, how did you and Shawn meet?"

Jefferson was halfway through his ice cream and cake. This meant that in the same way happy foods made one confess, when it was gone, it can also shut you down like Fort Knox. He responded to the question as he put another load of ice cream and cake into his mouth, "Let's just say we met at a competition for fighters."

Mrs. Cook smiled and nodded her head; she realized Shawn was an expert in martial arts, but he wouldn't exploit that skill just for competition. If he was competing, he had to have had good reason to put himself out there. She looked at Jefferson and asked, "What do you mean?"

Jefferson was almost done; the confession canal was slowly shutting down. He said, "Mrs. C, I'm not trying to be rude or anything, but I think you should speak to Shawn about that." Jefferson smiled as he shoveled another load of his ice cream and cake into his mouth.

Roberta Cook calmly nodded her head with a smile and thought to herself, *I sure will.* She knew whatever it was that Jefferson couldn't say about how he and Shawn met must have been very bad or under serious conditions; his loyalty was admirable. She smiled and continued, "Are you married, and do you have children?"

Ashley and Shawn were having a wonderful time. Their laughter and fun were wonderful to hear. Ashley squealing could be heard throughout the house; it brought a smile to Jefferson's face. He said, "They sure are having a good time." He lightly laughed; he was almost finished with his dessert.

Mrs. Cook lightly laughed listening to those two upstairs; she said, "Those two have always been so close, like peanut butter and jelly, and Serenity was like the milk." Jefferson smiled and nodded. Mrs. Cook asked again, "Are you married, and do you have children?"

Jefferson had about two more spoons to go; he ignored the question again. "Boy, this ice cream and cake sure hit the spot, Mrs. C!"

Mrs. Cook calmly asked, "Would you like more?"

Jefferson thought; he felt his flat stomach and said, "Uh, nah. No, thank you. I'm good, thanks." He looked at her and said, "Mrs. C, you would have been a good integrator. You are very cunning and smart and wise. You asked the right questions." He paused and continued, "Let me put it this way, and this is for the ice cream." He told her his story, the short version; but it was enough, enough to connect the dots.

When he was done, Mrs. Cook stood up, walked over to him, and hugged him like a mother would. She held him like that for a few seconds and said to him, "There is no replacement for a mother's love, but this is the closest I could give you." She held him. She could feel the tension in his body; she assured him it was okay, and she encouraged him to let it go. That was the word that busted open the gate of his heart as the tears started coming down, and his shoulders started shaking. There wasn't a sound at all from him, but she knew the buildup was about to be released; that dam was about to break. She could feel it. The tension, the pain, the guilt, the regret, the unforgiveness, the failure—all of it was being held in. She held on to him tightly, and the words he wanted to hear, no ice cream or cake could have done any better; he heard her say, "Jefferson . . . let it go."

When he got the permission to do so, the hardness of his heart crumbled as he cried, and the tears came streaming down his face; all that hurt, stress, and tension through the years came flooding down his face. Mr. Cook heard the commotion as he came into the kitchen just to be warned off by his wife as he dipped back out. He knew his wife had it under control.

Meanwhile, Mrs. Cook rubbed Jefferson's head as she hummed a song that only a mother could. The tears continued to pour down his face. Jefferson apologized to those he failed; he apologized to his mother, to his father, to God, to his wife and children, pleading and begging for forgiveness. "Mama, I'm so sorry. Dad, forgive me. Oh, God, help me, help me. Please help me." He cried. He wanted to do better. He asked God to help him do better, to get better; he wanted his family. His tears and confession were deep, hard, and real."

Mrs. Cook's tears started to flow. She held on to Jefferson as if he was on a cliff; she held on to him as if he was her only son, and he held on to her as if he couldn't and wouldn't let another person go in his life. They both cried and rocked back and forth and side to side—a friend finding a friend.

# CHAPTER 144

Shawn came down the stairs; he noticed how quiet it was. He looked around; the lights were dim. He went into the kitchen; it was clean as if Mr. Clean did it himself. He walked toward the back porch. There was a light on. *Perhaps it is Jefferson*, Shawn thought. He took a couple of steps and stopped; he took a few more steps when he heard his father call him into his study.

Shawn went into the study room and found his father at the reading table; he looked so scholarly, a man that excelled in what he taught himself. His father became a successful businessman who worked because he was bored. Travis Cook couldn't see himself retired and home every day; he knew that would either drive him crazy, or his wife would drive him crazy, or he would drive her crazy, or they both would become crazy at the same time. Every day he would put in a few hours here and there, get some rest and recreation in between, or even find a project to take on. He would volunteer his time at a junior high school or a high school for a couple of days, or he and his wife would just go on a cruise or to one of the islands for days.

Shawn walked in. "Hey, Dad." He looked around the dim lighting of the room.

Travis Cook was working on a five-thousand-piece puzzle with a piece of the mystery in his hand, looking where the mystery piece would go; he said, "I like it this way. It's peaceful. Different strokes for different folks." He looked up at Shawn and smiled. "Come have a seat." There was a pause. Travis Cook continued, "She finally knocked out?"

Shawn blew out an air of relief with a chuckle and said, "Well, to tell you the truth, she knocked out about thirty minutes ago . . . Girl is persistent."

Mr. Cook lightly chuckled. "An apple doesn't fall too far from the tree."

Shawn lightly smiled with a slight head nod and said, "I guess I'm her tree, and you were mine." They both laughed.

Mr. Cook looked at his watch and said, "Thirty minutes ago, huh? Well, I have an hour later."

Shawn lightly laughed and said, "Guilty, what can I say? It's my favorite cartoon, out of all three . . ." Mr. Cook blew out a whistle as Shawn smiled and said, "This was my favorite."

Mr. Cook said, "Is that the one with the boy who . . ." Mr. Cook described it perfectly.

Shawn responded, "Seems like it's your favorite one as well." Mr. Cook looked up at his son and smiled. Shawn continued, "Anyway, where's Jay?"

Mr. Cook didn't want to get too deep in the muck and mire and just shrugged his shoulders. "I think he's in the bathroom."

Shawn looked at his father. "You think?"

Mr. Cook nodded his head. "Well, where else could he be?" Mr. Cook was careful with the next line that came out of his mouth. "I think he was talking to your mother and . . ."

Shawn looked at his father, saying, "You think again? Is there anything that you could say you know for sure?" Shawn thought about what his father saw, Jefferson speaking to his mother. Shawn raised his hand as his father continued to talk about the last time he saw Jefferson. Shawn said, "Pop, say no more. If he was talking with Mom, I have an idea what may have taken place. The president should hire her as their best interrogator or their official priest. She could get a confession out of anyone, even the hardest of the hard criminals." He continued, "When Frank started living with us, remember how hard and tough he was? He wouldn't talk or cry or express emotions. He was rock-hard—"

Travis Cook jumped in, saying, "Until he met your mother. It took her about—"

Shawn jumped back in. "About . . . hmmm . . . less than a week. Frank was confessing and crying about every day." He and his father laughed. Shawn looked concerned. "Pops, what bathroom did Jefferson use? Upstairs, downstairs, the basement?"

Mr. Cook was becoming agitated; he was trying to concentrate on placing this missing piece. He blew out a frustrated breath. He pointed to the restroom just outside of his study. Shawn was heading toward the door to leave the study; he turned back and looked at his father. "Pops."

Mr. Cook put his glasses down to the bridge of his nose, looking really agitated. "Yes, Shawn?"

Shawn playfully motioned back as if he was scared and said, "Thanks." He laughed. Mr. Cook lightly laughed and jokingly looked around to throw something at Shawn.

Shawn walked out of the study, went to the bathroom, and knocked on the door. "Jefferson, you okay?"

Shawn heard Jefferson sniffle, and then sounding macho, Jefferson said, "What! Oh yeah, I'm cool. Uh, give me a minute."

Shawn slightly smiled and told Jefferson to take his time. "Nah, man, not rushing you. Take all the time you need, man." Shawn said to himself, *After dealing with Mom, he's going to need it.*

He heard Jefferson sniffle again and say in a low tone, "Damn . . . okay, thanks, bro. I'll be right out." There was a pause. Jefferson asked, "Yo, Wall Street, your mom out there?"

Shawn smiled. "Nah, why?"

Jefferson responded, "Nah, just asking."

Shawn knew he was pushing the limit when he asked, "Do you want me to get her?"

Jefferson said in a desperate tone, "Huh, what? No . . . no, absolutely not. I mean no no no, I'm cool."

Shawn said, "Okay, when you're done, I'll be in Pops's study." Jefferson made a sound that meant okay.

Shawn walked into his father's study, shaking his head. Mr. Cook shook his head and said, "She got to him, didn't she?"

Shawn slightly smiled. "Yep, that's not easy with Jefferson. He's one tough dude."

Mr. Cook looked at Shawn. "You know better than that. Your mother is tough, and you know that." Shawn nodded his head. Mr. Cook looked around; he went to the door. He opened the door and listened. He looked around, trying to make sure she wasn't around. He turned back to go inside and then said, "With her, she has catlike movement. You can't even hear her when she walks, even in a house where the floor makes that squeaky sound, catlike movement." Travis Cook was joking in a way, but there was some truth to what he was saying.

exaggerative buildup, "Son, did you know the government had offered your mother a great deal of money to be the head of their MWCW program?" Shawn repeated the acronym and looked at his father with a bewildered expression. Mr. Cook smiled and said, "No one in the family knows this except me and your mother and now you. It means 'Mothers with Catlike Walk.'" Shawn lightly laughed; his father looked at him and said, "It's true. The program was designed as a spy program against antiterrorist groups."

Shawn played along. "Really? So what happened to the program?"

Mr. Cook shook his head and said, "That idiot who kept saying he was going to make America great again decided to scrap the program and focus on building a wall around the world . . . He's still talking about that wall."

Shawn, still playing along, asked, "What, are you serious? Why didn't—"

Mr. Cook put his finger to his mouth. "Shh . . ."

Shawn whispered, "Why has no one ever told me about this?"

Mr. Cook, playing this down to a tee, looked over Shawn's shoulders and whispered, "Because it never happened." They both laughed. Mr. Cook responded, "But in all seriousness, it could happen. I've seen her in action, and man, she is good! Why do you think I have all of these cameras around the house? It's to keep track of those catlike movements." Shawn laughed, knowing that his father was just playing, but the man was good; he knew how to twine fable through truth. Ashley loved his stories.

Mr. Cook said, "Listen, I'm just trying to lighten the load you are under, son." There was a pause; then his father continued, "How are you holding up, son?"

Shawn stared down at the floor; he finally looked up at his father. "Pop, I don't know. I don't know what the hell I'm doing. I don't know if I'm doing the right thing or not. My mind is jumbled up . . . The dude is getting to me, Pop. He's breaking me down." Shawn rubbed his eyes as he continued, "I've turned to God more times than I ever have. All I could say, God is keeping me, Pop. It's like the footprints in the sand—two footprints and then there was only one set . . . His. When I can't go any further, He picks me up and carries me. I can't explain it no other way, Pop. Look at me—I'm broken, busted, bruised, and banged up. Yet he gives me the strength . . . My daily bread every single . . ." Shawn shakes his head. "I really don't know, I really don't."

Mr. Cook went over to his son, placed his arm around his shoulder, and said, "Hey, that answer is good enough for me."

Shawn nodded and said, "How's everyone? They don't know, right?" He was referring to his siblings.

Mr. Cook shook his head. "No, they just know bits and pieces they heard from the news and stuff."

Shawn nodded his head with satisfaction. "Good. The less they know, the better it is for them."

Mr. Cook tapped on the desk and said with concern, "So now what? What is this nutjob's next move?"

Shawn shrugged his shoulders; he squeezed his forehead with his fingers, which brought down to his eyes. "I don't know. I'm supposed to get this call anytime of the day. But so far, his calls have been early in the wee hours of the morning, two, three o'clock."

Mr. Cook said in frustration, "The man is sick. He's demented. I hate to say it, son. You know me. I wish bad on no one. I believe everyone deserves . . ."

They said it together, "A second chance."

Mr. Cook nodded his head and continued, "But this lowlife scumbag— sorry, son—but this punk-ass sucker needs to be taken out of this world and join his lowlife, demented brother in hell." He shook his head and said, "I hate talking this way, but this guy pushed all the wrong buttons, and he needs to be put down like a rabid animal." Shawn agreed; his father was on a tirade. "You could insult me, curse me, even want to fight me or even try to kill me. But the day you put your hands on my wife or children or grandchildren, you are a dead man. I'm taking your ass out of here, quick and fast." Mr. Cook slammed his hand on the desk.

Shawn quickly went over to him to calm him down. "Dad, easy. Don't let your pressure go up over this."

Mr. Cook looked at Shawn. "Too late. This shit is more than enough. This mother need to be brought down, dammit."

Shawn urged his father to relax. "Pop, calm down."

Travis Cook looked at his son. "I'm good, son, I'm good."

They were both quiet when Mr. Cook quickly got up; he startled Shawn. "Dad, whoa . . . Are you okay? Where are you going?"

His father waved for Shawn to come with him. He walked over to the wall unit. Shawn's father opened the door of the wall unit. Shawn was looking at his father's collection of albums. Shawn was impressed, "Wow, cool collection, Pop. I remember when I was young, you wouldn't even want us near this wall. Mom used to say you had your reasons, and that was it—no explanation, nothing."

Travis Cook nodded his head. "Yep, that is what I always told your mother to say when you and your brothers and sisters got that itch in wanting to know. I used to say to her, 'Roberta, just tell them I have my reasons.' She would look at me, but I knew that answer didn't sit well with her." Travis Cook slightly smiled.

Shawn gave a slight nod, looked at his father, and said, "You know that answer didn't sit well with me. I really wanted to know what you were hiding behind these cabinets."

Travis Cook gave a slight nod and said, "Okay, pass me that home improvement book in the bookshelf." Shawn went over to the bookshelf to take the book out. The book wouldn't come out. He made another attempt; the book was stuck. Shawn looked at the bookshelf, trying to figure out what was causing the book to get stuck. He tried taking another book out. No problem. The other book came out. He tried again with the home improvement book. Same result—it was stuck. He said, "Uh, Dad . . ."

Mr. Cook looked at Shawn and said, "Son, the book is right in front of you, home improvement."

Shawn looked at his father and said, "Dad, I know. I think I can read." He tried again—same results; he said in a frustrated tone, "It's stuck. I don't want to rip the book. The thing is old maybe . . ." He tried again—same results. "Pop, I don't know. It's stuck."

Mr. Cook looked at him. "What do you mean it's stuck? How?" Mr. Cook looked at Shawn as if he had some serious issues.

Shawn had a tense smile on his face. "How? I don't know. It's your book. What do you mean how? Look." He was showing his father. "Dad, look, huh? Stuck."

Mr. Cook looked concerned. "How is this possible? I was just reading it the other day."

He looked at Shawn as if Shawn had a magical answer. Shawn just shrugged his shoulders. "Pop, I can't answer that question." Shawn paused and said, "Hold up, let me try something."

Mr. Cook got up and went over to Shawn; he touched his arm. "Wait a minute." Mr. Cook walked up to the book and looked at it; he made the attempt to pull it out, but the book was stuck.

Shawn slightly smiled and said, "See? I know I wasn't . . ."

While Shawn was talking, Mr. Cook touched three books in the unit; the home improvement book slightly moved as the entire shelf of books opened up wide as they parted from each other. Shawn was surprised. "Whoa, wow! How did you?" Shawn paused and continued, still mesmerized, "Cool, I thought this thing only happens in the movies."

Mr. Cook slightly laughed and said in a spy-type voice, "The name is Cook, Travis Cook." They both laughed, slapping each other a high five. Mr. Cook continued, "And I'm a bad mother . . ."

Shawn looked at his father, and they both said it together, "Shut your mouth." That got another laugh from father and son. Both shelves had opened up like a book.

When Shawn saw what was inside the secret compartment, his jaws dropped, and he said, "Yeah, Pop, you are one bad mother, you know that."

# Chapter 145

Shawn looked at what he was seeing and said, "Wow."

From behind them, they heard, "Damn."

They both turned and saw Jefferson standing, looking mesmerized. "Damn, Mr. C, what are you running up in here?"

Travis Cook urged Jefferson to keep his voice down and to close the door with him on the other side of it. Jefferson looked dejected. Shawn advocated for him, "Pop, he's cool."

Mr. Cook looked at Shawn and said, "Yeah? Can he keep his mouth shut?"

Shawn jokingly looked at his father and said, "Come on now, you are asking for a lot."

Jefferson looked desperate. "Yo, Wall Street."

Shawn smiled and said, "Just playin'. Pops, he's cool."

Mr. Cook told Jefferson to come in and close the door. Jefferson went in with excitement. Mr. Cook looked at him and said, "Keep your hands to yourself. Do not touch anything, you understand?" Jefferson nodded his head like a boy on Christmas morning. Mr. Cook looked at Shawn, who gestured to his father that it would be all right.

Shawn and Jefferson looked at the arsenal of weapons, and Shawn shook his head. "Wow, I never knew you were into this, Pop. How long?"

Mr. Cook nodded his head, looking serious. "A long time, years. I started out collecting a few items here and there and then bang."

Jefferson added on, "You mean boom and kaboom."

Mr. Cook just looked at Jefferson with no expression. Mr. Cook continued as he took out a few automatic guns and knives of all kinds; some of them looked as deadly as guns. He took out hand-to-hand combat weapons and said, "Some of these weapons are so advanced, not even the armed forces know about them." Mr. Cook put a few more of them on the table; he said, "Take, for instance, this baby right here."

Jefferson was ready to pick it up. "Okay, don't mind if I do." He had his hand on the weapon when Mr. Cook slapped his wrist like he would a child. Jefferson jerked his hand back when he was hit and said, "Ouch, damn. I thought we were picking out the weapons we really like."

Mr. Cook looked at him and said, "No, I don't think so." Mr. Cook continued, "Don't touch the weapons, okay? Look and learn. You touch, you get another hit . . . pow, right on the hand."

Jefferson was still rubbing his hand; he said, "I know one thing—you and Mrs. C love to slap. She uses spoons, and you use your hands. Ouch, that thing is still stinging."

Mr. Cook brought his glasses down to the bridge of his nose and said, "It's the only way to get the message across."

Shawn lightly laughed. "You haven't seen anything. You need to speak to my brothers and sisters. They can tell you some stories. I know a few myself." Shawn shook his head with a slight smile. He continued to look at his father's collection and said, "Pops, Mom know about this?"

Mr. Cook blew out a breath and said, "Please, that woman knows everything that goes on in this house, can't keep anything from her. You hide something, she'll find it. You twist the truth, she'll find a way to straighten it out." Mr. Cook shook his head, slightly laughed, and said, "Yeah, but that's my girl."

Shawn was surprised; he said, "So she hasn't approached you about safety and how dangerous it is to have all this lethal stuff in the house?"

Mr. Cook slightly smiled. "Of course, she's given me the third and the fourth and fifth degree to put down the law—her law. Nah, I don't play with your mother when it comes down to this."

Jefferson was still looking at the weapons when said to himself, "You have the right to remain silent. Anything, and I mean anything, you say or do . . . blah, blah. You have a right to an . . . blah . . . blah . . . blah." As he was reciting the Miranda rights, Jefferson casually tried to pick up another weapon when Mr. Cook slapped his hand again . . . Pow. Jefferson pulled his hand back, letting the weapon go. "Ouch, damn."

Mr. Cook looked at him. "Hands off, that's the Travis Cook law."

Shawn ignored the two; he realized that his father really liked Jefferson. Shawn slightly smiled and said, "Pops, your collection is cool. I would have never guessed in a million years you had this stuff in here, so cool."

Jefferson added as he made another attempt to pick up another weapon, "Yeah, Pops, this is so—" Mr. Cook came down again with another slap. Jefferson reacted. "Ouch! What, your hands made of stone? I just wanted to touch it, ouch!"

Mr. Cook looked at Jefferson. "Just relax, okay, son? I'll take care of you. Your wish will come true. Just relax."

Jefferson's eyes beamed. "Really? Wow, how about this one? This is my favorite. No, how about this one? I like this one. It has—"

Mr. Cook cut him off, put his pointer finger to his mouth, and calmly said, "Relax . . . relax . . ."

Jefferson nodded his head. "Okay, okay, I'm relaxed, okay."

Mr. Cook smiled at Jefferson and said, "Good."

Shawn smiled and said, "Hey, Dad, Jefferson and I need to get ready."

Mr. Cook responded as Shawn was preparing to leave, "Okay, but I want you to take whatever you need to take down that son of a bitch. I have weapons, ammo—whatever you need, son, I have." There was a pause; then Mr. Cook continued, "I wish I could do it, but I can't, son. But you can. Take whatever you want and find that sucker and take him out."

Shawn was surprised his father had offered him any weapon; he said, "Dad, are you serious?"

Jefferson desperately added, "Yes, he's serious. Even serious or deranged, we'll take either one. Shawn, take it." Mr. Cook looked at Jefferson with his finger on his mouth. Jefferson nodded and kept still.

Mr. Cook turned his attention back to Shawn. "Son, I'm serious. Whatever you need, it's yours." Jefferson was biting his lower lip with suspense. Mr. Cook continued, "Listen, this guy is dangerous. I know you are more than able to take out an army with just your hands and feet, but you will be taking a risk with this nutcase. You need to prepare yourself for war." Shawn was ready to protest when Mr. Cook said in a firm tone, "I insist."

Jefferson put on his firm voice, saying, "Yes, me too, Shawn."

Mr. Cook smiled at Jefferson and said, "Jefferson."

Jefferson responded, "I know, relax."

Mr. Cook said, "No . . . it's your turn."

Jefferson was practically ready to jump out of his skin with excitement. "Are you serious, Mr. C? Thanks, now I would like . . ."

Mr. Cook was looking at his arsenal and said, "Ah, here she is."

Jefferson smiled with his eyes closed, saying, "Yeah, come to Papa." He had his hands out wide, knowing that he was going to get a large weapon. "Come to Papa, girl. I take care of you, and you take care of me." Mr. Cook put the weapon in Jefferson's hand. Jefferson, with a smile, opened his eyes and looked down to see what looked like Jimmy's first Christmas toy gun—something he could fit in his pocket. We're talking about his shirt pocket.

Mr. Cook looked at Jefferson's expression and said, "Ooh, my dear friend, you may underestimate the appearance. But you will respect the power. I guarantee it. This is my gift from me to you, son." He paused; he went from that fatherly voice to the tough man's voice, saying, "You better bring my baby back."

Jefferson looked at it, smiled, and said, "Okay, I will. Hmm, let's call him Little John." Mr. Cook nodded with a smile. Jefferson was still looking down at his new weapon, Little John.

His eyes popped wide open with a huge smile on his face when he heard Mr. Cook say, "Now, Jay, you could choose any two weapons you like." Jefferson looked at Shawn and smiled.

# CHAPTER 146

Shawn and Jefferson were heading back to Shawn's place. Shawn was allowing G to drive. He was riding shotgun; he hadn't felt that trust like he had in Complex. He just wanted to close his eyes for at least fifteen minutes, but he wouldn't and couldn't take that chance. Shawn looked over at Jefferson, who was still admiring and playing around with his new toys. Shawn watched him and inquired, "How you holding up?"

Jefferson held the weapon, looking at it, and responded, "Good, I guess. Hey, Wall Street, your pops is cool man, no joke."

Shawn nodded. Jefferson, still studying every detail, asked, "Has he always been that way?"

Shawn nodded his head. "Pretty much."

Jefferson smiled; just getting off the subject and looking at the weapons, he said, "I think he likes me."

Shawn's eyebrows went up. "Really? How do you know that?"

Jefferson was aiming the gun at nothing in particular. Shawn was starting to feel a little uneasy. "Hey, easy."

Jefferson responded, "Relax, bro, it's not even loaded."

Shawn replied, "Still, it's a gun. Better to practice safety. Plus you just need to know how you point that thing."

Jefferson nodded; still smiling and still looking at the weapon, he said, "Sure, no problem."

Shawn felt a sense of relief they were home; he said, "Gordon."

Gordon responded, "Yes, sir?"

Shawn smiled and said, "Good job, good driving."

He wondered if his back porch was bugged. His cell went off. Shawn touched his Bluetooth. "Commissioner Moore, no time no hear."

Curt Moore responded, "Yeah, well, I know you're probably happy not to hear my gravelly voice." There was a brief pause when Moore continued, "Cook, have you noticed when we first met, my voice . . ."

Shawn nodded and said, "Yeah, you were a dick."

Moore shook his head and said, "You think you're a badass, Cook, huh?"

Shawn responded, "You asked me a question, and I responded. When we first met, you were a detective. You know, 'dick' is short for—"

Moore cut him off. "Yeah, I know. But you find the right time to use that title in so many ways, Cook. Think you're slick?"

Shawn lightly chuckled and said, "Yes, I remember when we first met."

Moore lost his train of thought. "Oh yeah, my voice was normal, human. Now ever since I've taken on this case, my voice sounds like sandpaper. Thanks. I was talking to my wife the other night, trying to set the mood, and she said I sounded like a defective Barry White."

Shawn did not respond; he just made an emphatic sound and continued, "To tell you the truth, Curt, most of the time, I'm glad to hear from you, like now."

Moore nodded and knew Shawn was up to something; he said, "Really? Why now, Cook? You insult me and my men practically every time we speak, and now you want to hear from me? Okay, what is it you want?"

Shawn responded, "You are the man with the info."

The commissioner snorted. "Yeah right, like I said, you look at me and my guys as if we do nothing. But now we are resourceful. Come on, Cook, what is going on?"

Shawn lightly laughed and said, "I never said 'resourceful.' I would look at you guys as a hit-and-miss group." He laughed.

Moore didn't think it was funny. "Not funny, Cook. As a matter of fact, it's very offensive and insulting. But it's okay because one day, you will come to us looking and begging for our services. Watch."

Shawn was smiling and said, "So true. Okay, seriously, what's going on?"

Curt Moore shook his head and said, "SOS, we're working on it. We are getting closer, Cook."

Shawn nodded and said in a sarcastic tone, "Yeah, okay, sure."

The commissioner blew out a frustrated breath. "Dammit, Cook! Okay, we're no more closer than we were a week ago, two weeks ago, okay. And to tell you the damn truth, yes, it's freakin' frustrating to be stuck in the same damn spot every freakin' day, okay!" Moore inhaled and continued, "This mother sucker is like some kind of damn phantom. I don't have any consistent clues to nail the son of a bitch, okay? The bastard has people working for him that refuse to talk, and on top of that, we don't even know who these damn people are. So do I feel good telling you this shit that we're getting no closer? Hell to the no, Cook! But this is where we're at right now." The commissioner inhaled as his gravelly voice became hard as if gravel was rolling around in his vocal cords. "But we're going to nail that son of a bitch. Watch."

Shawn wanted to say something sarcastic but took a different route. "I gather Mrs. Stewart is still not speaking, for good reasons. That punk somehow sent his people to her husband and two boys to deliver a threatening message. This lowlife scumbag went on to her son's campus just to let them know, 'You talk, your mother is dead.' And he did the same with her husband." Shawn added, "How about putting them in a witness protection program?"

Moore laughed and said, "Are you out of your mind? I don't know who I can trust anymore." Then Moore cursed under his breath.

There was a pause; then Shawn responded, "I need to speak to Mrs. Stewart, just her and I."

Moore said in an aggravated tone, "Haven't you been listening to me, Cook? I have folks on the take. She talks. They find out, and she is as good as dead—her and her family."

Shawn slammed his fist down on the dashboard. Gordon said, "Easy, sir."

Jefferson added, "Keep your cool, man."

Moore asked, "What was that? Who was that?"

Shawn continued, "My nuts hitting against each other. Listen, Curt, I need you to set this up. Are all your men on the take?"

Moore shook his head. "No."

"Do you have someone you can trust?"

Moore thought and said, "Sure, yeah."

Shawn responded, "Put that person on the late-night tour and set up the meeting."

Moore hee-hawed before Shawn cut him off. "Curt, just make it happen, okay?"

The commissioner nodded and said, "I'll get it done . . . My way, Cook, like it or not, my way."

Shawn nodded. "Okay." He switched gears. "Curt, I need for you to send a few guys over to debug my backyard." Moore asked what happened. Shawn explained what happened the other night; he said, "I need to make sure. I would do it, but a friend has my stuff."

The commissioner nodded and said, "No problem. I'll let you know, Cook, when we're done. Take care." The phone disconnected.

# CHAPTER 147

Break day 1

Shawn was awakened by some noise in his backyard, voices and low laughter. He thought, *What the hell is going on?* In the midst of the chatter and the laughter, he could hear Jefferson's voice along with a few female voices laughing and squealing. He looked at his clock, 7:00 a.m. He overslept for an hour; he wanted to get up and work out, so that made him a little disappointed. His thoughts were interrupted by the noise in his backyard. Why did Jefferson have folks in his backyard so early in the damn morning, Saturday morning, laughing and talking and everything in between?

Shawn was leaning on his elbows when he crashed back down to the bed just to quickly rise back up with eyes opened wide, thinking, *These are Jefferson's get-high feeding buddies, looking like the* Night of the Living Dead *with Jefferson being the head zombie. Shawn* further thought, *In this community, in this quiet, peaceful community . . . These are hardworking folks with the beautiful houses and nicely mowed lawns and nice cars.* Shawn thought, ever since he moved into this community, it had always been quiet. Nothing went on after eight o'clock. This was a crime-free community with retired folks, but in one night, Jefferson stained and soiled it.

Shawn shot out of bed; he yelled for Jefferson. Shawn could hear Jefferson, but the little jerk was somewhere; he seemed to be moving, his voice traveling and trailing throughout the backyard. Shawn came down to the front door; he opened it and saw Jefferson heading toward the back of the backyard, where they could get their feeding on and where they couldn't be seen. *How nice and considerate of him.* What happened next sealed the deal for Shawn. *I'll kill him and his zombie friends.*

He called Jefferson's name, but Jefferson kept on laughing and walking. Shawn thought Jefferson was ignoring him; after thinking about it, Jefferson wasn't ignoring him. He had his headphones on, and the way he listened to music, not even a train blowing its horn would get his attention. Shawn hurried after Jefferson; as he turned the corner of the house, he ran into Commissioner Curt Moore. Shawn was totally caught off guard as he almost slipped on the grass. He said to Moore, "Whoa, what the hell is going on here, Moore?"

The commissioner was getting ready to respond when Jefferson responded, "I called him."

Shawn looked at Jefferson and pointed. "You? You called Moore?"

Jefferson nodded his head. "Yes, I did . . ." There was a pause; then Jefferson slightly smiled. "You seemed surprised. Being bugged is no joke. It's an invasion, not cool, bro. So I called Curt." Commissioner stared at Jefferson with a tough look. Jefferson raised his hand, gesturing an apology, and corrected himself, "Commissioner Moore."

Curt said, "Mr. Moore is okay, young man."

Jefferson smiled with a nod. "Noted."

Shawn shook his head and said, "But—"

Moore jumped in, saying, "Cook, your place is clean, bug-free."

Shawn was still stunned as he looked at Moore with a bit of confusion; he blinked as if he had missed something. "What?"

Moore waved his hand for his team to wrap it up. "Let's go, we're done. Good job."

Jefferson was getting the numbers of the two women that came with Moore. He said, "Okay, Detectives, be easy and go easy. And maybe when I'm in the neighborhood, I may need to be arrested, and I would be guilty as charged."

One of them laughed and said, "Charged with what?"

Jefferson smiled and winked at them. "I'll come up with something. Just keep those handcuffs handy, okay, Detectives?" They both blushed and laughed and blew Jefferson an air kiss; he acted as if he caught both of the kisses and laughed. The commissioner walked up to Jefferson. Jefferson smiled and said, "Mr. Moore, those two detectives are hot."

Moore looked at Jefferson and said, "They are not detectives. They are my nieces, and if you think I'm a ballbuster, their father is a ball blaster. Take care, champ." Moore softly tapped Jefferson on the cheek and walked away with a laugh. "Cook, I'll call you later about that thing we talked about."

Shawn looked confused, and then he remembered. "Sure, okay."

Shawn looked at Jefferson. "Why didn't you say something? I thought—"

Jefferson cut him off. "You thought I was up to no good, right?" He raised his voice and said, "Come on, Wall Street, be straight with me, man. Right? That's what you thought I am, right?"

Shawn hesitated and said, "Well . . . yeah, a little, but . . ."

Jefferson mumbled, "Yeah, it's the story of my life." There was a pause; then he continued, "Hey, no sweat, man. When you have a jacked-up life and your reputation follows you like shit on a stick, folks tend to hold shit against you . . ." There was another pause as he continued, "It sort of goes with the territory. Crap follows you wherever you go. I'm like a trash magnet."

Shawn was feeling terrible; he had just reinforced that image Jefferson had of himself. He looked at Jefferson; he was lost for words. Jefferson looked at him, turned, and walked away. He stopped, turned back to Shawn, and asked, "Do you mind if I use your gym?"

Shawn was surprised at the request. Up to this point, Shawn told Jefferson to make himself at home and do what he wanted to do; but now with this wedge between them, Shawn felt he had broken that trust. He said, "Of course, I don't—"

Jefferson said, "Thanks, I don't want to be accused of stealing, especially with this freakin' habit I have." Then he turned to walk away.

# CHAPTER 148

Shawn was grateful he had this break; he hadn't heard from the stranger. He decided to work off some of this extra energy he was feeling. He went down to the gym to work out on the heavy bag. Jefferson was over in the weight room. Shawn knew he had to smooth things over with Jefferson eventually.

Shawn started out with the jump rope just as a warm-up; he was excellent with the jump rope, better than the best of them. He could do all types of tricks with that rope, but right now, he needed to stick to the basics. He looked over at Jefferson, who was over on the bench press. He watched Jefferson lift the weight as his back arched as he pushed the weight up. Shawn knew that meant the weight was either heavy, or his technique was really messed up.

Shawn went over to the heavy bag; he did some basic strike blows. He went into his power body punching. The sound of the bag when hit was crisp as it echoed throughout the room . . . Body blow, smack was the sound, body blow, and then a hook to the side of the bag, kidney shot. *Thsmack*, that nice and crisp sound. He moved down to the speed bag; he got himself into a rhythm.

He looked over at Jefferson, who was struggling getting the weight back up; his strength was fading as the weight on the bar was slowly coming down. He was in trouble, Shawn thought. But he was too stubborn to ask for help even though he was in serious trouble. Shawn shook his head, went over, and spotted Jefferson as he stood at the top of the bench, encouraging and urging Jefferson to concentrate and lift and push. Shawn was helping Jefferson get the weight up with light assistance but had Jefferson to do most of the work. Shawn was there to make sure Jefferson didn't get hurt. Jefferson was bringing down the bar to his chest and struggling to push it back up. Shawn was encouraging him, "Jay, keep your back flat. Your strength is coming from here and here." He firmly touched Jefferson's shoulder and arms; he continued "And here." He tapped Jefferson's chest as he continued, "Your breathing, baby, come on now."

Jefferson nodded as he kept his back flat and pushed the weight bar up. He did it; he had it up. He gave a smile of accomplishment. He looked at Shawn and said with a look of determination, "Again."

Shawn nodded with a smile and said, "Really? Your call, baby. Do your thing." Shawn nodded his head as he got into position; ready and waiting for Jefferson, he said, "Track 1 'Determination and Momentum Workout' . . . with major kick-ass bass."

Jefferson looked at him with a perplexed expression while pushing the weight up; the music kicked in with that kick-ass bass, which was pumping and vibrating throughout the room. Jefferson nodded and smiled. "Yeah, baby, I'm feeling that."

He had a slight struggle on his face. Shawn said, "Always save your wind. It is the core of your energy. It is the main force behind you, underneath you, and around you, baby. It'll give you that extra push when you need it. All of that yelling and screaming takes you away from your core, which is the center of your strength. All of that other stuff, save that for Hollywood. Now come on and lift that mother . . ."

The music hit that note at the right time. Shawn was ready as he leaned in position to assist Jefferson just in case he got into trouble. Jefferson, with his back flat, pushed the bar up. He held it there for a second or two. Shawn smiled. "Good job, Jay."

Shawn was ready to guide the bar back to the bar rest. Jefferson looked at him, winked, and said, "One more."

Shawn was surprised; he thought Jefferson was done. "Are you serious?"

Jefferson nodded; he brought the weight bar off the bench stand and held the bar straight. His arms were shaking a little. Shawn was starting to become concerned; maybe Jefferson bit off more than he could chew. Shawn knew Jefferson was at the point of fatigue. Shawn questioned whether he should have stopped him; he did well and should just call it a day. A weight spotter could only do so much in this position to lift the weight to help the lifter due to the awkward position and the stance the spotter was in. Shawn thought and said, "Freak this. Track 22 'All You Got' track. Volume high, bass tight, now."

Shawn looked down at Jefferson. "Remember your breathing. Your core is your strength. Concentrate. Focus. Go, baby, go." Shawn got into his stance; he was ready because anything could happen when a lifter was tired and exhausted.

Jefferson nodded; he closed his eyes for a second or two. They shot open as if someone or something entered his body; he brought that 325-pound bar down toward his chest, arms shaking, legs slightly moving. He heard the beat of the music. He heard Shawn in the background, yelling and encouraging and pushing him, "Come on, Jay! Come on, baby! Your time, your moment."

Jefferson was struggling, but he was determined that he was going to push this bad boy up. Shawn was nodding his head and yelling, "Push, baby, push! Come on! Yeah! Yeah! Yeah! Push!" Jefferson's back was lifting up, which meant he was calling on every muscle in his body. Shawn kept yelling, "Keep that back flat, Jay! Use your core, baby. You're almost there. Come on, Jay!"

Jefferson strained out a nod and pushed up. He had not realized that he was working on his third lift. Something was wrong; something happened. The momentum had stopped; the lifting was caught somewhere. Jefferson was in trouble; he had a look of panic in his eyes. Shawn saw it; he'd been there before. He came down closer to Jefferson's side and said, "I'm here. You can do this. You're doing good. Just relax. Concentrate on your core. Remember the center of your power."

Jefferson closed his eyes and blocked out any outside noise; everything seemed to come to a standstill as those things started fading out. Shawn watched as Jefferson's muscles in his arms tightened up, his veins peeking boldly from under his skin, the grip on the bar tightening as the knuckles on his hand were turning colors as the blood shot through them. The sweat was pouring down his face into his eyes; he closed and opened them real tight. As he began to push the bar, he could feel strength coming from somewhere as his arms shook from the strain; he nodded his head toward Shawn, telling him he was okay. He could hear Shawn from a distance, yet so near. He was almost there as his muscles burned. Shawn was yelling with encouragement, "You want it? Earn it! Take it! Conqueror it! Now freakin' go for it! No one can stop you but you. Go go go go! Release that inner core NOW!"

Jefferson's eyes shot open, looking at Shawn, who looked at him and said, "Trust me."

Jefferson nodded; he pushed and strained every fiber of his muscles. If the timing was right, mission accomplished. If the timing was wrong, several things could go wrong, including serious injury. Jefferson bellowed out a war cry that seemed to give him that motivation to lift the weight up to the stand; then he brought the weight bar down into its stand. When he did this, his yell went from a war cry to a victory shout like they did when the walls of Jericho fell under Joshua. Jefferson felt that victory coarse throughout his body as he jumped up from the weight bench. "Yo, Wall Street, I did it, man! I did it. First time ever, man."

Shawn looked at him with a smile. Jefferson said, "First time lifting this much weight, man. I lifted almost twice my weight, man."

Shawn, still smiling, said, "Four times, man."

Jefferson looked shocked. "What! Get the freak outta here! Are you serious?"

Shawn nodded his head. "Serious, man. Four times, bro."

Jefferson thought about it, and the realization hit him as he yelled with a hoot and a "Hell yeah, baby!" He continued, "Yo, Wall Street, you are the man, dude. You know your stuff . . . Well, of course, look at you. You are like a Marvel Universe superhero, man. Yo, thanks, man." Jefferson gave Shawn a shoulder tap and a quick brotherly hug. He looked at Shawn and said, "Yo, what's next, man? I want to work out. Yo, I'm pumped, and that music . . . Yo, Wall Street, what can I say? You are the man."

Shawn looked at him with a slight smile. "So I'm the man now, huh?"

Jefferson put his head down and looked back up. "Oh, that? Yo, it's all good, Wall Street. You have proven your worth, brah."

Shawn lightly smiled and said, "I've proven my worth. Yeah, okay. Hey, come here. I want to show you something."

Shawn went over to the reactionary punching bag. He responded with a light punch to the bag. "This is a reactionary bag."

Jefferson asked, "Why is it called a reactionary bag?"

Shawn smiled and nodded his head. "I knew you would ask that question." He responded, "Because it trains you not to react on impulse, but to react with precision and patience and with timing. For example . . ." Shawn held up his finger as he continued, "AI, level 1, basic."

Jefferson, with surprise, looked around with wide eyes open when the lights on the computer came on. Jefferson smiled and said, "Yo, cool." Shawn nodded his head with seriousness; he walked up to Jefferson and placed five electrotype suction items on different parts of his body. Jefferson was looking at the connectors and said with excitement, "Hey, this is what those people who make those video games put on them in order to create a game! Wow, this is so cool. I remember reading this article where—"

Shawn held up his hand and said, "Just relax. All of this is coming at you so fast."

Jefferson smiled and nodded his head. "Yeah, man. I got this crazy sensation right now as if I'm high, man, and I haven't had anything within . . . Well, that's not important. Keep going. Sorry."

Shawn smiled and said, "AI, begin."

The lights lit up on different parts of the bag. Shawn punched the light when they came on. The lights would come on at different intervals, first slow. Shawn said, "AI, stop program." All the lights on the bag dimmed and finally off. Shawn looked at Jefferson and said, "Cool, huh? Now you can get excited."

Jefferson laughed and said, "Yeah, cool. Wow, a computer-generated sparring partner."

Shawn in a noncommitted way agreed more or less with Jefferson. "Well . . . I guess that's the layman's term."

Jefferson continued, "May I? I think I can do this."

Shawn smiled. "Let's see. Computer, basic program, begin."

Jefferson was caught off guard as he felt a sharp electric shock to his midsection. He responded, "Ouch, whoa! What the . . . I didn't know . . ." The lights came on the bag in different spots. Jefferson handled stage 1 with ease; as a matter of fact, he was talking while he was going through the lights on the bag. When it was done, Jefferson chuckled. "Cool, cute, child's play." Another chuckle escaped his mouth; he was taking off the electro gloves when he said, "I mean it's cool for beginners. Don't get me wrong. I like the concept, but it lacks something—something a little more challenging. There you go, challenging . . . Personally, after beating this thing a few times, I would actually get bored and lose interest."

Jefferson took off the gloves and put them on the table. He turned to head out of the gym when he heard Shawn say, "Computer, next level." Jefferson cut his eyes at Shawn with that Hollywood look; he said, "Not convinced, huh?"

Jefferson walked back over to the bag, Shawn tossed him the gloves; he put them on and stood there in the circle as he got into his fighting stance. "Okay, bring it. Give me what you got." The lights on the bag came on in different spots; that threw Jefferson slightly off. He expected the same sequence of lights, but it didn't happen; that's the thing that threw him off, but he seemed to recover as he nodded his head. "Come on." The lights were coming on and off more frequently, but the level was still easy for Jefferson as he punched at the lights that came on. Jefferson smiled. "Anything else? This is getting monotonous. Come on, where is the challenge?"

Shawn looked at him and smiled; he said, "Computer, workout program 1."

Jefferson looked at Shawn and said, "Are you serious, Wall Street, program 1? Come on, back to basics." He chuckled. "Whatever, just bring it." Jefferson lightly laughed. "Program 1." He shook his head, saying, "Whatever."

The lights came on; this time, on didn't spots on the bag, and this time a little much faster. Jefferson quickly jabbed the first two lights as the bag snapped from the jab. He smiled at Shawn, taking his eyes off the bag when the light came on, making a loud sound indicating that Jefferson missed the light. Jefferson felt the sting from the computer indicating he missed. His mouth dropped open. "Ohh, okay, okay. You got that one, AI." Jefferson was making that excuse up while looking at Shawn.

In the meantime, the light flashed; the sound blew out loud as Jefferson reacted to the electric sting on the left side of his face. Jefferson, surprised, said, "Whoa! I just turned my head for a second."

Shawn responded, "It only takes a split second to get knocked out or even worse. NOW PAY ATTENTION!"

Jefferson nodded with alertness. He was in his fighting position; he was ready. Shawn nodded his head, happy that Jefferson was taking this thing seriously. AI said, "Seventy percent, sir."

Jefferson, looking perplexed, said, "What was that?"

Shawn responded, "AI said you hit only 70 percent of your target." There was a pause; then Shawn added, "You would have to do better—70 percent in a street fight means your opponent has tagged you 30 percent. You may say, 'But I got 70 percent.' But in reality, it only takes the right punch in the right spot to knock your ass out, Jefferson. Don't get so cocky and arrogant and especially overconfident. AI, hold up on levels 3 and 4."

Jefferson went from looking at Shawn to the bag as Shawn continued to talk. "I've seen teams thinking that they had the upper hand lose to a team they thought they could beat with their eyes closed—boxers walking in the ring standing and showboating just to be carried out. There are no assumptions in a street fight. Don't get caught out there thinking you're all of that. It only takes one hit in the right area."

Jefferson wanted to look at Shawn, but he knew he had to keep focus. Shawn said, "Listen to me. Your opponent, adversary, enemy—whatever you want to call him—won't come at you the same way. Don't expect that. Expect for him to change up, switch up, if they know what they are doing. Remember Leon Spinks? Had one style, brawling, knock your ass out in the first round. He was knocking everybody out . . . until they caught on to his one-way style. And boom, bam, his career was done, baby. You just need to be ready. Computer, begin. Levels 3, 4."

AI lights flashed much quicker this time on different spots on the bag. Jefferson was trying to concentrate, but he was having difficulty hitting the lights. AI said, "Sixty percent."

Shawn said, "Come on, Jay. You're dropping. Come on, you're losing the fight." He continued, "Computer, switch to challenging mode. Jay, pay attention. I need for you to focus."

Jefferson looked at the bag in his fighting stance. He nodded his head, indicating to Shawn he was ready. Shawn said, "Begin."

The lights came on the bag, flashing much quicker in different spots. The buzzer was sounding frequently, which meant Jefferson was missing the target; he was off by seconds. Jefferson was becoming frustrated, and now he was striking according to impulse and not reaction.

Shawn raised his voice. "Stop reacting. Concentrate. Focus." The buzzer sounded again and again and again.

AI said, "Thirty percent, you lose. Next."

Jefferson was frustrated; he hit the bag out of frustration. "Damn." He struck the bag again, cursing to himself. Shawn laughed. "This is why it's called training."

Shawn lightly laughed as Jefferson stepped aside and said, "Here, let's see you do it."

Shawn smiled and said, "I have a bad shoulder."

Jefferson turned the tables back on him and mocked him, saying, "What? Not in a street fight, dude! You can't say, 'Hey, my shoulder is hurting. Let's fight next week same time.'" Jefferson looked at Shawn.

Shawn nodded his head. "You're right."

He stepped into the circle; the computer knew another challenger had stepped up into the circle. The computer said, "Welcome. Let's begin."

The lights started flashing on the bag. The speed of the flash started out average and started to pick up, and now it was a good decent speed. Shawn, in his fighting position, tagged the bag each time. His strikes were crisp with a snap. The flash came faster, but Shawn kept up. Jefferson just shook his head; he was impressed. AI proceeded to the next level. Jefferson was amazed and said, "Whoa, no, it didn't jump to the next level."

Shawn was throwing hooks, jabs, and body blows, snapping the bag quick and hard. AI's animated face had suffered considerably; the face was busted and bruised. The eyes were blackened and swollen. The mouth was swollen and bleeding; the nose was broken as Shawn continued to pound away, delivering death-defying power blow after blow. AI went to the next level.

Jefferson noticed everything about Shawn; he was a master of the art of fighting. He wasn't even breathing hard.

The program level was ending as AI came back with a flurry of lights. Shawn hit as many as he could. The bell sounded, and the percentage was displayed: 99.9 percent. AI said, "You are the winner, Mr. Shawn Cook. Congratulations."

Shawn stepped back. Jefferson was impressed as he patted Shawn on the back. "Wow, awesome display, dude! You just put on a clinic, made me look stupid."

Shawn smiled; he didn't even break a sweat. He looked at Jefferson. "If you want to do what I just did, train for it, want it. You have to desire it, Jay. It won't come to you. You have to go for it, and if you do . . . you will conqueror it." Shawn patted Jefferson on the back. "Time to fuel up."

Jefferson looked at him. "What?"

Shawn smiled. "Time to eat. I'm a starving man."

Jefferson smiled and said, "Now that language I understand."

# CHAPTER 149

Jefferson convinced Shawn to try this restaurant he'd been to when he was younger. It was a nice-looking building that had a pebble-rock parking lot. The place was slightly off the road. Jefferson bragged about the food—fresh, no canned stuff as far as he could remember; it had been so long.

They walked into the restaurant as the bell above the door sounded, indicating someone was either coming in or going out. Shawn looked around; there wasn't anything fancy about the place, very simple. The aroma from the food was breathtaking as customers ate and enjoyed their meals. The furniture looked about ten years behind time. The lighting was average, and the area between tables was spacious. There was a calmness in the place. The music that was playing was nice and low; a gospel R & B music was playing. Jefferson had a smile on his face.

The hostess welcomed them. "Welcome to Bell's. Eat in or eat out?" She was standing there, waiting for a response.

Shawn looked at Jefferson but focused his attention back on the hostess. His words got caught in his throat; he admired her beauty, no makeup or anything to enhance her looks. She was all natural. A lump formed in his throat; she reminded him of Serenity—that nice short hairstyle that went just a little past the nape of her neck, just like his wife's. She had such a wonderful smile with a hard, chiseled, toned body—not too much, but enough to say the gym was her friend. Jefferson looked at her, walked up to her, and kissed her on the cheek. Shawn thought the man was losing his mind, a complete stranger. She smiled at the nice gesture. He pulled back and slightly smiled. "Hi, Tina."

The younger lady looked at Jefferson with curiosity, broke out with a smile, and said, "Hi, Jeff, long time."

Jefferson nodded his head, looked at Shawn, and said with a slight laugh, "She is the only one that can get away with calling me Jeff, so don't get any ideas."

Shawn still looked confused and said, "Okay."

Jefferson turned his attention back to Tina and said, "Tee, this is Shawn Cook."

Shawn shook her hand and said, "A pleasure."

Jefferson said, "Yeah, Mr. Smooth Operator." Jefferson lightly laughed and said, "He's good people." Shawn smiled.

Tina playfully nudged Jefferson and said, "Look and learn."

Jefferson made a face and said, "How can I learn something I already know?" He winked at her.

Tina smiled at him and hugged him. "How have you been? Wow, I was just thinking about you the other day."

Jefferson's face slightly tensed; it was a look of difficult intolerance. He nodded his head quickly. "I'm good . . ." He looked outside the window and back at Tina. "I'm . . . good, hanging in there. And you?" Jefferson's tension became more evident; he was very serious, a very rare look.

Tina had an expression of sympathy as if she understood the feelings behind the look. She rubbed his shoulders. "It's been such a long time."

Jefferson tried to break the tension and smiled, but whatever was going on in his head, his heart was no doubt real. "Please don't start that. No pity parties, babe. I'm past that . . . don't need to . . ." He shook his head.

Tina nodded her head, silently agreeing with him. He kissed her on the top of her head the way big brothers kiss their younger sisters. Shawn looked on and observed, still confused. There was a brief silence when Jefferson asked, "Where's Pop?"

That made Shawn even more curious; he looked at Jefferson. He had so many questions; with all the stuff they've been through in a short amount of time, he felt all of it had just dissolved, and he had to find another starting point. Tina responded, "Where he's always, in the kitchen with Mom."

Jefferson smiled at Tina and said, "I'll be back . . ." He patted Shawn, who was still looking ambivalent, on the back; he said, "Yo, treat my road dawg as if he's at a five-star hotel and you're the pretty hostess." Jefferson walked back to the kitchen, yelling, "Hey, Pops, Mom!"

Pop and Rita Jones turned and saw Jefferson coming through the swing doors. Pop, smiling from ear to ear, wiped his hands on a towel hanging in the front of his waist; he was so excited. "Oh my god, my my. Wow, honey plum, it's Jefferson."

Rita May laughed. "Pop, I have eyes. I see my big boy even though I thought my eyes were playing tricks . . . God is so good."

She hobbled over to Jefferson; he looked at her with a huge grin. It's been such a long time. The last time he was here she was walking okay, a slight limp, but it looked as if Mr. Arthritis had been working overtime. He quickly moved toward her. She grabbed him and hugged him; she was just slightly over his midsection. They held each other in a tight embrace. He lifted her off the floor. Rita May laughed and said, "Boy, you better put me down. You're going to hurt your back. As you can see, I put on a few pounds."

Pop responded, "A few, understatement."

She looked over at Pop. "Hush up, Pop."

She laughed, giggled, and said, "Boy, you are still crazy."

Jefferson spun her around; she cried for him to put her down, but she loved every second of it.

"Jeff, you better put your mom down." That was Pop.

He did; as he wiped the corners of his eyes, he said, "I didn't know what happened to you guys. I came around . . ." He thought and said, "Some time ago, and I was told by the town folks you guys had moved."

Pop nodded his head. "We did. Rent was too high. Those darn Republicans and that fake-hair blond guy Mr. Chump." Pop laughed and continued, "Chump, that's what we call him." They all laughed as Pop continued, "So we packed up everything like the Beverly Hillbillies, and here we go. We love it."

Pop came over and grabbed both his wife and Jefferson with his strong arms and hugged them. Pop was slightly taller than his wife; the three of them hugging looked like the Smurfs and the giant. They broke the embrace. Pop kissed Jefferson on the cheek and said, "Boy, how are you?"

Jefferson smiled from ear to ear and responded, "Excellent now."

# CHAPTER 150

Tina offered Shawn a booth. He looked around and saw a few other spots that would have been equally nice as well; she said, "This is his favorite spot." Tina moved a little to the side and saw what looked like the shape of a stop sign. It said Jeff's Office. Tina pointed and said, "See? This is his spot."

Shawn lightly laughed with a smile. "Okay, here is where we park."

Tina looked at him with those cute big light brown eyes and asked, "Do you still need some more time?" He looked at her. She slightly smiled. "For your order."

Shawn looked at her and realized what she was talking about. "Uh, yeah . . . I'll just wait for Jefferson."

Tina smiled and responded, "I already know what he wants. It's the same thing. It's been the same thing for years when he used to come around. Maybe he's changed . . ." There was a pause; then she forced a smile. "I doubt it."

Shawn asked, "How long was that?"

Tina thought. "Hmmm, about five to seven years. It's amazing. He still looks pretty much the same." She looked at Shawn with a bit of curiosity in her eyes. "Sooo how did you two meet?"

Shawn, caught off guard, slightly smiled and continued, "Why did you look at me like that?"

, brushing back her hair, and responded, "It's been a long time, that's all. Plus Jeff is a loner . . . I'm surprised he has a friend . . . So I was wondering . . ." She laughed.

He looked at her with a smile in his voice and said, "What's so funny?"

Tina's laugh dribbled down to a ladylike chuckle; she said, "When you two came in, I thought you were by yourself. But when I noticed how he was right behind you, I was completely surprised."

Shawn nodded. "Jefferson is a nice guy, loyal to the core. I can't see anyone pushing him away or him being a loner, you know what I mean?"

She looked down and back up. "Things happen—sometimes bad things, sometime ugly things, things that folks don't want to let go and have no problem reminding you. People don't want you to forget." Tina was transfixed while she was talking when she looked at him with a smile. "Ready to order?"

Shawn shook his head and said, "Not yet, in a minute."

She gave a slight nod as she continued, "Sometimes people do things to push you away and make you stay away." Tina's mind drifted somewhere—some forbidden place, someplace painful, emotional.

Shawn could see her eyes getting glassy; he asked, "Are you okay?"

Tina seemed unable to break away from the thought; it didn't want to let her go. She'd been at this spot before; she knew how to break free from it even though it seemed to get harder and harder each time. She wiped her eyes and said, "Damn allergies." Shawn knew better; the season for allergies was over. Tina wiped her eyes and smiled. "Sorry. So wow, how did we drift over to that?" She wouldn't let go. "So how did you two meet?"

Shawn nodded and thought; he said, "Oh, at a mixed martial arts event."

There was a pause; she continued, "Wow, I didn't know Jeff was into that. Wow, just when you thought you know someone . . . wow."

Shawn was cool about it; he knew Tina was trying to get some info out of him, but he wasn't biting. "That's life . . . changes. Things you never ate before, all of sudden, you love. Things you used to eat, you can't stand it anymore . . . Life changes, what a difference a few years can make." Shawn slightly smiled. Tina nodded with a slight smile. Shawn knew from the look on Tina's face she wasn't going to give up that easily; he didn't know when or how, but he knew she was going to strike.

She smiled. "Are you ready to order?"

Shawn smiled and said, "Yeah."

Tina slid out from the booth and was sitting on the edge of the bench when she was getting ready to get up. Shawn asked, "So how did you and Pop meet up with Jefferson?"

Tina looked at him with an exasperated look. "You are persistent, aren't you?"

Shawn shrugged his shoulders. "That's what some people call it."

She was curious. "And others?"

He chuckled, saying, "A pain in the ass."

They both lightly laughed; she said, "Well, I must admit you are heading in that direction." She looked at him and shook her head. He just shrugged his shoulders.

She looked around the eatery; everything was okay. She turned back to him. She filled him in on Jefferson's story—his rise and fall, the uncut version, as she would call it. The rise to stardom and his hard crash, from having everything to having nothing, losing everything—family, friends, and almost his soul.

Tina started, "What can I say? He got mixed up or rather trapped into something, a web, a tangled web of drugs, deceit, and lies." She stopped and looked at him with an eye of curiosity. "I'm surprised Jeff never told you his story, and you said you've known him for how long?"

Shawn was caught off guard with that question; however, he recovered quickly. "Well, he did tell me some things. We never got a chance to finish."

Tina looked at him with questioning eyes and said, "Yeah, that sounds like Jeff." She looked around; folks were still eating and enjoying the nice, peaceful environment. She brought her attention back to Shawn. "Sorry, he was the best of the best, a professor at Hunter College. He moved up the ranks rather quickly, promotion after promotion. Jeff has always been a hard worker, an accomplished individual from start to finish, no matter how long it took. He became dean for the freshmen class, the youngest dean. He was loved by everyone. That crazy personality of his was his main ticket to bridging so many gaps. He was well connected to the staff and student body. He would take time out of his day to hold sessions in the student lounge concerning questions students may have had regarding tutoring or whatever. He was the man on the spot. You would find him in the student lounge just relaxing with the students. They loved him."

She stopped. Shawn looked at her and asked, "Are you all right?"

Tina wiped the corners of her eyes and nodded. "Yeah . . . sure . . . This usually happens when I go into Jeff's story." She paused, inhaled a breath, and said, "He got mixed up in some wicked shit, excuse me." Shawn's eyebrow arched. She continued, "He met this student. She was a small-time dealer. He wanted something to take the edge from his workload. He was on the brink of burnout. He needed a boost, and he found one." She paused and continued, "One boost always led to another boost and to another, and then you're ready to graduate to the next level—something harder, something a little more dangerous, something that works quicker and faster. And you tell yourself you can handle it."

Shawn was completely into what Tina was saying. She went on, "She gave him something called RX24."

Shawn asked, "What was it?"

Tina responded, "A pill from hell, and when I say 'hell,' I'm not speaking figuratively. It completely ruined him, destroyed everything he worked for."

Shawn asked again, "What was it?"

Tina shrugged. "Not sure, I don't think he even knew what it was. RX24, RX treatment from the inside . . . 24, twenty-four hours."

Shawn responded, "Damn."

Tina nodded her head. "Yeah, exactly." She continued, "He couldn't stop. It had him. It was doing something to him. He went from once a day to twice a day to three times a day." She shook her head. "I remember seeing him. He looked terrible. He was crashing fast. He knew it and couldn't do anything about it. That RX24 was tearing up his wallet. That crap even got into his bank account. That shit affected every corner of his life. Everyone saw the change. It was so damn evident."

Shawn looked at her. "He didn't see the change."

Of course, but there is something that is as powerful as believing in God, and that is denial. I told him the stuff was killing him. He would tell me he had it under control and that he could quit any time he wanted to—the devil's lie."

Shawn looked tense. "So what happened?"

Tina lightly chuckled. "I don't blame you for not wanting to hear the rest of the damage." Shawn did not respond; she continued, "It got so bad that taking the RX24 was more important than taking care of himself." Shawn's eyebrow went up. Tina caught the gesture; she said, "He just shut down. He stopped bathing, eating. He looked like a skeleton with skin. He was gone. He was done."

Shawn asked the obvious question. "His career?"

Tina looked at him. "What career?" She looked up at the ceiling as the tears flooded her eyes; one blink, and there goes the dam. She said,

"What do you think? But I'll play along. He was suspended several times until they had enough of the nonsense as they would call it. He lost his wife. She had about enough of his crap. She walked out, her and their baby daughter without a forwarding address. She shut this door, locked it, bolted it, and threw away the key."

Shawn, looking down, asked, "Do you blame her? Would you have stayed?"

Tina stared straight ahead in a daze. "No, I can't blame her. He did some serious damage beside the drugs, getting your freakin' ass kicked on a daily basis . . . No, I don't blame her." She continued, "The man you see now is not the same man back then, and to explain why I wouldn't stay . . ." She lightly chuckled, but it was a chilling chuckle, sort of diabolical. She continued, "If I would have stayed, I would have found a way to kill that son of a bitch, slice him up, and feed him to the dogs. My sister was nice in leaving." Shawn looked at her, stunned. Tina continued, "Jeff is such a wonderful guy, he really is. Even with this crazy drug, he tried to hold it together—you know, be himself. But you can't be yourself when something else has taken over your heart, mind, and soul." She continued, "My sister loved him, but it was just too much for her and the baby. The day she left was the day she found her life. She was living with a man who was dead and didn't know it."

That caught Shawn's attention; he said, "Jefferson's wife is your sister?"

Tina nodded her head. "Yep."

Shawn began to put the pieces together. "Ahh, I see. So that's where ten years come in."

Tina looked at him. "Excuse me?"

Shawn looked at her. "No, sorry. I was calculating something. So you haven't seen Jeff in some time?"

. "Yeah, you can say that even though 'a while' would be an understatement, but he did keep in contact. He was living in Las Vegas." She paused and continued, "He would write asking about my sister and my niece. I was told not to tell him anything, so I didn't. This is how I got details on what had happened to him. He would write pages after pages in detail. You got the *Reader's Digest* version." She lightly laughed. She continued, "He would call now and then or send a postcard. It was good to know he was still alive. He never mentioned how he was doing, but I just assumed the few phone calls and postcards and letters all indicated he was doing okay."

Shawn was surprised to uncover this part of Jefferson's life; he asked, "So today is the first day since he left?"

Tina nodded. "Yep, ten years ago today . . . A man that looked like he was run over by a bulldozer walked out of this door, and ten years later, he finds us and walks right back in."

Shawn responded, "You don't seem to be excited."

She looked at him with a serious expression and said, "No, I am excited. I'm just guarded. You're not going to waltz in and waltz out whenever you feel like it. I don't think so. I don't care how much I miss you or love you or care about you. I can't allow him to put me through that thing again."

Shawn slightly smiled. "I understand, but I got a strong feeling he's going to be sticking around for a long time."

Tina gave him an inquisitive look and said, "We'll see."

Shawn switched gears. "So he seems very close to Pop and Rita May. The relationship with the three of you is amazing."

Tina smiled. "Pop and Rita are my relatives, uncle and aunt." He looked at her, perplexed. She lightly laughed and said, "On your next rodeo when you come back, I'll tell you the story of how I came into Pop and Rita's life—too long to tell, cowboy. All I can say is my aunt and uncle stuck by Jeff's side no matter what he went through." She shook her head and lightly laughed. Shawn smiled. He paused and was ready to speak when she interrupted him. "Jeff, another long story how the three of us met."

She blew out a breath and said, "Whew! Thank you."

Shawn looked at her. "For what?"

Tina said, "For sticking close to Jeff. Not too many people in this town did that. So many abandoned him. He became a disappointment. When he was doing well, they lifted him up. And when he was going through his hell, they tore him down." There was a pause, and she continued, "He admires you. He respects you."

Shawn looked at her with a slight grin. "How do you know that?"

Tina held his hand and said, "I know my brother, and if he didn't respect you or admire you, he wouldn't be with you." She smiled and lightly squeezed his hand.

He smiled and said, "Well, I guess we are family because he treats me like a big brother." Shawn lightly squeezed her hand and said, "'Howdy' country style or 'what's up, sis?' Martin style."

They both laughed. Tina said, "You never told me how you and Jeff met. I guess it doesn't matter as long you watch over him, protect my brother." She paused and said, "Welcome to the family, Shawn."

Shawn smiled and said, "Why thank you, Missy Tee! That's mighty nice of you."

They both laughed.

# CHAPTER 151

Shawn and Jefferson enjoyed the meal as they were getting ready to leave, exchanging hugs, kisses, and tears. They put their phone numbers in their phones. Rita said, "So where are you staying?"

Jefferson smiled, nudged Shawn, and said, "Well, for now, I'll be staying with Shawn until I can get back on my feet."

Aunt Rita looked at her husband; they both looked at Shawn with concern, Shawn could see their concern and said, "He'll be fine. I have plenty of space."

Jefferson nodded his head with enthusiasm. "Yeah, nice and big."

Shawn continued, "Jay is like a little brother. Don't worry, he'll be fine."

Rita May said, "Well, if he gives you any trouble, send him back here. I have a strap with his name on it."

Shawn lightly laughed; he hugged Jefferson in a playful headlock and said, "He'll be fine, I promise." Shawn let Jeff go and smooshed his hair. Pop gave Shawn a nice manly hug, and Rita gave him a hug and a peck on the cheek.

Pop looked at Jefferson and pointed his finger at him. "Behave yourself."

Jefferson nodded. "Yes, sir." Pop, still pointing that Uncle Sam–looking finger, continued, "And no more running. We are here for you, you hear me?"

Jefferson nodded his head; as he was slightly looking down, he said, "Yes, sir."

Pop and Rita May went back to the kitchen as the three watched. Jefferson added, "Man, Tina, they're getting old. But what a team! One can't live without the other."

Tina nodded her head. "I know."

Jefferson looked at her and said in a serious tone, "Thank you for putting up with me, answering all of my postcards and letters and—"

She cut him off, saying, "Please don't ask about Tracey. Just wait. I speak to her at least twice a week. I'm sure she would be happy to know that you are doing well and that you're back." There was a pause before she continued, "Jeff, I don't know what else to say or to tell you. You know she doesn't want me to give you any information about her other than she is doing well and that your daughter is fine." Tina nodded her head and said, "Jeff honey, let it go and move on. This stuff is going to make you sick, and you can relapse. You don't want that to happen."

Jefferson whispered with clenched teeth. "I can't . . . I can't let her go. I love her, Tina."

Tina nodded her head. "I know you do, but there is a lot of stuff that has happen, like ten years of stuff. Just give it more time."

Jefferson looked at her, still apparently frustrated. "More time? Don't you think ten years is enough time?"

Tina did not say anything; she took out her cell phone, did something to it, and handed it to Shawn. "Take a picture of Jeff and I." Jefferson was surprised. Tina said, "Listen to me, Jeff. I will intervene this one time. After this, that's it. I will get these two pictures developed and send them to Tracey." She reached into her pocket and took out a pen; she looked at Shawn. "Give me your address please."

Shawn was caught off guard. Tina was standing there, looking at Shawn as if he was a special case; she said, "Address . . . please." Shawn gave her the address. She looked at Jefferson. "When the film is developed, I will tape a piece of paper to the back of the picture and send it to my sister, letting her know this is the address where you are staying. Now whether she responds, I have no control. As a matter of fact, when this is over, do not ask me any questions about Tracey."

Jefferson smiled and hugged and kissed her on the cheek. "Thank you, sis."

Tina wiped a tear from the corner of her eyes.

# CHAPTER 152

Jefferson was driving; there was silence for most of the ride. Shawn said, "I need to burn off some of this energy. Make a right at the next corner and then a left."

Jefferson looked at him and did as he was instructed. When he made that left, his face lit up with a smile. "Wow. Are you serious?" He looked over at Shawn, who was smiling.

Shawn said, "This is one way to get your mind off stuff that feels like it's weighing you down."

Jefferson barked out a laugh and said, "So you bring us to not a strip joint, but an arcade! Are you serious, an arcade?"

Shawn continued to smile. "No, not just any arcade, but the number one–rated arcade in the city. Here, park right there."

Jefferson responded, "You want me to park here? It says 'Reserve Parking Only,' Wall Street. Look, the sign."

Shawn looked at him and said to Gordon, "Release seat belt."

Gordon responded, "Yes, sir. Should I wait here in this illegal parking spot, sir? If I'm towed, it will cost you . . . let's see, ah, close to $400, sir."

Jefferson agreed, "That's right, G. You school him because Lord knows I don't have $400!"

Gordon replied, "Yes, Master Jefferson, good point."

Jefferson shook his head and said, "Nah, hold up, G. Please don't call me 'master,' okay?"

Gordon replied, "I apologize, sir. I was just being polite and respectful the way my program has been designed by my creator Tanya Jacqueline Hawkins, sir. How about 'mister'?"

Jefferson responded, "You mean like in the *Color Purple*? Hell no, keep going."

Shawn was very much concerned; he said, "Jay, listen, you really don't want to tamper with Gordon's program. It's etched in his memory data. TJ only gave him so much to choose from. It's a standard program. You shouldn't—"

Jefferson interrupted Shawn, saying, "Wall Street, chill. I got this, brah."

Shawn just shook his head, casually threw his hands up, and said, "Okay, do you, but I'm warning you not to . . ."

Jefferson looked at Shawn, who nodded his head and backed off.

Gordon continued, "Sir, I'm not sure what you want to be called. You detest being called 'master.' You don't like the term 'mister.' I am confused. What else is there, sir? I can call you these names in a different language if you like." Gordon started speaking the names in different languages; he said afterward, "So what do you think, sir? I mean, Master. No, sorry . . ." Gordon's lights started flashing off and on.

Jefferson was concerned as he turned to Shawn. "What's happening to him?"

Shawn responded, "You have overloaded his system. I told you he could only take but so much."

Jefferson was worried. "Okay, okay, Gordon, no more names. Relax, we'll work something out." He looked at Shawn.

Gordon replied, "Thank you, sir."

Jefferson said, "Listen, just call me dawg. 'Yo, dawg,' 'Hey, dawg,' for example." He smiled. "Yeah, that's it, G." Shawn just shook his head. Jefferson said to Shawn, "See? Cool, I have my own customized computerized car." He was excited. He said to Shawn, "Yo, Wall Street, are you sure you up for this, brah?"

Shawn responded, "Yep, need to release some of this energy."

Jefferson looked at him. "And you think you're going to get your satisfaction out on me?" He threw his head back and laughed out loud. He stopped and looked at Shawn and said, "I don't think so, Captain." Jefferson continued, "I'll have you to know I am the king of this thing called the arcade. I've mastered all the games, bro." He continued, "Now keep in mind, when you go inside, it's going to look different. You probably haven't been in one of these in years. And it's only fair to warn you they don't have those old crappy games like *Donkey Kong, Pac-Man, Ms. Pac-Man, Dig Dug*, huh, okay? New age, new era, Okay? Name them. They won't carry them. They are extinct. Okay, puff . . ."

Jefferson threw his head back and laughed real loud again; he continued, "Ah, games like *Asteroids*, *Pole Position*. The list goes on and on, bro. Surrender now while your pride and dignity are still in one piece."

Gordon made a sound and said, "Ah, yeah . . . you dawg."

Jefferson was hyper, but it seemed as if the air was slowly seeping out of him; the excitement of beating Shawn was fading. He said, "Gordon, listen. Don't say 'you dawg.' Just say 'dawg' or something smart and intelligent, okay?"

Gordon responded, "Whatever, you dawg from the hood."

Jefferson got excited. "Okay, take off the 'whatever,' but the rest is cool. It's my night. Come on, Wall Street, it's time to get that ass waxed."

Gordon added, "Yeah, wax that ass extra good . . . ah . . . dawg. And when you are done waxing it, come and wax mine. Buff it. Make it shine, dawg. I need a good ass waxing, you dawg."

Jefferson shook his head with a tense smile. "Okay, we need to work on a few slang mechanics, but the foundation is there . . . I think."

# Chapter 153

Jefferson got on the passenger side of the car. Shawn hopped in the driver's side in a much better mood. Gordon said, "What's up, dawg? Did you wax that ass, shine it up, buff it, and smacked it? My turn."

Jefferson stared real hard at the speaker system with a look of frustration. He said, "Yo, Shawn, I could have beat you, man."

Gordon responded, "Oh man, you got your ass waxed, dawg. Wow."

Jefferson, while looking at the speaker, wanted to say something but resisted. He heard Shawn say with a smile, "Which game, brah?"

Jefferson sarcastically chuckled. "Man, you're funny, bro."

Gordon, out of nowhere, said, "What's cookin', dawg? Besides getting your ass waxed with a buff and a shine."

Jefferson appeared agitated and looked at Shawn, who shrugged his shoulders and said, "I told you . . ." Shawn zipped his lips. "I'm not going to throw it back at you."

Jefferson rolled his eyes and continued, "What do you mean 'what game'? Every freakin' game."

Shawn replied, "That's right, every game."

Gordon raised his tone. "What, are you serious? Yo, what's up with that, dawg?"

Jefferson was now pissed as he raised his voice at Gordon, saying, "Gordon, do me a favor." He looked at Shawn, who shook his head and gave Jefferson a hard disapproving look not to say anything negative to Gordon. Jefferson responded with a low growl and said, "Ah, nothing."

Gordon continued, "Yo, dawg, check it out. I've been tightening up on my slang, dawg. I can spit some words out, dawg, that make sense. I'm getting there." Gordon continued, "Yo, dawg, at the rate I'm going, I'll be a master at this, my dawg."

Jefferson sneered and said, "I can't take this. I can't do this. This is too much."

Gordon replied, "Getting your ass waxed like that with a buff and a shine, I would probably feel the same way you feel right now, dawg."

Jefferson growled, "Shawn, please."

Shawn told Gordon to set the coordinates for home. Gordon replied, "Yes, sir."

Jefferson thought and shrugged, thinking, *That doesn't sound too bad.* He said to Shawn, "You surprised me, Wall Street. I thought this was going to be a walk in the park, a stroll, but you proved me wrong . . . good game." They gave each other a dap.

Gordon jumped in. "I must say . . ." Jefferson was just waiting for Gordon to slip up because he was ready to shut him down. Gordon began, "Sir, that was very impressive." Jefferson had the words in his mouth to let Gordon have it, but he stopped when he heard Gordon's compliment.

Shawn looked at Jefferson; his mouth was slightly open, and he looked as if he had something to say. Shawn asked Jefferson, "Now what was that you were going to say?"

Jefferson cleared his throat and said, "Uh, thank you, Gordon."

Gordon replied, "You are most welcome, sir." There was a silence when Gordon said, "Excuse me, sir. If I may, with your permission, may I stop with this dawg thing? I know you like it, sir, but—"

Jefferson cut him off as he practically stumbled over his words. "No, by all means, permission granted. It is an excellent idea, starting immediately."

Gordon continued, "I will continue if you want me to, but . . ."

Jefferson frantically shook his head. "No! I mean no, Gordon. What an excellent idea."

Gordon's lights flashed bright; he said, "Thank you, sir."

Jefferson blew out an exaggerated breath and said, "No, thank you."

# Chapter 154

Serenity was in the shower, enjoying the nice warm water and the relaxing steam. The accommodations that Evans has provided were wonderful. She was more than thankful he allowed her to call and speak to Ashley. Serenity smiled and was humming a song when she heard a sound coming from Evans's bedroom and now her bedroom as well. She listened as she turned off the shower water; she listened again. There it was again, that same sound. What was it? She listened.

Serenity called Evans; perhaps he was working on something or was maybe in the kitchen. She called his name again. Still no response. She reached for her towel on the outside rack. She still had not pulled back the shower curtain as she continued to feel for the towel; her hand landed on the towel when her hand was grabbed, and the shower curtain was pulled back with such a force and quickness. She screamed as the masked man smacked her; she was stumbling backward when he quickly, with such force, grabbed her by the arm and yanked her toward him. She came toward him with such resistance, screaming and swinging with her arms flailing. She was clawing at his mask; her blows and hits had no effect on him.

He laughed and smacked her again. It seemed the more she hit him, the stronger he became. He grabbed her by her hair and dragged her out of the shower. She resisted and fought hard, scratching and punching and screaming. As he dragged her out of the shower, her legs were being hit against the shower tile and metal, scratching and scraping and bruising up her legs. Serenity screamed and pleaded and cried; she called Evans, but he did not answer.

The masked man was strong as he dragged her by her hair into the bedroom as her body bumped and hit the walls. He grabbed her suddenly by her shoulders, squeezing them like a vice grip. Serenity howled in pain as he picked her up and threw her onto the bed. He started loosening his belt; as she tried to get away, he grabbed her by her waist as his fingers went deep into her skin. She kicked and screamed from the pain; his fingers felt like sharp claws. His voice was garbled and rough; he said, "So you want it nice and hard, huh?"

She continued to kick and scream; she turned on her stomach and tried to quickly crawl when he came down hard on her back with a hard elbow. The blow was so hard, it knocked the wind out of her for a few seconds. In that moment, that brief moment, she became helpless, defenseless. It was enough time for him to pounce on her. His huge hands grabbed her and placed her on all fours. Her head was spinning as she tried to cough the oxygen back into her lungs, but by this time, he had already dominated her as he straddled himself behind her. He reached into his underwear and took out his huge cock. He had her by her hair to keep her in place. She screamed and tried her best to get away; it was useless. She yelled and cried for Evans—no answer.

She heard the beast over her, laugh, and taunt her. He said something in his garbled language, something about placing his seed in her as he reared back and thrust that hard manhood in her. She screamed as the pain shot throughout her body; her scream penetrated into the air.

Shawn quickly sat up, yelling Serenity's name; he was drenched with sweat. He had to take a few seconds to get it together; his breathing was ragged and rough as he looked around. He sat there with his head in his hands; he cursed out loud. He bolted up. He grabbed and put a pair of sweat pants on, no tee shirt, no footwear. He went with such a determination to his gym. He walked in the gym room; the lights came on. AI greeted him, "Welcome, Mr. Cook, to another—"

Shawn interrupted AI. "Set your computer to the next level, your animation and my animation on." Shawn slipped on his vest without protective headgear. He attached electron prongs to different parts of his body. He said, "I want the blows of damage to be felt as well as show up on both animations. I want full damage on both. Ten-round fight. The match can't be stopped either way. Make five consecutive hits affect my animation and my skills."

AI said, "Sir, this is very dangerous, and it can cause all kinds of serious injury. Even—"

Shawn cut off the computer and said, "Begin program now."

If the computer connected with a blow to Shawn, he would feel every blow from the electro prongs attached to his body; he had them up to level 9—the highest level was 10.

The bell sounded. Shawn was in the circle moving; when he moved, his animated character would move as well. If he ducked, the animated character would duck as well. Shawn came out ducking and moving as he bounced on his toes, weaving and bobbing as he threw a series jabs. If he connected, the computer animation would light up and show where the hit took place; the same results would occur with Shawn's animated character. However, with Shawn's animated character, enough blows to any part of the body would slow down the animated reflexes to the extent enough blows the animated fighter would be unable to contend or compete. The blows would begin to show on the animated body as well.

Shawn moved with grace and precision. AI caught him with a quick jab to the face and a quick left and right hook combination to the face. Shawn's animation was stunned as its reflexes reacted a second or two late. Shawn felt the sting of the blows as he put his arms up and retreated a little, shaking his head, trying to shake the daze away. He tapped his gloves against his head as he recovered and went toward AI. He knew a few more blows like that, he was done. He realized he had to take out AI quickly. Shawn ducked and moved, bobbed, and weaved as he ducked a jab from AI and the same combination that connected a few minutes ago. This time, Shawn countered with two hard crisp blows to the body and the side of AI's face.

AI moved back and covered up against the ropes as he went into a defense/offense mode, trying to lure Shawn into his trap. Shawn came in carefully with abandoned aggression. AI was covering up, protecting himself, and trying to sneak in quick crisp jabs. Shawn moved left, right, and left, ducked, dodged, and countered with hard blows. The blows were starting to show on AI's face and body. Shawn knew that with this move he was making, his body would suffer damage as well; it was the price of fighting against a rope-a-dope fighter. The key was not to exhaust your energy and connect with the right spots to render your fighter helpless and then raise your game and throw out the trash.

Jefferson was watching from the shadows in amazement. Shawn did not know that he was watching. Shawn did some damage to AI, but he did not come out clean either; the blows from AI had did some damage to Shawn's animation as well. Shawn moved with such fluidity, but somehow

Shawn was pinned in the corner. AI came in for the kill. Jefferson watched in amazement; he knew Shawn was in trouble.

This fight was over as AI went in like a shark smelling blood. Jefferson shook his head as he watched Shawn somehow bring boxing skills to another level as he countered and reencountered and jabbed and punched, moving and bobbing, sticking and moving as AI was hitting and swinging and connecting with the air as the hard swings made hissing and swishing sounds. Shawn managed to get out of the corner when AI tagged him hard. Shawn's animated character staggered back but recovered. He knew one more of those, and it was over.

Shawn came back with such an aggressive force, connecting blow after blow. AI was slammed and backed up into the corner, stunned and dazed, trying to survive the round. Shawn did not let up as he threw a melee of punches, most of them connecting and doing sufficient damage. AI's animation was busted up very bad. It took each hit to the face, blood splattered. The eyes were almost shut; the body and the ribs were red, which indicated the ribs were broken.

Thirty seconds remained in the round. AI was still against the ropes. Shawn's jab connected twice as AI's head jerked back. Shawn came back with a left hook and right hook. AI's knees buckled; the onslaught continued with no mercy, ruthless abandonment—a hard right to the head, a left hook to the body. Shawn unloaded a Sugar Ray machine gunfire of blows. AI fell down on one knee but managed to stagger back up.

Fifteen seconds. Shawn had backed up when AI went down on a knee, but it was back up as Shawn stalked AI like Mike Tyson. Shawn did not waste any time; he picked up where he left off, hard crisp blows.

Ten seconds. Shawn was on a mission as his animated character was breathing hard as he threw haymakers and body blows; he threw everything he had. His fighting went from skills to anger as he expressed his pent-up anger and frustration as he yelled. Shawn threw a hard right hook and a hard upper cut, which sent AI to the canvas.     The ref started counting. AI was saved by the bell. Shawn was angry as he yelled out in frustration.

Jefferson was confused; he didn't understand where the anger was coming from, and then it hit him. His anger was a buildup of everything; it was coming from a deep, dark place.

Shawn stood there, breathing hard but smooth; his hands were on his waist with his head down as he was inhaling the air. The computer continued, "We are ready to start the second round."

Shawn was ready for the bell to sound when a towel came in from AI's corner. The different colors flashed brightly; the computer said, "TKO, sir. Congratulations. You remain the reigning champ, sir. However, there is a challenger that is waiting, sir, to fight you. Do you want to take on the challenge, sir?"

Shawn said, "No, not at this time." He removed the prongs from several parts of his body and said, "Save the program."

Shawn stood there with his hands on his waist, looking enraged and angry as he punched the heavy bag out of frustration.

Jefferson came from out of the shadows. "I wasn't spying on you. I didn't want to break up your concentration." He briefly paused as he continued, "Wow, you put on a clinic, son. I've never seen . . . wow."

Shawn ignored the compliment as he walked past him, saying, "I need to run. You coming?"

Jefferson looked at him. "Run?"

Shawn looked at him as he was putting on his running gear, "Yes, a run. That's the act of moving faster than a walk, in between a trot and slower than a sprint. Now that should cover all the bases. Would you like to come?" He looked annoyed.

Jefferson gave Shawn a brush-off look and said, "No need to play Sesame Street, okay? But to make sure I heard right, a run. Let's see, people run from the police, the bus, the train. I once ran my ass off when I was in the wrong hood and totally misunderstood."

Shawn did not crack a smile; he looked at Jefferson and said, "Okay, yes or no? I'll make it easier for you. You can ride the bike."

Jefferson smiled. "Okay, feed me, Seymour. Keep going."

Shawn looked at him, turned to walk out of the gym, and said, "Breakfast on me. Take it or leave it."

Jefferson smiled and said, "Like that dude on *The A-Team* always says, 'I love it when a plan comes together' . . . Deal."

# CHAPTER 155

They were on their final mile. Shawn continued to maintain the same pace he started with, calculating when he was going to make that move to the finish line. The terrain was a combination of hills and straight streets.

Jefferson had second thoughts about riding the bike. The hills were doing him in; he felt the strain throughout his body. He'd been trailing behind early on in the race, but he was determined he wasn't going out this way. He started whining about pain in his legs. "Shawn, my legs, I can't feel my legs . . ." He sounded like the character in the movie *Forrest Gump*. His complaining continued. "Shawn, my legs, are they still there? . . . Shawn."

Shawn was focused as he could see the finish line. Jefferson looked at Shawn; he didn't even look tired. Jefferson was just a few feet behind him. Jefferson's breathing was becoming somewhat hard; he said to Shawn, "Yo, brah, you okay?"

Shawn had that look of determination; he slightly turned his head toward Jefferson and said with determination, "Keep up, little man."

Jefferson repeated the "little man" when he all of a sudden saw Shawn take off in a sprint. It took Jefferson just a few seconds to realize that Shawn was challenging him. "Oh wow . . ." Jefferson cried out loud, "Oh, okay!"

He began to pedal as fast as his painful legs could go. The pain was shooting throughout his legs and back. He cried out, fighting against the pain. He was closing in on Shawn. Shawn could hear Jefferson's breathing and the sound of the bike tires on the smooth pavement. Jefferson was now equal with Shawn, neck to neck like at a horse race; this might be a photo finish as both men pushed. Shawn was starting to pull away. Jefferson said in a hard growl, "No, you don't! I don't think so, not on my watch!"

Shawn began to pull out with a slight advantage, looking at Jefferson, saying, "Come on, Jay. Come on, baby, push . . . push."

Jefferson put his head down and gave it his last shot as he began to jump out in front. He began to celebrate the moment of victory and Shawn's agony of defeat; he said with a smile of celebration, "I got this! I got this! I got you, Wall Street. This little man beat that big man. So who is the big man now, chump?"

Shawn was still running hard as he listened to Jefferson shout his premature celebrative moment. Shawn knew he was going to lose this one; as he continued to hear Jefferson rant and taunt him, he started getting angry. He started thinking about the dream he had last night; that began to fuel the fire, the flame, the torch as he began to close the gap between him and Jefferson—but it was too late. Jefferson looked in the side mirrors of the bike and saw Shawn approaching fast like a freight train as his arms were pumping and his legs were moving up and down like a piston. It was too late as Jefferson added a little more speed for assurance. Shawn came hard, yelling, "No pain, no gain!"

yell. Jefferson knew he had it as he laughed and taunted Shawn as he came toward the finish line. "Finally, I beat you in something." He continued, "That's right, I'm the man, the bomb, baby." Women were passing by, smiling. He continued, "Who are you going to call? Jefferson Newhouse, baby! I'm in the . . . oh shiiiit." His legs tightened up as he yelled in agony, "Damn, oh man!"

He was right about to cross the finish line and cruise over it, but not before Shawn crossed it first, passing Jefferson with his hands raised. He heard Jefferson curse and say, "Damn, freakin' cramp, son of . . . damn!"

Shawn had crossed the line and was bent over, catching his breath. He looked back and saw Jefferson off his bike and sitting next to it, rubbing the back of his legs, rocking back and forth; he said in frustration, "Damn, damn. Freak, I had you, Wall Street. I had you."

Shawn was standing over Jefferson as he knelt near him. "Cramp?" He helped massage his leg.

Jefferson nodded. "Oh yeah."

Shawn slightly smiled. "You almost beat me."

Jefferson stopped the massage and looked at Shawn. "Don't gloat and don't patronize me, but I had you. Damn, I had you, man." He cursed under his breath. "Man, I can't beat you in anything. That's a damn shame. Jefferson looked at Shawn, waiting for the smart remark; all he got was a humble smile.

Shawn moved Jefferson's hand. "Let me see that. And yes, you did—you had me. You rode like a warrior."

Jefferson blew out a breath of frustration. "The bottom line is you won, and I lost . . . again." He had a look of relief on his face. "Wow, that really feels good. Wow, who taught you that, your sensei?"

Shawn, looking serious, replied, "No, a very wise person."

Jefferson looked at him. "Who?"

Shawn smiled and did a fake bow of respect. "My mother."

Jefferson responded, "Oh, the slapper." They both chuckled.

Shawn's face turned serious as he stared out to nothing in particular. Jefferson looked at him and slightly nudged him. "What's on your mind? Something is happening tonight. You practically almost destroyed your heavy bag. That wasn't skill fighting—that was anger. What is going on? Are you okay?"

Shawn looked down and back up at Jefferson; they both got up off the ground. Shawn said, "No, not really. It's been three days, and this mother . . ." He bit his lower lip. He continued, "I'm in the dark. This sucker knows exactly what he is doing. He's playing games with my head, Jay. That son of a bitch knows what he is doing . . . Why haven't I heard from him?"

Jefferson limped a few feet away and said, "Keep in mind, he doesn't want Serenity—he wants you. Plus you have the advantage."

Shawn looked at Jefferson. "How so?"

Jefferson continued, "Whoever is watching Serenity seemed to be breaking his own boss's rules. I'm more than certain this nut has no idea what is going on in his own backyard."

Shawn thought about it and nodded his head. "Good point. But how long before the stranger catches on?"

Jefferson looked serious and replied, "True."

# Chapter 156

Day 4

Shawn's cell phone chimed. He was sound asleep. He heard the sound of the chime sneak into his dream. He quickly sat up and reached past the clock phone, which read 2:45 a.m. Shawn mumbled to himself, "What the hell?" He picked up the phone and said in an irritated tone, "This better be good."

There was a slight pause before Shawn heard the voice—the voice of the stranger. "Oh, I'm sure it's worth your while and your time, Mr. Cook, especially wanting to know where the beautiful and gorgeous Serenity is . . ." The stranger gave that laugh before he continued, "So now, Mr. Cook, is that . . . uh . . . good enough?" The stranger did that eerie laugh again as he continued, "Do I have your undivided attention, Mr. Cook? Because the bottom line still remains the same—I hold the cards."

Shawn's anger was beginning to seep back in as he gritted into the phone. "What do you want? Get to the point."

The stranger said with a smile in his voice, "Good."

Shawn did not say another word; he was afraid of putting Serenity's life in danger. The stranger responded, "I am sorry I'm calling so late or so early. But I figured since you haven't heard from me in the last few days, you know business before pleasure, you would be happy to hear my voice and what's the latest news on your lovely wife. But I stand corrected . . . maybe."

would call a person for several days without allowing any form of communication. Shawn was a businessman and couldn't think what type of business this could be, obviously some form of retreat. Right now, he could really use Complex.

The stranger interrupted his thoughts. "Did you hear what I said, Mr. Cook?" Shawn hadn't heard anything the stranger was saying. The stranger paused and said, "You could at least say thank you."

Shawn was trying to piece all of this together; something was missing. It was driving him crazy. Shawn decided to be the bigger man and played along; he said, "Thank you."

The stranger had a smile in his voice. "I was just wondering whether the game was getting a little boring to you. Maybe I need to spice it up a bit. I mean, here I am, away for several days and not having spoken to you—I would have thought you would be practically wondering what was going on with your wife, but . . . hmmm . . . interesting."

The stranger was waiting for the right emotion; he was testing Shawn at this point, and at this point, he didn't like the reaction he was getting from him. The stranger thought and asked, "Something is not right here. You don't seem so concerned about whether you hear from your wife or not."

Shawn knew he had gotten into the stranger's head, but he knew he had to be extremely careful not to get too much inside his head; he was walking a tightrope, and he knew it. It was true this guy Evans was breaking all the rules; he has allowed Serenity to call twice. Out of the two phone calls, he put his own life and safety in danger. Shawn knew he could not allow the stranger to figure out that he'd been double-crossed somehow; he had to keep the stranger off-balance.

The stranger continued to probe. "Hmmm . . . Mr. Cook, your enthusiasm is not the same as at the beginning of the game. You seem to be much calmer and cooler than I thought you would be."

Shawn knew this was it; the stranger smelled the scent and was going after it. He knew; he broke it down, and he knew. Shawn knew that the answer he was about to give would blow up the whole thing or continue to keep the stranger in the dark.

# CHAPTER 157

Shawn said in an agitated tone, "What do you want from me, you low-down prick? You're going to pay, punk. I will find out who you are even if I have to exhaust the very last penny. I'm going to bring your scum ass down. Mark that on your calendar, punk. I would do worse to you than I did to your bro . . ." Shawn stopped.

The stranger yelled in the phone obscenities and threats; he said, "Enough! Enough, I see your anger is still very much intact, Mr. Cook. But it is a shame you will not get a chance to take it out on me. You will, like you said, go to your grave with it. By the time, Mr. Cook, you find out who I am, you'll be an old useless man who will be haunted by your failures to save your wife."

Shawn was pissed, but he knew he hit the right nerve; whatever suspicions the stranger had seemed to be gone. Shawn came back and said, "We'll see. You're going to slip up, and when you do, I'll be right there to make sure you fall very hard."

The stranger laughed and said, "It must be very hard going to bed alone, Mr. Cook."

Shawn gritted his teeth; he sneered and said, "Equally as hard as talking to your brother every day. How does it feel hearing his voice and now nothing, huh?"

The stranger slammed his fist down on the desk; there was some noise in the background, but Shawn couldn't make out what it was. The stranger was fuming; he was trying to control it but was failing as he yelled into the phone, "Mr. Cook, you are going to respect me! You are going to show me respect! You might have a short memory span, but don't forget I have your bitch, and you are seriously pushing me to take it out on her because of your damn big mouth. Keep in mind, her demise would be your doing, not mine, Mr. Cook."

Shawn gritted his teeth as he yelled, "You touch her, if you lay one finger on her, you are dead, mother sucker! You're dead, asswipe!"

The stranger slammed his fist down on the table again. "Mr. Cook, your assignment has changed. You will be acting as a homeless man on the number 2 train starting at Forty-Second Street. You will take the train to 125th Street. You will be approached by four thugs. They have been instructed to harass you and then beat you to a pulp." The stranger continued, "These lowlives are our so-called future." Shawn started to say something when the stranger cut him off. "Excuse me, I'm not finished. Plus I think you want to hear this, Mr. Cook."

Shawn blew out a harsh breath as the stranger continued, "Mr. Cook, don't be upset. These are the worthless trash of society just taking up space. Plus they're arrogant and violent and rude. Listen to this. One of them is eighteen years old. His name is Joe Kelvin . . ." Shawn thought the name sounded familiar. The stranger must read his mind as he said to Shawn, "Yeah, Mr. Cook, you know Mr. Kelvin. You should know him since you worked with kids. He was a part of your group, one of the failing rejects." The stranger continued, "That's right, Mr. Cook. I did my homework on you. Anyway, this guy used to train at your gym. That's right. He was considered to be a high prospect to the pros. He was just in high school, and the scouts were looking at him like vultures, funny—and so were the drug dealers."

Shawn thought about Kelvin, and what the stranger was saying was true. The stranger continued, "Kelvin was the highlight in every sports page of the New York papers. He was better than good and superseded very good. He was great. He left his contemporaries so far behind him. Hmm . . . still can't recall who I'm talking about, Mr. Cook? Selective memory maybe." The stranger chuckled lightly as he continued, "Or how about Lemar James? He was once destined to be great, a superstar. He was once compared to the best athletes. Does James sound familiar, huh?"

Shawn did not say anything; the stranger said, "I understand, Mr. Cook. You don't have to say anything, Mr. Cook. This was your quote about this young man, 'great and destined to be a great player.' Does that ring a bell, Mr. Cook, huh?"

Shawn had to know; he asked, "Whatever happened to James?"

The stranger said, "Ah, the wrong crowd, negative influences, pride—you know, the whole shebang. Conceited, superior, self-important. This young man disregarded the warnings in his life, warnings that were clearly visible, clearly dangerous, and clearly undeniable. He ignored them and thought he was beyond average. Being normal was too good for him, so in turn, he gave up his dreams for the mighty dollar. He should have listened to the O'Jays' 'For the Love of Money.' Have you ever heard that song before? . . . Very profound."

Shawn, frustrated, blew a harsh breath into the phone. The stranger apologized and continued, "He didn't know how to play the game, and if you're going to be in the game, you better know how to play it. And if you don't know how to play it, the game will play you." He continued, "I just named two. There are two more, which I don't have the time for and you don't have time to listen to. But the bottom line is these are losers, a waste of raw talent. And because of this, these men will be dealt with."

Shawn yelled in the phone as his rage took over, "And so you want to play God and make that decision?"

The stranger shouted back and said, "You did! You made that decision, Mr. Cook, when you killed my brother without a second thought!"

Shawn gritted his teeth and sneered in anger, "Your brother, if I didn't stop him, he was going to kill hundreds."

The stranger was yelling so loud his voice cracked. "So you decided to take matters into your own hands and kill him, doing God a favor?"

Shawn shook his head and shouted with frustration and anger, "No, that's not true! That's not how it went down, dammit! It was either him or me. He left me no other choice. I did what anybody would have done. I protected myself!"

The stranger sounded sarcastic as he said, "Yes, the hero of the hour, of the poor and needy, God's champion." The stranger cursed, "So you didn't have no other choice but to kill him? Bullshit! You could have immobilized him to deescalate the situation."

Shawn yelled, "The son of a bitch fought me to the very end! I did what I had to do!"

The stranger said in a haunting tone, "And so must I, Mr. Cook, so must I."

Shawn went berserk. "Don't you dare touch her! Leave my wife out of this. You want me? Come and get me. Come and get me, you lowlife scumbag piece of crap! Tell me where, tell me where to meet you. Tell me! You are dead!"

The stranger lightly chuckled. "Mr. Cook, your promises are like clouds, just filled with air. But let me tell you . . . the two other guys, you try to help, but you fail. No, rather, they fail you." The stranger continued, "Do you remember a young man named Samuel Picket? A very talented football player from the peewee league to high school to college. You remember him? You should, Mr. Cook. You trained him. Well, at least he went to your gym."

There was a pause; the stranger continued, "The young man was amazingly gifted . . . but . . ." There was a slight pause as he continued, "The man was good, but he was so easily influenced by everything and anything. No self-control. C'mon, Mr. Cook, do you remember what happened to your protégée, your star, huh? You supported him in his court trial. The judge was ready to get that piece of crap off the streets. As a matter of fact, the judge labeled him as young and reckless and very dangerous. But you made the difference, the weight that tipped the scale. What a grave mistake you made."

Shawn did remember Samuel Picket, a natural by nature, could run the forty-yard dash in 4.0 seconds easy. The young man was from one of the toughest projects, Hidden Talents, which was a place like the projects has—talent that is just being wasted, hidden behind poor situations and single moms, whatever the case may be. A lot of these kids don't have the discipline or the patience, so they turned to other things—most of it destructive things. Shawn's thoughts were invaded by the voice of the stranger.

"Sad to say, Mr. Cook, your intervention fell on deaf ears. Or should I say, everyone heard it except Picket." The stranger continued, "Six months later, he ended up back in court, charged with attempted assault with a weapon. Funny how he used that same line he used the first time when he came to court. Maybe he forgot the judge he had the first time was the same judge this time. The judge realized he made a mistake the first time. He wasn't going for bullshit—pardon me—this time. As a matter of fact, the judge felt insulted." The stranger paused and continued, "Things may have been different if you were there, but unfortunately for Picket, you were out of town on a business trip. His own parents did not show up. He had no support from family or friends. The judge sent Picket up north for two years. He was a good boy. His sentence was reduced from two years to six to eight months with community service."

The stranger stopped. Shawn was silent. The stranger asked, "Has he stopped by your gym, Mr. Cook, to at least say thank you, huh?" Before Shawn could respond, the stranger continued, "No, he hasn't. He's been in mischief and trouble ever since he got out of the correctional facility."

Shawn had heard enough. "Okay, so what is your point?"

The stranger chuckled. "Ah, the payoff, okay. This young man, just like the other two, had so many chances. And they messed up, blundered it each time Mr. Cook, all these men are worthless. They have no dreams. They waste the taxpayers' money year after year on this piece of crap, thumb their noses at society, put their middle fingers up at those who try to help them. And with anger, Mr. Cook, they say in their rebellious way, 'F you, F the system, and now F off.'"

Shawn asked, "Are you a taxpayer, mister . . . ? I didn't get the name."

The stranger chuckled. "And you won't, Mr. Cook. Mr. Cook, don't take me for a fool. I'm smart. I know you are good at the art of fighting. Like I said, Mr. Cook, I study you, very carefully. I could hold my own, but I'd be a fool to fight you in the great condition you're in. So I'd rather break you down to make the playing field even."

Shawn snorted and said, "That won't ever happen. Keep dreaming. I will be your worst nightmare when I catch you."

The stranger smiled. "Anyway, one more you helped, and they told you in so many ways to F off." He continued, "The next loser is Mike 'Hit Man' Clark. This man was amazing in his day.

He was the epitome of boxing. Look at his accomplishments—five-time Golden Glove winner, came in tied for the gold in the Olympics. But he fell from grace." The stranger paused and asked Shawn, "Do you remember him? You should. He trained in your gym too."

Shawn countered, "Just because a person trains in my gym doesn't mean I know him."

. "I agree, but you trained this one yourself. Don't you remember?" Shawn was speechless. The stranger continued, "He was amazing, but one technicality in his tie for the gold in the Olympics dropped him down to silver. Silver is not bad, but hold up. What was going on got worse. Hit Man wanted to go pro, but a simple physical exam ratted him out." The stranger laughed. "How pathetic, how stupid . . . Don't you remember? He was juicing. He got caught. He wasn't expecting to get caught. What a loser! But in reality, getting caught was probably the best thing for this idiot because they saved him the embarrassment if he had gone pro. He would have lost everything, including his self-respect."

The stranger continued, "Sadly, all his gold medals were confiscated and endorsements snatched away. He lived with shame for years, in and out of shelters. The only thing that was working was his cock, and he misused that too. He got women pregnant and was the father of how many children, I lost count. He owed child support, which he would be doing for the rest of his life. In and out of jail, which has become his second home." There was a pause; then the stranger said, "You don't remember him?"

Shawn tried to defend himself, saying, "That's not how it happened. By the time he came to us, steroids had ruined his life. He was already washed up. If you're going to tell the story, tell it right."

The stranger lightly chuckled. "It doesn't matter, Mr. Cook. That is not my point. My point is you made an effort to help. And yet you don't receive anything, nothing, no recognition, no thank you for trying—nothing. This generation is worthless, corrupt, unproductive, and senseless. I can go on and on, Mr. Cook." The stranger's anger continued to come out. "This is one reason why they need to be destroyed. They have no motivation like you and I. We earned what we have. This generation wants us to hand it to them. They want it quick and fast and immediate—instant gratification. If you don't give, they take. If you give, they want more."

The stranger's voice was finally calming down as if there was a storm that just passed through; he said, "Mr. Cook, you and I could have changed the course of this destructive society. You and I could have presented this doomed culture with hope. You and I could have picked and chosen the elite, the select ones, and we could have built a society of the best of the best. You and I—"

Shawn cut him off. "No, sir, there will never be a 'you and I.' I know what it means to work. You don't. I know what it means to earn a paycheck. You don't, and I know what it is and how it feels to be poor . . . You don't." Shawn paused as he continued, "No, sir, there would never be a 'you and I.' I know what it is to break your ass every single day. I watch my father do it. How about yours? You are describing the hardships and difficulty of life. I've been there, but you haven't. So when it comes to hardships and difficulties, there is no 'you,' and there would never be an 'I.'"

The stranger chuckled. "Perhaps you're right. That's why you can't appreciate the cleansing my brother wanted to do." The stranger's anger came back as he started yelling into the phone, "My brother wanted to get rid of the scum of this society!"

Shawn gritted his teeth and said in a low hard tone, "You're sick like your brother . . . You need help."

The stranger laughed. "No, Mr. Cook, I don't need help. And neither did my brother. He had a solution to fixing this culture. He was going to go from city to city, starting here in New York. But you interfered, and for that, you will pay. You will be dealt with, sir. You took and destroyed, and now the one you love and adore will be snatched and taken from you."

Shawn was so angry that he starting shaking; he shook his head as he closed his eyes, trying to maintain some form of control. He could still hear the stranger's taunting voice; the stranger continued, "You see, Mr. Cook, these four hoodlums, degenerates you will encounter tonight are worthless, useless. Why keep them here? They are just taking up space. Do you see my point?"

Shawn responded in anger, "No, I don't, and I never will! You need help."

The stranger chuckled. "I need help just because I want to pick up where my brother left off, and that makes me insane?"

Shawn thought about it a few seconds and said, "Uh, yeah, think about it. Who in their right mind would want to destroy lives instead of saving and helping? You have the means and the resources to—"

he stranger cut Shawn off. "I would rather give . . ." Shawn heard that sound in the background again; it was too faint to make out as he heard the stranger continue, "My money to a homeless animal shelter." He continued as his anger flared out, "These are losers, hoodlums, misfits of society, Mr. Cook, that don't deserve not even a penny! They are toxic waste that will eventually destroy the world. I wish I can set them on an island far away from society and drop an atomic bomb on the island, destroying them."

The stranger, just like that, calmed down and said, "You see, Mr. Cook, these lowlives want something out of this, sir."

Shawn practically spit the words out of his mouth. "What the hell? All I want from you is two things: your life and my wife."

The stranger had a smile in his voice; he made a sound from a game show when somebody gets an answer correct. "Ding ding ding! Exactly, Mr. Cook, but please allow me to finish. They are desperate lowlives, hoodlums. They've been offered to cause havoc on the train, to deter and detain. They have no idea who you are, sir. They would get paid just for doing that." The stranger cleared his throat. "Now pay attention. This is very important." Shawn blew out a harsh breath; the stranger continued, "That's what they want, just a few bucks just to get high. But you need them because one of them has the key to set Serenity free, and if that happens, game over—you win." The stranger continued, "I have what they want. They have what they need. You see, Mr. Cook, everyone wants something."

Shawn cursed under his breath and said, "While you pull the strings, you like to be in control."

The stranger lightly laughed. "Who doesn't? Of course, somebody has to do it."

Shawn had no more to say. "May the Lord God be with your soul."

The stranger said, "Oh, he has, Mr. Cook. That's why he has called me—no, appointed me to throw out the trash. And that was what my brother was going to do before you spoiled everything."

Shawn was exhausted fighting with this man; he had nothing else to say and was determined to keep his word in regard to finding the stranger and making him pay for all the lives he had taken up to this point.

The stranger asked, "Mr. Cook, why are you so quiet?"

Shawn shook his head and said in a frustrated tone, "Are you done?"

The stranger picked up on Shawn's anger and said, "Mr. Cook, I mentioned to you before, this is not your fault. You were supporting losers, rejects. You were given a bad hand before the game started." The stranger cleared his throat and added, "Now the last candidate, his name is Hector Nieves." There was a pause; then the stranger continued, "That name should sound very familiar, Mr. Cook. This young man—"

Shawn cut him off. "I don't need for you to tell me about him. He used to go to the gym. I haven't seen him in a while."

The stranger chuckled and said, "You will tonight."

Shawn thought about Hector, a nice young man with great potential. He wasn't a tough guy. He enjoyed singing; he could win any singing competition, but his mom didn't enroll him into the school to sing but to learn how to fight. Hector was always picked on. One day, his mother took him over to the gym, where she met Shawn; she had heard so much about him that she wanted to meet him for herself. She signed Hector up; he came a few times, and that was it.

The stranger said, "He has great talent, great potential. He has not completely surrendered himself to the dark side like these other losers have, but he is easily influenced."

Shawn was curious. "So why is he on this list of your so-called losers?"

The stranger lightly chuckled and said, "Good question. Mr. Nieves wants to fit in. He wants to be a part of something, and at this stage in his life, he's vulnerable and easily influenced. But . . . I believe you can save him. You can discourage him, reroute him, and place him on the right path."

Shawn sarcastically said, "So you do have a heart. When did stone turn into clay?"

The stranger ignored the statement, which made Shawn even more frustrated. The stranger continued, "Mr. Cook, I wish we could continue this conversation, but perhaps at another time."

Shawn lightly laughed and said, "You should take the opportunity now because the next time we meet, I'm going to end your miserable existence and send you to hell, where people—"

The stranger cut him off, saying, "You have an hour and a half, Mr. Cook. I'm expecting to hear from you by three thirty this morning, sir. You need to be on the train by two thirty. You will be in the last two cars. I must warn you, Mr. Cook, anyone on that train gets injured or hurt in any way, Mr. Cook, I'm holding you responsible for their safety, sir. Anyone hurt, that would be a strike against your lovely wife. Three strikes, well, you know how the song goes." Shawn was ready to protest against the rules when the stranger cut him off. "I wish you the best, sir. God be with you." The stranger disconnected the call.

Shawn was livid; he was ready to throw the phone against the wall when he noticed his mainline phone was still on. He looked at; there was a red light coming from the phone. It wasn't the charge indicator; he looked at the charge indicator, which was fully charged. He looked at it again when the red light faded out. Shawn looked at his clock radio; he still had some time, but not much. Thinking about what he was about to do, he had to hurry. He had to try his theory; he picked up the mainline phone and dialed his own number. The phone went into the chime; he pressed a few buttons to bypass some of the instructions and to do what he had to do. He was asked by the answering machine to put in his password, which was "Serenity." The answering machine was going through messages. He skipped them until he came to the one he just had with the stranger. He pressed Save. He quickly got up off the bed and looked at the clock; he had to hurry up.

# CHAPTER 158

Shawn pulled over to a parking spot. Shawn said to Gordon, "If we're not back in about forty-five to an hour, set your GPS for my place."

G responded, "Uh, sir, are you sure you want me to do that?"

Shawn thought and said, "Why do you ask that?"

Gordon responded, "Well, going to your place is logical, sir. But that would seem fruitless. If something goes wrong, I would think you would have me program to go to the police station with a note for Mr. Commissioner Curt Moore, sir."

Jefferson just shook his head and said, "Why is it you two have great dialogue and chemistry? I mean good meaningful conversations. I get 'What up, dawg?' Well, sorry, you did say you won't do that. So what is it going to be, 'Here, little pussy'?" Jefferson lightly laughed and said, "Just kidding, G." There was some hesitation from Gordon. Jefferson became somewhat nervous and said, "Tell me that wasn't on your agenda."

Gordon said, "Well, sir, with my confusion, the thought did cross my mind. And even a little scenario where we were talking, and I said to you, 'Yes, Sir Pussy.' But . . . we worked it out, sir. My confusion is gone, sir."

Jefferson smiled. "Thank God we worked that out because going around having you calling me the p word is not cool and—"

Shawn interrupted the conversation with a frustrated look on his face; he said, "Jefferson, can you make an attempt to focus please? I need for you to be right here with me." He pointed to his heart and eyes.

Jefferson nodded with his game face on. "Sorry, Shawn, I'm good. Yo, Wall Street, I'm good. I'm cool. Let's do this."

Shawn nodded. "Okay, G, when we get there, stay put for further instructions."

Gordon responded, "Affirmative, sir."

Shawn and Jefferson got out at 125<sup>th</sup> Street, the heart of Harlem. In the wee hours of the morning, the street looked like it was early morning dawn. Even this early, the street vendors were still selling food, shoes, books, incense, and everything under the sun. That was 125<sup>th</sup> Street; that was Harlem. The smell of food wafted through the air; it was a totally different atmosphere. In one sense, the bright lights looked beautiful; but on the other hand, it looked scary and eerie. Everything seemed so bright even though it was late or early in the wee hours of the night; it couldn't be no more than 1:30 a.m., but it looked like 5:00 a.m.

Some of the women were dressed in very nice clothes, while others dressed so provocatively. Everything was short on them, starting with those tight Daisy Duke outfits or a very short skirt that left nothing to the imagination.

Shawn and Jefferson had to ride the train down Fourteenth Street and catch it back up. They were going to get Gordon to drive, but the traffic was bumper to bumper; if Complex were here, she would know how to drive through this traffic. So since they didn't have that luxury, they would rather take a chance with the train than fight with this traffic.

As they took a few steps down the subway stairs, Jefferson heard his name; he turned and saw a woman dressed in a very short skirt with high leather boots say, "Hey, Jay baby! Hi, it's me Honeywell . . ." She stretched her arms out. "Honeywell, Kittie." Jefferson looked around as if he didn't know who the young woman was talking to; how many guys could there be at two something in the morning named Jay baby? Jefferson slightly smiled, trotted back up the steps, and walked over to the young lady with a smile.

Shawn protested, "Jefferson! What the hell are you doing, man?"

Jefferson turned toward Shawn and raised his eyebrow, lifting up a finger. Shawn blew out an exasperated breath. He looked at his watch and said in a hard tone, "Ten minutes, bro, you have ten minutes."

Shawn heard him call the woman. "Hey, baby, what's up? You are looking exceptionally good."

Shawn's head quickly jerked up, looking at Kittie Honeywell with a slightly disgusted look and thought about Jefferson, *This dude needs glasses, or he's just running game.*

Kittie laughed all teeth and gums with a wide mouth. Shawn looked at his watch. "Yo, Jay, let's . . ." He watched Jefferson kiss Honeywell; he turned his head, shaking it. He heard Jefferson asked Kittie if she was usually around here. Kittie had a smile in her voice and told Jefferson yes.

Shawn thought, *Either here or her second home, the zoo. Take your pick. There are a few of them in New York.* She had a pass for each one, he was sure.

Shawn turned back toward them, and Jefferson was standing right there, just a few inches from Shawn. "Ready."

Shawn backed up just an inch and just looked at him. "How low and deep you went in the burrow to find that one?"

Jefferson looked at Shawn, confused. "What?"

Shawn waved a dismissive hand and shook his head. "Forget it, let's go. I'm on a time schedule."

Jefferson looked confused; he looked back at Kittie Honeywell. He turned and looked at Shawn. "Beauty is truly in the eye of the beholder."

Shawn and Jefferson started walking down to the train. Shawn said, "If beauty is in the eye of the beholder, you must be blind."

Shawn made a face and shook his head as he swiped his metro card and went through. He handed the card to Jefferson; he swiped himself through. He was pocketing the card. Shawn snatched the card from him and looked at him. Shawn looked up at the scheduled time of arrival, three minutes. Shawn looked at Jefferson. "Remember, we need to sit in the last two cars of the train. I'll be at one end. You'll be at the other end. Remember, don't do anything to hurt these young men."

Jefferson looked at Shawn. "Sure. But I will—and know this—I will protect myself. And if one of them gets hurt, not my problem."

Shawn nodded his head and said, "Fair enough."

# Chapter 159

Shawn was all the way at the end of the car; he was dressed in a black hoodie with the hood covering his head. He was lying spread out in the corner; his feet were on the floor. He positioned himself where he covered his head, but he was able to see the other end of the car, where Jefferson was. There were a few customers in the car.

Jefferson was at the other end of the car; he had his cap down on his face, but up enough where he could still see what was going on.

Before they got on the train, Shawn and Jefferson went over some hand signals. One finger meant everything was okay; the middle finger meant that things were about to get totally crazy and out of control, and three fingers meant to make a judgment call. A fist meant getting ready to do some physical damage, but nothing fatal.

Shawn was slouching in his seat; he had poured some water on the floor right beneath him to give the impression that he had urinated on himself. He took a quick glance at his watch; he had about two minutes. Within the next few seconds, a group of young adults came into the car; they were very loud, very rowdy. They were jumping around, swinging on the poles; one of them was jumping on the seats next to customers. Shawn recognized one of them without a doubt.

Joe Kelvin announced to the passengers, "Yo, those that want to get the hell off or go to the next car, you better do it now. This is your first and final warning because we will not be responsible for lost items such as your wallets or purses, your teeth, or your life."

Kelvin laughed; the others laughed as well. Kelvin continued, "Last call."

All the passengers got up and went to the next car except for Shawn and Jefferson. The group clapped and was going wild; they knew they were in control. They started wrestling with one another and fell on Jefferson, who wasn't expecting that to happen; he lost his cool and nudged them off him. The young man could feel Jefferson's aggression and said, "Yo, punk, what's the deal with the aggression? What's your problem, punk?"

Jefferson wanted to jump up and beat the snot out of this mother sucker. Jefferson's response was as aggressive as his aggressive nudge as he lay there in a half lying-down position; some would have thought this position was leaving him in a weak and vulnerable position, but for others, it was a good defense and offense position. The young man, no doubt, was Hector Nieves, who walked toward Jefferson and was still talking junk. His right hand was reaching for something.

Shawn quickly studied the situation; panic swept through him like a hard flood sweeping through an old city. Shawn thought, *Oh shit, Hector is reaching for something.* He looked at Jefferson, who was giving Shawn a hand signal of one finger. Shawn rubbed his eyes; he looked again as Jefferson was explaining to the young man he wasn't the one with the problem. At the same time, Jefferson was still flashing that one finger; it meant everything was okay. Shawn thought he must have gotten the signals mixed up. Shawn thought, *A one, is he nuts? Hell is about to break loose every which way. This place is about to turn into a war zone.*

The young man was yelling from the top of his lungs; he felt Jefferson play him in front of his buddies. His so-called buddies began to egg him on as they all came close to Jefferson.

Shawn thought, *This is not good.* Yet through all of this craziness, Jefferson was still flashing that one finger, which meant everything was okay. Shawn said to himself, *The hell it isn't.*

# Chapter 160

Jefferson also appeared to be reaching or at least making sure he could quickly get whatever it was he was reaching for. Shawn knew what Jefferson had; from what he saw, he knew the young man was packing something as well and was reaching for it. Shawn looked at Hector and concluded the young man looked the same a few years ago, short and skinny; he looked as if he did not belong or fit in.

Shawn wanted to interfere; the situation was becoming very intense, so why the hell was Jefferson still flashing the number one finger, meaning all was cool and under control? Shawn thought the man had to be out of his mind. The other thugs were still around Hector, encouraging him to take care of the situation. Jefferson's eyes opened up wide; he knew the odds were totally against him as he flashed a three.

Shawn thought to himself, *Really?* Shawn had a couple of empty beer cans as the train roared on in the express lane.

Shawn threw the cans hard against the door. The loud sound startled the four young men; it was a perfect distraction. Now three of them were coming toward Shawn. The one he wanted to come was Hector Nieves, but he was still dealing with Jefferson and was still reaching for something. Shawn looked at Jefferson as the three thugs were still coming toward him, making all types of noises, yelling and barking. Jefferson caught Shawn's eyes looking at him and flashed him a number one, which indicated, "Do you, bro. I got this." Shawn nodded with a wink.

# CHAPTER 161

Shawn had to stay focused; he had to get the keys from one of these guys. Shawn knew the key would take him to where Serenity was. He quickly glanced at Jefferson to make sure he was okay. Jefferson was doing fine. Shawn brought his attention back to the three punks. The one talking all the trash talk was Samuel Pickett; his lifestyle did a number two. That youthful appearance he once had was gone; as he was walking to the other end of the car, he said, "You have a problem, bum, huh? What's with the noise?"

Shawn pulled his hoodie down a little further; he eased on up on the bench. All three young men stood in front of him. Mike Clark said to Picket, "Hey, two bums for the price of one." They all laughed. Shawn laughed as well. They all looked at him. "What's so funny, bum? You worthless piece of shit."

Shawn chuckled with his head down, the hoodie still covering his face. "I'm a worthless piece of crap . . . yeah, okay."

Samuel Pickett said, "Yeah, that's right. You have a problem with that?"

Shawn slowly shook his head and said, "I play the part, while you and you and you and him"—he pointed down to Hector—"live the part, which makes you the real losers."

Kelvin nudged Shawn's shoulder. "Who are you calling a loser, punk ass? Look at you, you are in no position to talk, punk."

Clark said, "Not only are you a bum, you are an insane and delusional bum." They all laughed.

Shawn slightly smiled, trying to maintain his cool; head still down with the hoodie covering his face, he said to Clark, "I guess Momma was right—it's better to be an insane bum than to be a jackass that not only lost the little reputation he had but ruined his entire career. Now what was your definition of an 'insane bum'?"

Clark's friends snickered and made sounds that Clark was dissed. Clark felt embarrassed; he moved toward Shawn in a threatening manner. Shawn held up his hands and said, "Hold up, wait. This really doesn't have to go there."

Pickett responded, "So true. But you brought this on yourself, and now we're going to kick your ass."

Shawn placed his head down and slightly looked up. "Gentlemen, all I want to know is who has the key. That's it, and I'll be on my way. Simple as that."

Pickett said with a sarcastic smile, "No, it's not that simple. You made this complicated, and now we're going to make your life miserable and just a little more difficult." The young men looked at one another and laughed. Pickett said, "Why don't you find that out yourself, who has the key?" He spread his arms outward, smiled, and said, "You messed up, son."

Shawn shrugged his shoulders and said, "Umm, okay, I was hoping that it didn't have to come to this."

Kelvin James said, "Well, it has. Oops, your loss."

Shawn looked at all three young men, hoodie down on his face with sunshades; he just smiled and said, "No, correction—oops! No, your loss." Shawn gave a straight kick to Kelvin James's knees; the impact of the kick to the left knee was so hard that it snapped like a twig while the other knee made a loud-sounding crack. James fell to the floor like a sack of potatoes; he was screaming in pain.

The two, Mike Clark and Samuel Pickett, looked on in fear and horror; both men approached Shawn. Pickett connected with a right to Shawn's shoulder; this wasn't the bad shoulder. Nevertheless, the blow hurt. Mike Clark went to grab Shawn, but Shawn was too quick and evasive. Shawn quickly knocked Clark's hands away and delivered a devastating backhand blow to Clark's face, followed by a quick combination of left and right hooks, ending with a fiery straight kick to the midsection. Clark grunted in pain as he crashed his back into the seat.

Meanwhile, Pickett took a couple of wild swings at Shawn. Shawn swerved to the left and pivoted to the right, causing Pickett to slam his fist into the pole. The hard crack sound was Pickett's hand breaking. Pickett began yelling and cursing in pain. He was in so much pain that he was on the floor, rocking back and forth.

This was Shawn's opportunity to do some more damage as he approached Kelvin James. "Where is the key?"

Kelvin shook his head in pain. "What? What key? I don't know . . . please."

Shawn looked at him and said, "Stay. Don't move."

The train started going local as the doors opened; customers saw what was going on. Shawn looked at them and said, "This train is out of order. Next car. Thank you for your cooperation and riding with MTA."

Most customers quickly went to the next car or chose to wait for the next train. Shawn went back to Pickett, took the broken hand, and squeezed it. Pickett screamed in pain. "What the hell is wrong with you?"

Shawn squeezed Pickett's hand again; he yelled in agony. Shawn told him to get up as he led the 6'5" mammoth by his hand. Pickett had no choice but to follow like a child being pulled by a parent. Shawn looked down at Jefferson to see how he was doing.

Jefferson seemed to be doing very well. Hector was trying to talk his way out of getting an ass whipping. Jefferson was now standing up; he was about three inches taller than Hector. Shawn heard Hector Nieves practically begging Jefferson not to hit him. Jefferson said to him, "So you still want to talk crap, huh? So you're going to kick my ass? Come on." Jefferson took Nieves and slammed him hard against the door.

Hector cursed. "Damn, my back, my back! Easy."

Jefferson bitch-slapped Hector, who cursed. Jefferson said to him, "So what now, punk?"

, Shawn still had Pickett's broken hand and was putting pressure on it. Pickett was pleading and begging for mercy. Shawn said, "So now you want mercy? Before this, you were the big man who was going to kick my ass. Where is the key, punk ass?"

Pickett was bent forward in pain as he tried to look up at Shawn with confusion. "What? The key? What key, man?" Shawn squeezed harder. Pickett yelled in agony, "What key? I don't know what you are talking about, man! I don't have a key! House key, car keys—what key, man?" Shawn twisted Pickett's broken hand; the 6'5" mammoth cursed and yelled out in pain.

, who seemed to be recovering and was starting to move around. Shawn had to act fast; he cursed under his breath. He took Pickett's broken hand and slammed it against the door. Pickett screamed as he pleaded and begged, "Enough, please, enough!"

Shawn yelled at him, "Where's the freakin' key?"

Pickett yelled back in pain, "What freakin' key? I don't have a key! Check my . . ."

Shawn was really beyond being pissed off because he knew the punk was telling the truth. He slammed Pickett in the midsection; he cried out in pain as he bent forward. Shawn quickly grabbed the passenger handles and came down hard on the back of Pickett's neck with a double ax kick. The connection and sound were devastating. Pickett made a painful sound and fell to the floor. Shawn clenched his mouth tightly; he was beyond angry.

He looked down at Jefferson. Jefferson looked back at Shawn, and he could tell these punks brought Shawn to another level. Jefferson said, "Yo, this punk is no problem. Right, punk?" Jefferson grabbed Hector by the collar and slammed him against the door again. Hector made a painful face. Jefferson looked at Shawn. "I got this. This punk isn't going anywhere. Handle big man."

Shawn went through Pickett's pocket—empty. He went over to Kelvin James and frisked his pockets. *What was that?* he thought. Shawn was going to go inside the man's pocket when Mike Clark seemed to have recovered from his injury. Shawn looked at Jefferson and said, "Bring that punk ass over here and make him sit down. If he moves, kick his ass. Watch this one." He pointed to Pickett. "He's not going anywhere. Watch him anyway. I think I may have felt some keys in his pocket, but let me . . ."

# CHAPTER 162

Shawn cut short his sentence when he felt someone behind him. He turned, still with his hoodie and sunshades on. The hood was down, a little bit past his forehead. Shawn looked at Mike Clark in a fighting boxing position. He moved toward Shawn. Shawn cracked the bones in his neck as he moved it from side to side. He got into his fighting pose. Shawn looked at Clark, thinking about how he trained this fighter five days a week; he became good. He was trained by the best. He said to Clark, "You don't have to do this . . . You really don't."

Clark ignored Shawn and lunged after him. Shawn sidestepped and moved to his right as if Clark was a bull. Shawn said, "You've always had that problem. You've always—" Clark lunged again. Shawn said, "Yeah, that thing. What is that?"

This time, Shawn lunged as he quickly squatted low and came hard and fast with three hooks to the body—*bam*, left, *bam*, right, *bam*, center. Clark's knees buckled as he stood up, holding his ribs. Shawn looked at him and said, "You need to stop. Just give me the keys, dammit. And I walk, you walk." Clark looked at him as he hobbled toward Shawn, his fists up. Shawn shook his head. "Please don't. Last chance." Clark stood there, fists still up in defense. Shawn reached into his pocket and took out his brass knuckles; he shrugged and moved toward Clark.

Jefferson thought about the boxing game at the house. Jefferson, in a panic, shook his head and yelled, "Wall Street, no!"

Shawn had already thrown two brisk jabs, which snapped Clark's head back. Clark's head crashed into the door behind him. Shawn walked toward Clark in a stalking motion. Clark took a wild swing, and Shawn ducked and came up hard with a punch to the ribs. Clark doubled over. Shawn grabbed him by his collar, yanked him up hard, and slammed him into the door. Shawn went to work throwing body blows. Clark bent forward, and Shawn came down with a hard elbow to the back of Clark's head. Clark was leaning forward when Shawn held him up with devastating blows to Clark's face. Blood spattered everywhere. Shawn yelled, "Give me the key! Give me the damn key!"

Clark was a bloody mess; he shook his head. "I don't have the key."

Shawn got in Clark's face. "I want the key. Where is the key?"

Clark yelled, "I don't know!"

Shawn grabbed Clark by the throat and said, "I will choke you out, you son of a bitch. Who has the key? I won't ask you again."

Clark, choking, yelled in pain, "I don't know! . . . I really don't know! I can't breathe!"

Jefferson was trying to calm Shawn down. Shawn looked at him with a hard stare. Jefferson backed off. Shawn looked at Clark. "You're lying." Shawn kicked Clark so hard he crashed into the door and slid down to the floor. Shawn placed his foot into Clark's windpipe and pressed hard.

Clark struggled to speak as he was losing oxygen. "I don't have it." Clark emptied his pockets. Shawn eased up on the pressure. Clark was coughing, trying to get air; he said, "See, I don't have it."

Jefferson was heading toward them. "Wall Street, does he have it?"

Shawn shook his head. "Damn, he doesn't have the key." He looked around, frustrated and baffled; he said, "If these guys don't have it, damn, the stranger played me."

Jefferson looked at Shawn as the train came to the next station. Shawn asked, "How about him? You checked him?"

Jefferson turned and looked at Hector; he turned back and looked at Shawn. "No, I thought—"

that quick before the door closed, Hector Nieves quickly took off for the door before it closed. Shawn and Jefferson quickly looked at each other and at Hector as he barely made it out of the door. Shawn shot past Jefferson and held the door from closing with his bad shoulder; he grimaced in pain as he watched Hector take off the down corridor toward the stairs that led to the exit. The train doors opened as Shawn and Jefferson took off after Hector. Jefferson and Hector ran past the conductor. Shawn yelled at him, "Call NYPD Commissioner Curt, urgent, now!"

Shawn saw Jefferson was moving like a track star. Shawn was pushing it; after everything, his body was done. H was broken down; his body was hurting in so many places. Jefferson, on the other hand, had that spring and jump like a gazelle. Shawn looked at him. "I'm good. Get that punk. Go go go!"

Hector was running hard and looking back as he pressed forward; he wasn't a runner, but he had average speed. He was weaving, dodging, pushing, and shoving people. "Move, move, get out of the way . . . move!"

Jefferson couldn't see him, but the way the crowd was reacting, he knew it had to be that punk-ass chump. Hector ran up some stairs toward the exit. When he got to the top of the stairs, he noticed the exit was closed. The sign read "From 6 a.m. to 12 p.m., use the exit at the end." Hector cursed and shuffled back down the stairs, taking two at the time; he missed a step and fell. He got back up; he felt the pain in his knee as he continued to run toward the end of the exit.

Shawn saw Jefferson for a quick second; then he was gone. Shawn took out his cell and pressed a button; he heard the prompt. Shawn said, "Call Jefferson."

Jefferson tapped his Bluetooth and said in an annoyed tone, "Really, Wall Street, really? You call me when I'm in the heart of a crisis, and you want me to talk while I'm trying . . ." Jefferson took in a breath as he continued, "I'm trying to save every inch of air . . . right now, at this moment that I am losing. Really? For real?"

Shawn's breathing was okay; it was his aches and pains that were kicking his ass. Shawn said, "Sorry, man. I saw you, and then I didn't. You okay?"

Jefferson sucked his teeth. "Really?" He continued, "I'm right behind this snot-nosed punk-ass son-of-a-bitch mother . . . call EMS!" Shawn asked why. Jefferson said, "Because I'm gonna kill this jackass for making me run and chase after his trifling ass like this. He is dead. Call EMS. I haven't ran like this since being chased by the po-po in the projects in the Bronx." Jefferson continued, "Shawn, he's going up the stairs. If he gets out here, baby, in this hood, he'll be like a needle in a haystack, buddy."

Shawn cursed; he knew Jefferson was right. He said, "Keep going. I have an idea."

# CHAPTER 163

Shawn hoped his idea would work; if it failed, he would lose Hector Nieves, the key, and Serenity. He knew he couldn't get Commissioner Moore into the situation knowing that he's been warned not to involve outsiders; he knew that Gordon wasn't as sophisticated as Complex, but he was still able to follow basic demands, and this was a thing Shawn was putting all his chips on—he needed this to work. He called Gordon, "G, I need you to go to the 125th Street Station and park at the north-end entrance."

Gordon replied, "Sir, that is a sidewalk, and that is against the laws of safety and—"

Shawn cut him off. "G, you are my only hope. Please, just do it now."

Gordon was silent for a few seconds before he responded, "Sir, you know this is against my law-abiding programming."

Shawn cursed under his breath; he knew Gordon would have a problem with it. He knew he wasn't going to do it. "Damn, G, you were my last hope."

Gordon replied, "Okay, sir, I'm at the entrance of the north end of the subway entrance, and I hate this . . ."

Shawn smiled. "What! You're there? Wow, okay. Stay there. Don't move."

Shawn called Jefferson, who responded. He was still chasing after Hector; as he was closing in on him, he touched his Bluetooth. "Yeah, now what?"

# CHAPTER 164

Hector hobbled down the corridor; he saw the exit, his way of escape from this lunatic who was chasing him. Hector hobbled up the stairs; he was like a man who had been trapped in a cave. Finally, he saw the light of freedom.

Shawn explained briefly what was going on. "You have to make tracks, man. Having G there would only slow Hector down. He'll find a way to get around Gordon, so—"

Jefferson cut him off. "I know, I need to haul ass and catch this prick before he gets out of this subway . . . On it." He put his head down and picked up speed.

Hector looked behind him; he could hear Jefferson's footsteps running. He chuckled as he continued to limp up the stairs; he got to the top and was more than happy to step out of this nightmare into his free-at-last moment. Hector realized there was a problem; he couldn't proceed. There was a car there, blocking the entrance. Hector cursed to himself; he couldn't get out. He yelled for someone to move the car; there was no response. He started banging on the side of the car, begging and pleading. The car alarm went off, making several sounds of warnings. Hector went to cover his ears.

Gordon responded, "Please step back from the vehicle. Step back. Step back. Step back from the vehicle."

The bells and sirens went off again. Hector covered his ears, yelling in frustration.

Jefferson called Shawn and said, "The spider caught the fly, so that's all of that begging and pleading I hear upstairs. Homeboy is crying like a baby. I'm going to get this idiot and kick his ass for making me run."

191

Jefferson could see Hector's legs when he was almost at the top; he said to him, "Yo, my man, there's no place to run, punk. G, stand down." The alarm made several beeping sounds before it shut off.

Jefferson came closer to Hector and dragged him up the stairs. They had one more set of stairs to go; they stood on a small platform. Hector backed up right into wall behind him. His hands were up to his face, protecting what was about to come. He said, "Hey, man, what do you want? What do you need? I have connections."

Jefferson responded, "The only connection that is going to happen right now is my fist against your face."

Hector was still pleading, still trying to negotiate to keep his face in one piece. "I could give you whatever you want, and if I can't, I could get it in . . ." He smiled. He looked at his watch when Jefferson slapped him in the back of his head. Hector reacted. "Ouch! In twenty-four hours, man. Trust me, I can—"

Jefferson cut him off, saying, "Trust you? I trust you like I trust a dog with rabies." Hector watched Jefferson move closer. "All right, dude, game time is over. Now we're gonna play a new game. It's called Beat Your Ass, Punk. You had me running and chasing after you like a fool, but look and see who the bigger fool is, punk."

Hector put his hand up to cover his face; it was enough to distract Jefferson as Hector pivoted and shot up the stairs. Hector was almost at the stairs before Jefferson realized what just happened as he went to grab Hector's ankle. Hector, out of desperation, starting kicking Jefferson to break free from the grip he had on his ankles. He managed to knock Jefferson off his ankles, setting himself free. Hector made it to the top and was climbing out of the subway when he heard Jefferson yelling and cursing at him, "You son of a bitch, Hector! You're dead!"

Hector laughed, taunting Jefferson. "Hey, hate the game, not . . ."

Jefferson cursed when he heard a loud sound that sounded like a smack and Hector making a painful sound as he fell to one knee. He was dragged a few inches. Gordon was given the directive to move. Jefferson walked up the stairs and looked at Shawn with surprise. "How . . . how did you . . . ? Where the hell did you come from? How?"

Jefferson turned his attention back to Hector and wagged a pointing finger at him. "Bad boy." He slapped Hector hard enough for him to curse and yell from the hit. Jefferson looked at him like a parent to a child. "Watch your mouth, young man." He gave him another tap against the head. Jefferson looked at him and said, "You think that hurts?" Jefferson looked at Shawn. "How did you?" He looked at Hector with a look of disappointment. "Very bad boy." He slapped Hector in the back of his head. He looked at Shawn, baffled and perplexed. "Wow, I don't know how you got here so fast."

Shawn just shrugged his shoulders. Jefferson, with his hand on his chin, shook his head; he said with some confusion, "Wait, hold up . . . I'm trying to . . . hmmm . . ." Jefferson started adding it up as if it was a math problem. Jefferson continued, "The gate was locked, shut tight, I mean lock and chain. But how did you . . . ?"

Jefferson looked at Hector and said, "Naughty boy made Uncle Jay run. That wasn't right, was it?" Before Hector could respond, Jefferson kicked him on his butt; the kick was low impact. Jefferson said to Hector, "That's for making me run after your ass."

Shawn looked at Jefferson and said with a slight smile, "We'll talk about my Houdini."

Jefferson sarcastically laughed. "Indeed you will, indeed you will. Pop in, pop out."

Shawn turned his attention back on Hector; he grabbed him hard by his collar and threw him hard against the car. Hector slammed into the car with a hard thud.

Commissioner Moore and his men drove up and got out of their cars. Jefferson saw them first. "Uh-oh . . . Oh boy, here come Dudley Do-Right and the Keystone Cops."

Hector opened his eyes and saw the police; he yelled in desperation, "Help me! Help me please!"

Jefferson elbowed Hector in his midsection; the man made a painful sound. "Uggh." He bent over; then he slowly rose up and reached out his hand toward the police. "Help meee . . ." Jefferson was going for another midsection hit. Shawn raised his hand toward Jefferson and slightly shook his head.

Shawn smiled and greeted Commissioner Moore, "Hey, Commish, what's up?"

Jefferson waved to Moore, who just shook his head. Moore said, "Now how did I know you were involved, Mr. Cook?" Shawn gave Moore an innocent look.

Jefferson nodded. "Yeah, how did you know?" Shawn looked at Jefferson and shrugged his shoulders, dumbfounded.

Curtis Moore turned serious. "I'll tell you how. I just followed the damn trail of destruction, Cook, your trademark that you and little you over here have been leaving ever since this case started. And frankly, Cook, I'm getting fed up with this, cleaning up your crap." There was a brief pause before Moore continued; one could almost see the steam seeping out from his forehead. He was that pissed off; he continued, "You alone, Cook, are costing the city in the hundreds of thousands . . ."

Jefferson made a goofy smile and said, "Wow! What's the grand prize?"

Moore looked at Jefferson. "Five to ten . . ."

Jefferson said, "Million?"

The commissioner barked at Jefferson, "No! Years in prison, you idiot!"

Shawn wanted to laugh. Meanwhile, Hector was still trying to get the commissioner's attention. Moore looked at him. "What are you doing with this piece of shit?"

Hector looked at Moore. "Help me pleeeease. These guys are dangerous and deranged. Help me."

The commissioner looked at Hector. "You're just realizing that? You're late." Moore looked at Shawn. "I don't want to hear of a body that fits this idiot's description washed up at Orchard Beach, okay?"

Hector yelled, "No, help me please!"

Shawn gave Hector a quick backhand in his midsection. Hector bent over in pain. Shawn said, "Yeah, sure, no worries. He's in good, safe hands."

Hector's mouth dropped; he was shocked. "Hold up, wait . . . please help me . . . please."

One of the officers looked at the commissioner and said, "Sir."

Moore waved a dismissive hand at Hector. "Whatever. Let's go. He's in good hands." They turned to go. The commissioner, while walking back toward the car, raised his voice and said, "Cook, try to stay out of trouble."

Shawn responded, "I'm gonna try. I can't promise you anything."

The commissioner turned and looked at Shawn, who gave a slight smile. The commissioner continued, "Oh, by the way, Cook, the trash you left in the train car, we took care of it for you. Next time, dump your own junk."

# CHAPTER 165

Shawn looked at Hector, saying, "As for you."

Jefferson was rubbing his hands together and said, "Yeah, punk, as for you." Jefferson continued, "Forget the preambles and intros. Forget that crap." He grabbed Hector by the collar.

Hector made a sound, looking terrified. He said, "Wait, wait, please! I didn't know."

Jefferson looked at Shawn. "This dude must think we were born under a rock, right? He didn't know." Jefferson looked at Hector hard and slapped him in the head; most of it was just air. He looked at Hector and made a move, saying, "Right? You didn't know?" Hector flinched.

Jefferson said, "Yeah, punk, you need to be afraid. I'm going to beat you until I see three things from the beatdown, black or blue or your white meat, punk." He made another threatening move. Hector flinched. Jefferson moved a little closer to Hector and said, "Tsk, I'm sorry, I forgot to introduce you to my two best friends . . ." Jefferson raised his fist toward Hector and said, "This is Black, and this is Blue. Say hi to the punk, Black, and of course, you too, Blue." Hector cried out as Jefferson went to grab him.

Shawn stopped him. Jefferson looked at Shawn, surprised. "What? Oh, you want a piece of him first? . . . Hey, fine by me. Cool, just save some for me."

Shawn still had on his hoodie with the dark shades; he said, "Do you know me? Do you know who I am?" Hector had tears coming down his cheeks. Shawn raised his voice at him. "Look at me, look."

Hector looked and still didn't recognize Shawn; he pleaded, "No, I don't. C'mon, please. I don't recognize you."

Even with the hoodie and dark shades, Shawn felt Hector should still be able to recognize him with all the time he spent in the gym with him, day in and day out. Jefferson responded, "Well, time is up, punk. Maybe you recognize a Bronx-style kick-your-ass beatdown, huh?"

Hector wailed, "Please, oh my god . . . please!"

Jefferson looked at Shawn; he was balling up his fist and lightly punching his hand. Jefferson said, "I can't wait until it's my turn you, *pequeño* punk. Translation, Nieves, it means 'little punk.'"

Shawn took off his shades, looked at Hector, and said, "Have you ever seen me before, Hector?" Hector had saliva running down his chin.

Jefferson made a face and said, "Yo, now that's just pure straight-ass gross."

Shawn said, "Don't look at him. Look at me."

Hector was shaking; he pleaded and begged, "Please . . ."

Shawn grabbed him by the jaw and turned his face toward him. "Look."

Jefferson taunted, "Yeah, look at the one who is going to beat your ass, punk."

Hector's head dropped hopelessly. He shook his head as he lifted it up to look at Shawn. Shawn said in a hard tone, "Now do you know me?"

Jefferson, answering for Hector, said, "Nope, time for a hell-in-the-cell beatdown."

Hector wiped the tears streaming down his face and said, "Huh?" He looked at Shawn carefully; he was still sniffing and wiping his nose with his sleeve, saying, "Sir, I'm not trying to be difficult."

Jefferson cut in. "Well, you are! You're being difficult and stupid." Hector rolled his eyes at Jefferson. Jefferson responded, "What, punk! You better watch it! Roll your eyes at me again, punk."

Hector continued looking at Shawn. "I'm sure we've met, mister, and you do look familiar, but . . . I can't remember, sir. I'm being honest."

Jefferson said, mocking Hector, "Wow, somebody, bring me tissue for this snot-nosed punk. You're still getting an ass whipping, right, Shawn?"

Shawn nodded his head and said, "Yep."

Jefferson smiled and echoed Shawn's word, "Yep. I told you, you are going to get a beatdown, boy." Jefferson was still smiling.

Shawn continued, "But not today."

Jefferson was so caught up with the situation that Shawn agreed with him about the beatdown; without thinking, with his eyes closed and smiling, he said, "Nope, not today. Maybe . . ." Jefferson's eyes shot wide open as he looked at Shawn and said, "Are you serious? You've got to be kidding me! Do you know how much this SOB had me chase after him, and now you're going to set him free like a bird? Wee, wee, tweet, tweet! Come out of Jefferson's cage of beatdown and ass whipping. Fly, bird, go! Yo, that's bull . . . Nah, man, that's some crooked shit, man." Jefferson paused and continued, "Wall Street, do you know how much drama and trauma this little roach put me through, chasing after him?"

Shawn looked at Jefferson with understanding eyes; he looked back at Hector and reached out toward him. Hector flinched. Shawn looked at him. "Relax, I'm not going to hurt you."

Jefferson said, "That's true. He won't, but I'm going to beat you like a spoiled brat." He lunged for Hector; he was blocked by Shawn. Hector moved back. Shawn looked at Jefferson. "Jay, relax, okay? I got this." He winked and smiled at Jefferson.

Jefferson nodded his head. "Okay, okay, I trust you, Wall Street."

Shawn looked at Hector. "You are free to go."

Jefferson blew out a hard breath. "Damn."

Hector nervously fixed his clothes and was going to walk between Shawn and Jefferson when Shawn stopped him. Hector looked up at Shawn, who stood a good a good four to five inches taller. Shawn, still with the hoodie on as he slipped the dark shades back on, held out his hand. Hector looked confused. Shawn slightly smiled and said, "The key."

Hector looked bewildered and responded, "The key?"

Jefferson added, "What is this, English 101 or Hooked on Phonics? The key, butthole."

Hector made a surprised face as if a light bulb went off in his mind. He frisked himself briefly and then went into his pants pocket and took out a big single key. Hector looked at Shawn and said, "You mean this?"

Jefferson roughly grabbed Hector and pushed him hard against a parked car. Jefferson said, "Protect your face, protect your face." Hector's hands quickly went up to his face, protecting his nice, beautiful caramel complexion from any unnecessary damage. Jefferson added, "Assuming the position without asking, I love it. I control you, punk."

Hector was starting to get nervous again; he didn't know what Jefferson was up to. Shawn lightly smiled and said, "Excuse my partner's manners. He doesn't get out much. Don't take it personally."

Jefferson added, "No, take it VIP personal, kid." Jefferson frisked him. He looked at Shawn and disappointedly shook his head and said, "The punk is clean, damn." Jefferson looked at Hector and said up close in his face, "You see, if you had another key, that would mean you were lying to us, which means a beatdown. And I would have released the beast in me, punk. You better be glad."

Hector looked at Shawn, who was holding the key, and said, "What's so big about that key?"

Jefferson responded, "Your life, punk."

Shawn slightly smiled and said, "Getting back what belongs to me." Hector looked confused. Shawn added, "Don't worry about that . . ."

Jefferson was trying to find a reason to punch Hector out; he said, "Yeah, you need to mind your business, son."

Hector had about enough of Jefferson; he knew he couldn't beat him. Neither was he going to continue to let Jefferson continue to bash and bully him; he looked at Jefferson. "Yo . . ."

Jefferson, who was a couple of inches taller than Hector, walked toward Hector with his fists balled up and responded, "Yo? Yo what, Hector? You punk-ass piece of crap. You have something you need to say to me, huh? Here I am. Make your move, punk." Jefferson moved closer.

Hector looked nervous, but he wasn't backing down as he responded, "You need to let up, man."

Jefferson sneered at Hector, "What? Yeah, after I kick your ass."

Shawn casually held Jefferson back, saying, "Easy, Jay, easy."

Jefferson shook Shawn's grip off, looking at Hector. "Another time, another place, that I promise you, punk."

Hector looked at Jefferson. "Yo, what have I done to you?"

Jefferson made an intimidating move toward Hector. Hector nervously moved back. Jefferson gritted his teeth in anger and said, "You made me chase after you, jackass."

Shawn said, "Okay, enough."

Jefferson backed off. Hector relaxed. Jefferson was pointing to Hector as he was hitting his fist into his hand as a threatening gesture. Hector turned and looked at Shawn. "Can I go?"

Jefferson responded, "It's 'May I go?' jerk."

Hector ignored Jefferson. Shawn looked at him and nodded his head. "Yeah, sure."

Hector started to walk; he still had that terrible limp when he slipped coming down the train stairs. Shawn asked, "By the way, Nieves, how's your mom?"

Hector stopped and paused before he turned and looked at Shawn; he asked, "You know my mother?"

Shawn nodded his head and responded, "Yeah, we met a few times. Give my regards."

Hector gave a slight nod; he looked down at the ground and back up at Shawn. "Sure." Hector looked at Shawn, but he still couldn't make the connection who Shawn was.

Shawn continued, "Just tell her SC asked about her. She'll know."

He nodded with some hesitation and said in a whisper, "Sure, I will."

Shawn inquired as Hector was slowly walking away, "Hey, you guys still have that house and property upstate?"

Hector looked surprised; he wondered how Shawn knew so much. Hector looked at Shawn and still couldn't remember any connections with him; things were blurring in his mind. Hector responded, "She's still living there. I'm trying to live on my own."

Jefferson sarcastically smiled. "I guess that's not going so well for you, huh?" He chuckled.

Hector wanted to say something back but knew better; he just ignored Jefferson. Hector was clearly annoyed. He looked at Shawn, saying, "Things are rough, but it's . . . going to be all right."

Shawn looked concerned and said, "I'm curious, who is your father?"

Hector shrugged and said, "I have no idea . . ."

Jefferson continued to verbally bash Hector, saying, "Oh, a bastard."

Hector looked at Jefferson and said, "It takes one to know one."

Jefferson finally found a reason to knock Hector out. "What, punk!"

Shawn lightly held Jefferson's arm. "Relax, back up."

Jefferson looked at Hector and said in frustration, "Ooh, you're so dead, punk!"

Hector had slightly stepped back. He waited a few seconds before he continued to respond to Shawn's question. "My mom tells me my father is some rich dude that sends us money at least once a month."

Shawn inquired, "Have you ever spoken to him?"

Hector nodded. "A few times, I guess. Can I go now?"

Jefferson grabbed him by his collar, slightly lifted him off the ground, and stared into his face. "You better watch that attitude, homeboy. You're just barely getting out of here by the skin of your teeth. You better show some gratitude, punk." Jefferson released him. Hector was looking down, looking defeated and deflated.

Shawn had so many questions for Hector; when he came to his gym, Hector was a good and quiet kid. Something happened to that quiet guy. Shawn studied him and asked him, "So why would you get involved with a bunch of losers like these guys?"

Jefferson shook his head and said, "So now he wants to play Dr. Phil. He goes from mixed martial arts to the WWE John Cena and now to Dr. Phil, freakin' unbelievable!" Shawn ignored Jefferson, who waved a dismissive hand.

Hector shrugged his shoulders and said, "I don't know. It just seemed like a cool thing at the time, but I was wrong."

Jefferson added, "You weren't wrong. Who told you that? You were dead-ass wrong, jerk." Shawn gave Jefferson a look. Jefferson backed off with a look of disgust.

Hector said, "My father, even though I haven't met him, but he's set up a trust fund for me. I could go into it whenever I want, buy whatever I want."

Jefferson added, "No wonder you're so spoiled!"

Hector nodded. "Perhaps."

Shawn looked at him and in a stern tone said, "Get out of here. I catch you again hanging with the wrong crowd, I will personally kick your ass. You understand that?"

Hector nodded and said, "Yes, sir." He slid in between Shawn and Jefferson, who wasn't moving an inch.

Jefferson said to Hector, "You touch me or brush up against me or even breathe on me, I'm nailing you, homeboy."

Hector turned and looked at Shawn. Hector just shook his head. Shawn looked at Jefferson, who made a face of frustration as he cursed under his breath. He slightly moved back in order for Hector to pass. Hector inched past Jefferson. Jefferson just stared at him and said, "You better be glad your guardian angel is here. You are so lucky on the real tip."

Hector limped down the street; he flagged down a taxi and got in. The driver took a few seconds to pull off. Shawn and Jefferson watched the taxi slowly disappear in the wee hours of the morning.

Jefferson was highly upset with Shawn. Shawn knew it but refused to go back and forth over this young hoodlum wannabe. Jefferson said, "Man, you just don't understand, man. All the promises I made to that punk, not one was fulfilled. This makes me look weak. Bad street cred, man." He paused and continued, "Thanks, Shawn, thanks a lot."

Shawn looked at him. "It's done. Shake it off. Lay it down and don't pick it up. Come on, we have work to do."

Jefferson shook his head. "Why is it always 'we' when you want it to be 'you and I,' huh?" He paused again and continued, "Ooh, I just wanted to clock that spoiled smart-ass, word up, but did I get a chance? No, we can't do that. Me wanted to do it."

They got in the car. Jefferson, being sarcastic, said, "You want to drive, but me want to drive. But me can't because we don't trust my skills."

Shawn looked at him. "Are you done?" Jefferson was getting ready to say something when Shawn cut him off. "Are you hungry?"

Jefferson all of a sudden stopped complaining. "That's not cool, Wall Street. You know my weakness, which is a good meal, especially when sisters are putting their magic into the stuff."

# Chapter 166

Shawn sat across Jefferson; he said, "Wow, that was good."

The waitress, whose name tag read Peters, lightly chuckled. "I'm glad you enjoy it." She continued, "You gentlemen ready for some dessert? Mama's pecan pie with a spoon of whipped cream is soooo good, according to the customers and my waistline." She looked up at the ceiling and blew out a playful exasperated breath.

Shawn and Jefferson lightly laughed. Jefferson nodded with a slight smile and said, "Are you serious? You are gorgeous."

Peters slightly blushed with a smile. "Thank you."

Shawn looked at Jefferson and back at Peters and said, "Mr. Smooth Cat is on the loose. You better be careful. His motto is if he tags you, he'll bag you."

They all laughed. Peters smiled, looked at Jefferson, and said, "I don't think your bag can hold this 36-24-36. You better be carefully. Like the sign says, caution: slippery when wet."

Now it was time for Jefferson to blush as he slightly smiled. "Thanks for the warning." She smiled at him with a quick rub on the back of his hand; she looked at Shawn and just made an inquiring sound as if she was very much impressed.

There was a slight nervous arousal in the air when Jefferson stuttered quickly, picked up his glass of water, and took one large gulp. He said afterward, "Uh, uh, dessert."

They slightly laughed again. Peters said, "Let me stop. Yes, dessert."

She looked at Shawn, who chuckled. "No, thank you." Peters looked at him and gave him an "Are you sure?" look. Shawn nodded his head. "Maybe next time."

Peters smiled and nodded. "Okay." She looked at Jefferson. "Dessert?"

Jefferson rubbed his stomach and chuckled the way Shawn just did it; he stopped midchuckle and said, "Of course, bring that pecan pie over, my piece and his."

Shawn's eyes opened up wide. "What? Where does it go?"

Jefferson smiled, shrugged, and said, "I wish I knew."

They all laughed. In the middle of the laughter, Shawn's cell phone chimed; he looked at the face of the phone and shrugged. "Excuse me, I need to take this. I'll be back."

Shawn had a strong inkling who the caller was; he pressed his Bluetooth. Before he could say something, the stranger spoke.

"Mr. Cook, you amaze me every time, sir. I don't know how you do it, how you get these challenges complete, sparing your lovely wife another day. Well, bravo to you, Mr. Cook, bravo."

Shawn cut right to the point, saying, "Whatever, I have the key. Now where is my wife?"

. "My, aren't we anxious and very desperate?" The stranger made a sound of disappointment as he continued, "You just don't fit the profile, sir. I always thought you were so much better than that, cool under pressure. Obviously, I was mistaken. What a pity."

Shawn gritted his teeth. "I don't give a damn what you thought and how you look at me! We had a deal."

The stranger responded, "Be careful, Mr. Cook. You better remind yourself who is holding the cards, who is controlling this game."

Shawn wanted to tell this pompous asswipe there was another player at the table whose name was Evans. He didn't know how to look at Evans; he wasn't putting too much trust or confidence in the man in spite of what he had done so far for Serenity. A street lesson: never turn your back on a snake. Shawn gritted his teeth and sneered, "You are definitely dealing with danger, mister. And believe me, I'm going to nail your ass to the wall and introduce you to a new justice system . . . my system—no plea bargaining or pardon or any of that bullshit. It's just cold, hard justice. You have an appointment. You're done. You have an appointment with hell."

The stranger started off calm before his voice took off with anger. "More threats, Mr. Cook? You keep trying my patience, sir. You are either stupid or just an idiot. You are putting your wife's life in jeopardy. I want you to pay for what you did to my brother, but I don't mind taking your wife as a sacrificial substitute. I could end this game right here and right now, Mr. Cook. I could just tell you where to find Serenity—her body, that is. Of course, my men—"

Shawn yelled back in the phone, "You son of a bitch!"

The stranger responded, "She sure was that—I'm talking about my mother." There was a pause before the stranger continued, "Sir, don't play your little threatening games with me. I'm about fed up with them. You cross that line one more time, Cook, and you will regret it." The stranger cleared his throat; he sounded calm. "Okay, I will call you to let you know where Serenity is. That will be the final test of the game." The stranger continued, "Getting past all of our clashes and collisions, I must say, Mr. Cook, I'm impressed." There was a slight pause as the stranger continued, "I will be speaking to you. Take care."

Shawn was trying to get a word in before the call disconnected. He was furious when he went back inside the diner; folks knew it as they calmly sidestepped out of his way. Shawn sat down in his spot, still upset. "Damn, freakin' jackass disconnected the call before I could speak . . . ugh . . . argh." Shawn slammed his hand down on the table.

Peters, the waitress, was coming over, took one look at Shawn, and did a 180 back to the kitchen. Jefferson put his head down and said, "We'll nail that punk . . . We'll catch him."

# CHAPTER 167

Five days later

Shawn was putting up some shelves. Jefferson was working out for the third time today; he explained that every time he had an urge to feed with the drugs, he'd work out instead. So far, it'd been working. Shawn knew in reality Jefferson could not keep up with this crazy schedule.

Shawn's phone chimed; he did not recognize the chime. He looked at the window display; it said "Caller unknown." He cursed to himself; he wasn't in the mood to deal with the stranger, not today. Shawn didn't have a good feeling about this; things were quiet for the past five days, not a peep from the stranger. Shawn wasn't sure if this was good or not; the sick son of a bitch could be up to something. The quiet storm. Shawn was tired and exhausted, but he couldn't give up.

He looked over at the clock radio; it read 8:00 a.m, It felt much earlier; he hadn't been getting any sleep. In addition, his body was wrecked up. The fight on the train made his shoulder worse.

Shawn answered the phone with irritation and annoyance, "What!" He reached over and picked up to painkillers, which he was supposed to have taken much earlier, like two and a half hours earlier.

The voice on the other end, which he didn't recognize, said, "Come outside your front door, Mr. Cook."

Shawn looked at the phone and the window display again; he placed the phone back to his ear. "Who is this?"

The voice responded, "Just do as you're told, Mr. Cook."

Shawn reached under his pillow and took out his .44 Magnum; he reached under the other pillow and took out his Desert Eagle. He placed the Eagle in the back of his waistband. The phone on the other end clicked off. Shawn hung up his phone.

He called Jefferson, who came on the line, breathing hard; he said, "What's up?"

Shawn responded, "A possible code red."

Jefferson was getting excited. "Be right there. Where is it?"

Shawn responded, "In my backyard."

Jefferson responded, "Oh shit."

# CHAPTER 168

Shawn instructed Jefferson to go out the back door and box them in. "I don't know how many. My camera system is out."

Jefferson whistled and cursed under his breath. "These mother suckers know what they are doing."

Shawn nodded and said, "No doubt, and so do I. Keep your phone on vibrate."

Jefferson agreed and headed toward the back door.

# CHAPTER 169

The caller called again. "Mr. Cook, I'm waiting. I have things to do. It's either you come out, or I'm coming in. I don't have all day, Shawn Cook. Move your ass."

Shawn was surprised that the person called him by his first name; he looked confused. He looked at the window display again—nothing but "Unknown caller." Shawn responded, "Who is this?"

The voice responded, "Get your ass out here so I could settle this matter."

Shawn was baffled; he thought about the timing, even the personal greeting, and how this person knew where he lived. Shawn thought as his eyes opened up wide, *Unless that dude I caught in the backyard, the one I let go, maybe he said something. Damn.*

Shawn was baffled. There were too many things that weren't adding up and yet too many that were. Shawn, like a man in the dark, took a wild leap, so to speak, and said, "Tanya?"

Tanya Jacqueline Hawkins, also known as TJ, laughed and said, "Who else, baby? Now get your ass out here to the front door so you can tell this young handsome gentleman to get his Glock out of my face and come on."

Shawn said into the radio, "Jay, stand down. Everything is cool."

# CHAPTER 170

Shawn opened the front door and saw a nice, slick, sexy-looking car. He slightly smiled. "TJ, another car, cool and not cool."

TJ looked concerned. "Explain."

Shawn continued, "I really don't need another car. I mean this one looks good and sexy. That lean look, cool. And I know you said you're going to give me something to replace Gordon."

Jefferson jumped in, speaking to TJ. "Hi, I'm Jefferson. My friends call me Jay. You may also. I don't have a problem getting to know the creator of such beauties."

TJ smiled and, with her hand outstretched, said, "Tanya Jaqueline Hawkins. Folks I don't know call me Jacqueline Hawkins or Ms. Hawkins." She looked at him to see if he caught her drift. She said, "Either one for you is fine."

Shawn smiled, looked at Jefferson, and said, "You met your match, kid."

Jefferson looked at Shawn and said, "Maybe." He looked back at TJ. "Maybe not."

TJ said to Shawn, "You have a real charmer." Jefferson gave a big smile of confidence.

Shawn looked at TJ, who continued the dialogue. But he interrupted, saying, "Thanks, but no thanks. I'll just wait . . . Tanya, I really don't want another car."

TJ said, "I thought you wanted to drive in style."

Shawn nodded his head and said, "I do, but not without Complex. I really want Complex back." There was a pause before he continued, "I'll just have to wait until you fix her. Not a problem, I'll wait."

TJ responded, "How is that coming for you? You know, the waiting."

Shawn responded, "Not good. I don't mind the element of waiting if I know what is going on, but I feel I'm in the dark. What is going on with my car?"

TJ looked as if she was losing patience; she said, "Patience is not one of my strong points." She looked at him with some annoyance and said, "Keep in mind how we got to this place, okay?"

Shawn nodded his head. "Okay, okay, I'm sorry. This is my fault, but I thought she would be fixed by now. Sorry, too many expectations." He looked at Jefferson. "Don't you have something to do beside lip-read everything in this damn conversation?"

TJ looked at Jefferson. "Wow, poor guy, caught in the cross fire . . . hmmm . . . casualty of war."

Jefferson put on his best sad face and said, "You think you can help me?"

TJ said, "Not really. If he's your casualty of war, I'll be your death wish. You really don't want to piss me off, Jefferson."

Shawn just shook his head and said, "I have no other choice. You send me another car, which is my fault. Don't worry about it."

TJ looked concerned and sympathetic, but in a matter of seconds, she had a look that said "Grow up and stop bitchin'." Instead, she casually said, "Okay, either handle this grown-up stuff like a man and be patient. Or continue to sulk and bark and bitch, okay? Find out which one works for you."

Jefferson was impressed; he said, "I've never seen . . ." Shawn just looked at him, which caused him to relax. Jefferson apologized, "I'll just sit over here and just look at my phone."

Shawn just shook his head and said, "He's a pain in the ass, but he's the best friend anyone could have. Okay, I'm good. It is what it is. What is the name of the car?"

TJ responded, "Ask."

Shawn shook his head. "Whatever. What's your name?"

The car lights came on; the lights were going around the car like some type of spaceship. The wheels flipped with a shield to protect them. The car was showing all it could do. Shawn was impressed; the sunroof opened up. Shawn nodded with approval. "I like that, a big improvement from Gordon. Okay, nice, but . . ." He paused and casually shrugged his shoulders. "Okay, so what is your name?"

The car didn't say anything. Shawn turned to walk away and said, "Well, can't expect too much. TJ, take care. I'll wait for Complex, but thank you."

TJ shrugged her shoulders and said, "Talk to you in a few."

Shawn said under his breath, "Whatever."

He was walking back inside the house when he heard, "I better be the only bitch up in this piece besides my girl princess and queen, Serenity."

Shawn stopped as he quickly turned back toward the car; he looked at it and said, "Excuse me?"

The car shot back, "Yeah, there is no excuse for you throwing in the towel like that. That is not what you teach, and you know better than that." Complex paused and continued, "Now fix yourself up, and let's get started. We have some serious things to do, kid. That little attitude, leave it outside. Don't bring that crap in here."

Shawn could not believe it; he looked at TJ and back at Complex. "Complex?"

Complex replied sarcastically, "No, Cinderella. Of course it's me—the one and only, baby." Complex played a song, "How Do You Like Me Now?"

Shawn was feeling the groove as he bobbed his head to the music; he said with excitement, "Wow, unbelievable! Complex, you look, you look . . ."

Complex said, "Come on, big boy, don't get tongue-tied on me. Let me help you out. I look lean, mean, and sexy—one hot-ass bitch . . ." Complex blasted the music and said, "How do you like me now?" Shawn shook his head. Complex said, "My girl did not hold back anything. I mean, look at me, baby—from the inside to the outside, from the interior to the exterior. Yeah, baby, I am the one, no question."

Shawn dialed TJ Hawkins. She picked up on the first ring; she said, "So what do you think? Are you still mad at me?"

Shawn laughed. "Tanya, you did a wonderful job! And no, I'm not mad at you. I love you. You saved my buddy."

TJ warned Shawn, "Shawn—"

Shawn cut in, saying, "I know, I know she is a computer. But I care about her."

TJ nodded and said, "I know."

Shawn paused and said, "TJ, you're the best." There was another pause before he continued, "Why didn't you tell me? I was acting like a spoiled child, sulking, and yet you knew. Why?"

TJ lightly laughed and said, "You know me. I love me some Shawn—not like that. Well, maybe that way too. But you know if I could, I would do anything for you. You are a good man, Mr. Shawn Cook."

Shawn smiled and responded, "You're right. You are the best."

Complex cut in. "She is the best of the best. Thank you, girl."

TJ smiled. "To answer as to why I didn't tell you, well, our girl wanted to tell you. She wanted to surprise you."

Jefferson just shook his head. "Yo, this is madness—a conversation with two humans and a computer. If I would tell anyone this, I'd be in the Looney Tunes blue room with Bugs Bunny as my therapist and Donald Duck as his assistant." There was a pause; then Jefferson continued, "But I like it."

TJ and Shawn laughed. Complex's lights flashed off and on. TJ smiled and said, "Was happy to do it. Well, got to go. Enjoy. Oh, by the way, Mr. Cook, I put a reminder when you need to bring Complex for a checkup. I gave you a three-month-in-advance window. You screw that up, as much I love you, you and I are going to have some serious problems. Now go."

Shawn nodded. "Thank you. Don't worry about that. I learned my lesson."

TJ slightly smiled and said, "Good, I could talk about all the changes I made to my girl, but I think I'll leave that up to her. It's such a beautiful day. Take her for a spin."

Shawn smiled; he reached for the handle to get in when Complex said, "Wait!"

Shawn had a concerned look on his face. "What happened?"

Complex responded, "Stand back."

Shawn stood back as the doors opened up scissor-style like a Lamborghini. He smiled and nodded his head. Complex's image on the monitor smiled; she said, "Hop in." Shawn jumped in. Complex said, "Ooh, baby, you've lost a few pounds. Before the weight was bam—just right, nice, and solid. Now it's like, where are you, baby?" There was a pause; then Complex said, "We're going to have to do something about that."

TJ came on, saying, "I forgot to tell you guys something—"

Complex interrupted TJ. "Sorry, babe, but I need to get this thing off my chest." TJ told Complex to go ahead. Complex continued, "Thank you. Shawn babes, I wanted to apologize for all I said and did. It wasn't me. Well, it was, but I had no control. I was out of control. So can you forgive me? I just needed to say that."

Shawn smiled and said, "All is forgiven, girl."

TJ continued with a smile in her voice, "Okay, first, I kinda left the attitude in place. Complex thought it was a good idea."

Shawn nodded and said, "Yeah, I hear it. Not a problem, a little edge."

TJ said, "Well, it's more than a little edge."

Complex's animation on the monitor smiled and laughed. She said, "Good, I want to be known as BAD."

Shawn responded, "I hate to ask, but I need to know."

Complex's image covered her mouth with a light laugh and said, "Badass diva. And when I'm really pissed off, badass bitch."

Shawn said, "Oh-kay."

Jefferson nodded with excitement. "I like that. You're going to get one or the other. No matter which one, she is going to be bad."

Complex smiled and said, "I like him. Can we keep him?" Shawn just shook his head and smiled.

TJ said, "Okay. If you look down at the knob, it says, 'Attitude Adjustment,' from 1 through 10. See that?"

Shawn nodded. "Yeah, I see it."

TJ continued, "Long story short, the higher the number, the more the attitude. The more the attitude, my girl can do some mean, nasty, horrific, disastrous stuff."

Complex told Shawn to try it as she took off out of the long driveway and made a left slide and peeled out; her image smiled with excitement, screaming, "How you like me now?" They hit the highway.

TJ said, "Shawn, listen to me. You really don't want the high numbers unless you're in a situation where you don't give a damn or if you have no other choices or alternatives or options, then by all means, crank that son of a gun up and activate that attitude adjustment."

Shawn wanted to test Complex's steering and control; he went in and out of cars. He smiled and nodded his head, saying, "Nice."

Complex responded, "Not bad, hon. Let me show you, baby, how it's done."

Shawn let go of the steering wheel, took his foot off the accelerator, sat back, and watched Complex do her thing. Shawn smiled as Complex dipped in and out of traffic. Complex's lights flashed brightly as the image on the screen smiled and blew a kiss at him.

Complex was excited. "Ooowee, baby, the bitch is back!"

Shawn smiled as he continued to let Complex control the driving, saying, "Yes, you are."

# CHAPTER 171

Complex said to Shawn, "There is so much I need to tell you about the new me, BAD. But first, it's time to air this baby out. You with me?"

TJ came on, saying, "Complex, don't."

Complex said, "Shawn."

TJ said, "Complex, don't you dare put Shawn—"

Shawn said, "Girl, go for it."

Complex's colors flashed brightly; the image of Complex on the monitor was smiling. She screamed with delight, "Sit back, handsome!" Complex's image became dark; she said, "It's time for some attitude adjustment. You mess with my family, mister, you mess with me. I'm coming after you, ghost, stranger, whatever, whoever, or whatever your name is. I'm BAD, and BAD is back, and I'm going to kick your ass!"

adjustment meter began to climb—2, 3, 4, 5, 6, 7 . . . Complex yelled as the song "Bad" by Michael Jackson played; she continued, "Complex went to lunch, but BAD is here. Badass bitch or badass diva, you take your pick, but I'm coming for you." Complex screamed.

As the music blasted, she zoomed past the highway patrol, who didn't even bother chasing. One of the officers said, "Wow, did you see that?"

His partner said, "Wow, it was a quick blur."

"Because I'm bad . . . Come on, you know I'm bad . . ."

Complex said, "Baby, we are going to take this mother sucker down. I have an assortment of weapons—rocket launchers, a torch, grenades, six Uzis, three on each side of the hood. That's just the start. Ghost, you are going down . . ." Complex screamed out of anger and frustration as she zoomed down the highway.

# CHAPTER 172

Complex coasted into Shawn's driveway with the song ending, "Who's bad . . . ?"

Complex stopped; her sensors came on. The control panel went through a sequence. The flamethrower weapon was chosen. Shawn looked on in shock. "Complex, what are you doing?"

Complex calmly responded, "Just taking out the trash for you."

Shawn looked at the monitor, which was focused on Gordon. He looked at Gordon and back at the monitor with Complex aiming; he said in a panic, "But that's not trash—that's Gordon!"

Complex ignored Shawn and said, "You'll thank me later."

Shawn was still baffled. "Complex!"

Complex responded, "Baby, give me a minute—4, 3, 2, 1 . . ."

Shawn yelled, "Complex, I said stand down NOW!"

Complex's light flashed bright; her image on the monitor was laughing, "Shawn sweetie, calm down. I'm just playing even though I want to get rid of that piece of—"

Jefferson came up to the car; he knocked on the window. Shawn gave instructions for the window to come down. The windows came down. Jefferson had a smile on his face. "Yo, bro, what is this? This is hot to the core. I saw her in the yard, but she looks much better up close. Wow, nice, sleek, and smooth, bro!"

Shawn said, "You own me."

Jefferson looked at him with confusion. "What?"

Shawn waved him off. "Never mind, I'll explain later." He continued, "Jefferson, meet Complex. Complex, Jefferson."

Jefferson's breath got caught in his chest. "What? This is Complex, dude? The one you've been bragging and boasting about as if she was your woman?" He paused and said, "I wish she was my woman, my homegirl."

Complex's colors flashed bright. "I like him. Can we keep him please?"

Shawn responded, "He's already kept. He's a fixture."

Jefferson was amazed. "Hold up, she speaks with colors as well? Wow, what an improvement!" He looked over at Gordon and said, "But I'm grateful for what I have." Jefferson continued, "So she's like Gordon—you know, somewhat limited in expression and communication?"

Complex's flash turned bright red; her animation on the monitor had an angry face. Shawn wanted to laugh; he knew Jefferson had stepped on a minefield of explosives and really didn't know it. He had just opened up a hornet's nest. Shawn stepped in and said, "Complex." He gave Complex the green light to respond.

Complex said, "Limited, you said 'limited'? Wait, where is your better half?"

Jefferson looked around. "Who said that?" Jefferson looked at Shawn, who was pointing to Complex. Jefferson's eyes opened up wide. "Get out of here! Wall Street, are you serious? Are you really serious?"

Shawn nodded his head and said, "You heard her."

Jefferson was excited. "A talking car that can express herself and with animation expressing those expressions—get out of here!"

Shawn raised his hand, warning Jefferson not to refer to Complex as a car, but it was too late. He said, "Final round."

Complex added, "A car? Look at me, young man."

Jefferson peeked inside the car; he said with amazement, "Wow, awesome! It's so cool in here."

Complex continued, "Yeah, this must be Butt-Head, and that clunk of whatever it is must be Beavis."

Shawn and Jefferson turned and looked at Gordon; he was just sitting there, doing nothing. Jefferson looked around; he was clearly uncomfortable. He asked Gordon if he was okay. Gordon took a few seconds to respond.

Complex added, "Hmmm, brain delay dysfunction. Listen, boy, I'll run circles around you and your outdated clunk of a car. Now speaking of cars, that is a car." There was a pause; then Complex continued, "Let's get this straight, sweetie, from jump street—I'm not a car, Butt-Head. I'm a state-of-the-art miracle, okay?"

Jefferson was smiling. "Wow, I love it! She insults and gives put-downs at the same time. Wow, so cool."

Complex's animation shook her head. "Listen, before you came over here, I was going to do you a huge, ginormous, astronomical favor . . . I can still do it, for the love of humanity."

Jefferson, looking at the animation and speaking with it as if Complex was a real human, said, "Wow, me? What was the favor?"

Complex said, "Oh . . . uh, just walk over and . . ." She cleared her throat and continued, "Get inside your car. I'll do both, two for the price of one. Oh yeah, baby. Hey, of no charge."

Jefferson smiled, turned, and headed toward Gordon. Shawn lightly grabbed him by the arm. Jefferson looked at him. "What?"

Shawn calmly said, "You'll thank me later."

Jefferson looked perplexed and shrugged his shoulders. "Okay, whatever. Anyway, Wall Street, you have to speak to Tanya."

Complex responded with an attitude, "Ms. Hawkins to you. You forgot what she said."

Jefferson continued, "Please speak to Ms. Hawkins about upgrading Gordon."

Complex's animation laughed. "What? That thing needs more than an upgrade! I don't think my girl has any spare parts for that thing. Me, I'm different. I'm unique. If my name wasn't Complex, it would be Unique with a little bit of mystique."

Jefferson responded, "Wow, state of the art. What are you, or rather, who are you?"

Complex said, "I'm your mama. I'm your daddy. I'm that brother and sister in the alley. I'm that badass mother sucker . . ."

Jefferson was fired up. "Get outta here! Man, Complex is amazing!"

Complex's animation slightly smiled with a nod. "Shawn, I would have to admit, this one has potential after all."

Jefferson smiled and said, "What can I say? Women adore me."

Complex laughed. "Oh, he's so modest too. I like him. But that clunk of junk, that scrap piece of metal—"

Gordon cut her off as he continued, "I beg your pardon? I'll just have you know I am made of the same precious stuff or, as you put it, this clunk of junk that you are made of. The only difference, missy, is yours is—"

Complex finished the sentence, saying, "More advanced, better, and longer lasting . . . state-of-the-art, baby. I'm ten to fifteen years more advanced than any car, including yours, bucko."

Gordon replied, "The name is Gordon, not this bucko, okay?"

Complex shook her head and said, "Whatever, Gordon. Your parts have a few more years, and then boom, junkyard heaven!"

Shawn was amazed two cars were going at it, but he heard about enough. "Okay, enough, no more!"

Gordon said, "She came at me first, sir. I was just trying to defend myself against this bully."

Complex responded, "Bullying? I could show you what bullying looks like, tough guy."

Gordon responded, "Thank you for seeing me as a tough guy. Well, actually, to be honest, I'm—"

Complex cut him off. "Gordon, some of your parts must be defected or used. That wasn't meant to be . . . forget it. I'm done. I have no more to say."

Gordon added, "Wow, a miracle."

Complex's animation appeared contemplative; she said, "And neither do you. So hush it."

Gordon replied, "Ms. Complex, I will not hush it, and you can't make me."

Complex responded, "Really?" Complex's dashboard came on with a few beeps, and that was it. Shawn knew something happened.

Jefferson, concerned, said, "What happened? . . . Shawn?"

Shawn raised his hand to Jefferson for him to calm down; he looked at Complex. "Complex, what did you do?"

Complex responded, "He'll be fine."

Shawn asked, "Okay, but what did you do?"

Complex seemed a little upset and responded, "I just temporarily blocked his speech controller. He talks more than a woman."

Shawn was surprised. "Which means he can't talk."

Jefferson was upset; he was looking at Complex's animation. "You did what! Shawn!"

Complex responded, "You'll thank me later. He talks too much and can't even back it up."

Shawn wanted to laugh. Jefferson must have caught him wanting to laugh; he said, "Yo, Wall Street, this isn't funny, man. You need to put your car in check, bro. She is clearly out of control."

Complex responded, spitting out the words, "I'm out of control? No, your outdated piece of sh . . . piece of metal is!"

Jefferson responded, "So what? . . . You think you're the cat's meow, sweetie?" He was now pointing at Complex's animation on the monitor. "Let me school you and tell you something, you cyborg Albert Einstein . . ."

Complex smiled and said, "Insulting, but so true. Continue."

Jefferson made a frustrated sound as he continued, "You may be all of that for now, but others will follow just like you."

Complex's colors flashed brightly. "You are correct, Butt-Head, follow! They will follow because this cyborg bitch will always lead the pack, baby."

Jefferson paused and thought about how he set up his own argument that turned against him; he shook his head in frustration as he looked over at Gordon and said, "Shawn!"

Shawn nodded his head. "Yeah, okay. Complex, enough. Restore Gordon's vocal system . . . now please . . . Thank you."

There was some hesitation; then there was a sequence of beeps and a long-sounding beep. "There, happy?"

's system was still where it left off. "And I so eloquently put it will be upgraded to your status, and there will be two of us, sister." Gordon's lights blinked quickly. "Wait! Come to think about it, we are technically brother and sister. We come from the same designer."

Complex's animation looked intense. "Shawn and Jefferson, back up. I'm going to disintegrate your clunk of junk."

Jefferson ran over to Gordon. "No, you're not. Then you will have to disintegrate me as well."

Complex calmly said, "Not a problem . . ."

Shawn said calmly, "Complex, stand down."

Gordon repeated the phrase, "Yeah, Complex, stand down."

Complex made a face of annoyance and said, "Whatever. Gordon and Jefferson, you can kiss my tailpipe."

Gordon replied, "Your tailpipe? That is rather nasty because the fuel and all of that . . ."

back would be too logical, making both of them look ridiculous; he said through clenched teeth, "Gordon, enough. Just don't say anything."

Gordon's light was dull; he said, "But, sir, I was only trying to . . ."

Jefferson, with a look of impatience, said, "Not now, enough."

Gordon added, "Yes, sir. But if I may, sir, one more thing, sir, to Ms. Complex, sir. It would only be a couple of minutes, sir."

---

Jefferson just shook his head. "Two minutes, Gordon, two minutes."

Gordon's lights blinked. "Ms. Complex, I am fully aware what you have done. Your name is like an icon at Central. Ms. Tanya Jacqueline Hawkins can't stop talking about you. You are her pride and joy. We all want to be like you, with all of that sophisticated, future, advanced computer stuff in you. Yes, it is true you are way ahead of us. I may not be as sophisticated as you, but my level of intelligence is rather decent, I think." Gordon paused and continued, "For the last few weeks or so, I kept Mr. Cook and Jefferson alive while you were away. So I can't be all that bad, can I?"

There was another pause. Shawn slightly smiled and thought, *Touché, Gordon. Well said.*

Complex's lights slowly dimmed; she said very softly, "Ouch."

Jefferson responded, "Wow."

Shawn said, "Okay, we're good. Now let's get to work and find my wife."

# CHAPTER 173

Shawn was in the gym in his Jacuzzi; the stranger had been calling him with assignments two to three o'clock in the morning. His body was bruised, battered, and broken.

Jefferson walked in the room and looked at Shawn, who was hunched over in the Jacuzzi, just taking in the water massage. Jefferson sat on the steps; there was silence for a few seconds when Shawn said in a whisper, "Jay, I'm tired. I'm broken. I'm angry and frustrated. He's beating me, Jay. He's winning this freakin' battle. He has the advantage . . . my wife. He holds the cards. I hold nothing. How long can I endure this? He's always three steps ahead of me. I can't catch up. I just want to throw in the towel."

Jefferson looked at his best friend. "I don't think so. Listen to me, Shawn. My body is all messed up too. I'm broken and bruised. Do you think I've put my life on the line just for you to give up, huh? You've got to be out of your freakin' mind!" There was a pause. "Listen, this is exactly what he wants you to do . . . give up. This is exactly how he wants you to feel, hopeless. The son of a bitch wants to break you down, bro, to dust and sweep your remains in the trash."

Jefferson stood up; he was adamant. "The son of a bitch wants to break you down to the point you have no fight in you. Listen to me, Shawn. You can't, and I won't let you do that to yourself. I know what it's like to be broken, to have your spirit ripped out of you to the point you want to end it all. I know what that feels like. I could write a damn book on that shit, man. I've been there. But one day, I met a very wise man that once told me, 'If you want what you want, you have to go out and get it.' I believe in that person. I would give my life for that person, even to this day."

Shawn knew the person Jefferson was referring to was him. Shawn smiled, gave Jefferson a power-grip handshake, and said, "Thanks, man."

# CHAPTER 174

Two hours later

Shawn gathered around the cars and Jefferson. "I wanted to give you guys an update on where we are right now." He took a breath, released it, and said, "The same spot where we were three days ago—nowhere. Every time we think we have something, it's not enough or is obsolete . . . The man is like a phantom, a ghost. The man is dangerous. He has one thing in mind: steal, kill, and destroy. He is out to avenge the death of his twin brother, Phillip Keys. I'm the target. And Serenity, my wife, is the bait. Jay and I were trying to figure out how to stop this guy, but the problem is not stopping him, but first finding him."

There was a pause; then Complex said, "A lot of things have happened before I left, and now that I'm back, I have to make a lot of adjustments—thanks to TJ for adjusting those sensitive areas in my system that, as Gordon has pointed out, will soon become obsolete. And, Gordon, thank you. It is true—we are made of the same material. Okay, mine may be advanced. But we have a great designer that can work wonders, which she will in me and also with you, Gordon. We will be equal with different skills and talents. But keep in mind, I'm the boss, okay?" They all lightly laughed. Complex's image on the monitor looked at Shawn. "Babes, we knew it all along, but now we can prove it."

Shawn looked baffled. "What?"

Complex continued, "The stranger, ghost, the phantom, whatever you want to call him. The man you killed."

Shawn looked away with his head down and said, "Next subject. I don't want to gloat over what I have done. I feel awful already. This is why my wife is not with me. Please move on."

Complex tried to reason with Shawn. "If you give me a minute."

Shawn looked at the image on the monitor. "Not even a second. This discussion is over, Complex. Everybody, get back to your stations."

They all started slowly moving when Complex said, "No! Everybody, stop."

Shawn was surprised. "What! You are going against me, Complex." He said, "TJ must have missed something because you must be out of your spark plugs."

Gordon laughed. "Spark plugs . . . that was a—"

Jefferson told Gordon to be quiet. He said, "Shawn."

Shawn held out his hand toward Jefferson. "Back off. This is between Complex and me. Now, everyone, go to your stations."

Complex boldly said, "Nobody move."

Shawn looked at Complex and said, "Complex, shut down."

Complex said, "Not before I say what I have to say, Shawn."

Shawn looked around, frustrated, and said, "You have twenty seconds."

Complex said, "I need only fifteen seconds." She continued, "The man that has Serenity is not a twin of Phillip Keys. He's not even a blood relative."

Shawn's mind was racing; his head was spinning. He mumbled to himself something; then he looked at Complex. "Go on."

Complex looked at Shawn and said, "I can't."

Shawn, looking confused, asked, "Why?"

Complex responded, "My fifteen seconds are up, Mr. Cook."

Jefferson turned his back, smiling. Shawn looked agitated and mumbled for Complex to continue.

Complex said, "I'm sorry, Mr. Cook, I didn't hear that. What was that? Speak louder please."

Shawn knew Complex did a checkmate on him as he sneered, "I said to go ahead." Complex's image smiled. Shawn asked, "By the way, how did you get this information?"

Complex explained, "While TJ was working on me at headquarters lab, I was listening to the recordings of this nutjob. I compared his voice to thousands of speeches, and I finally found a match."

was. His cell chimed. Shawn cursed under his breath; he wasn't going to answer at first. He tapped his Bluetooth. "Moore."

Commissioner Moore spoke with some urgency in his voice. "Cook, I have some information I think you may want to hear—"

Shawn interrupted the commissioner, saying, "The same here. I'll call you back in twenty-five minutes."

Moore nodded and said, "No problem, twenty-five minutes. I think you would want to hear this."

Shawn needed to know something. "Moore, give me an idea. Can you do that?"

Curtis Moore said, "Ms. Stewart is ready to confess. She is ready to tell it all."

Shawn thought and asked, "What's the catch?"

Moore said, "As long as we make sure her family, her husband and two sons, are safe. We're working on that right now."

Shawn responded, "That can take hours. Hold off on that move, Moore. I think I have something hot. Call you back."

The commissioner wanted to know. "Come on, Cook."

Shawn, in an urgent voice, said, "I'll let you know." He disconnected the call.

Shawn felt bum-rushed with all of this news coming in at the same time; he sat down on his steps and put his head down.

Jefferson sat next to him, "Yo, bro, you okay?"

Shawn nodded his head. "Yeah, a lot going on. This woman who worked for the stranger is ready to confess everything, but there is a catch—she wants to make sure her family is placed in a safe house until they catch this guy."

Jefferson was excited. "Good news! One step closer to getting Serenity back."

Shawn looked at Jefferson and said, "True. But if Complex is on target, we're not only a step closer—we will be right in this lowlife's circle."

# CHAPTER 175

Shawn said to Complex, "Finish what you were saying concerning what you found."

Complex continued, "In my research, your mystery man is James Hollingsworth."

Shawn stopped her. "Hold up, the Hollingsworth . . . the same one that . . . ?"

Complex's image on the monitor began nodding her head. "Yes, the filthy-rich billionaire that is on the *Forbes* list as the richest men in the world."

Jefferson inquired, "Wall Street, where do you fit on that *Forbes* list?"

Shawn responded, "Jay, this is not the time nor the place to discuss such a question."

Jefferson smiled. "That low, eh?"

Complex, defending Shawn, responded, "Well, at least he's on that list."

Jefferson nodded. "True that. I was just trying to break up some of this tension."

Complex continued, "Look, take a look at James Hollingsworth." A photo came up with Hollingsworth's face. Complex continued, "Watch this. Here is Phillip Keys, you know, the one you killed."

Shawn, defending himself, said, "It was in self-defense. Why can't some people get that? Like this Hollingsworth. It was in self-defense. It was either him or me."

Complex responded, "Personally, I don't give a rat's ass." She continued, "Personally, I'm glad you did what you did. That scumbag was corrupt. You did right by taking him out of this world."

Gordon was still on the "rat's ass" part; he said in a contemplating voice, "Hmmm, a rat's butt or behind. I'm not allowed to use such words."

Jefferson said, "Gordon, you may on this one."

Gordon responded, "A rat's ass. Sounds nice . . . a rat's ass. I don't give a darn about your rat's ass. But what does a rat's ass have to do with this topic of discussion?"

Jefferson said, "I'll explain later."

Complex continued, "Look at the pictures side by side. Do you see something?"

Jefferson said with a surprised tone, "Wow, get out of here! Wow, they could pass for twins!"

Complex responded, "Yeah. But through a detailed inspection, one could see the subtle and slight difference, can you not?"

Jefferson was looking at the pictures very hard until he had to rub his eyes; he looked again, and he saw it. He said as if he discovered gold, "Oh yeah, I see it. Now I see. Wow, why didn't I see that before?"

Gordon added, "Sir, the human eye and the mind are very complex . . ."

Complex's lights flashed, and her animated character smiled. "Gordon, I'm beginning to like you more and more. Good thing I didn't blow you up when I had a chance."

Gordon responded, "I'm sorry. What was that?"

Complex hesitated and said, "Nothing, just thinking about something. It's all good." She quickly continued, "Hollingsworth looked up to Phillip Keys like a big brother. As a matter of fact, according to this photograph, look at it. Now look at this one." Another picture came up on the screen. The screen was split; now Shawn was even stunned by what he was seeing.

# CHAPTER 176

Shawn said, "Wow, what a major difference! This dude had some serious work done to his face."

Jefferson pointed to Gordon. Even though Gordon wasn't as sophisticated as Complex, he was somehow keeping up. Jefferson tapped Gordon's hood. Gordon's lights flashed on and off.

Complex responded to Jefferson's remark that Hollingsworth had extensive work done to his face, "Yep."

Jefferson asked, "But why?"

Complex said, "The only logical solution would be—"

Gordon interrupted. "I'm sorry, may I?"

Complex responded, "Yes, please."

Gordon continued, "Our Mr. Hollingsworth was trying to look like the terrorist Phillip Keys. He apparently was obsessed with his life to the extent the thought took over every aspect of his life. Therefore, he began to find ways to look like Keys to the extent he claimed he was the twin."

Complex responded with flashing lights and sounds of trumpets going off. She said, "You go, boy! Damn, you're good. Move over, Dr. Phil. Dr. G is in the house." Complex played the sounds of a standing ovation at a ball game.

The fanfare slowly died down when she said, "But let's take this one step further. Hollingsworth, that loose nut, wanted to look like Keys so he could live his life as Hollingsworth and strictly live as the twin of Phillip Keys or, even sicker, to claim Keys had been brought back from the dead to carry on the destructive plan Keys had in mind for all the cities of the United States." Complex paused and continued, "But there were so many obstacles and barriers that got in the way. So many things went wrong."

Shawn, with his hand cupped on his chin, asked, "Like what?"

Complex's animated picture smiled. "Okay, keep in mind all of this is just speculative stuff, okay?"

Jefferson asked, "How did you get all of this information?"

Complex winked at him and said, "If I told you, I'd have to get rid of you."

Jefferson wisely thought about it and said, "Gotcha . . . never mind."

Complex continued, "Smart man. Shawn, you know already Hollingsworth is very dangerous and especially now that he is in the middle of personalities. One part of him has Phillip Keys's persona, and the other has his businessman persona. But I think it's safe to say the Phillip Keys's persona is slowly taking over." She continued, "Which means the man is dangerous and evil. He needs to be stopped because, at this point, we haven't seen anything yet." Complex looked concerned. "For example, one of the plastic surgeons was found in the river . . . dead."

Shawn said, "Let me take a guess. Hollingsworth no doubt, and no doubt he had an airtight alibi, which was he's filthy rich and had the best lawyers. And even according to rumors, he paid off the judge."

Jefferson added, "I do remember that case. I didn't bother to read it. I mean, who in their right mind would go up against one of the richest men in the country?"

Shawn nodded. "True, but we are. I don't care how mentally deranged he is or how many personalities he may have—one or twenty, every single one of them is going down."

# CHAPTER 177

Shawn was pacing back and forth. Jefferson was listening to Complex, who said to Shawn, "Shawn, you need to relax. Your readings are very high. You can't function like this. You are asking for trouble. Look at this. Your brain functions are starting to decline, 70 percent and dipping."

Jefferson was amazed; he said, "Wait a second. This is unbelievable. I don't know if I'm hearing right." He paused, thinking; he shook his head. "Okay, I had to digest what I thought I heard. Are you telling me, Complex, that you can sense Shawn's vitals, blood pressure, heart rate, brain function?" Jefferson was astonished; he grabbed his head with his hands as his voice pitch went up an octave. "Oh my god, this is beyond amazing! So in other words, you can tell if someone was about to get sick—you know, heart, kidney, etcetera, etcetera."

Complex said, "Pretty much. But it's not always accurate, but always in the ballpark, so to speak. It's just a good guess."

Jefferson was still blown away. "Oh my . . . Shawn, is she for real?"

Shawn was ready to respond when Complex questioned Jefferson, "Are you doubting me, Mr. Newhouse?"

Jefferson was shaking his head. "Uh . . ."

Complex said, "I'm called Complex for a reason. And in reality, if you think this is a breakthrough, you haven't seen anything yet, kid." Complex's image smiled and winked as she continued, "I move from complex to perplexing, from perplexing to baffling the minds. And from there, I'll leave you dumbfounded or simply dumb."

Jefferson was overwhelmed. "Yo, I have to get me one of these."

Good hunting, kid. There is only one me, baby." She played a soundtrack of a crowd being amazed. She smiled. "Now may I continue?"

Jefferson was speechless as he nodded his head with astonishment. Complex continued, "Okay, so Hollingsworth had extensive work done on his face. He was so enthralled with the idea of looking like Keys to the point he wanted every aspect of this man's face—every dent, every dimple . . . even childhood scars. I wouldn't be surprised if Keys had dimples on his ass. Hollingsworth would want that as well, the sicko. And for the most part, he got what he wanted from the untrained eye. But there are flaws, and he knew it. That's why he had it done several times. He was obsessed." There was a pause; then Complex continued, "It came to a point that Hollingsworth was trapped. He fell deeper into Keys's psyche. He wanted to emulate a terrorist."

Jefferson responded, "That's sick, man."

Shawn said, "Not if that is your goal, your mission."

Complex said, "Exactly, and that is what it became for Hollingsworth. He wanted to be completely consumed by Keys, and eventually, he did."

; of course, this was all theory and speculation, but Complex was hardly ever wrong. Shawn said, "Okay, we know that we are dealing with a sick mother sucker that has some serious issues." He paused and continued, "But that doesn't help us in regard to nailing that bastard. He still remains a mystery. I want to know—I need to know—something concrete. Theory must move from theory to concrete before I present this to Commissioner Moore."

There was another pause; hope was slowly diminishing, and Shawn knew it. This was the closest he had ever been to getting Serenity back, and even this was dwindling fast. Shawn felt the impact of his thoughts and cursed under his breath.

Complex responded, "Shawn, do you have any recordings of Hollingsworth leaving a message for you?"

Shawn shook his head. "Every phone call, I picked up. I had no other choice. He would have harmed Serenity. What choice did I have?" He shook his head. "Damn, this is no good." Shawn thought and said, "Hold up. The only thing I have of this asswipe is two conversations regarding this last assignment."

Jefferson snuck in, saying, "Where you kick major butt, ooh rah!"

Shawn continued, "That taping was by mistake. I went to answer the phone and by—"

Complex cut Shawn off. "I get the idea, and at this stage, details are not what we need. Just the facts, baby, that's all I want." She asked, "Do you still have—"

Shawn stopped the flow of the conversation as he looked over at Jefferson. Jefferson looked at his watch; he looked a little uptight, nervous. Something was wrong. Jefferson said, "I have to step off, sorry."

Complex said, "Shawn, Jay's vitals are not good at all."

Jefferson slightly raised his voice. "Stop reading me, dammit!"

Shawn was surprised at the tone; he said in a hard tone, "Hey! Easy."

Complex responded, "It's all good. Let him try that crap again. I'm going to run his ass over. One more time."

Shawn looked at him immediately; what was going on with Jefferson? He said to him, "Can you give us—"

Jefferson cut him off, shook his head, and said, "I already did. I pushed the limit. I need to go." He started shaking slightly. Shawn nodded as Jefferson headed toward the gate. "Sorry, I have to feed the need." He gave a slight painful smile.

Shawn nodded as if he understood, which in a way he did. He said, "Hey, aren't you going to take Gordon?"

Jefferson shook his head. "Nah, sorry, Gordon."

Gordon responded, "Not a problem, sir."

Jefferson slightly smiled. "Finally, he got it right." He was referring to Gordon with his crazy language. Shawn knew what he was about to hear next he wasn't going to like it; he braced himself for impact. He wanted Jefferson to finish what he was going to say. "Where I'm going is pretty close."

Shawn looked at him and asked, "How close, Jay?"

Jefferson wasn't in the mood, but he knew he had to show and give respect; he said, "Within the gates."

Shawn looked at him as if to say "Give me more."

Jefferson blew out an impatient breath and said, "A few minutes before you hit the main road . . ." There was a pause; then he continued, "Shawn, this is a beautiful community, but your community is not as perfect as you may think. And trust me, it didn't start with me." Shawn gave a look of frustration. Jefferson knew Shawn was upset and said, "I ran out of the other stuff. Look, this is not going to be the norm."

Shawn's frustration came out in his tone. "You're damn right it's not. All you need is one or two people to allow for it to happen, and the next thing you know, the sucker spreads like a disease. Not here, Jay, that's not going to happen in this community. It's one thing to keep that shit under wraps. But when you have the boldness to pull the covers off that monster, that means you don't give a damn who is affected, young or old."

Jefferson was listening, getting more and more agitated and fidgety; he said, "I wouldn't even do this if I wasn't caught up in—"

Shawn cut him off, saying, "Don't go there, Jay, okay? Just take responsibility. It makes you sound more like a man than blaming others for your actions, and I'd rather have you sound like a man who admits his failures than one who find excuses and blame others, okay?"

Jefferson wanted to say something but decided wisely not to say anything; he just nodded his head and turned with some hesitation to leave.

Shawn called him. Jefferson turned toward Shawn, who tossed him what looked like a medium-sized button. Jefferson caught it and looked at it with a puzzled expression. He looked up at Shawn with that same look.

Shawn said, "It's a tracker. Turn it on."

Jefferson turned the gadget on; there were two beeps coming from it.

Shawn said, "This baby saved your life once. Always play it safe."

Jefferson nodded and said, "Thanks."

Shawn just gave a "Whatever, no problem" look, but he cared for Jefferson like a little brother, and Jefferson knew it. Shawn, still looking at Jefferson, said, "Take Gordon. I need you back here ASAP."

Jefferson hesitated, gave a brief nod, and said, "Sure, no problem."

# CHAPTER 178

One hour later

Jefferson came in the yard looking much better. Shawn walked up to him, "You okay?"

Jefferson slightly smiled. "Yeah, pretty much." He hesitated and said to Shawn, "Don't give up on me. That would crush me if you did . . . I'm going to beat this thing."

Shawn gave Jefferson a big brother–little brother neck hug. "I'm with you, bro, through thick and thin. I made that promise to you, and I plan on keeping it." There was a slight pause when Shawn said, "I have confidence in you, man. I know you're going to beat this thing." There was another pause when Shawn removed his hand off Jefferson's neck and looked at him, asking, "You're good, you sure?"

Jefferson nodded his head and said, "Yeah."

Shawn nodded back with a slight smile. "Cool. Here, come over here. I have Complex analyzing a couple of phone calls that came in from Hollingsworth a couple of nights ago."

Jefferson was looking and feeling mellow, but he had this look of concern on his face; he said, "So what?" He paused.

Shawn didn't hear him respond. "What was that?"

Jefferson looked at Shawn, then looked away. Shawn looked at Jefferson and knew something was on his mind. Jefferson said, "I was asking what—"

Shawn interrupted him. "Hold up, time-out, bro. What's going on?"

Jefferson looked at him and said, "Nah, I'm good. I'm cool. I'm—"

Shawn interrupted him, saying, "Full of crap, man. C'mon, Jay, I need you to focus. We are a step closer to nailing this SOB, and right now, right now is not the time to retreat, man. I need you to man up and be up front with me. Now what the hell is going on?"

Jefferson paused; he looked every which way and then finally looked at Shawn. "Yo, I feel like I'm slowing this team down, man, and I don't want to do that." Jefferson stopped, thought, and continued, "Come on, man. I have a damn habit. I'm trying to control it . . ."

Complex said, "Jay, you have more drama in your life than a soap opera."

Shawn admonished Complex, "That would be enough, Complex. Your criticism at this time is not needed. Is that understood?" Complex's lights flashed dull. Shawn repeated, "Have I made myself clear, Complex?"

Complex responded, "Yes, sir."

Shawn turned his attention back to Jefferson. "I know you're dealing with what you are going through, and I think you're dealing with it pretty well . . . I mean, give yourself some credit. You've been in the trenches with me, keeping up with me. I don't see a regression. I see a progression . . ."

Jefferson chuckled sarcastically. "Yeah, like this morning, where I had to cut out on you guys. That wasn't cool."

Complex said, "You got that right."

Shawn said to Complex, "Complex, that's strike 2."

Jefferson said, "Complex is right, man. It's frustrating. You just don't know."

Shawn nodded his head. "You're right, I don't know. I only know what I see and what you tell me and what Complex may pick up reading you . . ." He paused and continued, "But this is what I see. I see a man who has more courage than anyone I know."

Jefferson looked down, listening, and said, "Thank you for the encouraging words, but let's be real here. I abandoned you guys this morning, and who knows if it may happen again."

Shawn looked at Jefferson and said, "No, you didn't abandon us."

Jefferson looked at Shawn with a look of bewilderment as if Shawn was crazy; he said, "Come on, Wall Street, I did. Yes, I did. Come on."

Shawn looked at him straight in the eye, man-to-man, and said, "You didn't abandon us. To abandon, Complex."

Complex quickly responded, "'Abandon,' according to the *Webster's Dictionary*, means, 'cease to support or look after, to desert, dump, forsake, ditch.'"

Shawn said, "That is the definition of what 'abandon' means. You ran off, you left, but you came back. To me, that is not abandonment. That's courage under fire, man."

Jefferson contemplated what Shawn was saying and said, "Wow, I didn't think—"

Complex said with urgency in her tone, "I think I have something."

# CHAPTER 179

Shawn and Jefferson sat in Complex's front seat while Gordon pulled alongside of Complex. Complex began to explain what was going on. "Okay, I apologize it took the time it did to get this information. I was trying to do it under an hour, but there were other pressing matters to attend to."

Jefferson lightly chuckled and asked, "Like what? Recharging your system or playing computer games? What could have possibly been the reason?" He let off another light chuckle.

Complex's image became slightly intense; she said, "For one, butthole, my system automatically charges itself. You keep forgetting, I'm complex and perplexing and don't forget unique." Complex smiled and continued, "So what was the delay? Very simple, monitoring your funky butt and making sure you weren't walking into an ambush."

Jefferson looked at the animated image and said, "Oh, you care that much about me, Complex?"

Complex smiled and winked, "Ahh . . . of course not. No, I follow directives. It wasn't personal, baby doll, but all professional, honeybun."

Jefferson loved the back-and-forth; he said, "Do you think you can find a human being like you? I mean, if you were human—"

Complex cut him off. "I would run circles around you, kid." Complex played the sound of tires peeling out.

Jefferson, curious, asked, "What was that sound?"

Complex responded, "Me leaving your ass in the dust. If I was human? Little boy, please, save some of that oxygen to live, baby."

Jefferson smiled and said, "Every day coming home to that . . . I love it."

Complex responded, "You like punishment, you little freakazoid?"

Jefferson still had the smile plastered on his face; he said, "Yeah, you and me and a human Complex, I would love it."

Complex gave Jefferson a dismissive look and said, "Yeah, in your dreams, bucko."

Gordon responded, "That's the name you called me . . . bucko."

Complex responded, "You've graduated to my assistant. Jefferson, despite that mouth, I have to admit, I like you. Shawn, I like him. Can we keep him." Complex jokingly smiled. Her smile faded as she became serious again. "Shawn, I analyzed the recording from your phone, but what made you record the conversation?"

Shawn shrugged his shoulder. "To tell you the truth, I pressed the Record button by mistake. I didn't realize I was recording that idiot. Why? What do you have?"

Complex said, "I'm not sure. Listen carefully. I'll play it for you." She continued, "I blocked out the conversation between you and Hollingsworth."

Jefferson responded, "What, in order for us to hear only the background sounds?"

Complex responded, "Correct, Jay, you are so smart. This is why I tolerate you. You have so much potential. Shawn, can we keep him?"

Shawn asked Complex to focus. Jefferson was all smiles from Complex's compliment.

Complex continued, "Listen . . ." There was a lot of clattering noise, making the background sound difficult to understand. There was the sound of bells and a public announcer, sounds of cars, and something else that neither Jefferson nor Shawn could make out.

Shawn said, "Complex, rewind that. Let us hear it again."

Complex nodded and said, "I'll do better than that. I'll play it again and will eliminate some more of the background noise."

Shawn nodded. "Okay, cool."

Complex said, "Okay, boys, here we go. Listen." She played it again. There were the same sounds, clatter of voices, and the PA announcer; but this time, there was the sound of children playing. There was that loud PA announcer repeating the same thing over and over. Shawn and Jefferson still couldn't make it out; they both were getting frustrated.

They both heard the same sounds—talking, traffic like fire trucks and ambulances and car horns, bells, the PA speaker, children playing; they now could hear someone giving away a free paper.

Complex asked, "Anything yet?" They both shook their heads.

Shawn said, "I really don't know."

Jefferson agreed with Shawn. "Nothing."

Complex said, "Okay, let's start eliminating other sounds."

Shawn and Jefferson agreed, but it was obvious they were fed up. Complex's animated picture smiled and said, "Isn't this fun?"

Jefferson wanted to say something sarcastic but thought otherwise. *This is not the right time*, he thought to himself.

Complex said, "Okay, enough, my bad boys are getting tired and frustrated. Okay, I'm going to eliminate all the sounds, but just the ones I think are important. Okay, listen up."

Shawn and Jefferson were listening when they heard the same repeated phrase every few minutes by what sounded like the PA announcer. "Welcome to . . ."

That woke Shawn up; he said, "Hold up, wait. 'Welcome to' some place, and then it becomes fuzzy."

Jefferson, also excited, said, "Yeah, that's what I heard too."

Shawn said, "Complex."

Complex responded, "I'm on it, big guy. Cleaning it up . . . Okay, how about now?"

"Welcome to the Hil . . . Enjoy your sta . . . at the Hil . . ."

Shawn responded, "Damnit, I hear it, but I can't seem to break through those last couple of words . . ." He paused and continued, "But for some reason . . . hmm, strange."

Jefferson asked, "Wall Street, what?"

Shawn, looking baffled, said, "I've heard or I thought I heard that announcement before. I just can't . . . damn."

Jefferson was equally frustrated. "We are so close. I know we are."

Complex said, "Okay, let me try one last time to clean it up."

Gordon responded, "I'm sorry, I was just listening to everyone. I wasn't distancing myself. I was trying to figure out what was said as well. Complex, do you mind if I take a shot?"

Complex responded, "Gordon, let me clean it up first."

Gordon quickly responded, "No . . . sorry, I sounded too aggressive. Sorry, what I meant to say was please don't. I'd rather go for the challenge round like everyone else." Gordon's lights flashed brightly and corrected himself. "Well, at least that is what they say on these game shows, challenge round, or is it bonus round? Yes, I correct myself, the bonus round. Uh, may I?"

Complex smiled. "Of course, yes, go ahead."

Gordon said, "Apparently, it's a male's voice. And it's pleasant, very much nonthreatening, which means it's a business environment we can safely say rather than at a ballpark." Gordon continued, "There are children in the background, a lot of happy noise."

Complex interjected, "Gordon is right. According to my information, there are buses taking children to a music theme park. It has been posted for weeks. Sorry, Gordon, continue."

Gordon continued, "The PA announcer is saying, 'Hello, welcome to the . . .'"

Shawn and Jefferson were practically on pins and needles as they waited with anticipation for Gordon to reveal what he thought was being said. Gordon continued as he repeated the words, "'Hello, welcome to the Hilton.' Yes, that is the missing word, 'the Hilton'!" Gordon continued, "And then he would say, 'I hope you enjoy your stay at the Hilton.'" Shawn and Jefferson were surprised as Gordon continued, "Complex is accurate. The tour bus is for the children to a theme park."

Shawn's breath got caught in his chest; he couldn't believe what he had just heard. Jefferson said, "No way!"

Gordon responded, "Uh, yes way, sir. The Hilton Hotel. I could have Complex play it again if, of course, she doesn't mind."

Shawn looked at the animated picture of Complex on the monitor. "Complex, confirm."

Complex nodded her head. "Confirmed. Good work, Gordon. Yes, Shawn, the Hilton Hotel."

Jefferson couldn't believe it; he was shaking his head. He said, "Wait a minute, you mean to tell me that that crazy, sick son of a bitch has been under our noses all this freakin' time?"

Shawn was still shocked and baffled. "But how? How did he accomplish that, and why the hell didn't the commissioner at least pick this up?"

Complex responded, "Well, don't pick on him. He didn't know. He was as lost as you two. And as for me, well, I was all messed up courtesy of your neglect. And you can't blame Gordon because he was new to the game, so . . ." Complex played the sound of drums getting ready to reveal a winner; she said, "The winner goes to . . . you, Shawn Cook. Plus the commissioner wouldn't have figured it out anyway because he's the back end of a donkey." She continued, "Apparently, Hollingsworth knew he was being deceptive according to the recording."

Shawn looked at Complex, confused. "I'm missing something. What do you mean? Expound please."

Complex said, "If you recall during that conversation you had with Hollingsworth, apparently, he was interrupted. He was sounding very upset about it."

Jefferson jumped in, saying, "His flow was being interrupted, I guess."

Complex responded, "And you guess wrong. He wasn't upset because he was interrupted. He was upset because . . . Just listen to this."

"Welcome to the Hilton, Mr. Collingsworth."

Complex said, "Did you get that?"

Jefferson said, "Yeah, the man called him Collingsworth and not Hollingsworth."

Complex said, "Jay, does your brain shrink every time you speak? Don't say too much. A mind is a terrible thing to waste." Jefferson waved a dismissive hand at Complex.

Shawn's eyes lit up; he was stunned. "Son of a bitch, he's going under another name."

Complex said, "Well, actually, Collingsworth is his real name. He interchanges between that and Hollingsworth."

Jefferson asked why. Gordon said, "So nothing could be pinned on him. As Mr. Collingsworth, he's considered an outstanding citizen."

Shawn replied, "But we've seen his true colors. The punk ass is anti-American and dangerous. All of this so-called name-changing crap is poppycock. The real question is, what is he doing in New York?"

Complex responded, "I'm not sure. Maybe to finish what his so-called brother started."

Shawn looked concerned. "Complex may be right." He added, "Complex, patch me in to Commissioner Curtis Moore. I don't give a rip if this man is in a meeting with the mayor or Como or this dude in the White House. I need to speak to him right now. Tell them it is of high urgency and safety."

# Chapter 180

The commissioner broke up the meeting he was having with the leadership of the city as he came over to Shawn's place with a two-car escort.

Shawn and Jefferson could not believe the commissioner wasn't convinced; he said in frustration, "So you expect me to walk into the Hilton Hotel and place one of the wealthiest men in the world in cuffs based on a tape from your answer machine?" Moore pointed at Shawn. "I heard the tape, and there is so much background noise. How the hell do you expect me to figure it out, huh? Come on, Cook." The commissioner continued, "It would take weeks for that tape to be analyzed and figured out if that's Collingsworth. I can take the machine, and—"

Shawn, in frustration, raised his voice, saying, "Curt, we don't have time for that. Trust me, he's your man. Listen, Moore, I haven't been wrong yet, have I?"

Curtis Moore responded, "You have a hunch, Cook. I bring that to the court. His attorneys would have the man free as soon as he sits his ass down in the chair. Come on, man!" The commissioner looked at Cook. "I have to give you credit, Cook. You are one ballsy smart-ass, no matter how you do it or how you get the job done your way. Anyway, no way. It's not going to happen. I'm not going to make myself look like an idiot. Sorry, wrong guy." There was a brief pause, Moore added, "Do you know what this man has done for this country? How many jobs he has opened up for the unemployed?"

Shawn yelled, "Yes, I'm very much aware of the stats! But this man is either a great liar, a good deceiver, or a nutcase!"

Jefferson jumped in. "This is bull crap! The man has presented you with facts, hard-core facts. We have explained in detail this man's background history and—"

Commissioner Moore cut Jefferson off. "And you need to have a seat. Stay out of this. I could arrest you for the drugs. Yeah, I know what you are doing."

Jefferson responded, "I wasn't hiding."

Moore said, "Keep beefing with me. As a matter of fact, you look stoned right now." He looked at Shawn. "What the hell are you running here, Cook? A drug den or a junkies' corner?"

Jefferson was now standing up; he was pissed off. "Yo, don't call me a junkie. I'm not a junkie, sir."

The commissioner looked at him and said, "Really?" He slightly laughed.

Jefferson responded with attitude, "Really."

Shawn knew Jefferson was getting worked up, so he intervened. "Why are you beating up on Jefferson? He's trying to get his shit straight, man. You really should be going after that psycho bastard Hollingsworth, Collingsworth, that sick mother sucker."

Jefferson responded, "Nah, Shawn, it's all good. I'm cool. Thanks for the backup, but this man put no fear in my heart."

Commissioner Moore said, "Sure, you are good, no doubt about that—good and feeling good . . . You look like you're just coming down from a trip, my man. I should run your ass in, give you thirty days with some dude name Bubba."

Jefferson looked at him. "And how about you, sir? What are you coming down from? And this Bubba dude, you seem to know him very well. Are you making this a personal reference?" He blew Moore a pretend kiss and laughed.

That took the smile off the commissioner's face as he quickly looked at Jefferson. "Excuse me. You start any rumors, you will regret it."

That was supposed to cause Jefferson to back down, but it made him more determined; he refused to back down. Jefferson slapped his chest a few times, "No fear here, bro. I've been through it, man. When you can shake death's hand and say 'Maybe next time,' your threats are nothing but Play-Doh."

There was a pause; then Jefferson moved closer to Moore; he was being held back by Shawn. Jefferson sneered in frustration, "So what are you coming down from, Curtis?"

Moore looked at Shawn. "You better talk to your boy. He's one step to making a jail cell his home for the next thirty days."

Jefferson's voice was rough. "You're going to arrest me for what? Telling the truth?"

Shawn added, "No one is getting arrested on my watch."

Moore responded, looking at Shawn, "Your watch? Whatever, Cook. You stand in the way of justice, I'll haul your ass in also. Martial artist or not, I'll stun gun your ass, having you on the floor kicking like you lost your senses . . . Be careful, Cook." Moore looked at Jefferson; he wanted him to finish what he was saying, "You were saying what? What about me, huh?"

Jefferson stood his ground, "You take one look at me, and you could tell I'll flyin'. Cool. I take one look at you, I could tell you got that cheap bottle of wine for a dollar nine."

Moore moved toward him. Jefferson, seizing the moment, said, "Wait, can you walk that straight line, Commish?"

The commissioner looked at Shawn. "You better call your watchdog off, Cook. He doesn't know who he's messin' with." The commissioner sarcastically chuckled. "I'll have your ass so fast in jail." He shook his head. "You don't know me, son."

Jefferson looked at him with a sneer. "And you don't me, coon." He shrugged his shoulders.

Shawn knew what that meant; that meant Jefferson was about to let the chips fall wherever. Shawn was trying to calm Jefferson down. The commissioner smiled as he turned to leave as he signaled his men to leave. Jefferson looked at Shawn and shook the light grip he had on his arm. Jefferson broke free as he pointed his finger at the commissioner, who was walking back to his car. Jefferson slightly smiled and said, "You know what, Commissioner, the difference between my addiction and let's say yours . . ."

Moore quickly stopped and turned around to face Jefferson. The commissioner pointed at Jefferson, saying, "I'm warning you."

Jefferson plowed forward, not giving a damn as to what the consequences might be; he said, "You started this, so I'm going to finish it. Now I get stoned, nothing to hide. But you get drunk. My high wears off rather quickly, Commissioner, compared to yours, which may take all night and even the following day. It's a hangover, too much on the brain. There is no difference between you being a functional alcoholic and me a functional drug user."

There was a pause; then Jefferson continued, "Commissioner, at least I can get in your face and talk. You have to keep poppin' those round ball mints until your breath starts smelling like old mothballs." He continued, "So before you start placing labels on folks, Commissioner, you need to see your own label. I'm not a junkie. I am a functional substance abuser. You, on the other hand, are a straight-up hard-core alcoholic with a messed-up liver."

Moore went after Jefferson. "You son of a bitch, I'll break you in two, punk!"

Jefferson went after Curtis Moore. "Bring it you, punk-ass bitch! I'm going to beat your old turkey ass. I'm going to beat your butt. I'm going to knock out whatever alcohol that is in you. I'll be your twelve-step program, punk."

Moore's men held him back while Shawn held Jefferson back. Commissioner Moore looked at Shawn and said, "You better talk to your friend, Cook. Things happen. Things happen. Accidents happen."

Jefferson yelled at Moore, "Be careful how you creep on me, punk! You better not sleep on me, Moore! Your naps will turn into nightmares, son! Believe that!"

Shawn was holding Jefferson back, allowing him to vent; he knew Moore had crossed that line with Jefferson whether he knew it or not. Jefferson said, "You have to try to set me up, sneak up on me like in elementary school. Be a man for once, coon. Why don't you come and kick my ass yourself? You have to get others to do your dirty laundry." There was a pause. Jefferson said, "Come down to the gym. Three rounds, we can settle this the old-fashioned way. The loser has to go to a twelve-month program."

Commissioner Moore was getting back in the unmarked car with his men when he heard the challenge; he felt his men were waiting and looking at him to see if he was going to accept the challenge. He sensed they were looking at him differently and that if he didn't accept the challenge, they would no doubt lose respect for him. Jefferson had called him out; he had to make a decision. Moore paused and then said, "When this thing with Cook is over, I accept your challenge. If you beat my ass, I'll go to a twelve-month program."

Jefferson added, "Not some classy cruise type of program where you sit on your ass all day and eat that high-class 'three meals and two snacks a day' crap."

The commissioner looked at him, responding, "Not a problem. I need to know what size you wear in shirt and pants." Jefferson looked at him inquisitively. Moore said, "I'm going to need the measurements to make sure the prison outfit fits you perfectly. It'll be ready for you." Moore's men chuckled as they got into the car.

Shawn knew he couldn't rely on Moore to help bring in Hollingsworth; he had to find another way to save Serenity.

Moore pointed to Shawn, "Whenever you're ready to go after that lowlife sucker, let me know, Cook. We'll nail the bastard. And, Cook, you better be right." Shawn's eyes lit up with hope. Moore continued, "Hey, send me a photo of him. I'll put a tail on him, follow him like a disease."

Complex played a soundtrack of a football game where the crowd was going wild.

The commissioner wasn't thinking about the fanfare; his main goal was hoping he wasn't making a mistake. If Cook was wrong, a lot of careers would be over, including his. He pointed to Jefferson, who stared back at him without flinching as Moore told his driver to go.

# CHAPTER 181

Jefferson had that nervous energy as he paced back and forth; he said to Shawn, "I don't know how you can be so calm. This dude has your wife."

Shawn nodded his head as he was punching and kicking the heavy bag; his punches and kicks were crisp and quick. He came up with an uppercut, follow by a left hook and then a right hook with a high kick to the bag. If this was a real person, they wouldn't have a head left.

Jefferson insisted on talking about the situation. Shawn tried to ignore him, but Jefferson wasn't having it as he continued to press the issue. He wanted Shawn to become angry; he wanted Shawn to feel what he was feeling. He wanted Shawn to have some kind of reaction.

; the punches and kicks hitting the bag sounded crisp, giving off nice-sounding pops that echoed throughout the room. Shawn said as he continued to punch and kick the bag, "Don't go by what you see. Never take your enemy for granted. If you would only go by the way they look, major mistake." He continued, "I may look calm, but trust me, deep within . . ." Shawn delivered two hard pops to the bag as he continued, "I'm just a train wreck about to happen. I'm just a few seconds from snapping, cracking, and popping, baby . . ." He delivered a hard kick and an elbow to the bag. He continued, "So don't look at what you see . . ." Shawn delivered a hard, crisp combination, left, right, uppercut. With each hit, the bag made a crisp popping sound. Shawn stood up and hit the bag with three hard rights. *Pop, pop, pop* was the sound of the bag; he looked at Jefferson. "That's lesson number one."

Shawn went over to pick up the heavy medicine ball and threw it at Jefferson, "Heads up, stay alert." He continued, "Do you know what I'm saying about not going by what you see?"

Jefferson caught the heavy ball as he grimaced. He threw it back at Shawn, saying, "Yeah . . . but . . ."

Shawn caught it while he was continuing the conversation, "You see what . . ."

He tossed it back at Jefferson, who caught it with a grimace on his face, saying, "I understand where you're . . ." He tossed it back at Shawn, who caught it as if it was a beach ball.

Shawn said, "Do you really understand my emotional pain?" He tossed it back at Jefferson with force. The heavy ball made a loud pop when it hit Jefferson's midsection.

"Uggh . . . uh, I'm trying to . . ." He tossed it back at Shawn.

Shawn caught it and was still talking. "My pain, Jay, is deep within." He hurled it back to Jefferson.

The impact slammed him hard in the stomach, causing him to move back. "Uggh, argh . . ." Jefferson lifted up the ball and didn't have the strength to throw it. He fell to one knee as he dropped the solid ball; his head was slightly down. He was out of breath and in pain.

Shawn walked up to him, placing his hand on his shoulder. "Hey, you okay?"

Jefferson was still on one knee with his head down; he looked like the statue of *The Thinker*. In this case, he looked more like the praying man. Jefferson waved Shawn off with a nod; in between breaths, he said, "I'm good."

Shawn looked at him with concern. "Are you sure?"

Jefferson gave Shawn a weak thumbs-up with a head nod just as week. "I'm . . . I'm o . . . I'm o . . . kay."

Shawn, still looking concerned and worried, slightly smiled and touched Jefferson on the shoulder. "Okay, I'm going for a run. Want to come?"

Jefferson, with the other hand, gave a thumbs-down as he slowly shook his head. In between breaths, he told Shawn to enjoy. "Nah, you go ahead. Knock yourself out. While I'm down here on my knee, I might as well meditate and pray."

Shawn asked, "Cool, when did you start that?"

Jefferson replied, "Uh, just now."

# CHAPTER 182

Shawn got back from his run; he looked tense. The run helped him to refocus. He had his headset on.

Complex said, "Shawn, I can do a quick scan and check all the phone calls you received and see if there is anything we could use."

Shawn shook his head. "No, keep the line open. The man is airtight, but he's going to slip up. We just have to be ready when that happens."

Complex agreed, then said, "When you get a chance, check on Jay." Shawn asked what the problem was. Complex responded, "What did you guys do this morning?"

Shawn replied, "We worked out."

Complex's colors flashed. "Uh-huh, so that's why he kept asking me for painkillers and Epsom salt and, oh, sports cream. I asked him which type of sports cream. He said he didn't care." She continued, "I can tell just by his movement, he was walking as if he was walking on pins and needles and glass. Shawn, why did you work that boy so hard?"

Shawn laughed. "Oh, so he's sore from the workout . . . He didn't say anything to me. I left him here in a praying position."

Complex said, "Well, hmmm . . . okay."

Shawn laughed, saying, "Oh, he's sore from the workout, huh? Interesting." He laughed again. "I could imagine if he had a full workout, he'd probably be crawling . . . Where is he now?"

Complex said, "I think in the backyard nursing his wounds."

Shawn gave a dismissive wave of his hand with a light chuckle. "He'll be okay."

Complex just shook her head and said, "I'm beginning to like Jay. He has that swagger about him . . . I can see why you like him."

Shawn slightly smiled. "Trust me, it has nothing to do with his so-called swagger. He's just a good—"

Complex said, "Incoming from the commissioner."

Shawn asked Complex to put it through. "Commissioner, what's up?"

Curt Moore sounded tense and agitated. "Anything?"

Shawn shook his head and said, "Not yet. We know he's no longer at the Hilton."

Moore asked, "How do you know that?"

Shawn responded, "I have my sources."

Moore, getting more agitated, said, "You and your damn sources, Cook. Who are these people?"

Shawn lightly laughed. "I couldn't tell you that. It would blow their cover."

Moore made a gruff sound as he continued, "Regarding this sicko Hollingsworth, I can put the squeeze on his ass and flush him out and make him make a move."

Shawn responded strongly, "That's a negative. He may be an ass, and I can't stand him. But he's good, and he's dangerous and has connections, connections as far as the White House. No, let him keep thinking he's in control. When I drop that load on him that I know who he is, that's when I'll need your men to step up and step in and nail that sucker . . . No half steppin' on this, Moore. Make sure all the men that you are using are clean."

Moore nodded, even more frustrated because Shawn was speaking to him as if this was his first time on the merry-go-round; he said, "Cook."

Shawn got the message, saying, "Okay, your party."

The commissioner responded gruffly, "We'll handle it. We'll nail the son of a bitch."

# CHAPTER 183

Two hours later

Complex called Shawn, who was playing a one-on-one basketball game with Jefferson. "Shawn, I think it's him. The number is unknown."

Shawn said with a little bit of nervous energy, "Okay, patch him through and try to trace the number and the possible location—"

Complex cut him off. "I know, babe. Incoming."

Shawn waited a few seconds just to control his breathing. "Hello." He recognized the voice immediately.

"Mr. Cook, the game is getting interesting, isn't it? We are coming down to the final showdown, Mr. Cook. Isn't this exciting?"

Shawn was starting to get agitated even though the ball was in his court; just hearing the stranger's voice sent his frustrations into overdrive. The stranger continued, "Mr. Cook, I know you're not really up for talking, and that is okay. So I'll talk for both of us." There was that stupid laugh as he continued, "But as I was saying, you have been a worthy opponent. If it wasn't for the fact that I want to destroy you, you and I would have been an exceptional team."

Shawn barked back, "I don't think so, not in a million years! You are sick! You don't need a business partner—you need a straitjacket in a blue room, you crazy sick son of a—"

The stranger raised his voice. "Be careful, Mr. Cook. I still hold the cards, and I still hold the beautiful Serenity Cook in my hands. So you better be careful—no, you better be extracareful."

Shawn blew out a breath of frustration and said, "Skip all of that. I have the key. Where is my wife?"

The stranger looked puzzled. "The key?"

Shawn sneered into the phone, "Yes, the key that I got from the young man on the train, that key!"

The stranger smiled. "Oh, that key. What about it?"

Shawn raised his voice. "I have it. Now where is my wife? Keep your end of the bargain, stranger."

The stranger took it lightly. "Oh yes, that . . . Hmmm . . . well, the score is tied, Mr. Cook."

Shawn Cook felt his blood boiling. "You lying son of a bitch, my last challenge put me in the lead! You need to keep track of what the hell is going on."

Shawn heard Complex say, "Shawn, I got it."

The stranger raised his voice, saying, "Your wife will pay for that one, Mr. Cook, but back to business. You may be right, sir. But since I hold the cards and control this game, I make the rules of this game, and that can't be disputed. It's not open for discussion."

The stranger told Shawn he would keep in touch and hung up the phone.

to himself; he was waiting for one more phone call to come in, and then he'd put his plan in effect. The stranger told Shawn he will keep in touch and hung up the phone. In the past, Shawn would have been pissed off at the stranger hanging up on him. He would have thrown the phone against the wall or something else crazy. He couldn't stand the idea of someone backing out of a deal, but it said a lot about the person he was dealing with; and with the stranger, Shawn knew he was as dangerous as a poisonous snake. A person with no class, no character, no foundational substance or integrity is very dangerous in every way. In a way, Shawn wasn't surprised; businessman or not, the stranger was a lowlife piece of crap, but at least he knew how he was going to approach Hollingsworth.

Shawn had received more information on the man from Complex; the man was a walking disaster, a troubled soul as he was referred to by Hollingsworth's priest. Hollingsworth had everything that would make any person them feel satisfied and content, but this man had always chased after his father's approval and always fell short. According to sources, Hollingsworth would have bent over backward to kiss his own ass if he could just to please his father. His father was a straight-up no-nonsense straight shooter; he always looked at his son as weak, a weak link in the chain; he even told him that. The disappearance of his father rocked the business world, especially Wall Street. They found his body floating in the ocean weeks later; the body had decomposed so badly they had to use dental records to identify that it was Hollingsworth's father.

Hollingsworth took over the business; he brought out his siblings and fired everyone that worked with his father. He didn't want to have anything to do with his father.

Shawn asked, "Where did you find this information?"

Complex's animated picture smiled and said, "I have my sources, baby."

Shawn said, "Complex."

Complex said, "His brothers and sisters wrote a book called *Caine and Abel*." There was a pause; then Complex continued, "But I found this out also—Hollingsworth's family name is really Collingsworth, which we now know that Hollingsworth uses both names."

; he'd put it on the back burner of his mind to keep it warm. He said, "Complex."

Complex knew what Shawn wanted. "I have it. It took some doing. He covered his tracks very well. It is an unlisted number."

Shawn was impressed. "How did you manage to get the information?"

Complex responded, "I'm good at what I do. You know that, baby."

Jefferson echoed, "Baby."

Shawn responded to Complex's comment, "Yes, you are good at what you do. And the 'baby' thing is a designer thing. I'll tell you later."

Complex smiled and winked, then continued, "Okay, baby, what's next?"

Jefferson replied, "If I was eavesdropping, I would have thought you guys were lovers. I mean babe this and babe that—if I didn't know better, sounds like hot stuff."

Complex smiled and flirted with Jefferson, saying, "Sounds like the little boy is jealous. You want Mama to call you baby also?"

Jefferson just thought about how Complex changed her voice and made it sound so sexy; he responded, "Yes, I mean no, I mean . . . maybe."

Complex responded, "Ah, no. You want that to happen? Earn it." She let out a throaty laugh and smiled at Jefferson.

Jefferson looked at the image, shook his head, and said, "Wow."

Shawn interrupted the moment, saying, "Hey, Jay, you and Gordon could have the same thing."

Gordon added, "I could put that in my memory chip."

Complex responded, "Yeah, sounds like a great idea."

Jefferson responded, "Uh, no, I don't think so. I mean, Gordon, you're cool with the whole nine. But we need to keep what we have professional. You going around calling me baby with that male voice is not cool."

Gordon responded, "Well, sir, at one time, you wanted me to call you dawg."

Complex reacted. "Dawg."

Jefferson responded, "Long story, right, Shawn?"

Shawn responded, "Huh?"

Jefferson responded, "Traitor. You know exactly what I'm talking about." He continued speaking to Gordon. "We're cool. That's enough for me."

Gordon responded, "No problem, sir."

Jefferson nodded his head and said, "Good."

Shawn said, "Okay, folks, let's get back to work." He said to Complex, "Get me the commissioner."

A few seconds later, Commissioner Curtis Moore came on the line. "Moore here."

Shawn wasted no time. "Give me an update on what's going on."

Moore said, "We have located the husband and placed him in a safe house, and even as we speak, I have my men picking up their two sons and bringing them to the safe house."

Shawn was concerned. "These men of yours, are they clean? Can you trust them?"

Moore said, "Yes, handpicked by me. Plus they are related to me. They try some monkey business, I know where they live, where they go to work out, and which ones are coming to dinner for Thanksgiving. Don't worry, it's covered."

Shawn nodded his head. "Sounds good. Anything else?"

The commissioner said, "We're waiting for you to let us know when to get this lowlife piece of crap."

Shawn said, "Well, at least we're on the same page on what Hollingsworth is doing." There was a pause; then he said, "Stand by. We're about to make that move."

# CHAPTER 184

he commissioner, "I'm going to shoot some hoops." Jefferson could tell Shawn was restless; he thought about going for a drive. He had this nervous energy he needed to get rid of; he thought about it and said to himself, *If I go for a drive, that will break some of this tension I'm feeling. But then again, to disappear at a time like this isn't a very wise idea.* He decided he needed to stay close.

Two hours later

Shawn and Jefferson played a couple of games. Jefferson lost both games. He thought Shawn was going hard the entire game; he looked tense. He jammed the ball twice while Jefferson was checking him; he apologized for playing so hard. "Sorry, bro, a lot of pent-up anger and frustration."

Jefferson just nodded his head when Complex called Shawn. "Incoming call from Moore." Shawn was still feeling on edge.

Moore said, "Okay, Cook, we have the husband and their two sons settled. Now what?"

Shawn, still looking tense, said, "Time to flush this punk out. Be on standby."

Forty-five minutes later

Complex said to Shawn, "Shawn, forty-five minutes is up. You ready to do this?"

Shawn took in a deep breath and replied, "Yeah."

Complex dialed the number; there was a silence, and then there was a voice that had a surprised and unsure tone. "Hello." Shawn could tell the person was caught off guard. "Hel-hello, who is this? Hello." Shawn did not say anything.

The stranger was getting upset. "Listen, if you can't speak, please hang up the damn phone. You have the wrong number. This is a private line. Whoever you are, you have the wrong number. WHO IS THIS, AND HOW THE HELL DID YOU GET THIS NUMBER!"

ed for Complex to hang up. Complex disconnected the call. Jefferson was surprised the call disconnected; he said, "What are you doing? You had homeboy crapping on himself. Why did you let him off the hook? You had that son of bitch. You should have finish him." Jefferson shook his head.

Shawn said, "Complex."

Complex smiled and said, "Yes, sir. Mr. Cook allowed this lowlife piece of crap to think, just to think about what just happened. Right now, he is doing a number two in his pants because no one is supposed to have that number. Mr. Hollingsworth is very concerned. Right now, he is probably calling up the phone company and cursing them out. He wants to use another phone, but he wouldn't dare do that because his ego and his pride are too big . . ."

Jefferson finished the assumption, saying, "Therefore, he's anticipating another call from the phone company, and that's when Shawn will . . ."

Shawn smiled. "You were doing good, kid."

Jefferson looked confused. "What? That's when you . . ." Jefferson stopped when he saw Shawn shaking his head.

Shawn said, pointing at Complex, "Not me, but Complex."

Jefferson looked at Complex's picture, and she smiled; he smiled as well and said, "Ahh, sugar, honey, and iced tea, go with your BAD self, baby. Do your thing."

Complex smiled and said, "Stay and watch, honey." She added, "It's showtime."

# CHAPTER 185

Hollingsworth paced his hotel room; he had already called the phone company. They informed him that the only thing they could do was issue him a new phone with a new number. Hollingsworth yelled at the person on the line, "I'm a businessman, you measly little idiot! I change my number, all my contacts will be lost, or they wouldn't know how to reach me, you imbecile! Do you understand that? Now somebody better fix this problem!"

The agent apologized for what had happened. He was more concerned about being reported by Hollingsworth. Hollingsworth couldn't care less about some freckle-faced young punk; he just wanted the situation to be fixed. Hollingsworth said to the manager, "You better launch an investigation while I'm still here, and I want to know what the outcome is. You understand that?"

The manager said, "Yes, sir, Mr. Hollingsworth."

Hollingsworth paused and continued, "I want to know who had the nerve, the gall to call me on my private phone, and how the hell he got my number." The manager asked him if he wanted him to use his phone to call who he needed to call. Hollingsworth yelled, "No, you idiot! I'm expecting a phone call. For the person to call me, I can't have this line tied up."

The phone chimed. Hollingsworth touched his Bluetooth; his voice was loud. "Hello."

The voice on the other end said, "This is the operator, sir. We are trying to track down the person who is calling you, sir. So far, we narrowed the search down, which is pretty good, to about one thousand people."

Hollingsworth repeated the number. "What! A thousand! I don't have time. You have to do better than that."

Complex, who was acting like the operator, said, "Sir, we are doing the best we can. Oh, by the way, is this the first time you are speaking to someone?"

Hollingsworth was starting to get upset; he wasn't used to incompetence. He was used to identifying the problem and fixing it. Hollingsworth yelled in the phone, "NO!"

Complex said, "Sir, no need to yell. Please lower your voice. I can hear you very well."

Hollingsworth raised his voice. "Don't you tell me how to speak and—"

Complex cut Hollingsworth off; he couldn't believe she did that as his breath got caught in his throat. Complex said, "Sir, if you continue to yell and scream and act like a jackass . . ."

Mr. Hollingsworth stuttered as he made an attempt to catch his breath; he was shocked—no one ever spoke to him in such a manner.

Complex continued, "As I was saying, if you are determined to continue this conversation, you will give me no other choice but to put my supervisor on the phone."

Hollingsworth wanted to laugh. "Put your what?" Complex tried to repeat what she had said about putting her supervisor on. Hollingsworth said, "I heard what you said, you annoying bitch. Put your supervisor on the damn phone. I—"

Complex disconnected the call. Hollingsworth stood there, looking at his phone. "Hello? Hello? Hello? Stupid whore hung up on me." He slammed the phone down hard on the desk. People began to stop and look to see what was going on. Hollingsworth, still seething, looked around at the faces staring at him; he said, "What are you looking at? Mind your own damn business!"

Hollingsworth's bodyguards and personal aide tried to calm him down; the aide said, "Sir, you are creating a scene. You are drawing attention, which is the last thing you want, sir." The aide gently took him by the arm. "Sir, please, let's go upstairs."

Hollingsworth snatched his arm from her light grip. He, at this point, had lost his cool; he said, "Keep your hands off me! Who do you think you are? You can shine my shoes and clean up the mess I make, nothing else. Do you know who I am, huh? Don't you ever forget. You better recognize who I am. I pay your salary, and I pay you well, bitch. Don't you ever put your hands on me again, you understand?" She nodded her head.

Shawn said to Complex, "Put the squeeze on him. Time to reel that SOB in, and if I'm right, he'll react. We just have to be ready. Patch me into the commissioner."

# CHAPTER 186

Hollingsworth had gone up to his room; he had apologized to his staff. He was now pacing the floor, trying to figure out how someone got his unlisted number; he was thinking when his cell chimed. He answered the phone, sounding exhausted; all that fight seemed to have gone. He'd never experienced this before. Hollingsworth answered, "Hello."

Complex said, "This is the operator."

Hollingsworth recognized the voice; it was the same woman that hung up the phone the last time they spoke. His anger was returning. "What the hell do you want!"

Complex said, "Sir, let's not . . ." She stopped and said, "I'm not going there with you, sir. Been there and done that. It's not going to happen." There was a pause; then Complex added, "We are trying to help you, sir, but this nasty attitude really needs to be put in check and—"

Hollingsworth cut her off and said in that menacing tone, "Be so ever careful. You really don't know who I am, do you? I will find out who you are, and I will make sure that the only job you will find is making buttons in a sweatshop. I promise you that! Now put your supervisor on."

Shawn hesitated for a second, and then he spoke.

# CHAPTER 187

Shawn slightly altered his voice, making it sound a little deeper. "Yeah."

Hollingsworth was caught off guard; he gave a surprised look, looking at the phone. He said under his breath, "Yeah? What the hell is going on around here?" Hollingsworth said, "What do you mean 'yeah'? Didn't that dizzy broad explain to you what was going on?"

Shawn replied, "You need to watch your mouth, sir, or I will disconnect this call."

Mr. Hollingsworth made a light chuckle. "Do you know who you are speaking to?"

Shawn responded, "I don't give a damn who you are—president, pope, or pauper. You just watch your mouth and show some damn RESPECT."

Mr. Hollingsworth said, "What, excuse me?"

Shawn replied, "There is no excuse for you."

Hollingsworth was shocked having someone speak to him like that; his voice rose a bit as he sneered, "Who is this? I demand to know."

Shawn made his voice regular; he said with anger seeping through every single word, "Game over, you lowlife scumbag piece of crap."

Hollingsworth was caught off guard again, but he recovered rather quickly even though his voice still sounded shaky. Hollingsworth said, "Well, Mr. Cook, you are a very resourceful adversary. There is no doubt in my mind you a good, worthy opponent." He lightly chuckled. "Tell me, Mr. Cook, I wondered how you got my number . . . Well, it doesn't matter . . . I guess it's my move."

Shawn asked, "Is it really?"

Hollingsworth chuckled; then with a tinge of doubt, he asked, "Isn't it, Mr. Cook?"

Shawn did not say anything; he wanted the doubts in Hollingsworth's head to swirl around like a revolving door. Shawn finally said, "No, it's not, Hollingsworth. I'm sorry, I meant to say Collingsworth." Shawn could hear Hollingsworth's breath get caught in his chest. Shawn continued, "Yeah, that's right. Got your name, your unlisted phone number, and now where you're staying. Sorry, I was meaning to ask you, how is the Hilton?" Hollingsworth was still holding his breath. Shawn said, "You're going to pass out if you don't start breathing." He lightly laughed.

Hollingsworth said with disgust, "What are you talking about?"

Shawn responded, "It's over, Hollingsworth. You lose. I'm coming after you, Hollingsworth. You are a dead man. As I promise, you will die a more terrible death than your so-called look-alike fake twin brother. You spent a lot of money to make your face look like his. and in the end, earth to earth and dust to dust, ashes to ashes." Shawn disconnected the call.

Hollingsworth was still in shock as he continued to hold the phone, just staring at nothing; he was stunned. He felt as if he was about to throw up his food. He was still standing there, staring at nothing in particular when he realized that everything was starting to unravel. Hollingsworth didn't know how Shawn got the number; maybe someone gave it to him. He thought only one person could have given him that number; it had to have been Evans. He'd been acting somewhat strange as if he had something to hide. Every time he called there, Evans seemed so preoccupied, busy, or busy doing something; those times when Hollingsworth asked what he was doing, Evans told him he was just relaxing playing solitaire, probably not by himself, but with Serenity.

worth took a paperweight and threw it against the wall. He had to think fast; he had to stay two steps ahead of Shawn.

Hollingsworth signaled his driver to go and get the car. He signaled for the bodyguards to come over; he wrote an address down and said to them, "This is where you need to go. Set the explosives near the kitchen area." Hollingsworth continued, "I don't care how you do it. Don't disappoint me."

One of the bodyguards asked him what they should do with the rest of the explosives. Hollingsworth looked at them and said, "I don't give a damn what you do with them. Use your imagination. When I call, you set off the explosives. You understand?"

They both nodded and then turned to leave. One of the bodyguards asked his partner, "Do you know where this place we have to go is?"

The other bodyguard looked at the address and said, "Yeah, this is Shawn Cook's restaurant." Then they drove off.

# CHAPTER 188

Hollingsworth looked at his watch. "We must leave. Let me call Bobby Lee. He owes me a favor. Time to pay up."

# CHAPTER 189

Shawn told Complex to connect him with the commissioner. Moore immediately came on the line. "What's up Cook?"

Shawn said without hesitation, "Arrest Hollingsworth. He's up to something."

Moore said, "We'll get him."

About twenty minutes later, Hollingsworth called Shawn. "Okay, Mr. Cook, I surrender. A deal is a deal. Here is the address to where your wife is."

Hollingsworth was getting ready to give directions on how to get to the place when Shawn cut him off. "I know how to get there."

Hollingsworth nodded his head. "Good." He disconnected the call.

Complex said, "Shawn, look at me." Shawn turned to look at Complex, who said, "Good, you don't have 'stupid' written on your forehead . . ." She became serious. "Please tell me you realize this is some kind of a trap, babe. It has ambush written all over it."

Jefferson walked up to them. "What's up? Just by the look on your face, Wall Street, something is not cool."

Shawn said to Jefferson, "I just received a call from Hollingsworth. He's surrendering. He also told me where to find Serenity. I can come and get her . . . game over."

Jefferson was excited. "Are you serious? Wow, it's over! He's waving the white flag of surrender. You won . . ."

Complex said to Jefferson, "Jay, look at me." He turned to look at Complex, who said, "Really, Jay?"

Jefferson thought, and then it hit him. "Wait a second, Wall Street, we're talking about Hollingsworth the snake, not Santa Claus. That's got to be a trap, man . . ."

Complex responded, "Whew! I was getting ready to give you the Dumb Ass Award." She continued, "Thank you, somebody is on the same page."

Jefferson smiled. "That's right, babe, we—"

Complex cut him off. "First of all, don't call me babe. And second, as for being on the same page, blue moons do occur every now and then." Jefferson looked dejected; he looked at Complex's face on the monitor. She smiled, winked at him, and said, "Relax, big guy, just pulling your chain."

Shawn said in a serious tone, "Can we get back to this?"

Complex flat-out said, "Get back to what? Shawn honey, it's a trap. He's trying to set you up."

Shawn fired back, "I agree, you guys are right! I know it's an ambush. But he has me against the wall, between a rock and a hard place. If I don't go and Serenity is there, I may lose her forever. If I go and get there and the place is rigged, we all die. Do you guys see what I'm saying?" He looked at Jefferson.

Jefferson said, "Not really." He looked at Shawn with a question mark on his face.

Shawn said, "For better or for worse, in sickness or in health, till death do us part. I love that woman, man. I would die for her, and if this is an ambush, they better hit me with everything they have because this will be the day that whoever will find out my love and devotion and commitment to the woman I love so deeply and dearly without a question inseparable."

# CHAPTER 190

Serenity knew something wasn't right. For the last forty-eight hours, Evans had been acting strange; he hadn't been himself. He had seemed more guarded and more protective of her; he didn't want her out of his sight. It wasn't that he didn't trust her; it went deeper—it was as if he was protecting her. He was cautious even when he would go into one of the rooms of the house; he wanted to go first to make sure it was safe. He covered up all the windows in the house so no one would be able to look in. There was no doubt in her mind that he'd been very kind, extremely kind to her, but something else was going on. Serenity could sense it; she could see it in his attitude and behavior. She had caught him working out more on fighting techniques. She wanted to ask him what was wrong, but she wasn't sure how to start such a conversation, but she knew.

Some days, she found Evans in a room by himself, thinking out loud as if he was planning. From the time he kidnapped her, she always saw him as quiet and reserved, which she had come to know the man, but what she had been seeing for the last few days had been someone else. Something was on his mind; he would take phone calls into another area of the house. Serenity could hear him on the phone at times becoming aggressive. She knew it wasn't the stranger, his boss; it was someone else that he had been business partners with, someone with whom the partnership and friendship had crashed.

Serenity asked Evans one day if he was okay; he looked at her, not in a sexual way. Nevertheless, the look frightened her; it was as if he was looking through her into the very depths of her soul. That troubled her; she didn't know what to make of it. Was he about to snap?

She had come to like the man that was holding her hostage, if that is what you want to call it. Even though Serenity had come to like Evans, her heart, mind, body, and soul longed for her husband.

One day, Serenity and Evans were at the table playing a game of Spades when his phone chimed. He pressed his Bluetooth, already knowing who was calling; he responded, "Yes, sir?"

Hollingsworth was on the other end. "Evans, how are things coming along?"

Evans immediately knew something was wrong; something was in the stranger's voice. Evans nodded his head. "Good, sir." He added, "What's up?"

Hollingsworth lightly chuckled and said, "Evans, that's what I like about you. You like to get to the point, no time for chitchat or small talk, no time for game playing. I hate when someone tries to play me . . ." There was a pause; then the stranger continued, "I like to keep things businesslike. If something is not working out as expected, cut your losses. You and I are like that, aren't we?" Evans did not respond as the stranger continued, "I've always admired that in you, Evans."

Evans looked at the phone; he looked at Serenity, who wrinkled her nose at him, indicating she was baffled. What was going on? He shrugged his shoulders as if to say he didn't have a clue what was going on, but something was odd with the conversation. It seemed as if the stranger was hinting at something, as if he knew something Evans did not know. That bothered Evans; he asked, "Sir, are you okay?" He gave a fake laugh of assurance after he asked the question. Evans had to be careful how he worded any question; if the question had certain implications of overconcern, it would make Evans look as if he was hiding or avoiding something.

The stranger gave his own light chuckle. "Of course . . . why do you ask?"

Evans hesitated at first; then he spoke. "You don't seem like yourself."

The stranger responded, "Interesting . . . I'm sitting here thinking the same thing about you. Isn't that interesting?"

The stranger let out that fake laugh again; it caught Evans's attention and not in a good way. His instincts were blasting all over the place. Maybe he was just nervous. The stranger knew Evans wasn't new to this game; he didn't want to give him any ideas to think otherwise. The stranger said,

"No, I'm fine. I'm just running behind schedule. I have one more task to do, as much as I hate to do it. But business is business, right?"

Those vibes, those instincts Evans was just feeling were getting stronger. *But why?* he thought.

The stranger changed the subject; both men could feel the tension building up. "Oh, how is our guest doing?"

Evans was trying to put this jigsaw puzzle together; something was definitely wrong. He was thinking hard when the voice of his employer interrupted his thoughts. "Evans, are you still there?"

Evans nodded. "Yes, sorry, sir. I was just thinking about something. I'm good."

The stranger said in an eerie tone, "I know you are, Evans. You're very good."

Evans didn't know what to make of that last statement. His thoughts once again drifted, and he was brought back by the stranger; this time, what the stranger had to say really had Evans's attention.

# CHAPTER 191

Evans disconnected the call, looking very troubled. Serenity, with a concerned expression on her face, looked at him. "What?" He shook his head. She pressed the issue, "Evans, what is it? Tell me."

Evans looked at her and said, "My employer is coming here."

Serenity nervously smiled. "When? Today? Tomorrow? When?" She evaded the reality of the present moment as she tried to duck into another day to put off the inevitable. "Talk to me." She rubbed his forearm. "Please."

Evans looked at her; she was so beautiful. He looked at her hands and how nice it felt against his skin; he slowly pulled away. He had to; her magic was too strong. As he pulled away, he noticed her hands were slightly shaking; she started nibbling on her lower lip. She pushed back her hair behind her ears; she knew this day was going to eventually come. She swallowed a dose of reality. Serenity looked at him, nervous; trying her best to stop shaking, she asked, "Is this it, Evans? Is this where this story ends, huh?" Her glassy eyes dropped a tear or two. She had to hear it from him.

Evans sincerely shook his head. "No, it couldn't be. There are things I'm more than certain that still need to be completed." He didn't know that Shawn knew his employer's identity. He paused and said, "If I inquire, that makes me look suspicious. I have to go along with it for now." He paused and said, looking right into her beautiful button eyes, "I'm not going to let anything happen to you . . . I promise."

Serenity was taken aback by his declaration; she looked down in her lap. With her beautiful long eyelashes, she looked up at him. "When?"

He looked away from her, and the word came out like a whisper. "Today."

Serenity's breath got caught in her throat as she covered her mouth, saying, "Today? Tonight? This afternoon? This—"

Evans cut her off and said, "Sometime this morning . . . He's on his way now."

The air in Serenity got sucked up as she made a suction sound covering her mouth. He noticed she was still shaking, even more; he had to comfort her. He had to give her words of hope. "Don't worry, I'll be right here. Even if he looks at you the wrong way, I'll carve his heart out of his chest or anyone that tries to hurt you, for that matter."

Evans's hand; it felt so strong. She was grateful and thankful for him as she put her head down as the tears fell on her hands. It was such a strange feeling, yet it felt that there was such a strong connection there sealed by her tears. He would have had sex with most women, sex for protection or the simple fact he had such a strong presence about him that women seemed to fall for the idea of that positive and confident attitude and they developed a dependable attraction for him. But with Serenity, there wasn't a desire just to have sex—he just wanted to protect her, with no strings attached.

Evans slowly pulled away from her hand; he hesitated. With a slight stutter, he said, "Li-listen, we need some food in this place."

She asked, "You want me to go with you?"

Evans said "yes" in his head, but "no" came out of his mouth. He said, "I would love your company, but I think it's safer to stay here and lie low. The stranger is up to something. With you out there, you become an easy target. At least here, you have options of flight or fight."

Serenity nodded her head. "Okay, I understand."

He wanted to grab her and kiss her so bad. He slightly stuttered a bit and said, "I'm going to get a few items like some . . . some . . . ah, some . . ." Evans's arms were moving, trying to explain what he needed to get from the store. Serenity turned her head to avoid from laughing; he stopped with the hand movements and said, "As you can see, I'm not used to this . . ." He stopped and looked at her. "Wait. Admit, are you laughing at me?" Serenity covered her mouth and shook her head, trying her best not to laugh; he said, "Serenity, you are indeed laughing at me."

She tried to compose herself as she was trying to catch her breath; she said, "I'm sorry, you look so adorable." She continued, "I'm not laughing at you."

Evans looked around and back at her. "Correct me if I'm wrong, but I don't see anyone else."

Serenity started the giggles again, covering her mouth; he thought the way she giggled, the way her hands covered her mouth was so priceless. She said firmly, "I wasn't laughing at you." She paused and said, "Well, maybe a little."

He chuckled, and then he started laughing as well, a very rare occasion since she'd been with him. Evans said, "Wow." He shook his head. "Listen, this food-shopping business is all new for me."

She had composed herself and said, "This would look great on your resume—big and strong kidnapper is a teddy bear deep within that knows how to go food shopping." Serenity looked at him with a slight smile; he looked at her with a slight blush. She added, "That also blushes."

Evans wanted to make a move toward her, but she already belonged to someone she so dearly loved. He said, "Shawn is a lucky man. You are everything a man would want in a woman." He stood there as if he was glued to the floor. She looked up at him with those cute big light brown button eyes, a beautiful nose with her perfect, he could only imagine, multipurpose mouth that provided wonders of satisfaction. Evans was starting to feel uncomfortable in a shy way; he looked around, blew out a breath of relief, and said, "Sorry, I'll be back."

Serenity asked him again if she could come; she thought afterward that the word "come" might not have been a good choice at the time, in that moment. He cleaned it up and told her again it wouldn't be safe or wise; it would be best if she stayed here. She thought about it again and agreed.

Evans turned and left; he said, "I'll see you in a few. Just stay in your room. We need to play it safe like the real thing, okay?"

She nodded her head. He didn't want to leave her; he wished she could be with him forever.

# CHAPTER 192

Hollingsworth called Shawn. "It's unfortunate things must end on such a terrible note. I wanted this thing to play itself out. Really, I did. I wanted this story, this saga, this epic, this drama to end between good and bad, between right and wrong, between evil and redemption." He paused for a brief second and continued, "Yeah, Mr. Cook, we've had our differences and preferences—"

Shawn cut him off. "No, Hollingsworth, we didn't. You make it sound as if your brother's doing wasn't wrong, but you are sadly mistaken and deceived. His act was pure evil to the tenth degree. If you can't see that, you are as blind as he was." Shawn was getting worked up again as he gritted his teeth and sneered into the phone, "Your brother—humph, if that's what you want to call him—was evil incarnate like you! You may feel you have a certain purpose or destiny, and you do because folks like you and your brother go to hell every day because of the lies and deceptions they believe in. They're all down there—Hitler, Capone, Napoleon, Manson. The list goes on and on. When I catch you, that's where I'm going to send you, along with them and your brother. You are pure evil, and you will pay for it in eternity!"

Hollingsworth was angry. "You're waving your righteous flag like your ancestors did. They were punished and killed in the most brutal way, and yet they are in our so-called history books not as heroes, but as martyrs. At least my brother was going to take action against the hypocrisy and abuse of this country against innocent people."

Shawn yelled into the phone, "So what your brother was going to do was kill innocent people that had nothing—absolutely nothing—to do with his crazy cause!"

Hollingsworth casually said, "Sometimes sacrifice is needed."

Shawn said, "And yours would be appreciated. The bottom line, Hollingsworth, Collingsworth—whatever the hell your name is—is you are going down like I promised you. And oh, by the way, all of your assets are being shut down, frozen as we speak, you lowlife piece of crap."

Hollingsworth's anger was boiling like a pot on the stove; he said, "You made a grave mistake, Mr. Cook! You want to hijack my hard-earned money—"

Shawn cut him off. "That you had folks slave for you and sacrifice for you! I know who you are, Hollingsworth. You're like an apple where you may look red and nice on the outside, yeah. But on the inside, you're rotten and poison. You may have some people fooled. But I got your number, and I'm coming for you, punk!"

# Chapter 193

Hollingsworth nervously called and spoke to Bobby Lee, who was the one whose skull Hollingsworth planted a chip in to track his every move. If Bobby Lee traveled too far, the chip would send a terrible pain to his head. Bobby, who was watching the house where Evans and Serenity were staying, said, "Yeah, Evans is leaving the house. The chick is in there by herself."

Hollingsworth said, "Excellent! Move quickly while Evans is out. Go in the house and bring that bitch to me." Bobby Lee consented. The stranger continued, "Meet me in the rear of the Bay Plaza parking area." Hollingsworth disconnected the call.

# Chapter 194

Evans had completed what he called a mission, a major mission—food shopping. He couldn't believe how many machines or computers he wasn't used to; he knew he looked like someone that came out of the Dark Ages. That's what happens when a person is so disconnected from the real world—mass confusion. It took a few shoppers, mostly women, to guide and help him; they thought it was so cute. This big, strong man was like a child in a big store looking for their mommy. He thanked them, and some of them smiled with a phone number. "Any time you need help, give me a call. I'm just around the corner. You could probably see that nice brick house from here." Evans thought to himself, *Oh yeah, among the rows of other brick homes.* Her voice brought his attention back to her. "At 2675 King Boulevard." She smiled with a flirtatious wink and headed off to her car, swaying her ass off.

All of this was new to Evans. He never went shopping, maybe for a soda or something sweet. Other than that, he was working on one of his contract assignments; or his maid would come in at least three days a week to clean, stock up the refrigerator, or leave his meals out labeled for each day he was expected to return. One day, she left instructions on how to use the microwave and the oven. She would do his laundry, except for the underwear; he'd drop those off with Susan, the owner of the Laundromat. Susan was kind enough to bring it to him, of course, for payment in return, not necessarily money.

So now Evans was getting a taste of what or a fraction of what his maid did; but he felt this was something he could do once he learned. In the meantime, he would make sure she'd get a bonus for Christmas. Overall, he was proud of himself that in one day he became domesticated, the first steps of becoming a homemaker. Serenity was going to be so proud of him.

He was coming to grips that she wasn't his and would never be; he thought and slightly smiled. He could live with that. These last several days with Serenity Cook opened his eyes.

His phone chimed; he didn't bother to see who it was. Evans touched his Bluetooth. "Yeah?"

Hollingsworth was surprised; he repeated the street greeting, "Yeah? Interesting, Mr. Evans, your professionalism since this case has started has declined . . . hmmm . . . somewhat. Don't you think, sir, hmmm?"

Evans tried to downplay it. "No, sir, I'm still on board. I'm still sharp, sir. I'm very much aware of what is going on, Mr. X."

Hollingsworth said, "Oh, I hope so, Mr. Evans. I would be truly disappointed if that wasn't the case, sir." There was a pause; then the stranger caught Evans by surprise.

Mr. Hollingsworth asked, "May I speak with Mrs. Cook, sir?" Evans snapped his fingers and cursed under his breath. Hollingsworth asked, "What is the problem, Mr. Evans?"

Evans hesitated. He sounded a little nervous at first, but he recovered quickly. "Uh, nothing, Mr. X."

Hollingsworth responded, "Good. Please put Serenity Cook on the phone, Mr. Evans."

Evans knew he had to come clean, not to try to squirm out of it; he said, "Mr. X, uh . . . I left Serenity, I mean Mrs. Cook . . ."

Mr. Hollingsworth said to himself, *Too late, hmmm . . . first-name basis again.*

As Evans finished his sentence, saying, "Back at the house, but the place is secure, sir."

Hollingsworth sounded calm. "You left Mrs. Cook by herself? Mr. Evans, isn't that risky, let alone dangerous?"

Evans swallowed, thinking. "Yes, sir, if she wasn't secure. But she is secure. The room I have her in is also secure. plus I have the key to get in or come out of the room. The house has been shut down, sir."

Hollingsworth was nice and calm, which made Evans think that something wasn't adding up. Normally, the man would have gone berserk with threats and all kinds of things; but not today, he was calm and cool. Hollingsworth said, "Okay, okay. Easy, Mr. Evans, I believe you." Evans heard the affirmation, but something was still not right. Hollingsworth continued, "Okay, moving on. The reason why I'm calling, Mr. Evans, is to let you know that, unfortunately, my event to come out to the place has been postponed until further notice. So I won't be coming out today, and I'm not sure when. Some more pressing issues have come up."

Evans's voice was elated as he replied, "Really? Sorry to hear that."

Hollingsworth responded, "Are you, sir?"

Evans responded, "Ah, yes."

worth was convinced that Evans had compromised the mission; he had allowed the Cook bitch to interfere with what he was supposed to do. Hollingsworth's disappointed look turned into a slight smile; his plan that was about to happen was perfect.

# CHAPTER 195

Thirty minutes earlier

Serenity was in her room watching the news; something came on about her husband. The report was sketchy; that's when she heard the front door close. She was happy Evans had returned. She practically skipped out to the front area of the house. She didn't see anyone; she questioned whether she heard the front door. It sounded like the front door, she thought. She looked at the front door, trying to figure out what or where that sound came from.

Serenity casually walked toward the door. She reached out for the door handle; for some strange reason, she felt compelled to turn the knob. The front doorknob turned; she was starting to get nervous. She knew she had locked the door when Evans headed out, even turned the knob to make sure the door was locked.

She opened the door slightly. Serenity carefully looked outside; she looked left and right. It was quiet; the only sounds were the birds and other animals scurrying through the bushes. This was weird; she shook her head. She closed the front door, and that's when she knew something was seriously wrong.

# CHAPTER 196

From the corner of her eye, Bobby Lee stood there. Serenity quickly turned to face him. He appeared to be in some kind of discomfort. He reached for her. She shoved him away; he said, holding the side of his head, "I don't want trouble, and I don't want to hurt you. Just cooperate and come with me."

Serenity slightly backed up when he lunged at her again; this time, she sidestepped him and shoved him forward, where the momentum of his weight drove him forward into the wall unit. He hit the wall with a solid hit; he stood back up, cursing, "Bitch." Bobby Lee came at her again. She tried to run, but he caught her by her blouse. The blouse ripped. He held his head and said, "Please stop. I don't want to hurt you. I just want to do what I need to do and stop the pain in my head . . . please." Bobby Lee bent forward, holding his head.

In order to get to the front door, Serenity had to run past him. She thought about the back door, but the distance was too far. She dashed to the front door; she was slightly in front of him, catching him off guard when she felt a hand grab her by her hair. She screamed and yelled in pain. Bobby Lee had a good grip. Serenity remember a technique that Shawn taught her; she grabbed his closed fist and dug her nails into it. Bobby Lee clenched his teeth and grunted in pain. It was enough to cause him to let go of his grip. She made her move as she twisted his arms as they got tangled up in each other; he was bent over when she delivered a stunning blow with her knee into his nuts. He doubled over in pain, cursing at her.

Serenity remembered Shawn telling her there were a few moves that could leave an adversary powerless when they were in this position. She went right for the side of his knees, kicking it as hard as she could. She heard a cracking sound, causing him to yell out in agony, "Arrgg, you bitch!" As if he wasn't hurt, he lunged after her; she screamed as she moved and dodged, throwing whatever she could get her hands on—a lampstand, remote controls. She yanked the cable box from the socket, throwing that at him and hitting him in the head; that made him even more angry. "I'm going to get you! You're dead, arggg!" She tried to run toward the back door, her only chance to get away from this madman.

Bobby Lee recovered and took off after her, knocking over tables and chairs. She was in the crosshairs of his anger as he took a lunge at her, driving his hard body into hers. They both crashed hard into the wall unit, causing the unit to topple. They were both on the floor in pain when they looked up and saw the wall unit coming down toward them. They both pushed off each other and rolled away from each other as the heavy wall unit came crashing down hard into the floor between them.

Serenity managed to get up slowly, dazed and shaken. This was her chance to run away from this psychopath; she was trying to run, but he tripped her. She hit the ground hard. She moaned in pain. They both struggled to get up. They were up as they grappled with each other. She came up with a hard knee aimed toward his stomach. He slightly turned, causing the blow to miss its target. Bobby Lee grabbed her by the shoulder; she yelled in pain as his hands were moving toward her neck. He said to her, "I need you to stop. I have to make this pain go away."

Serenity thought he was crazy as he came up with a hard knee to her stomach; it connected full contact. She made a sound as if the wind was knocked out of her, but she was able to recover as she broke the grapple by slamming both her arms down on his, which also left his front body completely open. She drove a straight chop to his throat; he grabbed his throat in pain. His eyes bugged out in surprise. Serenity came back with a hard clap against his ears as she heard a crunch, which was his eardrums cracking. Bobby Lee screamed in pain, grabbing his ears, but he was still strong. Something was keeping this guy standing.

He reared back and backhanded Serenity in the face; she was hit so hard she went airborne. She hit the floor with a loud thud. He staggered over to her, coughing and still holding his throat as blood was dripping down from his ears. Bobby Lee lifted her up by her hair. He stood her upright as if she was a prize he had won. Serenity was slightly dazed; she was bruised up pretty badly. He was getting ready to delivered a knockout blow. He reached back to hit her as her hands fumbled for anything she could use. Her hands came across a hard porcelain object; she gripped it and swung it with such force, hitting him in the jaw. She heard his jaw shatter as he let go of his grip as he spun around and hit the floor hard.

Serenity stumbled up to him to make sure he was out cold. She staggered past him, tripping over his body; she was able to maintain her balance as she quickly hurried toward the back door when a hand grabbed her by the legs and yanked her hard. The force of the pull on her leg split her legs open as she could feel what felt like a tear to her leg. The pain shot through her like a searing-hot iron. Serenity cried out in pain. Bobby Lee slowly stood up staggering; somehow, she was able to stand up. She couldn't put too much force on that leg. He went to grab her; she was in such pain, but she was able to grab him.

They both were now in a grappling position in front of the full-length living room window; she broke free from his grip and hit him with a flurry of blows, most of which were connecting. Bobby Lee tried to block them, but they were coming too fast and too quick, striking and hitting its target. He was grunting and making all kinds of sounds of frustration; he was yelling for her to stop, but Serenity kept on hitting and connecting. He was so angry he let out a loud and wild yell as he lowered his shoulders and rammed right into her. The impact caused her to let out a harsh grunt as they both crashed through the full-length window. They both crashed to the ground hard. They both lay there; no one moved.

# Chapter 197

Evans was so happy; he hadn't been this excited in such a long time. He was determined to find a way to take Mr. X out of this equation. This wasn't business; this was personal—a favor for Serenity. Whatever problems Mr. X had with Shawn, that was between Mr. X and Shawn, not Serenity. Why didn't he see this before? He was too blind to see not the reality, but the truth.

Evans pulled up in the parking lot; he was so excited to tell Serenity his good news that he failed to see the figure up in the trees, with weapons set to fire when given the command. He grabbed the bags from the back of the car; he excitedly went to the front door. He couldn't reach for his keys, So he took a chance to open the door; the doorknob turned. Evans slightly smiled and thought, *I thought I told this girl to keep this . . .*

He could sense something was wrong; he could feel something wasn't right. Evans dropped the bags of groceries and reached back in his waistband to pull out his Magnum. He cocked it; he looked around slowly. He walked a few steps and stopped; he couldn't believe the damage in the living room. Chairs were toppled over, and pictures from off the walls shattered; even the heavy couch was moved from its spot. Evans began to panic. "Serenity . . . Serenity . . ."

He looked down and saw blood drops; apparently, the injury was serious. The drops were practically on top of one another, but whose blood was it? He called out frantically, "Serenity . . . Serenity!"

Nothing—not a moan, no movement, not even the slightest noise, no response. Evans thought the worst; the woman wasn't a fighter. Serenity was too soft and delicate, not a vicious bone in her body to hurt anyone. That just wasn't her; she wasn't wired that way, he surmised.

He had an awful feeling who was behind this; at that moment, his cell phone chimed. Evans didn't recognize the ringtone; he touched his Bluetooth. Before the caller could respond, Evans spoke. "Where is she? Where is Serenity, you low-down son of a bitch?"

Hollingsworth said, "I'm tired of folks calling me that derogatory name, so inhumane and so disrespectful, don't you think, Evans?"

Evans ignored him and yelled, "Where is she, Mr. X? I'm going to rip you apart with my bare hands."

Hollingsworth dryly said, "Well, you would have to take a number and get in line . . . Wait your turn." A slight laugh came out. Hollingsworth continued, "Evans, you are losing it, And the ironic thing, my dear friend, is she belongs to someone else. But soon, the tense will be changed to 'was.'" He chuckled.

Evans was furious and said, "You're a coward. You made your move while I was out."

Hollingsworth responded, "Well, of course, I'm not stupid. I am no match for your skills, sir. You probably would crush me . . . I know that. That's why I did the 'Now you see her, and now you don't and won't.'"

Evans was furious. "I will hunt you down, you lowlife piece of shit! You know me. I won't stop until—"

Hollingsworth cut him off, saying, "You're getting sloppy, my friend."

Evans, with determination in his voice, said, "Where is she?"

Hollingsworth chuckled. "My, my, Mr. Evans, I've never seen you like this before. And you know, you and I go back a few years, my friend."

Evans growled into the phone, "That's changed! You are no longer a friend, but an adversary! And you already know how I treat my enemies! Where is she?"

Hollingsworth slightly smiled. "Evans, I know you all too well. I'm one step ahead of you, always have been and always will be. But this time, I admit, you fooled me. I wouldn't in a million years have thought your downfall would be caused by a bitch."

Evans cringed when he heard the derogatory term. "You better watch your mouth."

Hollingsworth said, "What is also amazing is she is not even yours, but you act like she is."

Evans said, "I will find you, Mr. X, I promise."

Hollingsworth said, "Maybe. Maybe not. And by the time you find me, my plan of revenge would have been carried out. And oh, by the way,

Mr. Evans, this Mr. X no longer exists. The name is Hollingsworth. Yes, you've been working for a very rich man that gives to every possible charity cause. And yes, I am one of the richest. Just ask Mr. Forbes." There was a pause; then the stranger continued, "I didn't think you would have taken the bait, leaving the house and leaving the beautiful Serenity Cook there by herself just to buy some food. Well, I guess you will be eating alone tonight. But I thought to myself, 'He's not going to go for this.' The next thing I knew, you went for it . . . You've become very sloppy. You've lost your sharpness, your keen awareness. I always thought you had this extra awareness. I would have never thought that this special talent would be your downfall, but overconfidence can be a bitch sometimes."

Evans interjected, "And your pride and self-conceit and egotistical attitude will be yours!"

Hollingsworth said, "It's been a pleasure working with you, my frenemy. Too bad you've become a disappointment. I knew you were slipping. It was just a matter of time before you fell, and I guess this is that time. I will use your serious mistake to accomplish my final goal and purpose. Take care, Francisco Evans."

# Chapter 198

Hollingsworth called Shawn. Complex said, "The jackass is calling you." Shawn was heading toward the address where Serenity was said to be by Hollingsworth. He was about ten minutes away. He told Complex to put the call through. Complex sent the call through. Shawn responded, "What do you want, Hollingsworth?"

Taunting Shawn, Hollingsworth pouted and said, "Why are you treating me so, Mr. Cook? I kept my word about getting your wife back." Shawn made a sarcastic sound as Hollingsworth continued, "I've been extremely kind to you, Mr. Cook, and this is the thanks I get? A nasty attitude! You can't be good to folks these days."

Shawn sneered into the phone, "You and I, that's all you need to know."

Hollingsworth overdramatized catching his breath. "And now you're threatening me. Maybe this will wake you up. Several days has passed, and the beautiful Serenity Cook is still alive. You need to look at that, Mr. Cook, because to tell you the truth . . . hmmm, I was supposed to eliminate her on the third day. But I kept her not only alive, but also safe, you ungrateful son of a bitch." He was becoming angry as he started yelling in the phone, "I altered my plans, Mr. Cook! I changed my mind a dozen times, Mr. Cook! I've done so much to keep your wife alive . . ." Hollingsworth was furious as his voice continued to rise. "So instead of whining and bitching and threatening me, you need to take a step back and show me some damn respect, you ungrateful bastard! You need to thank me for what I've done. You got that? You caught that? You understand that, Mr. Cook?"

Shawn was silent for a few seconds; when he spoke, Hollingsworth could hear the intensity in his voice. He could feel the fire. Hollingsworth could feel the chill going up and down his spine. Shawn was not yelling or shouting; he spoke in a cold and deadly calculating tone. "Hollingsworth, you are a dead man. You may not know it. You have no idea of how or when, but you are a dead man. The only advice I'll give you is you better get your house in order, sir. I'm coming for you. You will pay for your actions."

Hollingsworth didn't realize he was slightly shaking as Shawn continued, "I strongly suggest the little capital and little investments you have, you put them aside for Hector. You know Hector, the one who had the key?"

Hollingsworth's breath got caught in his throat; he said, "How did you acquire that information?"

Shawn said, "What? That information about your son, Hector? It's who you know, Hollingsworth, and I know a lot about you. My sources gave me the information. It was like a puzzle, but I sort of put the pieces together. And once they started coming together . . . it wasn't hard to put it all together." There was a pause; then Shawn continued, "You were the one who was sending money to Hector's mother. He is your child out of wedlock, which, according to your religious beliefs, is a serious problem. So you tried to fix the problem. You were the one who moved them into that nice mansion, Hollingsworth. It didn't make sense at first, a single mom moving out of the projects into a mini mansion in Upstate New York. It wasn't lotto, you never know. But this one, I did know."

Shawn paused and continued, "Those gifts weren't your benevolence or of your generosity. Those gifts and that mansion were hush money for as long as she wanted to ride that train, and I think she's been riding that train for a while, but now the money train is broke. No more money on the train."

Hollingsworth, seething, said, "I want to know, Mr. Cook, how you came into this information."

Shawn responded, "Well, to tell you the truth, you piqued my interest. And if you didn't do that, I would have thought Hector was another kid that was about to bite the dust, another loser."

Hollingsworth said, "But how?"

Shawn said, "When you asked me not to hurt him or go hard on him, that he still had a chance, I figured something was up. And of course, my research sealed the deal, and that it's just who you know. That's all you need to know."

Hollingsworth responded, "Not bad, Mr. Cook. The destruction of my life is thorough, complete. You have wiped out my finances. You have destroyed my business. You have demolished my future, and you have wiped out the trust and faith my religious community had in me. Well done, Mr. Cook. But now I have one for you, sir."

# Chapter 199

"Well, do you know, Mr. Cook, that as you're heading to save your gorgeous wife, I have your family? You know, Mom, Dad, your brothers and sisters, and, of course, pretty little Ashley and her mutt—all have been invited out for just an appreciation celebration cause."

The hairs on Shawn's back arched up as he listened to Hollingsworth, who continued, "I'm having them followed. As I understand from my sources, Mr. Cook, they are heading toward your restaurant." Hollingsworth paused and said, "Hey, don't be surprised, sir. Remember, it's who you know. You are so right about that statement. And by the way, Mr. Cook, you may have inflicted harm on me. But I'm a businessman, and as a businessman, we are always ready for that rainy day. It probably may take a while, but I will eventually bounce back, of course under another name. But let me get back to your family."

Shawn's heart practically stopped when he mentioned his family; he said in a harsh tone, "What have you done?"

Hollingsworth said, "Correction, sir, not what I have done—it's what I have planned for that nice restaurant of yours. And look, it falls on a day when your family is meeting there." There was a pause; then Hollingsworth continued, "All of this big talk, you shut down my money, my resources, my community. You ostracized people in political power against me, even caused the religious community to probably reject my membership. But now it's my move, I believe, to ruin and destroy what matters most to you, Mr. Cook. So I decided to go after your family." Hollingsworth paused and came back with a smile in his voice. "Oh, look, I just got word they have just arrived at your restaurant. Excellent."

Shawn wanted to tell Complex to stop and turn around; he was between a rock and a wall. Complex said in Shawn's headset, "Remain calm. Just remain calm, easy . . . easy . . ." He pulled up to the house. Complex said, "Shawn, according to my view radar, you have one hostile in the trees. He has what appears to be a weapon, a high-powered weapon."

Shawn put Hollingsworth on mute. He could hear him, but Hollingsworth couldn't hear Shawn. Shawn asked Complex, "What is the hostile is waiting for?"

Complex responded, "I'm not sure. I need to neutralize him or distract him or simply take his ass out."

Shawn responded, "Negative on the third option." He took Hollingsworth off mute; all that time, Hollingsworth was just going on and on about his accomplishments. Shawn said, "Hollingsworth, what do you have planned?"

Hollingsworth chuckled. "Oh, by the way, you should be at the house." He continued, "You can have your bitch back. I have bigger fish to fry, as they say."

Shawn responded, agitated, "What do you mean by that?"

Hollingsworth said, "You wanted your enemy. Then you shall meet him. Goodbye, Mr. Cook."

Shawn yelled in the phone, "What do you plan on doing, Hollingsworth?"

Hollingsworth casually said, "I plan on escaping, Mr. Cook, not before I keep my promise and repay you when this saga started—an eye for an eye and a life for a life. You took mine. Now I'll wipe out yours."

Shawn yelled at Hollingsworth, "You sick bastard! What are you planning on doing?"

Hollingsworth said, "Hmmm . . . Put it this way, Mr. Cook. You can't be at two places at the same time, not even you." There was that menacing laugh as he continued, "You choose to save Serenity—not a bad choice. But the consequences of making that decision come at a price."

Shawn sneered into the phone, "What do you mean?"

Hollingsworth said, "While you're saving Serenity, your restaurant is filled with explosives. You know, like at the mall, you remember?"

Shawn growled into the phone, "You sick son of a bitch!"

Hollingsworth hunched his shoulders. "Can't please everyone. I can't help you decided to save your lady over your family—your choice, your decision." He thought and said, "Hmmm . . . true, I think I would have made the same decision. Anyway, time is running out, Mr. Cook. Those explosives are about to go off in . . . let's see . . . hmmm, about twenty-five minutes, sir. Good day, Mr. Cook." Hollingsworth disconnected the call.

Shawn's wind got trapped in his throat as panic swept through his body; he struggled to get the word out of his mouth. "Complex."

Complex's animation shook her head. "Shawn, even if I was the Concorde, there is no way I could get back in time . . . Shawn, I'm . . . I'm sorry."

Shawn cursed, "I have to get in touch with Jefferson. Complex, patch me—"

Complex quickly responded, "On it, babe."

Shawn continued, "Complex, tell him of the plot. Tell him to call Marcus and the both of them head over to the restaurant."

Complex responded, "Shawn, if I may ask, why Marcus?"

Shawn said, "He has some experience in dismantling explosives." He paused as he was getting out of the car. "Complex, I want to know everything that is going on."

Complex nodded. "Of course."

Shawn got out of the car and said, "Complex, shut down all systems."

Complex protested, "Shawn, that could be . . ."

Shawn nodded. "I know, disastrous. But if we could detect them, more than likely, they may be able to detect us."

Complex shook her head. "I don't like—"

Shawn cut her off, saying, "This is not the time. Can you isolate the hostile when I go inside after Serenity?"

Complex hesitated and said, "Yes, but—"

Shawn said, "No time for debate. Just do it."

Complex nodded and began the shutdown progress. As Shawn reached the door and was getting ready to walk inside the house, her detector went off; it was a silent alarm—only she could hear it. Shawn's system was down; she tried to override it but couldn't. Complex realized he was walking into a trap.

# CHAPTER 200

The hostile in the tree rose up on one of the branches and was aiming right at Shawn. Complex's system posted a warning, but Shawn's system was down. Complex programmed her sniper guns to come out. She was aiming at the hostile; the red sniper dart was aiming right at the hostile's chest, at least three or four red dots. The hostile dropped his weapon, looking around to see where the sniper was hiding at. When the sniper put his gun down, Complex said, "Bitch, you better recognize your reward. You get another chance to see another day."

Shawn had walked in the house. The door was unlocked; as soon as he walked in, he knew something was wrong. He called her name; there was panic in his tone. He tried to keep the tone even, but he couldn't. "Serenity . . . Serenity . . ."

Shawn's cell chimed; it was Complex. She said, "Shawn, the call is important. It's Hollingsworth."

Shawn snarled in the phone, "Patch the ass in." He went straight to the point. "Where is she?"

Hollingsworth lightly laughed and said, "You got the wrong guy, Mr. Cook. Don't ask me."

Shawn called her name again, "Serenity!"

The place was a wreck; not even a demolition crew could cause so much damage. Shawn's mind was thinking the worst. *Maybe she's out back, beat up bad and unconscious.* Panic struck his voice. "Serenity!"

The stranger had already added fire to the fuel and hung up the phone. Shawn stood there in the midst of the chaos.

Evans came out of one of the rooms. "She's not here. He has her."

Shawn looked at him; he recognized the face. "You son of a bitch, where is she? What did you do to—"

Evans said, "I didn't do—"

Rage took over as Shawn came after Evans. Shawn reached inside his pocket, took out three ninja stars, and threw them with good accuracy, one right behind the other. *Swiss, swiss, swiss.* Evans quickly picked up a two-by-four piece of wood; he quickly blocked two out of the three. The third one got stuck in his hand. Evans cringed but held on to the two-by-four, saying to Shawn, "You are making a mistake. I—"

Shawn was now up close, just a few inches away as Evans swung the two-by-four. Shawn ducked and came with a low and hard punch to Evans's midsection. Evans made a painful out-of-breath sound. "Ooph." He shook it off as he recovered from the hard blow. Then he came back with a hard kick to Shawn's stomach and a quick kick to his head. The kick to the stomach connected hard; but with the kick to the head, Shawn was able to lean his body back, causing the kick to miss by a few inches.

Evans tried to explain, but Shawn didn't want to hear it. Evans said, "You got this thing all wrong! You don't understand, Cook. He's—"

Shawn came with several quick blows. Evans blocked them and came back with his own melee of punches. Shawn moved and ducked as he bent and blocked; he was like a dancer. Evans picked up a pole about twelve inches long and swung it over his head. As it was coming down, Shawn blocked it and countered with a strong kick to Evans's midsection. The kick moved Evans back up; as he was holding his ribs, he said, "Listen, Cook, don't you see what—"

Shawn went after him. Evans ran toward the wall. Shawn knew he had him now; there was no place for Evans to run. Shawn was close enough that he lunged after Evans. Evans could feel Shawn was about to grab him. He ran up the wall enough to flip over Shawn and ended up behind him. Evans now had the advantage as he threw a barrage of punches and quick chops, attacking different parts of Shawn's body. Shawn tried to cover up, but the blows came too fast and too hard, hitting the right spots. Evans came with a shoulder pressure point that rendered Shawn to one knee as he howled in pain. Evans moved slightly back as he continued to release hard and sharp blows to Shawn's body.

At this point, Evans could have ended the fight, but he was just giving Shawn enough to stop him. Shawn used the wall to balance himself as he surprised Evans with a strong kick to his upper body; it was enough to give him some room. Shawn pushed off the wall, enduring the pain of his injured shoulder as he came back with two hard straight blows to

Evans's shoulder and the right side of his head. The two blows rendered Evans helpless as he bent over, trying to recover. Shawn took advantage and took two steps to do a Superman punch to finish Evans off. Evans caught the punch in midair and flipped Shawn over his back; their arms were now locked into each other as they struggled to get the advantage. Shawn flipped Evans over his back. Evans rolled over Shawn's back and landed on his feet as the two of them were still locked in that position, struggling to break free.

As they stood in front of the wall-to-wall window, all of a sudden, a barrage of bullets came shattering through the glass. The two were so tangled up they couldn't separate themselves from each other. They tried to duck to avoid the bullets, but they were too tangled up. Evans yelled, "We need to flip and roll over each other to get to a safe spot."

Shawn agreed, saying, "I start. Flip to my left, behind that couch."

Evans yelled, "Okay, go!"

They began to flip toward the couch as the shooter continued to shoot at them. They flipped, rolled, and crashed to the floor; they struggled to shake themselves free. Shawn was overaggressive.

Evans said, "Hold up, Cook. Relax, we need to move together."

Shawn spat back the words, "You need to freakin' relax, punk ass! Your own men are turning on you."

More bullets rang out, getting close to them. Shawn relaxed and was able to painfully free himself from Evans. The two sat there behind the couch with their backs against the wall. Evans said, "Listen, Cook. These are not my people, and if I wanted to take you out, I could've."

Shawn responded, "In your dreams, punk."

Evans raised his voice as more bullets came close to them. "Would you stop with the macho man shit?"

More bullets. They ducked.

Shawn said, "Well, whoever it is, they are toying with us. Those bullets are getting closer and closer . . ." He paused and continued, "The two more barrages of bullets will probably take us out."

Evans thought out loud, "Where are they coming from?"

Shawn sarcastically said, "Why don't you stick your head up and see if you can tell where they're coming from?"

Evans looked at him. Shawn apologized and continued, "There was one shooter when I first came. I took him out."

Shawn picked up his headset; he pressed a couple of buttons, hoping that he could activate it. He should never have instructed Complex to shut everything down; she was the only one that could turn it back on. He pressed the buttons and waited; he cursed, "Damn, nothing."

Then he heard, "Boy, what the hell are you doing?"

Shawn was elated, saying, "Complex, we're under heavy fire. We are trapped in here. The shooter has us pinned."

Complex responded, "I've been trying to get you for the last fifteen to twenty minutes, and what do you mean by 'we are'?"

Shawn responded, "Long story. Tell you later. Can you help us? Where is the shooting coming from?"

Complex said, "Apparently, there are perhaps two shooters in the tree. The one I stopped earlier hightailed his ass out of here. He made the right move because I—"

Shawn interrupted Complex. "Complex, take them out. Try to spare one."

Complex said, "Whoa, Shawn. How do you expect me to do that? I'll just take the son of bitches out? This is not 'Have it your way, Shawn.' This is Complex's way."

Shawn said, "Not this time. Just try. I need one."

Complex, annoyed, said, "Okay."

Shawn said, "Complex."

Complex responded, "Yes, Master . . ."

More bullets came flying very close to Shawn and Evans. Evans cursed, "Damn, that was close."

Shawn, trying to sound calm and not doing very well, said, "Complex, please do that now. That last barrage was close. The next one—"

Complex cut him off, saying, "Okay, Shawn. No problem, babe."

Shawn said, "Find out what is going on with Jefferson and Marcus. Patch me in, hurry."

Complex responded, "Okay. Is there anything else, sire?"

Shawn said, "Complex."

Complex said, "Sorry, just trying to . . . Never mind."

Shawn knew those barrage of bullets were coming any minute, and this time, the shooters were going to hit their target—Evans and him.

# CHAPTER 201

Evans looked over at Shawn and said, "What, you have a team?"

Shawn looked at him and said, "I want answers—not start a conversation as if we're good old friends as if we haven't seen each other for years. Where is Serenity? And explain all of this. What the hell is going on? Who are these bozos?"

Evans, a little nervous knowing the bullets would start flying soon, said, "That's what I was trying to tell you. Mr. X."

Shawn stopped him. "Mr. X?"

Evans responded, "That's what I've been calling him for years. His identity is unknown."

Shawn responded with a sarcastic chuckle, "A lot of blood on your hands, buddy. You'll probably get the book thrown at you." Shawn looked at him. "Not the prison book, but God's book."

Evans shrugged his shoulders, saying, "Not proud of what I've done to keep food on the table and a roof over my head. If I had a chance to do it over again . . ." He stopped when they heard something like a hard thud hitting the ground. Evans asked, "What the hell was that?"

Shawn simply said, "Complex."

Complex informed him a call was coming in; he heard Jefferson's voice. "Shawn, we're at the place. Now what?"

Shawn, with urgency in his voice, said, "Find Rosetta and tell her what is going on. The main thing is get folks out of there. Clear the area." There was a pause; then Shawn continued, "Call the commissioner. Tell him about the bomb. In the meantime, have Marcus start locating the bombs."

Jefferson asked, "You okay, bro?"

Shawn looked at Evans and said, "I'll let you know." Shawn disconnected the call.

Evans peeked up over the couch and saw a body under the tree; he looked up in the tree and saw another body just leaning on a branch. He looked as if he was sleeping, but he was barely moving. Shawn said, "Your so-called Mr. X's real name is Theodore Hollingsworth or Collingsworth, depending on the personality that has taken over his psyche . . ." There was a slight pause when Shawn continued, "So you've been working with a nutjob."

Evans responded, "I never linked the names together. There was always a name on the board of directors named Theodore Hollingsworth . . . I never . . ." His voice faded off.

Shaw, with sarcasm in his words, said, "Well, that's the lowlife scumbag you've been working for all these years." He looked at Evans and said, "Says a whole lot about you." Evans shot him a look.

They both stood up. Shawn was still on guard for anything that Evans might try to throw at him. Evans was at a slight distance but stood casual and ready for anything Shawn might do to him. He said, "Look. Can't you see, Mr. X Hollingsworth wanted us to take each other out? He set this up. I went to the store to stock up."

Shawn gave him a look after that statement; he said, "So I guess you had plans on staying here for a while, stocking up." Evans ignored the remark and told Shawn the whole story. Shawn said afterward, "So let me get this straight. Are you telling me this was it for you? The last rodeo, the last stop—however you want to phrase it. This was it?" Shawn paused as he looked at Evans and said, "So this was it? After you deliver my wife to that piece-of-crap lowlife, and of course, in return for whatever money you make, you just walk off." Shawn, at this point, wanted to slam Evans in the face.

Evans shook his head and said, "No, I wasn't going to deliver anything."

Shawn was now shouting. "So what was the plan, Evans, huh? What was the damn plan?"

Evans, for a brief second, put his head down, raised it back up, and said, "I was going to try to win her heart."

Shawn stepped back, looking at him. "What! You must be on some type of new drug called dumb ass. You must be one dumb-ass mother—"

Evans cut him off, saying, "No, I was going to give it a try."

Shawn pierced his mouth, trying to control his anger, and said, "So what happened?"

Evans looked out at the shattered glass and back at Shawn and then said, "She is madly in love with you."

Shawn stood there; his defenses were slowly coming down. He soberly nodded his head. He had to ask, "Did you and Serenity—"

Evans shook his head before Shawn could finish the sentence and said, "Nah, man, not even a handshake."

Shawn slightly smiled; he looked at Evans and said, "Thanks for taking good care of her. I'll take that in consideration when this is over, and I'm beating your ass."

Evans looked at Shawn without blinking and said, "Hey, not a problem, Cook."

Shawn continued, "This thing between us is far from being done, Evans. In the meantime—"

Evans cut him off and said, "You tell me when and where, and we can settle this. But right now, we both need to work together to save the same woman we both care so much about."

# CHAPTER 202

Jefferson and Marcus were heading toward the restaurant. Jefferson had his headphones on. Marcus asked, "Is that legal?"

Jefferson looked around. "Sure, uh, why not? I'm . . . I'm listening to my GPS—not a crime the last time I checked." The headphones were connected to Gordon's system.

Marcus, very worried and concerned, asked, "So what the hell is going on?"

Jefferson responded, "Look, Marcus, I'm not sure. I was just told that Shawn's restaurant is rigged with explosives, and we need to get everyone out. That's all."

Marcus, imitating Jefferson, said, "Oh, that's all? What do you mean 'that's all'! I've been through this already." He continued, "Okay, how much time do we have?"

Jefferson hunched his shoulders. "I don't know. All I know is we have to get there ASAP. The place is busy around this time, including Shawn's parents and Ashley and his other siblings and . . ."

Marcus looked shocked. "Oh shit . . . and so is my wife. Yo, Jay, put that pedal to the metal. Get us the hell over there."

Jefferson said, "Gordon? Help us out. Just break."

Marcus looked at Jefferson. "Who are you speaking to?"

Jefferson forgot that even Shawn's closest friend, Marcus, did not know about Complex or Gordon. He looked surprised he got caught. "Uh, I'll talk to you later about that." Jefferson asked Gordon, "Gordon, can't you go faster? I need for you to go faster."

Gordon replied in Jefferson's headset, "Sir, this is the speed limit. You can override my system, sir, if you like."

Jefferson said, "Sure, overriding system, now go."

Marcus looked around, trying to figure out who Jefferson was speaking to; he said, "Uh, the name is Marcus and not Gordon, and I can't go faster because you're driving."

Jefferson made a crazy laugh, waved a dismissive hand at Marcus, and said, "Listen, pay no attention to me. When I get nervous, I start talking to my imaginary friends."

Marcus looked around and back at the door. *Damn, it's locked.* He said, "Listen, Jefferson, the restaurant is just a few feet away. Uh, let me off. I can run to the restaurant from here."

Jefferson was still concentrating on the road. "Yo, just chill, man. There's nothing wrong with me. I'm harmless."

Marcus said, "It's like what the judge said to the man charged with attempted murder. He said, 'I'm not that much concerned about you. I'm more concerned about the twenty other personalities you have.'" Marcus did a fake laugh, looked at the car door again, and wondered if he could jump, tuck, and roll.

Jefferson asked, "You think I'm crazy, right? Looney Tunes out to lunch with the crew?"

Marcus nodded his head. "Uh . . . the thought has crossed my mind."

Jefferson let go of the steering wheel. "Gordon, take over, bro."

Marcus nervously jumped as he looked at Jefferson as if he lost his mind. "Who! Take over what? And my name is Marcus, and who the hell is Gordon?"

Jefferson stuttered as he continued to put his weapon together; he said, "Oh, Gordon? Oh, that's my road dog, my ace. Well, Shawn is really my ace. Gordon comes in a close second."

Gordon had to be hitting about sixty-five miles. Marcus nervously saw the car make a hard left without Jefferson even touching the wheel. Marcus nervously asked, "Is that your . . . uh, imaginary friend doing that?"

Jefferson was caught off guard with that question; he smiled and said without thinking, "Yep, yeah."

Jefferson caught on to his mistake, but not before Marcus asked nervously and praying at the same time, "Is . . . is this the s-same one that is the driving the car?" Marcus did not wait for Jefferson's response. He casually nodded his head and said, "Oh, okay, I see. Hmmm . . ." He looked at the door, slightly smiled, and started yelling, "Get me the freak out of this car! I'm in a vehicle driven by the invisible man named Gordon!"

Jefferson asked Marcus to calm down and told him he would explain everything later. Marcus, wide-eyed, looked at the wheel and looked at Jefferson turn this way and that way while the car was still going at least sixty miles per hour. Marcus asked again, "Who's driving?"

Jefferson said, "Not you."

Marcus responded, "And neither are you."

Jefferson said, "So what are you worrying about? Gordon, get us there."

Yes, sir."

# CHAPTER 203

Serenity lay in the back of the car on the floor; her hands were tied behind her back. Bobby Lee said, "Look, I just want this thing out of my head. That's it, and you are the key to getting this pain to stop."

Serenity complained of having a cramp. "I need to sit up, my leg."

Bobby Lee was driving with one hand, and the other hand was holding his head. "Damn . . .," he said in pain. He was getting tired of hearing Serenity's voice. "No, you need to shut the freak up, bitch. Your voice is making my head hurt even more." Bobby Lee continued, "I know this is not your fault. If your stupid dumb-ass man would have surrendered, you wouldn't be going through this cramp. I wouldn't have this stupid thing in my head . . . Oh, my head! Help me, somebody!"

Serenity's legs were definitely hurting. She knew it was more than a cramp; it might have been a fracture. She said, "I need to—"

Bobby Lee, frustrated, said, "Okay, okay, just shut up! Stop that damn whining, okay?" He pulled over; he was right before the exit before Connor Avenue in the Bronx. Bobby helped her sit up.

Serenity said, "I need to get out."

Bobby Lee made annoyed sounds; he yelled at her, "Get out! Get out right now!"

She looked at him, saying, "Can you at least untie these shackles so I can—"

Bobby Lee growled and said, "Lady, you are a pain in the ass. You need this. You want that. Is there ever an end with you? Turn around." He took off the restraints and said, "I'm not in the mood, lady. You try to run away, I feel that would be a very stupid thing to do."

Serenity looked at him. "Look at me. How far do you think I can get, huh?" She got out and stretched. She thought about running, and even though she was a runner in college, the fight back at the house did some serious damage to her body. If she ran, she wouldn't get too far; the second best thing was to buy some time. She grimaced in pain as she stretched the kinks out of her body. Bobby Lee was turning his neck from side to side; he started rubbing his neck, shaking his head every now and then. She was looking at him; he looked at her. "What are you staring at? Do your stretching and mind your damn business."

Serenity responded, "I'm looking at you."

Bobby Lee rubbed the side of his head. "Keep it up. You must want another beatdown, huh?"

Serenity chuckled and said, "Really? Look at you and look at me. Who do you think got the worst of this so-called beatdown?" She paused and continued, "Take these restraints off, and I'll beat you like your mama should've done."

Bobby Lee countered, "My mama never beat me."

Serenity responded, "I believe you."

He said in an annoyed tone, "You sure have a lot of lip, lady, for someone who is helpless right now. You talk a lot of crap . . . Are you done?"

She looked away and then back at him. "Sure."

Bobby Lee was holding his head; he was in so much pain. Serenity looked at him as she was stretching. "What happened to your head?"

He turned toward her and said, "Here we go, not even a minute and you're already asking questions." He paused, looked at her with a scowl, and said, "You happened to me. Your husband happened to me." He growled in pain. "I wouldn't wish this on my worst enemy, like you and your husband maybe." Bobby Lee made a strange growling laugh and cursed. "This thing never lets up."

Serenity said, "If I had a Tylenol or something, I would—"

He cut her off, saying, "Lady, it would take more than a simple pain pill, maybe a whole bottle just to take me out of this cruel existence. Nah, this is not your everyday pain. I'd rather have three times of a migraine than to have this thing." Bobby Lee yelled in agony, punching his head.

Serenity felt somewhat sorry for the man; she asked, "So what happened?"

Bobby looked at her and growled, "A persistent little bitch, eh?" He shook his head and started hitting it again, saying, "Get out, get out!" Serenity was becoming concerned; he looked at her and said, "I would be concerned also, lady. This pain would make you do some crazy shit." He paused and said, "Mr. X, the same man that is after your husband—no, that's an understatement . . . the one who wants to kill your husband. Yeah, that sounds better." Bobby Lee grinned, making a painful sound as he continued, "Well, that bastard planted this tracker in my head, sort of like the ankle thing convicts wear. Well, this mother sucker is in my head . . ." He yelled out in pain. "I can't take it, and I can't take it out. The more you attempt, the more severe the pain becomes. And the further away you are from it, the pain gets even worse, and right now"—he yelled—"this bitch hurts!"

Serenity asked why. Bobby Lee looked at her. "You're a nosy little thing, aren't you? Why? Because the man doesn't trust me. He knows without this thing in my head, I'm making a dash for the cash." She looked at him; he looked at her in frustration. "I'll run. I'm a flight risk, lady, and you know what? He's right. I've been running and ducking and dodging and hiding from this cat for a long time. Somebody snitched on my whereabouts." Bobby Lee continued, "There's also the fact that the man has people on his list looking out for his interest. He has more eyes watching out for him than a spider." He looked at her. "This is why I need to get your pretty sweet ass to him so my debt would be paid in full, and he can take this crap out of my skull, my crane. Whatever." He laughed with a nervous tic.

Serenity was thinking, trying to buy time. She asked, "What if Mr. X double-crossed you?"

He looked nervous as he fought off the urge not to scream; he said in pain, "You mean cancel the deal and still have you?" She nodded; he gestured with his hands as he grabbed his head, looked at her, and said, "He would do some crap like that. He is a cold-blooded SOB." All Serenity could do was cover her mouth. Bobby Lee had something else to think about; he said to her, "Enough with the thousand and one questions. Your cramp is gone. Get in and lie down."

Serenity slightly pouted. "Please let me sit up." He thought about it. She looked at him and said, "Please."

Bobby Lee was fed up and said, "Whatever. Just get in. Sit up, lie down, stand on your head—just get in the damn car." Serenity smiled and was ready to get in when he stopped her. "Hold up, turn around." She hesitated before Bobby Lee said, "Lady, you are racking my nerves. Turn around." She did as he put the restraints back on her wrists; he said, "You can't get everything your way. Now get in the damn car."

Serenity thought at least she stalled him for about twenty to twenty-five minutes. She could feel them. They—Shawn and Evans—were coming for her.

# CHAPTER 204

Complex told Shawn that Hollingsworth was calling. Shawn said to her, "Trace the call and see if you can get his location. Put him through."

Evans followed Shawn in his car. Shawn had no choice but to trust him and keep him close.

Shawn answered, "Hollingsworth, surprised to hear my voice?"

Hollingsworth nodded his head. "Indeed, sir, you are so resourceful, Mr. Cook. I wish I had one of you compared to twenty of my own men." There was a pause; then Hollingsworth added, "To tell you the truth, Mr. Cook, to beat Evans is amazing in and of itself. The man is as good . . . Well, I take that back—not as good as you." There was another pause as Hollingsworth continued, "My curiosity is eating at me, but I may assume Evans got the worst of it."

Shawn was silent; then he said, "Talking to me should give you a clear indicator of the answer to your question."

Mr. Hollingsworth was amazed. "Wow, bravo for you, Mr. Cook! You defeated a strong foe."

There was another pause when Shawn spoke. "Hollingsworth, I am making it my top priority—and I need for you to know this so there wouldn't be any surprises—that after I get my wife back, I'm coming after you, you scumbag. And I'm going to kill you. So I'm telling you this so that you can get in order the things you need to get together with your son, Hector."

Hollingsworth's breath got caught in his chest; he tried to sound casual about it but wasn't doing too well. Shawn responded, "Yeah, that's right, Mr. Holy and Right. I would have to admit he's a nice kid—a little misdirected and misunderstood, which is understandable seeing that his father is a prick."

Hollingsworth looked around as if others could hear his telephone conversation with Shawn. He shook off the initial surprise message from Shawn. "Whatever, Mr. Cook. Serenity is on her way to me. I will show you how it's done, Mr. Cook."

Shawn felt his anger boiling and said, "We will see. I'm closer than you think, Hollingsworth."

Hollingsworth laughed. "Yeah, okay, if you say so. You are a terrible poker player, Mr. Cook. I seriously doubt you are close, but it is a nice try. Well, this is where we part, Mr. Cook. You took mine, and now I take yours. Nice working with you." He disconnected the call.

Shawn knew Hollingsworth was correct; he didn't have anything—no clue, no idea at all. He asked Complex, "What's going on with picking up Serenity with the DNA that was at the house?"

Complex stated, "Difficult, Shawn. Working on it."

Shawn said with disappointment in his voice, "Complex."

Complex responded, "But I'm Complex. I found her."

Shawn practically jumped in his chair with excitement; he said, "What! Complex, serious?"

Complex's image on the monitor smiled, winked, and said, "She's heading up 95 south."

Shawn nodded with enthusiasm. "Okay, okay, great. The sounds in the background, can you make them out?"

Complex responded, "I'm still working on that."

Shawn responded, "Complex—"

Complex cut him off and responded, "Don't. I said I'm working on it, okay? I've narrowed it down from six hundred sites to five, babe. Now just relax."

Shawn looked surprised. "Wow."

Complex responded, "Yes, now let Complex do her thing. I know what I need to do."

Shawn nodded. "Okay, okay, sorry." There was a brief silence when he asked Complex to patch him to Jefferson.

Jefferson picked up. "What's up, Wall Street?"

Shawn, looking concerned, responded, "You tell me."

Jefferson said, "We are here. We got everybody out of the place."

Shawn said, "Good. Now get out of there and get everybody as far as you can from the restaurant."

Jefferson said, "What? Sorry, Wall Street, we're going to defuse this bomb."

Shawn shook his head and said with urgency, "No . . . no, Jefferson! Get out! Get out of there now! Let the professionals handle that. You and Marcus get the hell out of there now! You've done your part. Get out!"

Jefferson said, "Not this time, Wall Street."

Shawn was feeling exasperated. "Jay, you and Marcus get out! The bomb squad is on their way. Let them—"

The phone disconnected. Shawn looked at the phone. "Jay . . . Jay . . . Damn, he hung up."

Marcus looked at Jefferson and asked, "What did he say?"

Jefferson hesitated and said, "He want us to do what we can."

Marcus sucked his teeth. "I knew it."

Jefferson, concerned that time was running out, said to Marcus, "How will we find out where the bombs are planted?"

Marcus hurried over across the street to Rosetta. "Rose."

Rosetta responded, "Hey, baby, can we go back in now?"

Marcus shook his head and said, "No, sorry. We are still trying to figure out what's going on."

She said, "Figure out what, Marcus? I mean, is it a gas leak? Carbon monoxide problem or a simple fire drill?" She said hi to Jefferson, who came on over.

Jefferson smiled politely and said, "Ms. Rose."

She smiled. "A gentleman."

Jefferson slightly smiled; he wanted to get to the point without coming off rude. He told her thank you and continued, "Did you see anyone strange or doing something strange or acting strange?"

Rosetta, covering her eyes from the sun, responded, "No, not really. Just two repairmen, nice-looking men."

Marcus said, "What two men? Were they expected today?"

Rosetta thought and said, "I don't know, maybe. We have folks coming and going all the time."

Marcus didn't like what he was feeling. "What two men? Where did they go?"

Rosetta was getting a little nervous from the way Marcus was questioning her; she nervously said, "They said they had some orders from the owner. They went down to the basement. They said they had to repair a gas leak."

Jefferson asked, "How long ago?"

She thought and said, "Hmm . . . about ten minutes before you guys drove up."

Jefferson asked Rosetta if she could remember anything about the men. Rosetta said, "Other than they were handsome."

Marcus blew out a breath of impatience; he said, "Rosetta!"

She apologized, "Sorry. They wore a hat that said 'Core Leaks.' 'Core Leaks,' that's right."

Jefferson walked over to Gordon. "Did you get that? Core Leaks."

Gordon said in Jefferson's headset, "Yes, but there is no company by that name, sir. I could run a double-check."

Jefferson shook his head. "This should be—"

Rosetta called both Jefferson and Marcus over and said, "The two walked toward their car." Then she said, "They were dressed just like those guys." Rosetta looked again. "Wait a minute—as a matter of fact, those are . . . That's them!"

Jefferson looked at them; he yelled at them, "Hey, you, stop!"

The two men casually looked around and all of a sudden took off running. Jefferson and Marcus took off after them. Jefferson said to Marcus, "I just need one of them." He was closing in on the two. Marcus was at a slight distance behind. The two men all of a sudden split up. Jefferson cursed; he frantically pointed to Marcus to follow the man who went left. Jefferson didn't feel comfortable with that decision; he wasn't sure how Marcus's fighting skills were. Jefferson was now a few feet from the alleged bomber when the man quickly turned around to face him. The man had a knife in his hand, motioning Jefferson to come. Jefferson noticed the guy was shaking; he was nervous. Jefferson walked toward him. "Listen, it's over. You don't have to do this, okay? I'll make a deal with you. Give me the detonator, and I'll let you go—that simple."

The young man was thinking. Jefferson continued, "All I want is the detonator, that's all."

The young man smiled and said, "If you want it, come and get it."

Jefferson shook his head. "Damn, why dudes never take me serious? They look at me and think I'm a punk. But in a way, I was really hoping you would resist. You see, this way, I have a good reason to beat your ass and to deter you as well as to prove to you crime does not pay. But . . . hmmm . . . all right, here we go."

The young man was tossing the knife from hand to hand, saying, "Come and get some of this, punk."

Jefferson just looked at him; he looked distracted, but he was focused. He said, "Hey, where did you learn that from? You must have seen the movie *West Side Story*, you know, tossing the knife back and forth like the way you're doing it. Cool." Jefferson looked around and picked up a stick. He said with some annoyance, "I told you I don't have time for this." He walked toward the man.

The young man lunged at Jefferson, who pivoted to his right and at the same time came down hard with the stick and connected with the man's hand. The young man yelled in pain as he dropped the knife. The man bent forward in pain, holding his hand. Jefferson took the stick and made a backhand move, connecting the stick into the man's throat. The man gasped for air as he tried to catch his breath; he looked stunned and surprised. His eyes were open wide as he tried to breathe. The man fell to his knees as he continued to hold his throat, gasping for some air. Jefferson walked behind him. "I warned you, didn't I?"

Jefferson came down with the stick hard into the man's shoulder, cracking his collarbone. The man cried in agony, begging Jefferson to stop. Jefferson grabbed the man's broken collarbone and pressed down hard. The man howled in pain. "What the fu . . ." The young man could not get out the last word.

Jefferson said, "You want me to stop? Give me the detonator, you lowlife bastard!" The man fell to the ground. Jefferson grabbed him by the broken collarbone and yanked him up. "Son of a bitch, where is it? Or I'll break the other collarbone. I mean it. You have five seconds. Talk. One . . ." The young man, in enormous pain, was now taunting Jefferson as he heard him count down.

Jefferson said "Five" and was coming down with the stick toward the young man's other collarbone when the man yelled, "You're too late! It's too late!"

Jefferson came down hard with his elbow on the man's shoulder; the man yelled in pain. Jefferson said, "Last time, punk. Give me the freakin' detonator." He delivered another blow to the broken collarbone. The man cried, begged, and pleaded.

Wide-eyed, the man looked at Jefferson, who was coming down with the stick again when the man yelled out, "Wrong man, wrong man, butthole!" The man laughed hysterically and said, "My partner has the detonator, you idiot."

Jefferson looked at him; he was extremely pissed. "No, you're the idiot." He looked around and found a milk carton; he placed it by the man who was still on his knees. Jefferson went behind the man and grabbed him by his shoulder; the man yelled out in pain as Jefferson pulled him down hard on his back. Jefferson went down to the man's legs and placed his feet on the hard plastic carton box.

The man was yelling, pleading and begging. "What are you doing? What are going to do?" Jefferson ignored the man. The man yelled, "Wait . . . wait! I told you what you wanted."

. "A little too late." He picked up about a thirty-pound cinder block; he laid it on the young man's broken collarbone. The young man screamed in pain. Jefferson ran, got another one, and put the other block on the other shoulder; the man screamed in pain. The blocks were holding the man down; he continued to yell in pain. "I'll tell you what you need to know! Just take this damn block off me!"

Jefferson looked at him and said, "Stay here, don't move." The man howled and cursed. Jefferson headed out back to Marcus. Jefferson wasn't sure if Marcus had any fighting skills. Jefferson's cell phone chimed; he touched his Bluetooth as he was breathing hard. "Shawn, bad timing, bro."

Shawn's voice was urgent; he was concerned the way Jefferson sounded. Jefferson explained to Shawn they got everyone out of the restaurant and that his family was okay. Shawn asked, "The bombers, what about the bombers?" The police cars and the fire truck sirens made it almost impossible to hear anything.

Jefferson responded, "One is caught. I'm going . . . I'm going . . ." He continued, "Shawn, are you still there?"

Shawn said, "Yes."

Jefferson said to Shawn, "I can't even hear myself. I'll call you when things calm down. Shawn . . . are you okay? Shawn, can you hear me? Are you okay?" The noise level was too much. He disconnected the call.

Jefferson ran over to the spot where the two bombers split up. He frantically looked around. *Where's Marcus?* he thought. He looked and saw Marcus running toward him with something in his hand, waving it. Jefferson looked past Marcus and saw the bomber stretched out on the ground. Marcus ran up to Jefferson; both men were exhausted and slightly winded. Jefferson said, "I hate running when I don't have to."

Marcus nodded his head in agreement; he asked Jefferson, "Where's your guy?"

Jefferson responded, "Oh, him. I left him back there. He's carrying a lot on his shoulders." Jefferson was still looking past Marcus at the man who was stretched out on the ground.

Marcus turned to see what he was looking at and said, "Oh, that. A fighter doesn't have to look like a fighter to look like a fighter. Don't be fooled by looks. Plus C-4 taught me a few moves. As many times as he kicked my butt in sparring sessions, I had better learned something behind those behind-whipping sessions."

Jefferson smiled; he looked at the detonator and said, "We need to move our asses and get this thing to the bomb squad leader."

Marcus looked at the timer on the detonator; he cursed and said, "Yo, we have two minutes."

Jefferson responded, "Two-minute warning, baby, and then kaboom."

Both men were exhausted. Marcus said, "Can you get there in a minute?"

Jefferson was about to respond when Gordon pulled up without a driver. Marcus had to take a second look at the driver's seat; he just shook his head. Gordon said in Jefferson's headset, "I can. Hop in."

Jefferson smiled and said, "Gordon, we are glad to see you." Marcus quickly looked in the driver's spot.

Gordon said, "Thank you, sir. It's a pleasure to see you in one piece, sir."

Jefferson smiled and said, "We don't have much time, my friend."

Marcus looked at Jefferson and said, "The name is Marcus . . . forget it." He looked at Gordon. "What the! Who the hell is driving—"

Jefferson cut him off and said, "Long story. Just get in. I promise to explain everything." Then he said to Gordon, "Gordon—"

Gordon said, "Sorry to cut you off, sir, but I think by now I know the routine—haul ass and get us there."

Jefferson smiled and said, "That's my dude."

# Chapter 205

Complex's front panel was on, and it was flashing and blinking; it was her radar system, searching and looking for Serenity. Shawn was amazed. "Complex, TJ hooked you up. She gave you a serious makeover."

Complex responded, "That's my girl! Through thick and thin and through and through." She continued, "Thank you for the compliment, but right now, we need to locate my girl Serenity."

Shawn asked as they continued to travel on I-95, "Did you get the location of Hollingsworth?"

Complex's animation shook her head. "But I am narrowing down the search, Shawn."

He said, "Last time, you said you had it down to five."

Complex responded, "Well, that wasn't the complete truth."

Shawn, surprised, said, "Complex, you lied to me?"

She smiled bashfully. "A little. It was one of those lies your species makes, a white lie."

He was surprised. "Wow."

Complex said, "Don't act surprised. Your current president has been telling all kinds of lies since he took office—white little ones, dark big ones, and gray. I don't know where this one fits, so don't 'wow' me."

He continued, "Okay, starting now, talk to me. How many more places you have to check?"

Complex, with a confident look, said, "Oh, we're doing okay. I have about 150 other sites, but we are—"

Shawn was shocked; he said, "Complex, are you serious?"

She said, "As serious as a computer virus."

He shook his head. "Damn."

Complex said, "Shawn, I wish I could tell you something different."

Shawn looked upset. "Yeah, like the truth."

Complex was getting frustrated; she said, "Oh, we're back on that block again. I said I was sorry, so let it go, babe."

She was ready to say something else when she stopped; the visual alarm went off. The alarm caught Shawn off guard. He looked at the panel and said, "Complex . . . what's that?"

Her animation looked at Shawn with bewilderment and those serious eyes; she said, "I've found Serenity."

# Chapter 206

Shawn was excited; he had to be sure that Complex was on target. "Complex, are you sure?" There was some hope and doubt in his voice.

Complex said with enthusiasm in her voice, "Shawn, listen to me. My analysis is usually 98 percent correct, and you know that. I was designed to get at least a 99.9 percent accuracy." There was a pause; then she continued, "Shawn, more than certain. Shawn, it's her. The blouse and the blood you asked me to analyze match the blouse and the blood. What are the chances of a person having the same analysis! It is virtually impossible—not even for twins . . . No, Shawn, this is our girl. This is our Serenity."

Shawn's doubts were starting to fade; he said with confidence, "Complex, give me her exact location."

Complex's panel was lighting up and blinking. In a matter of seconds, Complex said, "Okay, Shawn, I have our girl's location." She paused as a picture of a map came on the screen. Complex added, "Shawn, according to this map, the driver pulled over and got off at the Corner Street exit."

Shawn thought out loud, "But why did he get off the highway?"

Complex just shrugged her shoulders. "I don't know. There had to be a reason."

Shawn said, "I agree, but what?" He told her to hurry over to Corner Street. He said to her, "Put on your siren and police lights."

Complex said to Shawn, "I don't think that's a good idea."

Shawn asked, "Why?"

Complex said, "Because this is not the drop-off site. This is not where the driver meets Hollingsworth."

Shawn looked concerned. "Complex, what was the purpose of pulling over to the side?"

Complex thought and said, "I'm not sure, but it couldn't be the drop-off because we have movement again."

He looked bewildered. "Complex how far are we from that site?"

She smiled. "I could get there in fifteen minutes."

Shawn, looking serious, responded, "Do it."

Complex put on her police lights and sirens. Shawn moved over to the passenger side as the police inflator came up on the driver's side. He looked back and saw Evans was still following; he said to Complex, "Pull over to the side for a second. I need to meet with this dude for a second."

She pulled over. Evans pulled over behind Shawn. Evans cautiously watched as Shawn got out of the car and headed toward him. Evans got out and watched Shawn. "What's going on?"

Evans was in a "get ready to throw down" stance. Shawn reached into his pocket. Evans flinched a bit and quickly looked around for a weapon or something. Shawn looked at him and said, "Relax . . ."

He tossed Evans something. Evans looked at it and looked back at Shawn. Shawn said, "It's a tracker indicator."

Evans looked perplexed. "Who am I tracking?"

Shawn turned to head back to Complex and said, "Me."

Evans looked really baffled. "I don't understand . . ."

Shawn said, "You will. We found Serenity."

Evans's eyes brightened up.

# CHAPTER 207

Shawn got back on the passenger side. "Let's do this."

Complex's extra restraints hooked over Shawn's shoulders; she smiled at him. "Have to keep you safe, babe." She looked at him. "You know Evans won't be able to keep up."

Shawn nodded. "I know. I gave him a tracker."

She smiled. "Good, he's going to need it. Ready?"

He nodded. "Yeah. Keep that punk on the radar. Once he meets up with Hollingsworth, move in on them."

The music came on, something jazzy with a nasty *Mod Squad* beat. The rage meter went from 0 to 5 and continued climbing.

Shawn cursed under his breath. Complex's image changed; she looked at Shawn and said, "Time to catch that son of a bitch."

# Chapter 208

Jefferson instructed Gordon to pull to the side at least a few feet from the restaurant. "Listen, we need to be safe and park here." Marcus looked at Jefferson as if he was on some kind of delusional trip. Jefferson said, "I understand. I've been through it. It freaked me out also."

Marcus looked at him with concern. "Really?"

Jefferson said, "I'll—"

Marcus said, "I know you will explain later."

Jefferson said, "Listen, we need to get this detonator to the bomb squad. We don't have much time."

Marcus added, "We hardly have any time, and we're going to run up in the midst of God knows how many explosives that have been planted to hand off a detonator. We don't know how much stuff have been planted, maybe enough to blow us up to kingdom come. If that happens, this entire block and the next block will be blown up, and who knows what other damage this thing will cause! And sitting here is not helping. We need to get this thing—I need to get this thing to them."

Marcus was still thinking about what Jefferson said. Jefferson waved his hand. "Forget it." Jefferson got out. Marcus, looking surprised, got out. "Wait, damn it. All I know is that sucker better not blow up." They both took off running toward the commissioner and the bomb squad.

Gordon said in Jefferson's headset, "Sir, I could protect you and your paranoid, neurotic friend if a blast should occur."

Jefferson said, "Thanks, Gordon, we'll be fine."

Marcus looked at Jefferson as they both continued to run toward the commissioner. "Was that your imaginary friend you were talking to?"

Jefferson nodded. "Yes, come on."

# CHAPTER 209

Jefferson and Marcus ran up to Commissioner Moore. Jefferson said to him with urgency, "Here, you guys are going to need this."

The commissioner looked at it and said, "What's this?"

Marcus, being a wiseass, said, "It's a remote for a flat-screen television. Yo, this is a detonator to those bombs planted in Shawn's restaurant. Here."

Moore looked at Jefferson and said, "So I see you found your long-lost twin, Jackass 1 and Jackass 2." Jefferson was ready to step toward Moore, who looked around at the officers gathered around him and said, "You'll be one stupid SOB. Back the hell up, Jay."

Jefferson, with a little reluctance, backed up and just looked at Moore; words did not have to be said. It was clear just by the looks on their faces. Moore snatched the detonator from Marcus. "Give me that!" He looked at it.

Jefferson cursed impatiently, folding his hands behind his neck. "Oh my . . . Moore, it's a detonator. Can't you see that?"

Moore looked at it. "Obviously, it is a detonator—not to a bomb, maybe to something else. But why give it to me, and where did you get this?"

Jefferson, still frustrated, cursed and said, "Moore, listen to me. Time is running out. We took it from the bombers who planted the explosives. Oh, by the way, you may want to pick them up. One is over here, and the other is down this way . . . Ah, he's not going anywhere." Moore shook his head.

Marcus, getting serious, said, "Listen, Moore, we took this from them. It has a timer on it. Would you look at it? Dammit! Or give it to the bomb squad leader."

Moore nodded. "Okay, enough. Gentlemen, thank you. We got this. We will have our men and the dogs deal with this one, and to set the record straight, this a remote control to some type of toy or something."

Jefferson was fuming. "What! Are you serious? This place is going to blow up any minute."

Moore said, "You heard what I said. Now either move the hell out of my way, or I'll have you moved to Rikers Island for thirty days. Now back off!"

Marcus stood his ground. "Moore, you are making a serious and grave mistake. You are putting all our lives in danger. If that restaurant blows up, it's going to be a serious chain reaction, Commissioner. Houses and everything at least two to three blocks from it will be destroyed . . . There are a set of bombs in my best friend's restaurant that are about to go off." Marcus grabbed Moore's hand with the detonator, looked at the time, and said, "Dammit. We are almost out of time."

Moore looked at Jefferson and Marcus. "Move out of my way. Go over there with the other folks."

Marcus and Jefferson were heading across the street when Jefferson stopped in the middle of the street and said, "I have to get in touch with Shawn. Maybe he could talk some sense in this idiot."

Shawn picked up on the first ring, sounding concerned and urgent and desperate, "Jay . . . Jay, what's happening? What's going on with the bomb situation? Was Marcus able to defuse it? Talk to me."

Jefferson understood the urgency in Shawn's tone. He continued, "Easy, Wall Street. Slow down, man."

Shawn apologized and said, "So much is going on. You got your hands full over there, and we think we're closing in on Serenity."

Jefferson was excited. "What! Serious?"

Marcus wanted to know what was going on. Jefferson covered the speaker part of the phone and told Marcus, "Shawn believes he's closing in on Serenity."

Marcus smiled and got on one knee, pumping his fist. "Yes, yes!" Jefferson slapped Marcus a high five.

Shawn said, "Hell to the yes! Complex did it, man."

Jefferson said, "Yo, I want one of those."

Complex in the background said, "You can't afford me, handsome. One of the nuts on my tire is worth more than your life, kid."

Jefferson smiled. "No change there."

Complex said, "Were you expecting one? I'm Complex, baby. You keep forgetting."

Shawn could see the conversation between these two could go on and on, so he said, "Talk to me, Jay. Is everybody out and safe?"

nodded. "Yeah, man, we're good with that, including your family. Ashley and her canine are good. Everybody is moving away from the restaurant just in case the place should go kaboom." He heard Shawn say something to Complex; he said, "Well, if push comes to shove, it's a good thing that Complex can defuse the bombs."

Shawn thought about Jefferson's comment and said, "Wait a minute, wait a minute. Back up a second. What do you mean 'if the place should go kaboom'? What do you mean 'kaboom,' Jay? What the hell is going on over there? Didn't Marcus defuse the bombs?"

Jefferson said, "We had to call in the bomb squad. He wasn't sure how many explosives there were or if each one is on its own time limit. Marcus believes he can do it . . ."

Marcus in the background said, "I can do it, Shawn."

Shawn asked, "Okay, so what's the problem?"

Jefferson continued, "Your boy, that asswipe, is telling us that what we took from the ones that planted the bomb—the detonator—is a decoy, that it's some kind of remote for a toy and not a detonator."

Marcus added, "Shawn, he won't let me in."

Shawn was angry; he was ready to rip Moore's head off his shoulders. "What! What the fu . . . Where is he? Put that ass on the phone! Is he crazy?"

Jefferson was already walking back over to Moore; the officers stopped him and Marcus. Marcus said, "We have a message for Commissioner Moore. Move out of the way, Lurch." The officer moved toward Marcus.

Moore said, "Let them through." He looked at them and said to Marcus, "I used to like you. Then you started hanging out with . . . this."

Jefferson retorted, "Your mama is a 'this.' People used to say to you about her, 'Uggh, what is this thing? Your little cockroach?'"

Moore shook his head. Jefferson handed him the phone. Moore was already annoyed; he looked at the phone and said, "Get that thing out of my face."

Jefferson, equally frustrated, said, "It's for you, butt face."

The commissioner snatched the phone out of Jefferson's hand; he growled into the phone, "Yeah, who is this?"

Shawn did not bother to share pleasantries; he came straight to the point. "Moore, listen to me. I've never been so serious before. Listen, just keep your trap shut for a minute."

Moore grunted. "I'm listening. You have a minute."

Shawn continued, "That device that was handed to you is not a toy. It's a detonator, either to stop the bomb from going off or to blow up the next three blocks." He continued, "Listen, you may be right. Maybe it is a toy. But I was told by Hollingsworth about the explosives, and I seriously doubt that this nutcase would be carrying around a toy remote control in his pocket, Commissioner. Think, man." Shawn continued to plead with Moore. "Wrap this around your brain, Moore, and I'm going to say it only once. If you don't listen to what I'm telling you and it turns out it was a bomb, you might as well kiss your political career goodbye. You will be the shame of the city. That thing is the real thing. I don't care what it looks like." There was a pause; then Shawn continued, "Okay, listen."

Shawn called Complex, "Complex."

Complex replied, "I got you, babe, yes?"

Shawn told Complex to hold it; he said to Moore, "Curtis, here are the spots where the bombs have been planted. Complex."

Moore said, "Complex?"

Shawn shushed him. "Listen."

Complex said, "There is one in each bathroom. There are two in the basement and one in the back of the building where you keep that extra supply of gasoline." Shawn asked Complex if that was it; she said that was it. Shawn said, "Shit, Commissioner . . . Wait, Complex . . ."

Complex said, "I don't know. They all may have different timers, Shawn. I'm not sure, but one thing's for sure, babe. Butt face has about five minutes to defuse all those bombs."

Moore said, "Okay, I understand, Cook. But if you are wrong, you make me look like a paranoid nutjob. I'll be the laughingstock of New York. Have you thought about that?"

Shawn countered, "Not really. This is what I was thinking—you would rather have folks laugh at you and call you a paranoid worrywart. But at the end of the day, I would rather be a hero, and it shows in the polls. And right now, the city is on edge—has been since 9/11 and even the Boston Marathon. At least you'd be considered a paranoid protector, and that's a good thing, Moore. In this case, Moore, it's a win-win situation."

Curtis Moore thought and said, "Cook, you're right."

orders for his men to get in that restaurant. Moore outlined where each bomb was placed. "Get your asses in there and deactivate those bombs now! We have three minutes . . . go . . . go . . . go!"

Jefferson was speaking to Shawn. "Whatever you said worked. I like him, and then again, I can't stand him. So what's up?"

Shawn's voice still sounded urgent. "Listen, I need you and Gordon to meet us behind Bay Plaza. There is a sale on old cars parked in the back of Bay Plaza. Lie low there. Gordon should blend in." Jefferson wanted to know what was going on. Shawn said, "Complex."

Complex took over, saying, "I think this is where the exchange is going to be. I can't see any other area on my GPS."

Shawn jumped in and said, "If we missed that drop-off, it's over. I lose Serenity for good, you understand?"

Jefferson nodded. "Of course. Let me get Marcus."

Shawn quickly said, "No, no. Let Marcus stay there. I need someone to make sure that my restaurant stays in one piece and folks are okay and safe. I know Moore is on board, but he has a history of flip-flopping. I'll call Marcus to let him know what is going on. Thanks."

# CHAPTER 210

Jefferson hopped in the car and said to Gordon, "Listen, Gordon, I need to get to Bay Plaza, the rear entrance."

Gordon responded, "Sir, the best and the quickest route is getting on I-95 according to the traffic from my GPS. Plus the roads are pretty clear." Jefferson told Gordon to go for it. Gordon agreed, "Yes, sir. Uh, sir, do you want me to break any speed limit laws?"

Jefferson was surprised; he said with a light chuckle, "Gordon, are you okay? Do you have enough oil or antifreeze? Maybe your gas is low, and you're running on fumes." He laughed, knowing that he was just joking with Gordon.

Gordon took the matter seriously. "Sir, I am perfectly fine. All my readings are very good, thanks to you, sir. I asked that question, sir, because I have broken the laws of the road since meeting you and Mr. Shawn Cook, aka Wall Street, which means not only one or two laws, sir, but a plethora, an overabundance, sir—breaking the word down, sir. If I were human and if I were arrested, they would throw away, as they say in this country, the key, sir. So now I figured since I have incorporated in my system breaking the law of the road, breaking one extra law wouldn't make much of a difference, now would it?"

Jefferson thought and said, "Wow, we have corrupted your system."

Gordon agreed, "Yes, you have indeed. I guess the next step is swearing and cussing."

Jefferson thought about it and said, "Oh, I can teach you that in three easy lessons. In the meantime, welcome to the club."

Shawn followed from a distance the car that Serenity was in. He instructed Complex to use her viewfinder. She put the zoomed picture on the screen. Shawn asked her to zoom in a little more. She did. Shawn was frozen; he couldn't move. There she was. All this time, he longed to be with her. He ached every night for her body to lean against his. He missed her enticing natural aroma, which permeated, pervaded, and penetrated from her skin her beauty. She was just fifty yards away, fifty yards of having her back.

Shawn told Complex to zoom in more; she did. He looked as anger was beginning to take over; he could see the bruises on her face, her ripped clothes, the cuts and bruises on her body, the dry blood. He said under his breath, "He will pay for what he did." Shawn wiped his eyes.

Complex said, "Shawn, you've come too close to mess this up. We will take care of it. He will pay for what he has done to our girl, I promise."

He said, "Complex, keep following. No more than five car lengths."

Complex's image nodded. "Yes, Shawn." She continued, "Shawn, I can feel my girl's vibe. She's a warrior, babe. We need to take this son of a bitch and Hollingsworth out. I would love to do the honors."

Shawn was still staring at the viewfinder at Serenity; he said under his breath, "Hang in there, baby. We're coming."

Serenity felt a strong sensation that caused her to shudder; she shook as she could feel the goose bumps going up and down her spine. Bobby Lee looked at her and sneered, "What's your problem?"

Serenity smiled. "Nothing. Everything is going to be all right." She whispered to herself, "Come on, baby. I don't know where you are, but I know you are close. Come on."

# CHAPTER 201

Bobby Lee drove the car to the back of Bay Plaza Mall as he had been instructed to do. It was late in the afternoon, yet the sunrays were still beaming down the damaged ozone layer; it had to have been at least eighty-five degrees and climbing. The weatherman reported from his nice cold air-conditioned building that it was a beautiful sunny day. The back of the mall looked as busy as the front. The only area that was quiet was the area where they were building another clothing store, as if the mall wasn't already swarming with clothing stores for every size, height, and weight. There were about three to four already; one more to throw in the overflowing pot wouldn't hurt—at least for the consumers, no monopolizing here. They loved it until some of the stores waved the white flag to surrender and move to another state and start the war somewhere else.

Hollingsworth was standing in the middle of the construction site, surrounded by beams, pipes, bricks, tons of bags of cement, trucks, and bulldozers; he looked somewhat ridiculous. He was dressed in a white suit, just standing there in the midst of all of this mess. He smiled as he was surrounded by his men; he was the monkey in the middle.

Shawn asked Complex to zoom in on the dude with the white suit; she did. He looked at the man and said, "That's the one, Complex."

Hollingsworth was surrounded by some tough-looking dudes; one of them had muscles behind his muscles. Shawn watched as another car drove up. Who emerged from the car put Shawn in a slight bit of a panic; it was the twins from the fighting pit in Hell's Kitchen. Shawn knew these men were getting paid handsomely just for the day.

Hollingsworth took out a cigar and lit it up when he saw Bobby Lee and Serenity approach him and his crew. He leaned over and said to the one with the muscles, "Put the tablet to the news station. I want to see my handiwork . . ." He laughed as if he had lost his mind. The one with the muscles smiled and laughed; a special report cut in on the news. Hollingsworth smiled and took a long puff of his cigar; he said, "Watch poetry in motion, gentlemen."

The news anchor said, "This just in. A bomb threat in Downtown Manhattan at the restaurant of entrepreneur and philanthropist Mr. Shawn Cook . . ."

Hollingsworth almost swallowed his cigar; he yelled, "A threat . . . a threat, that's got to be some kind of mistake! Turn to another station!" It was the same message. Hollingsworth snatched the cigar from his mouth and threw it hard on the ground.

The bodyguard with the muscles was still looking at the screen when he said, "Hey, boss, the restaurant is still standing intact. Wow, a miracle."

Hollingsworth angrily said, "Not a miracle, you muscle-bound idiot, but Shawn Cook, no doubt! Damnit, how did he pull this off?"

The news showed the two men who were beat up and handcuffed were placed in a police car. Hollingsworth cursed. The news reporter said, "Thanks to two unknown Good Samaritans that foiled the plan and saved countless of lives."

One customer had this to say, "Whoever did this was a fool. You can't stop what God has destined to be, no matter how hard you try."

The reporter came back on, saying, "That was just one of many who felt the same way this man felt. Reporting live from Downtown Manhattan, I'm Tate Jones."

Hollingsworth heard enough; he said calmly, "Turn it off . . . turn it off. I said turn it off, dammit!" He found an iron pipe and started smashing the tablet; he was furious, "Damn it, damn it!"

One of the twins said, "That Cook guy is tough."

Hollingsworth ignored the village idiot; he looked at his men. "We are getting ready to get the hell out of here." He looked at Serenity, who flinched just a bit. He said to her, "Your husband may have foiled my plans, but I still have you as bait."

Bobby Lee, holding on to Serenity, was excited. *Finally*, he thought, *I can get this thing out of my head.* He said, "You see, I have her, Mr. X, like you asked me to. I kept my word."

Hollingsworth smiled. "Good, Bobby, you've done well."

Bobby had developed that tic; he said, "Like I said I would do, sir. I kept my word."

Hollingsworth nodded his head. "Yes, you did, Bobby, very good."

Shawn said to Complex, "Complex, can you give me an open window to hear what is going on?"

Her animation made a doubtful face and said, "I'm not sure, I'll try. Let me see." Complex's panel began to light up.

Shawn could hear part of the conversation; he heard Hollingsworth tell Bobby Lee that he'd take good care of him as he had promised. Shawn said to Complex, "Complex, Hollingsworth looks like he's holding something in his left hand. Can you . . . can you zoom in on that?"

Complex responded, "I'll try."

Shawn looked and said, "Try to zoom it some more . . ." He kept looking as his breath got caught in his throat. "Oh sh . . ."

# CHAPTER 202

Shawn was too stunned to get the words out of his mouth; panic came over him. He said, "That looks like a detonator of some sort . . ." He looked around. "Dammit, where is the bomb?"

Complex said, "Shawn, my system is not picking up any bombs in the area, and that device, babe . . . doesn't look like a detonator. It looks like a remote control or something."

Shawn looked baffled. "A remote control to what?"

Complex's image shrugged. "I don't know, sweetie, but that dirtbag is up to something."

He nodded. "Agreed."

Complex zoomed in more on the device in Hollingsworth's hand. Shawn said, "Perhaps you're right. But whatever it is, if that punk has it, it has to be dangerous." He spoke on the radio to Jefferson. "Okay, let's meet up by the exercise building now."

Jefferson was curious and said, "'Let's' as in 'let us'? Wall Street, who is the 'us'—you and I and Complex and Gordon?"

Shawn said, "No, 'let us,' as in our special guest."

# Chapter 203

Jefferson pulled up first and got out; he gave Shawn a dap and said to Complex, "What's up, baby girl? Are you still looking for a human who looks like you?"

Complex's image smiled at Jefferson. "Not yet, I'm checking mental institutions."

Jefferson laughed. "My girl."

Complex said, "Keep dreaming." Jefferson loved the back-and-forth. Complex said, "Hey, Gordon, how's my roughrider?"

Gordon responded, "You are so right. I was asking Mr. Newhouse to have a set of shocks put on me. Rides do get bumpy sometimes."

Complex smiled and said, "Gordon, stay the way you are. Avoid following after your owner."

Gordon said, "I will take that into consideration, Ms. Complex."

She said, "Jefferson, take lessons."

Jefferson smiled and turned his attention back to Shawn. "What's up, Wall Street? What's up? Who is our special guest?"

Shawn said, "He should be here any minute." He continued, "The bomb squad shut down five bombs in the restaurant."

Jefferson said, "Damn, they meant business."

Shawn nodded. "Yep, that's the kind of nutjob we are dealing with, a real psychopath." He paused and continued, "Well, his party is over today. Complex."

Complex stated, "Nothing. They are still in that same spot."

Jefferson asked, "So where is this rest of us?"

Shawn said in his headset, "Complex, keep me posted on what is going on."

She responded, "You got it, hon."

Jefferson said, "I want that. I wish Gordon would speak like that to me. It sounds so cool."

Shawn, looking serious, asked, "You mean call you 'hon' and 'baby' and 'sweetie,' stuff like that?"

Jefferson stepped back. "Yo, dude, chill! I didn't mean it that way. You know what I mean."

Shawn said, "Like a masculine car."

Jefferson said, "No, something natural, open, and free, no restrictions. You guys talk as if she is human. It's so cool."

Shawn covered his mouth. "Don't tell anyone, but she thinks she is human." He chuckled and then became serious. "No, seriously, Complex's program costs a lot of money. And it costs about the same amount to keep up the maintenance stuff. Our girl is high-maintenance. No cheap stuff goes in her." He continued, "It may look easy—he communication, all of that stuff. All of this costs a lot of money, man. Plus there is a lot involved. It took TJ years to get Complex to where she is right now. What you see is the finished project. You missed out on the hard part."

The car pulled up.

"I hear you, bro." Jefferson said with a smile, "We'll get back to that. Now let's see who is going to . . ." He looked again, this time with anger and rage; he was pissed off.

As he slammed his car door, Gordon said, "Easy, easy."

Jefferson said to Gordon, "Easy my ass." He looked at Shawn. "Do you know who that is, Shawn, huh? Do you?" Shawn was ready to respond when Jefferson continued, "This is the mother sucker who was trying to choke me out, that son of a bitch." Jefferson reached for his weapon. Shawn put his hand on Jefferson's hand. Jefferson looked at Shawn's hand.

Shawn said, "Calm down."

Jefferson looked at Shawn. "Calm down? You calm the freak down! This punk tried to kill me, Shawn, and you're standing there asking me to calm down. Hell freaking no!" He continued, "Shawn, listen to me. You can't trust this dude. He's like a snake. Don't turn your back on him. I'm telling you."

Shawn was trying to calm Jefferson down; he placed his hand on his shoulder and said, "Jay, listen to me, he's working with us. He knows the deal, okay? Just relax." There was a pause; then Shawn continued, "I promise you, you have my word. If he gets out of hand, I'll shoot him my damn self."

Jefferson lightly smacked his forehead. "This is unfreakin' believable!" He added, "Yo, Wall Street, I hope you know what you are doing, man."

"Yeah, me too."

# Chapter 204

Complex said to Shawn, "Hollingsworth is up to something, but whatever it is, you need to make that move. It seems that he's about to break out and go ghost. You need to make that move, babe."

Shawn nodded his head. "I know. That is what he thinks. Complex, give me a rundown on Hollingsworth's team. I need a plan to take them out in order for me to get to Hollingsworth and get Serenity."

Meanwhile, Evans and Jefferson were going at it. Evans said to Jefferson, "Hey, no offense, man, I had to—"

Jefferson angrily responded, "No offense? Really, dude? You tried to choke me out, and now you're going to stand up there and say 'no offense' as if it was a regular day at the office! Freak you, punk! I got your number."

Evans responded, "What do you mean 'tried'?"

Jefferson cut him off. "You heard what I said, 'tried.' You tried to choke me out, you freakin' bastard."

Evans looked at him and said, "Evans looked at him and snorted. "Hold up, son. If I really wanted to kill you, I could've. I wanted to teach you a lesson."

Jefferson moved toward Evans. Shawn held him back. Jefferson raised his voice. "A lesson in what?"

Evans slightly moved toward Jefferson. Shawn put up his hand for Evans to stop. Evans said, "You came after me. Don't you remember?"

Jefferson said, "Clearly. You had something that wasn't yours."

Neither was she yours. What's your point?" He looked at Jefferson and said, "Plus like I said, you came after me. What was I supposed to do? Let you take me out? No, kid. You came for a fight, and I gave you one." He continued, "Next time, you better know what battle you're going to fight."

Jefferson looked at him and said, "Kiss my ass, punk."

Evans responded, "First, I beat your ass, and now you want me to kiss your ass? Hmmm . . ." They both stared at each other.

Jefferson said, "Another time."

Evans said, "In another place. Right now . . ."

They both turned and looked at the small group of men Serenity was surrounded by.

Shawn heard Complex say, "Shawn, Hollingsworth is making his move, babe. He's getting out of Dodge with Serenity. We need to do something." She continued, "We need to take them out two at a time."

Shawn agreed and said, "Who do you have?"

Complex said, "I need to take out the two sharpshooters. This way, you guys could deal with the others. Once I take out the sharpshooters, the two goons patrolling the front and the rear and on the side can be dealt with."

Shawn was looking serious. "Let's do this." He handed out headphones to the team. "Okay, listen up. Complex is in charge."

Evans, checking his equipment, asked casually, "Who's Complex?"

Jefferson was also checking his equipment; he smiled and said, "She is the baddest bitch you will ever meet."

Shawn said, "Complex, a quick intro."

Complex said, "I was already introduced. I'm the baddest bitch you will ever meet and the most dangerous one if I'm betrayed. If you think my sister Karma is bad, I give a whole new meaning to the word 'bad.'"

Evans responded, "Hmmm, nice voice."

Complex said, "We need to move. Hollingsworth and his men are breaking out, Shawn."

Evans said, "Man, she's hot."

Complex responded, "I know that. Let's go. Evans, take out the first two. Shawn, take out the twins."

Shawn responded, "Damn."

Complex responded in concern, "Damn? Damn what? What's the problem?"

Shawn shook his head. "Nothing. Let's go. Let's do this."

She responded, "We are, but I need to know what the 'damn' was for. I need you at your peak. You go out there with doubt, you put all of us in serious danger. Now what the hell is going on?"

Jefferson responded, "Yo, Wall Street, just tell her."

Complex said, "Okay, tell me what? Time, gentlemen, we are on the clock."

Shawn raised his voice. "I'm cool."

Jefferson said, "Shawn fought against these guys back in Hell's Kitchen. He beat them, but they almost killed him."

She was shocked. "What! When?"

Shawn said, "When you were being fixed. Hollingsworth had me do different task assignments in order to keep Serenity alive."

Complex said, "So can I safely assume the twins was one of your assignments?"

Jefferson said, "They almost killed him."

Complex looked concerned. "I can switch you with Jay."

Jefferson responded, "That's right, throw me to the lions."

Shawn responded, "Okay, enough. Stop. I need to face my adversaries. I need to do this."

Complex, with concern, pleaded, "No, you don't. If something happens to you, who will take care of me?"

Jefferson said, "I will. I got you, babe, all the way—365, 24/7."

She said, "That is so sweet of you, Jay."

He said, "Well, I just—"

Complex said, "NO! I don't think so."

Jefferson smiled and said, "The chick is hot."

Evans cut in, saying, "I really love this dialogue, but knowing my former employer, homeboy is going to be out. We need to make that move now. So all of this bullshit and chitchat need to cease."

Shawn agreed. Jefferson blew out a breath. Shawn said to him, "What happened before, that was then, and this is now. New chapter, new book. Let's kick some major butt." Then he asked Complex if she was ready.

She said, "Ready, no doubt."

Shawn smiled. "Give our friend a surprise call."

# Chapter 205

Hollingsworth looked at his watch. "We need to go. I'll take Mrs. Cook." He grabbed Serenity's arm firmly.

Bobby Lee said, "Mr. X, you said you would help me."

Hollingsworth put his arm Bobby Lee's shoulder and said, "Bobby Lee, yes, I will help you. Just be patient and—" Hollingsworth's phone chimed; he was already upset as they were already slightly behind schedule. He pressed his Bluetooth. "HELLO!"

Complex said, "We have the name of the caller who has been harassing you, sir."

Hollingsworth responded and said, "Good, but I'm not interested in that anymore." He disconnected the call and said to Serenity, "My dear, we will soon be on my island, and you're going to be my slave—sex slave. Let me put it this way, my all-purpose slave until the day you die."

Serenity told him where to go and to take a gasoline can with him. Hollingsworth laughed, then grabbed her by the jaw. "You will pay for that remark, bitch."

Shawn's muscles tensed up, and so did Evans's. Shawn said, "Complex, now."

Complex called again. Hollingsworth touched his Bluetooth; before he could say hello, Shawn said, "Hey, Hollingsworth, you're a dead man. I told you I was coming for you."

Hollingsworth nervously looked around and said, "You're bluffing." He looked around frantically as he began to perspire from his forehead; he said, "Like I said, Mr. Cook, you are a poor poker player."

Shawn came back and said, "And you are a fool."

Hollingsworth let out a quick laugh when two of his men went down hard, a perfect shot right between the eyes.

He looked at them and then quickly looked around as panic stripped his heart; he grabbed Serenity and put her in front of him, looking around frantically. He yelled out, "It's Cook! It's Shawn Cook! He's close by. Find him now!" His men flared out. He grabbed Serenity, who screamed.

Shawn heard it as he moved in that direction. He said to Complex, "Girl, cover me."

Complex replied, "Like a blanket, babe. Go."

Shawn hurried in that direction when one of the twins came toward him. He cursed under his breath. He thought, *Damn, which one is this?*

One of the twins said, "Different time, punk, not this time. I'm sober, and you are going to get an ass whipping. That night, you made my brother and I look bad. Now it's our turn."

Shawn thought, *Our?*

Now the other brother was coming from the opposite side; they were going to do a sandwich on him. Shawn said to Complex, "No matter what happens here, you keep your eyes on Serenity."

Complex said, "Shawn, I can take out both brothers in one shot."

He shook his head. "Thanks, but I need to do this. Just keep your eyes on Serenity." Complex was getting ready to speak when Shawn disconnected the call.

He reached into his pocket and took out something as he ran toward one of the twins. He looked slightly back to gauge how far or close the other twin was. The other twin was picking up momentum; these were not the same guys Shawn fought several nights ago. He met one of the twins in the center of the construction site. He studied the twin and knew he was dealing with the one called Cyclops.

Cyclops said, "I see you very clear this time around, punk."

Shawn looked at Cyclops and said, "Good. So can you see this?" He threw the first punch, which Cyclops dodged; the move surprised Shawn. He couldn't believe the man could move that quick. With the attempted blow missing its target, it left Shawn off-balance as Cyclops took advantage and came hard with a kick to the back of Shawn's leg. The blow felt as if he was kicked by a horse; he grunted in pain.

Cyclops laughed and said, "I told you I was going to kick your butt, punk."

The other twin grabbed Shawn's bad shoulder and squeezed hard. Shawn felt as if his shoulder was in a vice; he yelled in pain as the other twin reared back and came down hard on that injured shoulder. Shawn howled in agony. The twin went back to that shoulder as he grabbed it again in that vice grip. Shawn tried to fight, but he was no match for the Twins of Destruction, especially with his separated shoulder. While the other twin had Shawn in this grip, Cyclops walked up to Shawn and kicked him hard in the midsection. Shawn felt himself going out. He knew he had to stay awake; if he fainted, he knew it was all over. The Twins of Destruction would kill him, and he would lose Serenity forever.

The kick caused Shawn to break free from the vice grip as he staggered backward trying to maintain his balance. The Twins of Destruction laughed at what was going on; this was a totally different fight from the first one. The brief moment of breaking free gave Shawn the opportunity to go inside his jacket pocket; he grabbed what he was looking for, but the other twin grabbed him and swung him hard toward his brother, Cyclops. Shawn knew he had just a split second to pull this move off. He slid between Cyclops's legs; it happened so fast. Cyclops stood there dumbfounded as Shawn went back into his jacket pocket and bounced up with what look like a six-inch stick. The twins looked at him and laughed.

Cyclops said to his brother, "Is he serious? A stick? I'm about to shove that stick down your throat."

Shawn looked at him and motioned for him to come.

# Chapter 206

Meanwhile, Jefferson went after Hollingsworth. Bobby Lee came toward Jefferson; he was shaking and twitching. Whatever was happening was causing serious tremors throughout his body. Bobby Lee was grabbing different parts of his body, especially his head. He was completely out of control as he yelled and made weird sounds.

Hollingsworth was heading for his car, dragging Serenity. "Come on, bitch." She was putting up a good fight. He grabbed her and slapped her. Serenity yelped in pain as Jefferson, Evans, and Shawn watched helplessly.

Jefferson knew he couldn't let Hollingsworth get to his car; he had to stop him somehow. He moved in that direction, but Bobby Lee stood in his way, going through his ticking and twitching; the man was in serious pain and discomfort. Jefferson looked at him pleading and at the same time watched Hollingsworth; he said to Bobby Lee, "Look, we can help you. We can find a cure for that, but I need to stop that man right there."

Bobby Lee turned and saw Hollingsworth struggling with Serenity, who was putting up a good fight. Bobby Lee said in his pain, "Sorry, but I need that man. He can stop this. He can stop all of this, and I'll do whatever is necessary to get that done. He planted this damn thing in my head, and he is the only one that can take it out. So . . ." Then he looked around, picked up a pipe, and came at Jefferson.

Jefferson reacted, saying, "Whoa!" He took one more look at Hollingsworth, who was near the car. Jefferson yelled at Evans.

Evans was busy himself. He turned toward Jefferson, who pointed to Hollingsworth, who was still struggling with Serenity. Evans felt the urgency; he had to stop Hollingsworth. He tried to reason with the man with the muscles on top of muscles whose street name was Bulldozer. Evans said to him, "Listen to me. You really don't want to do this. I've worked for Hollingsworth for years as his private contractor. The man is a selfish, egotistical bastard that cares only for himself. I wish I never met the scumbag. You can still walk away. I'll make sure you get double what he's paying you or supposedly promised to pay you. Just walk away and do the right thing."

Bulldozer smiled as he gripped the pipe in his hand. "You mean like you did, Evans, like the way you walked away, made your dough, and now you want out. But it's funny—you don't want anyone else to make the money you made. Believe me, your name is legend in the streets. You get major cred and respect and, on top of that, money, dough, cabbage. I want that. I want to do it the way you did it, Ghost, your street handle." There was a pause; then Bulldozer continued, "You got me into this, which I've done well, not as good as you, but okay. And like everything in this life, Ghost, all things must come to an end. Time to either step down or be put down. The choice is up to you."

Evans nodded as he watched Hollingsworth still having a hard time getting Serenity to the car, but he was making progress. Evans turned his attention back to Bulldozer. "I wish I would have done things differently, like now. I regret it then, and I'm about to regret it now. So last chance to turn and walk away."

Bulldozer looked at Evans; he shrugged his shoulders and said, "Perhaps you're right . . ." He lightly chuckled and said, "Again." Bulldozer turned to walk away as Evans's concentration focused on Hollingsworth, who had Serenity near the car, still struggling as he grabbed her by her hair. Security screamed. Evans pivoted to run toward them when he heard Jefferson yell "Look out!"

But it was too late—Bulldozer had already plunged the long knife into Evans's back. Evans yelled with a growl in pain. Bulldozer pushed the blade further as Evans grunted. Bulldozer was right behind him by his ear, with the blade still stuck in his back. Evans's legs wanted to collapse like a deck of cards, but he willed himself to stand; as he stood in that tense position, he knew he had to try to control his breathing and not to panic.

Shaking his head, Bulldozer whispered in a taunting way, "Did you really think that I'd believe that you would just walk away? I don't. I don't trust that you're capable of doing it, so I have to make sure that you do it and stay away."

He snatched the knife out of Evans's back and was getting ready to plunge it back in again to finish him off for good when Evans turned. He dropped to one knee as he stuck out his arms and moved his fingers just a small twitch as two six-inch blades came shooting out right into Bulldozer's stomach; he made a painful surprised sound. Evans moved his fingers again; the sharp blades came jutting out back onto the holder on his wrist. He got up in a crouched position and sent the blades back out again right into Bulldozer's midsection. Evans brought the blades back out as the blood came gushing out of Bulldozer's stomach. Bulldozer dropped his knife; he looked up at Evans as life was slowly oozing from him.

Evans looked at him still in pain and said to Bulldozer, "You should have accepted my offer. It would have worked for you." Bulldozer slowly nodded his head.

Evans looked at Hollingsworth; he was trying to get Serenity in the car. Evans looked down at Bulldozer and noticed that he was reaching for something in his waistband. Evans wouldn't be distracted twice; he slapped Bulldozer's hand away. "Stop."

He brought out the two blades out again; then he painfully and casually walked behind Bulldozer and plunged the blades into his back. Bulldozer made a sound as his body stiffened. Evans snatched the blades out as he watched his former apprentice that he pulled from the streets crumble to the ground. Evans turned away from the body that he once laughed, trained, and hung out with. He hated this life. Evans felt weak but strong enough to respond to the woman he kidnapped and fell in love with, Serenity Cook.

# CHAPTER 207

The two brothers looked at Shawn's little pipe and laughed; one said, "You plan on using that little pipe on the Twins of Destruction, eh?"

Cyclops laughed and said, "Don't worry, brother. He's dreaming. He's having a pipe dream." They both laughed and slapped each other a high five.

Shawn looked at the six-inch pipe, chuckled, and said, "Sometimes dreams turn into nightmares. And this, gentlemen, is going to be your worst nightmare."

Cyclops looked at Shawn with anger and agitation; he clenched his teeth and said, "Enough! You're done, punk." The twins then came running toward him like wild bulls.

Shawn said, "Yeah, I agree, enough is enough."

The six-inch pipe turned into a twelve-inch pipe when he pressed the button on the pipe. Shawn stood there in his battle mode position, waiting; the timing had to be precise. He had to quickly take out one of the twins before taking out the other; he chose Cyclops. Shawn swung and connected with Cyclops's jaw. The burly giant was stunned by the hit as the blow stopped him right in his place as his knees buckled. Shawn knew Cyclops's brother was near, coming behind Shawn fast. He was still facing Cyclops as he jammed the pipe into Cyclops's midsection. Cyclops staggered back and fell to the ground. Shawn stood there looking at Cyclops hit the ground hard while Cyclops's brother was almost on. Shawn just stood there.

He heard Jefferson and Evans yell for him to turn around. Cyclops's brother was practically on top of him. Shawn quickly looked over at Jefferson and at Evans and winked. He put his head down as if he was in deep thought. Cyclops's brother also made it a little easier to track him when he yelled out his frustration. In Shawn's focus, everything was blocked out except for the sounds of Cyclops's brother feet hitting the pavement and his heavy breathing. It was enough for Shawn to quickly calculate how close Cyclops's brother was.

Shawn, still in that thinking position, pivoted back; he brought that pipe back over his head and came down hard with it on Cyclops's brother's shoulder, snapping his collarbone. The brother yelled in pain.

Meanwhile, Cyclops got up, staggering; he was still out of it. Shawn walked up to him as Cyclops took a wild swing at Shawn. Shawn ducked and dipped low; he took the metal pipe and swept Cyclops off his feet. Cyclops hit the ground hard. Shawn turned back to the other brother and came down hard three times in his midsection and chest. The only thing the brother could do was moan and groan in pain as he collapsed to the ground, holding his chest and midsection. Shawn looked at the twins as he pressed the button, causing the pipe to go from twelve inches to three. He said, "Didn't I tell you my pipe dream will turn into your nightmare?"

Shawn was heading toward Hollingsworth when Cyclops recovered. He was up and staggering as he swayed from side to side. Shawn heard Cyclops struggling; he could not believe the man was on his feet. He cursed under his breath; he knew he had to make sure that Cyclops would no longer be a problem. He did not need any more distractions.

Shawn watched Hollingsworth heading to the driver's side. He said to Complex, "Distract him. Don't let him get into that car, but he's mine."

Complex drove over to Hollingsworth driver's side to block him from getting in. Hollingsworth yelled; whoever was driving the tinted car was blocking him. "What the hell are you doing?" In anger, he said, "Get out of my way!" Hollingsworth took out his radio. "Do you really think this is going to stop me?" He said something in his radio, some type of code.

Jefferson heard, and yet he didn't hear; he was still dealing with Bobby Lee. Evans heard it and said, "He's calling for backup, code 99. He's calling everyone who is in the area—in other words, he's calling an army." Evans grimaced and said, "We need to hurry. Those sons of bitches are coming, and if they come, this place is going to get really freakin' ugly. We need to get outta of here."

Hollingsworth looked at Evans and said, "Ah, you remembered. Come back and work for me. We make a great team."

Evans did not say a word. Complex told Hollingsworth, "Step away from the car."

Hollingsworth tried to look in the dark-tinted windows of the car and said, "Freak you, whore!"

Complex said calmly, "This is your last and final warning. Step away from the car."

Hollingsworth still tried to look into the car and said, "Go to hell."

Complex said, "No, but that's where you will be heading soon. Oh, and by the way, I'm not a whore. You must be referring to your mother. I'm a bitch. Now move."

Before Hollingsworth could say anything, Complex squirted him in the eyes with the burning liquid that was worse than tear gas. Hollingsworth screamed as he let go of the door. Complex said, "I thought so. And by the way, you called me a whore, but I see you have a little bitch in you."

Shawn walked up to Cyclops and said, "You should have stayed your ass down and just stayed there until the storm was over. But it looks like you have entered into the eye of the storm, the perfect storm."

Cyclops got off one wild swing. Shawn came back with a flurry of blows; he started with a left jab and a right jab as Cyclops's head jerked back. Shawn exploded with a flurry of blows that were quick, massive, and deadly. The blows were coming so hard and fast that they were holding Cyclops up from collapsing.

Evans looked on in amazement and said, "Damn."

Jefferson smiled and said, "Go, C-4! End it, baby."

Shawn came with two roundhouses, one from the left leg and one from the right leg.

Evans looked on in amazement and thought, *The dude is freakin' magnificent.*

Shawn stopped as he stood in his fighting pose like Bruce Lee. His eyes were intense like fire. His mouth sneered with anger; his muscles were taut and visible through his shirt. He watched and looked at Cyclops amazingly still standing, staggering back and forth. Cyclops's brother was slowly recovering as he was gradually getting up. Shawn put his head down with his hands on his waist and just shook his head; he cursed under his breath. He knew this had to come to an end, or this was going to be a rematch of a rematch. He thought, *Not this time.*

Shawn nodded his head as he looked at the twins, thinking; he was looking intense. Cyclops's brother was bending. Shawn took off running toward the Twins of Destruction; he took out two ninja stars and tossed them with force into Cyclops's shoulder. One went into his left shoulder.

Cyclops jerked with pain as he howled in agony. The other star went into his right shoulder, which caused him to jerk in that direction as he yelled and cursed with pain. The pain was so severe that Cyclops leaned down forward, staggering in pain. The bending was enough for Shawn to run and use Cyclops's back as a springboard; he heard a crack as he projected himself off Cyclops's back. Cyclops then collapsed.

Shawn flipped in the air, reached into his pocket, and took out three ninja stars. As he was coming down toward the other brother, Shawn threw all three stars in quick succession; two went into the throat, and the last one went right between the eyes. The brother made a sound as he fell hard to the ground. Shawn quickly went to him and grabbed him by his hair as he was getting ready to deliver the final blow. As his hand was high in the air, Cyclops, the twin brother who was still seriously injured on the ground, pleaded with Shawn. "Wait, please spare my brother's life. I beg you please."

Shawn looked at Cyclops and said, "And exchange for what?"

Cyclops looked at his brother's semiconscious body and then at Shawn and said, "Our loyalty and respect forever."

Shawn thought about it, looked at Cyclops, and let go of the death grip he was about to perform. He looked at the brother and said, "Loyalty to me, no matter what?"

The brother nodded and said, "Yes, loyalty."

Shawn said, "You break your word, I will hunt you and your brother down. And when I get finished with you and the better half of your ugly twin, you would wish you were never born. Don't try me." The brother nodded.

Meanwhile, Jefferson was jabbing Bobby Lee with the right hand and the left—left jab, right jab, a quick double jab, a quick combination jab. The hard and quick blows did little harm to Bobby Lee as he kept on coming. Bobby grabbed his head as the pain persisted. Jefferson came out with an arsenal assault of blows. Bobby Lee just shook them off like nothing. Jefferson said to him, "We can do this all day, B. All—"

Bobby Lee surprised Jefferson with a right hook, which rocked Jefferson, causing him to stagger and knocking him off-balance. Jefferson was in trouble, and he knew it; he knew he had to stay on his feet. If he fell, he knew he was a dead man. The blows from Bobby Lee kept coming. Jefferson's guard was up, blocking a lot of the blows, but the ones that were connecting were doing damage. Jefferson tried to cover up and duck and dodge, bob and weave, but the bottom line was simple—he was in trouble.

Shawn saw Jefferson was in serious trouble. He went into his pocket and took out his brass knuckles; he made a whistling sound to Jefferson. The noise got Jefferson's attention and, at the same time, distracted Bobby Lee as he turned toward Shawn. Shawn tossed Jefferson the brass knuckles. Meanwhile, Bobby Lee delivered a massive blow to Jefferson's midsection. Jefferson bent over in pain, trying to catch his breath. Bobby Lee stood over Jefferson and said, "You don't understand. I have to get this thing out of my head . . . uggh." He came hard with elbows to the back of Jefferson, who howled in pain as he slowly fell to the ground on one knee. Bobby Lee said, "Can't you see it my way?"

Bobby Lee went to pick Jefferson up; he stood him up and kicked him on the side of his knee. Jefferson yelled in pain as he fell like a deck of cards collapsing. Bobby Lee said, "I can't let you or anyone else get in my way." He picked Jefferson up with one hand; his strength was enormous. He stood a staggering and bleeding Jefferson up.

Shawn wanted to jump in, but he had to stop Hollingsworth. Plus Jefferson waved him off with the one finger, which meant he was okay. Shawn thought, *Like the hell you are.* He was ready to jump in to help Jefferson when he heard Hollingsworth yelling and slapping Serenity. That was it; his mind provided the answer on what he had to do.

Meanwhile, Bobby Lee had Jefferson up. Jefferson was still staggering. He looked at him and slightly smiled. "That's all you have? I've fought tougher dudes in Hell's Kitchen ring. This is just—"

Jefferson couldn't finish the sentence. Bobby Lee came hard into him with a clothesline blow, which flipped Jefferson over to the ground.

Shawn told Jefferson to get up.

# CHAPTER 208

Shawn hurried over to Hollingsworth. Evans also made his way over to Hollingsworth. He grabbed Hollingsworth by the throat in a choke hold. Evans said, "You need to watch your mouth and keep your damn hands to yourself." He put more pressure on Hollingsworth's throat. Hollingsworth was coughing and gasping for air. Evans looked at Shawn. "I got this. Your friend needs help. Go." Evans held out his hand to Shawn, indicating for him to go. Shawn noticed that Evans had the situation under control.

Evans still had Hollingsworth in that choke hold. Hollingsworth was still gasping for air. Shawn said to Evans, "I need that bastard alive, Evans. He's going to pay for what he's done."

Evans nodded. "I understand. I got this. Go help out Jefferson."

Hollingsworth was saying something to Evans. Shawn couldn't hear the exchange, just bits and pieces.

Evans was looking at Hollingsworth, who said, "I mean it, seriously. All yours. Evans, we've been friends . . ." Hollingsworth looked at him and said, "Okay, maybe not close friends, but good associates for years, haven't we?"

Shawn didn't have the time to figure out what was going on as he hurried down to Jefferson.

Shawn ran over to Jefferson and helped him up. Shawn looked over at Evans; something wasn't right. Evans didn't have his choke hold on Hollingsworth, and the two were talking. Whatever they were talking about, Shawn didn't like it; something was absolutely wrong. Shawn knew he had to hurry.

He said to Jefferson, "Hollingsworth had called for backup. His men will be here like a swarm of bees. I need to get Serenity, but we need to take care of this dude." Shawn helped Jefferson up. "Listen, I got this. From what I could put together, he put his hands on my wife. From my hood, this is my fight."

Jefferson said, "I had him, Wall Street."

Shawn said, "I know, I guess that's why I'm picking you up off the ground, eh? This is my fight."

Jefferson understood; he raised both hands in a surrender fashion. "Not a problem. Help yourself. Be careful. Whatever Hollingsworth did to him, the man has enormous strength. He's twice as strong."

Shawn looked at Jefferson and said, "Good, twice as strong. Good, so am I. When you put your hands on my wife . . ." He walked up to Bobby Lee, who was going through his tics and shaking his head. Shawn said, "You put your hands on that woman." Bobby Lee looked at Serenity.

Shawn looked at Evans and Hollingsworth; he didn't like what he was seeing. Something was going on between the two.

Shawn focused back on Bobby Lee. "You put your hands on my wife. Put your hands on me, punk."

Bobby Lee looked at Shawn. "I tried to reason with her, but the bitch put up a fight, so . . . you know."

Shawn looked at him and said, "And now you know." He shrugged his shoulders. "You need to watch your mouth, punk." Shawn came with a quick roundhouse to the side of Bobby Lee's head. The kick would have knocked a horse unconscious, but Bobby Lee backed up a few feet and gave a painful smile as he walked toward Shawn.

Bobby Lee said, "This thing must stop the pain." He continued to walk toward Shawn, who slowly backed up.

Jefferson backed up with Shawn and said, "What is he referring to?"

Shawn said, "How the hell should I know!"

Bobby Lee went to grab Shawn, but he eluded the grab and came straight up with a palm blow right up Bobby Lee's nose; under normal conditions, that should have shifted his brain from the front to the back of his head. Bobby Lee shook it off and said in agony, "Get it out! Get it out! Arrgh!"

Shawn swung at Bobby Lee, who blocked the blow and came back with a hard backhand to the face. Shawn went airborne and landed hard on the ground; in pain, he cursed, "Son of a bitch!"

Jefferson jumped in and threw a few quick hard blows and combinations. Some connected; most of them were blocked. Jefferson was amazed. Bobby Lee grabbed Jefferson and tossed him like a rag doll. Jefferson hit the ground with a thud. Bobby Lee was going to finish the job as he came after Jefferson, who was still in a haze trying to shake off the blow.

Shawn had to do something quickly; he reached in his breast pocket and took out the six-inch pipe and ran toward Bobby Lee from behind. He swept Bobby Lee's feet from under him. Bobby Lee hit the ground and bounced back up as if he never fell. Shawn looked and said, "Damn."

The move gave Jefferson time to get up as the two men circled Bobby Lee. Jefferson said to Shawn, "What now? Suggestions."

Shawn looked perplexed. "I'm working on it."

Jefferson said, "Work harder please because King Kong is ready for round 2."

Bobby Lee made a sound of agony as he grabbed his head. Shawn asked Jefferson, "How strong is your back?" Jefferson looked at Shawn with a perplexed expression. Shawn said, "Jay, serious. I need to borrow it. I'm trying my best not to take this dude out. So come on, how strong is your back?"

Jefferson, still looking as if it was a trick question, said, "Uh, decent." Shawn said, "Good."

Bobby Lee cried out in agony again. "Take it out! Take it out! Arrrrg!"

Bobby Lee was up rocking and reeling slightly from side to side. Shawn cursed and quickly said, "Let's do what we practiced when we were working out. I just need your back."

Jefferson finally caught on and said, "Okay, okay."

Bobby Lee staggered toward them; he was angry as he was breathing heavy, making angry sounds. Jefferson fell on all fours; he looked at Bobby Lee and back at Shawn and said, "Oh shit, Wall Street. Come on! What are you waiting for?" Shawn put up his pointer finger, indicating for Jefferson to wait. Jefferson looked at Bobby Lee still coming. "Shawn, this dude is gone. He's lost it. Come on, man."

Shawn, looking at Bobby Lee, still had his finger up, indicating to wait; he said, "Timing is everything. Remember that song with the words 'Good things might come to those who wait'?"

And Jefferson quickly replied, "And that next verse, 'Not for those who wait too late . . . Just the two of us.' Yeah, yeah, Bill Withers."

Shawn nodded and said, "Now brace yourself." He ran as he jumped off Jefferson's back with a victory shout as he came straight-up hard into Bobby Lee's face with a kick that sent the man into a bunch of steel beams, pipes, and bricks. Shawn landed as he tucked, rolled, and bounced up.

He went into his pocket and took out his brass knuckles; he turned to Jefferson, who already had his brass knuckles on. The two walked up to Bobby Lee as he was getting up; they stood on either side of him. Shawn said, "I've had about enough of your craziness."

Bobby Lee yelled out in frustration as he came out at Shawn with a thick two-by-four piece of wood. He swung the wood at Shawn, who grabbed the wood as it was coming toward him. Shawn gritted his teeth as he shoved the wood hard to the side. Bobby Lee's body went with the force of the shove. He turned back around, looking at Shawn with anger as he came at him again, this time with such determination. Shawn did not move; he stood his ground. With his feet planted, he ducked and dipped and dodged Bobby Lee's punches. He leaned left and right; he was a moving target that couldn't be touched.

Bobby Lee was getting aggravated as sounds of frustration came from him. Shawn let loose a flurry of blows, and at the same time, Jefferson opened up his store of flurry whip ass of blows as Bobby Lee was being tagged from both sides. Whatever Shawn did, Jefferson was doing to the point they started moving in sync as if they were reading each other's mind. It was a symphony of kick ass in motion.

They started from the bottom of Bobby Lee's legs and moved up to his midsection with a flurry of blows; they moved up to his upper body, tagging him, and started going back down the same way they went up. Bobby Lee could do nothing; he was starting to show signs of fatigue, signs of breaking. Shawn reached down and picked up two thin pipes about ten inches long each. He stood there in Bruce Lee fashion, just focusing on Bobby Lee. Jefferson looked and said, "Oh crap, time to bring down the house."

Jefferson stepped back. Shawn moved the two pipes he held in his hands so fast it was as if he was moving frame by frame; it was unbelievable. He connected with Bobby Lee with at least five to seven nasty blows to the man's shoulders, face, and legs randomly. Bobby Lee grunted in pain; the look of pain registered on his face. Shawn stopped as he watched Bobby Lee stagger. He was wasted; he was done.

Shawn looked at Jefferson, who nodded; he was ready. Jefferson grabbed Shawn by his hands. Shawn began to swing Jefferson around in a circle until Shawn picked up the momentum and speed as he spun Jefferson in that circle. Jefferson was completely in the air. Shawn growled in pain as he let Jefferson go. Jefferson did this crazy body spin in the air, coming hard with a devastating punch into Bobby's Lee face. The man fell hard to the ground.

Shawn ran over to Jefferson and helped him up. They both looked down at Bobby Lee; the man was out cold. Jefferson brushed the dirt of his shoulders and chest and said, "You better recognize, punk. Welcome to the House of Pain. S and J are not only in the house—we rule the house . . . punk." Jefferson went to hold his left shoulder. "Yo, that sucker hurt like a mother. Nah, next time, you can do the fly and connect."

Shawn took out some handcuffs and tossed them to Jefferson. "Cuff him." Shawn looked over at what was going on with Evans and Hollingsworth. He hurried over there; something was going on.

# Chapter 209

looked confused; she had been forced into the car. She couldn't understand why Evans didn't do anything, why he allowed this to take place. Evans and Hollingsworth looked relaxed. Shawn looked at Evans and asked, "Evans, what's going on here?"

Hollingsworth chuckled and said, "Mr. Cook, it's simple. Can't you see? Money talks and bull . . . well, you know the rest, which I'm going to do . . . is walk."

Shawn looked at Evans. Hollingsworth blew out a breath of frustration and said, "Evans and I have made a deal, you nimrod. Okay, it took me emptying out a good amount of my stash. But there is nothing like freedom, Mr. Cook." He paused and continued, "The money is nothing. I'll put that back in time. For example, this construction site that you're standing on is mine. The money I will make from this will be sweet. I told you, Mr. Cook, you will not win. I told you what you have I will take because you took from me."

Shawn looked at Serenity, who was crying. Hollingsworth continued, "Remember, Mr. Cook, an eye for an eye, a tooth for a tooth . . . a life . . ."

Shawn looked at Evans, who shrugged as if he was in tremendous pain. "Sorry, Shawn, I need something to fall back on. I apologized to Serenity. I really did care for her. You are a blessed man."

Shawn looked at Evans; he gritted his teeth from the pain, from the deception, from the exhaustion, from everything. Hollingsworth laughed and said, "No, correction, was a blessed man. But it appears as if your blessings have run dry and out, Mr. Cook."

Shawn made a step toward them. Hollingsworth got nervous. Evans held his gun out, pointing it at Shawn. Hollingsworth slightly smiled. "Now, now, Mr. Cook, it's over."

Jefferson came over, pulling Bobby Lee with him. Jefferson was furious, enraged; he said, "I told you not to trust this backstabber, punk-ass malicious traitor."

Evans reacted, saying, "Ooh, big words! Do you know what they mean?"

Jefferson scowled at him and said, "I'll look it up. I'm sure your picture will be right next to it."

Evans looked at Jefferson and said, "You would have done the same thing. You don't break your loyalty to those that have shown you appreciation."

Hollingsworth smiled and said, "And him and I go way back—that's loyalty, folks." Hollingsworth's signal went through, showing that the money had gone through. He said, "Well, Mr. Evans, 30 million American dollars has just been put in your account in the Swiss Bank, sir."

Jefferson said, gritting his teeth, "You sellout son of a bitch! I bet your father's name was Judas, and I guess you're Judas Jr. He sold Jesus for thirty pieces of silver. You 30 million."

Evans smiled and said, "Inflation is a bitch."

Hollingsworth sarcastically sighed. "Oh well, gentlemen, time is quickly slipping away." He looked at Evans. "As always, Mr. Francisco Evans, it was nice doing business with you. I'll call you."

Jefferson was peeved; he said to Hollingsworth, "Don't forget to take your trash." He was referring to Bobby Lee.

Hollingsworth, looking at Bobby Lee and back at Jefferson, responded, "Oh, that . . . Well, I really don't have a need for that trash."

Jefferson shot back, "You dirty piece of scum! You use them and then throw them out!"

Hollingsworth thought about the statement and said, "Well, yeah, something like that . . ."

Jefferson just shook his head and said, "Bastard."

Hollingsworth continued, "Bobby Lee did what I wanted, and I must say, he did better than what I thought. Instead of catching Mr. Cook, I have him and his bitch and his errand boy. Good day, wouldn't you say, uh . . . Jeffrey?"

Jefferson shot back, "Get it right, pea brain! It's Jefferson Newhouse, punk!"

Hollingsworth had a carefree look on his face; he said, "Whatever. As I was saying, I can't use such baggage. I need to be free of trash. Plus I really don't believe in recycling trash." He laughed.

Jefferson said to Evans, "You hear that, Evans? You are done in his eyes. You're nothing but a used-up piece of crap." Then he said to Hollingsworth, "I just want you to know—and you probably heard it a million times, but here is a million and one—you are one cold son of a bitch."

. "Yes, I have heard that phrase before. Thank you. And to set the record straight, Bobby Lee is a loser just like you, Newhouse. Oh, I know all about you—everything. But that one, Bobby Lee, is dying . . ." He looked at his expensive watch and said, "I'll make this quick. You're going to die today anyway. That pain in Bobby's head is a tracker bug I planted and this"—he showed Jefferson the controls—"this controls the amount of pressure that is in his head. This controls the level of pain I decide to send to his head. Right now, I have it on, let's see, 3 and 4. And you see the strength and the power he has. I could make billions of dollars off this gadget." Hollingsworth continued, "When I'm done with his service, which is today. I will turn the pressure gauge to10."

Jefferson looked shocked as Hollingsworth continued, "And now get this—the farther I move away from him, the more the pain and pressure until his brain will have an overload and his head will self-destruct like a watermelon."

Jefferson shook his head and said, "You are not only sick—you are pure evil! Not an ounce of good is in you, Hollingsworth."

Hollingsworth looked at him and said, "Thank you, you keep in mind that my donations to the poor and needy exceed those of all these so-called charitable organizations."

Jefferson looked at him. "Buying and trying to bribe God will not make up for the evil you have caused in your lifetime."

Hollingsworth smiled and then looked at his watch. "Time to go. Good day, Jefferson."

Shawn felt as if the world had caved in with him in it; he felt so worthless, so useless. All of this—getting so close, putting his life and Jefferson's life on the line, getting so close on so many occasions, getting close to the prize just to have it snatched away from him. He looked on in defeat; he looked up at Serenity. She looked at him with such compassion, the eyes of forgiveness; she loved him so much. She just shook her head;

she knew it was over. She knew she would no longer see the man she loved. Tears began to stream down her face.

Shawn was perplexed; he didn't know what was happening. He felt he was in a bad dream. He couldn't understand why Complex wasn't doing something. Shawn came to the conclusion that she had malfunctioned somehow. He knew he wasn't quick enough to go inside his pocket for his weapon; he was in too much pain. Plus Evans would have that gun on him before he knew it . . . It was over. All his options were gone; he would lose Serenity forever. He put down his head; he consented to defeat. The bad guys not only won—they also took the prize of his life.

He looked at Hollingsworth and said, "I will find you, Hollingsworth, and I will make you pay. You have a date with destiny."

Hollingsworth walked up to him, smacked him hard in the face with his back hand, and said, "Really, Cook? I guess I missed the first appointment." He slapped him again and yelled at him, "You couldn't do it the first time! What makes you think you can do it the next time? Plus I hate to pop your bubble, but you won't be able to do it." Shawn looked at him. Hollingsworth casually said, "Do you know why, Mr. Cook? Because I'm going to kill you today. That's why, you cocksure bastard." Another smack as he continued, "It's going to be done, Mr. Cook, right now. Well, not right now, but today as soon as my army soldiers arrive."

Hollingsworth laughed. He looked at Shawn and spat in his face. Jefferson took a step toward Hollingsworth. Hollingsworth looked at him. "Don't be stupid. Be smart and enjoy the next fifteen minutes left of your life."

Jefferson was confused; he couldn't understand what was going on with Complex, all those weapons. He came to the same conclusion—malfunction. He knew Gordon did not have it in his program to do anything; they were doomed was the bottom line.

Hollingsworth walked back to the car and said to Evans, "Last order, okay? Get rid of them, execution-style. Let's get out of here." He looked at Evans and asked, "You okay? Come on, I need to leave. I need to catch a flight. Let's go."

Evans said, "Okay, I need to . . ." He put his weapon down on the roof of the car; he bent over, trying to deal with the pain from his wound. He came back up and reached for his gun, but it was gone.

# CHAPTER 210

He looked at Hollingsworth, who had his weapon; he was pointing it at Evans. Hollingsworth said, "You're a fool, Evans. You messed up big-time. Never leave your firearm, soldier. Out of all people, you should know that." He continued, "You're such a cocksure street punk, Evans, always have been, from the very first day I met you up till now. A lone ranger jackass, ghost . . . what a joke."

Evans looked at him. "You really don't get it, do you?"

Hollingsworth shook his head with a slight smile and said, "What is there to get? What? I win, and you lose." He held the gun toward Evans and said, "And now you die." Hollingsworth confidently held the gun out.

Shawn said in the headset, "Complex, do something. What the hell is wrong with you?"

Complex replied, "Shawn, there is nothing I can do, but . . ."

Hollingsworth said, "Nice knowing you, Evans."

He pulled the trigger; the gun clicked. He did it again; another click. He did it faster. *Click, click, click* . . . Hollingsworth began to panic; he made a desperate sound as he clicked again and again. "Shit . . ." He looked at the gun; he was astonished, amazed. He was still looking at the gun. "What the hell . . ."

Evans looked at Hollingsworth. Hollingsworth looked at Evans. Evans walked over to Hollingsworth and smacked the gun out of his hand. Evans said to him, "I'm the fool, and you are a bigger fool, I guess. A good soldier knows his enemy, and he keeps them closer than a friend. And with you, I made sure I was on you like flies on crap." Evans looked at Shawn briefly and back at Hollingsworth, who had his hands up, pleading and begging for mercy.

"Evans, I was just testing you, that's all. I really didn't have any intentions of—" Evans turned and smacked Hollingsworth so hard it knock him to the ground. Hollingsworth cried out for mercy, "Please, please, Evans!"

Evans walked over to him, picked him up off the ground, and said, "Hollingsworth, I don't need this weapon to kill you. I am a trained assassin, a trained killer. I could kill you in thirty-one different ways, like Baskin-Robbins's thirty-one flavors—that's every day of the month, you lowlife piece of shit. I don't need this." He showed Hollingsworth the gun; he took it and, using the butt of the gun, slammed it into Hollingsworth's face, breaking his nose and knocking out some of his perfect teeth. Evans kneed him in the nuts. Hollingsworth's mouth opened in pain, but nothing came out until finally a howl of pain escaped from his mouth.

Evans raised his hand to come back with another hit when Hollingsworth pleaded, "Wait, wait . . . Evans . . . Mr. Evans, I could make you rich."

Evans looked at him. "Don't you remember I took practically all of your money? I am rich, $30 million richer, you idiot!" He gripped the back of Hollingsworth's neck with his hand and slammed his face against the hood of the car. Evans still had his neck and said, "Do you really think I would become that careless, Hollingsworth, so you can take advantage of me?"

Hollingsworth pleaded, saying, "No no no, nooooo!"

Evans stepped back and gave him a hard side kick to the stomach. Hollingsworth cried out in pain as he slammed hard into the car and bounced off the door, leaving a huge dent in the door. Hollingsworth was moaning and begging when Evans grabbed him and snatched him up. Hollingsworth's face was a bloody mess; he had a broken nose and missing teeth. The once-handsome 5'9" rich man looked smaller than ever; he appeared worthless, inferior, and pathetic. His expensive suit looked tattered; he was now the image of shame.

He felt Evans's strong hand on him as Evans squeezed Hollingsworth's shoulders. He screamed in pain. Evans said, "You caused me to lose my family, my wife and children, but I won't fully blame you. I made that decision. I allowed you to convince me with your so-called pipe dream, you lowlife scumbag piece of crap."

Hollingsworth's words could not come out right; his face was swollen and his teeth knocked out. Evans grabbed him and slammed his face against the window of the car and said, "Apologize . . ."

Hollingsworth was still dazed. Evans said it again with more force as he put a strong hard grip to the back of Hollingsworth's neck. Hollingsworth flinched with pain, "Ahhhh." Blood was on the window.

Evans said, "I said apologize now."

Hollingsworth slowly lifted his eyes and looked at Serenity and looked back down; he looked back up and said, "I . . . I apologize." Serenity looked at him.

Evans dragged Hollingsworth from the front of the car door as Serenity got out. She looked at Hollingsworth, who was now on his knees, as she smacked him in the face once, twice, and thrice. She cried as she turned and walked over to her husband and looked up at him; there were no words. It was all in the tears of pain, joy, and hope. She fell into his arms as she cried a hard cry—it was a type of cry that came from deep, deep, deep down in her soul. Serenity hugged the man she loved so much. She held on to him as if no one would ever take him away from her arms; he held on tight and felt the same. She was beaten, battered, and bruised; and despite all of that, he found that his love for her was inseparable as he held back his tears. She could feel him shake as if he was ready to explode; she knew he wanted to cry—a howling cry, an agonizing cry. *Not here*, she thought. She knew when they go home. *Home*, she thought, *he will let the tears* go. She thanked God her man, her husband, was a warrior. God had place his enemies as his footstool. Hollingsworth was the first one.

Serenity broke the embrace and went over to Evans; she hugged him, a hug of respect and gratefulness. He'd been a true friend to the very end. The hug wasn't anything close to the way she hugged her man. Shawn saw it; he felt that. He was okay with that.

Serenity told Evans thank you; as she pulled away, her hand touched his side. She felt a heavy moisture. She quickly pulled her hand back and saw the blood. She was shocked as she gasped in panic, "Oh my god, Evans, you're—"

He shushed her, "It's okay. It's just a little wound."

She repeated his downplayed words, "Evans, a little?" She turned and looked at Shawn. "Oh my god, Shawn, Evans needs to get to the hospital."

Evans raised his hand and shook his head weakly. "No hospitals. I'll be okay."

Serenity, looking concerned, said, "Shawn." She looked at Evans. "No, you won't. You will die if . . ." She looked back at Shawn. "Babe, we need to get him some medical help."

Shawn nodded his head; he thought about his doctor and said, "Give me a minute."

Hollingsworth chuckled, saying, "He'll be joining me."

Evans said, "I don't think so. You'll be taking the express to hell. Say hi to your brother for me."

Hollingsworth's head dropped in defeat.

Serenity looked at Shawn; he nodded. "I'll take care of it."

He looked at Evans. "You need to trust me." Evans, looking skeptical, closed his eyes and nodded.

Shawn walked up to Hollingsworth; he just looked at the man who was his main threat; now he was harmless. Shawn shook his head. Hollingsworth looked up at Shawn and said, "You struck first. You took my brother and so—"

Shawn heard enough as he grabbed Hollingsworth by his collar and jerked him to him; he said, "Stop it, stop it, stop the bull crap, Hollingsworth! Phillip Keys wasn't your brother, you sick son of a bitch! You convinced yourself that he was, but the truth is out." Shawn paused and continued, "It takes a sick mind to get tons of surgery done just to look like a killer. You pay in the billions to get this done, you sick bastard!"

Hollingsworth's eyes opened up not at wanting to look like a killer, but at the idea to spend all that money just to look like a killer. Shawn said, "Yeah, I know what you've done, and so will the world. You're ill, Hollingsworth. You need help."

Shawn came with a right-hand cross to Hollingsworth's jaw; the punch knocked him out.

# CHAPTER 211

When Hollingsworth came to, he found his movement very limited; he tried to move, but he was confined with a restraint of some sort. He pulled hard; he heard someone yell, "Hey! What the hell are you doing?" Hollingsworth turned his neck quickly to the left and to the right, back to the left and to the right. He was still groggy. He heard the voice say, "Keep still, you idiot."

Hollingsworth stopped moving and thought; he finally said, "Bobby Lee, is that you?"

Bobby Lee said, "No, you, jackass. It's your mother, stupid."

Hollingsworth yanked on the restraint. Bobby Lee yanked back. Hollingsworth yanked again. Bobby Lee yanked hard again. Hollingsworth said, "Wait, listen . . ." He paused and continued, "Listen, if we could work together instead of fighting against each other, we may be able to get out of this."

Bobby Lee did not say anything; they both heard voices as Shawn snatched the hood off Hollingsworth and then Bobby Lee. They looked around and noticed they were handcuffed to each other. Hollingsworth said, "What are you doing, Cook? Is this some kind of a joke? If it is, it's not funny. I fail to see the humor."

Shawn turned toward Hollingsworth and grinded his teeth, saying, "You think I'm joking? You think all of this is one big joke?" Shawn looked at him with anger beaming out of his eyes as he continued, "You think this a hoax of some kind? How about this?" He smacked Hollingsworth hard in the face. "Do you still think I'm playing with you, punk? Did that feel real to you?"

Hollingsworth shook his head frantically, "Okay, okay." He looked at Shawn nervously and said, "Okay, what do you want, huh? I can make it happen."

Shawn said, "At one time, yes, but now no more. You are broke—no money, no gas in the gas tank. It's over, Hollingsworth. You're done."

Hollingsworth nodded his head and tried to negotiate with Shawn, "Okay, I could still make it happen. I still have connections. People still owe me. Tell me what you want. What do you need? I can make it happen."

Shawn grabbed Hollingsworth by the jaw, squeezed, and said, "You don't get it. You messed with my family. You messed with me. You know what I want, Hollingsworth?"

Hollingsworth's eyes opened up with hope. "What? Tell me, tell me, I can make it—"

Shawn cut him off and said in a hard eerie voice, "I want an eye for an eye, a tooth for a tooth, a life for a life, you sorry, no-good son of a bitch."

Hollingsworth nervously smiled and said, "I did not mess with your family."

Shawn, out of anger, grabbed him by his collar. Hollingsworth gasped with surprise at Shawn's aggressive behavior. He was shaking. Shawn said, "You still want to play semantics with me, mother sucker? I'll make it clear to you—this is payback for what you did to Phillip Collins and that woman and whoever you introduced into their lives to wreak havoc, and . . ." Shawn smacked Hollingsworth in the face and said, "My wife, you lowlife bastard."

Hollingsworth desperately yelled in a panic. "That's bullshit, Cook! Those folks—"

Shawn cut him off. "Had no choice, no voice, no representation. You became their judge and jury and executioner. And now I'm yours—your jury, your judge, and your executioner." He reached into his pocket and took out that control device Hollingsworth had.

Hollingsworth's eyes opened up wide in fear and panic. "That's mine. That belongs to me."

Jefferson walked up to Hollingsworth and said, "Oh well, sorry, finders keepers, losers weepers. So start weeping, you scumbag."

Shawn pierced his eyes on Hollingsworth and, with his voice low and deep, said, "You will pay for what've you've done, Hollingsworth, just like your mentor."

Jefferson added, "End of the line for you, punk."

Bobby Lee screamed in fear; he pleaded and begged, "Wait, wait, I did not have any choice. This bastard put some device in my head. He had complete control over me . . . please."

Shawn replied, "I know, that is unfortunate for you. You got caught in the cross fire, the collateral damage. I don't blame you."

Bobby Lee desperately asked, "So can you help me get free from this lunatic?"

Hollingsworth jerked him hard. "Who are you calling a lunatic?" Bobby Lee grunted in pain and jerked back hard. Hollingsworth cried out in agony, "You stupid ass, don't jerk!"

Bobby Lee said, "You don't jerk. I blame you for getting us into this. Now look at us. This is all your fault, you jackass."

Shawn said to Bobby Lee, "Just your association with Hollingsworth disgusts me. Your request is overruled and denied."

Bobby Lee protested the decision. "But this isn't my—"

Shawn looked at him and said, "Like I said, I'm the jury, judge, and executioner." He looked at Hollingsworth and said, "What happened to your army soldiers, Hollingsworth? Everyone must have heard you are broke. Word gets around quick." He looked at Complex.

Hollingsworth was frustrated. "I don't know . . . I don't understand. They were supposed to be here." His head dropped in defeat.

Serenity turned and looked back at Evans; she asked him, "Will you be all right?"

He nodded weakly and said, "I've been in worse situations." He smiled with a sheer bit of doubt on his face. "I think so." Evans grimaced as the pain became even more intense; he cursed, "Damn."

Jefferson came over to the car. "Listen, bro, I really didn't like you from day 1. I couldn't stand you when it was your ass getting out of the car here." He paused and continued, "But seeing what you've done here, yo, bro, you've earned my respect. Much respect, bro. You have heart, man, heart of a lion, a warrior. Hang in there, kid." Jefferson came closer to Evans, hugged him, and gave him a shoulder tap. They let go of each other.

Evans nodded and slightly smiled; the pain was kicking his ass bigtime. He gave Jefferson a thumbs-up.

Shawn came over to Jefferson and Evans; he said, "Okay, pep talk is over."

Complex said in Shawn's headset, "Incoming call from the commissioner, aka asswipe."

Jefferson heard it through his headset; he laughed and said, "Yo, Wall Street, in all seriousness, I need to get Gordon fixed like this, man! Serious. Check it, incoming calls can be screened. I mean, I could avoid all kinds of drama—female drama, bill collections, and friends you don't want to speak to." He continued, "The good part, I would know all of this ahead of time. So cool. TJ has to hook me up for Christmas. This will be my only Christmas gift, serious."

Shawn instructed Complex to send the call through. He said, "Moore, what's up?"

The commissioner said, "Cook, you are up to something. I know you are. So don't 'What's up?' me. You tell me, huh."

Shawn shrugged his shoulders. "Sure, I'm about to close the book on this chapter."

He got Curtis Moore's attention. "What do you mean?" Shawn did not give an answer. The commissioner was becoming agitated. "Cook, what do you mean?"

Shawn said, "I'll call you later. This is not the place nor the time."

The commissioner yelled in the phone, "Shawn . . . Shawn . . . Shawn! Dammit, Cook!" Complex disconnected the call.

Shawn took out the remote control. Hollingsworth's eyes opened up wide; he said in a panic, "Mr. Cook, what are you doing? What are you doing, huh?"

Shawn told him and Bobby Lee to get up; they both struggled in getting up. Both men were hurt and battered. Hollingsworth was breathing hard; he had one damaged lung. Shawn said to them, "Now this is the deal. I'm going five miles in my car. If you keep up, the reward is that you shall live. If you don't keep up and fall behind, well, the results are obvious, I think."

Hollingsworth cried out, "What, are you mad? Are you insane? Keep up! Cook, look at me." Shawn was doing something when Hollingsworth yelled, "Would somebody please look at me! Look at my condition . . . please!"

Shawn looked at him. "I haven't gone mad, and I'm not insane. Do you know what I am, Hollingsworth? I'm just freakin' pissed off, especially with you. You keep up with the car, and you will live. I am a man of my word. I will set you free."

Jefferson protested, "What! This bastard needs to die, Wall Street."

Shawn ignored Jefferson as he continued, "If you don't keep up . . ." He stopped.

Hollingsworth had a look of horror on his face; he asked the question he already knew the answer to. "Then what?"

Jefferson walked up behind him and said in a low tone, "Pop goes the weasel—in this case, that thing of evil on your shoulders you call a head."

Hollingsworth gave Shawn a desperate look and said, "Cook, I'm sure we can work something out. How about you let me live? And I promise you would never ever hear from me again."

Shawn thought about it. Jefferson could see he was considering it. Jefferson was completely bewildered; he said, "Shawn, don't fall for that. The man is no good. He's a liar, a deceiver, just pure evil. Shawn, you know that man."

Hollingsworth smiled with his Halloween-looking jack-o'-lantern face. He made a low laugh that had deception written all over it; it was sinister, dark, and evil. He said to Shawn, "Come on, Cook, show me the man you are. Take the challenge. You let me live, I disappear. C'mon, Cook."

Bobby Lee said, "How about me? I'm the one with the time bomb in my head that you placed there. How about me?"

Hollingsworth thought about it and said, "Hey, your problem, your issue, not mine."

Bobby Lee snickered. "You dirty son of a bitch, you told me that once you kill Cook and turn his wife into your sex slave, you would!"

Hollingsworth had a horrible look on his face as he looked at Bobby Lee and said, "Shut up, shut up, you idiot! Keep your mouth shut!" Shawn looked at Hollingsworth.

Bobby Lee continued, "You did this to me, and now you don't have the decency to undo your wrong, you lying bastard!"

Hollingsworth ignored Bobby Lee and focused on Shawn. "Pay no attention to him. He's delusional. So what do you say, Cook?"

Jefferson said, "He says—"

Hollingsworth looked at Jefferson. "Mind your business. I'm speaking to Cook, you insignificant little nuisance."

Jefferson casually walked over to Hollingsworth, stood in front of him, and smacked him in the face; before he was going to smack him again, Shawn grabbed him. Jefferson said to Shawn, "Don't do this. Don't believe this liar. Even his own man, Shawn. C'mon, the man . . . Complex."

Complex said, "Shawn babe, listen to me. I would never guide you wrong, and you know that. If I felt this was in your best interest, you know

I'm with you no matter what, babe. This man is no good, and deep down in your soul, you know it."

Hollingsworth was still recovering from Jefferson's smack. Complex was speaking in Shawn's headset. Hollingsworth shook his head slightly and said, "What's the problem, Cook? You're getting cold feet?" He laughed and said, "Cook, in the long run, you win. You still come out on top."

Shawn looked at Serenity and nodded his head. He said to Hollingsworth, "Hollingsworth, we're both businessmen, right? And businessmen sometimes have to take chances or gambles, right?"

Hollingsworth, looking somewhat confused, slowly nodded his head. "Uh . . . right."

Shawn continued, "And in business, it's that strange feeling of feeling it in the gut. I mean some business folks could make some crazy decisions just based on that gut feeling, right?"

Hollingsworth was starting to smile. "Yes."

Shawn continued, "Sometimes the majority is saying no, but that gut feeling is saying yes. And sometimes you just have to go with that gut feeling. Are you with me?"

Hollingsworth, with his busted mouth, smiled and said, "With you all the way." Jefferson just shook his head. Hollingsworth, mocking some folks in the church, said, "Yes, preach on, preacher!"

Jefferson just threw his hands up in defeat. "Oh shit, I'm done."

But there are times when the majority is saying no, and your gut is saying yes. But sometimes you have to go with the ones that care about you, those who've been in your corner from day 1, that have been there for you, in your ups and downs. And maybe, just maybe, Hollingsworth, your gut is wrong. Do I still have a witness?"

Hollingsworth's smile was slowly coming off his face; he was confused. "What? Huh? What are you saying, Cook?"

Jefferson threw both fists up in the air. "Yes, let the church say amen."

Complex's colors flashed brightly; she said in Shawn's headset, "Good call, handsome."

Shawn smiled and winked at her. Serenity couldn't hear the exchange, but from the reaction, she knew her husband had made the right decision; she just smiled. Evans looked at Shawn and gave him a weak thumbs-up with a nod.

A car was coming their way. Jefferson looked at Shawn. "You expecting company?"

Shawn slowly shook his head. "Not me."

He instructed Complex to get her weapons ready. The approaching car stopped a few feet from them. The windows were dark. Shawn asked, "Complex?"

Complex responded, "I'm not sure. But from my readings, not a threat, no hostile. But remember there is a 5 percent chance I may be wrong." Shawn had his hand on his revolver. The door opened.

Jefferson had his hand on his little gun he called Big Ben; he said under his breath, "Say hello to my little friend. I finally get a chance to use this." He smiled with satisfaction.

A woman got out and walked toward them. Shawn looked; he was surprised. It was the same woman who gave him details about Evans, the one who tossed him the phone and took off. She stepped up with her hands extended. "Mr. Cook."

Shawn gave her a short nod; he was confused. He looked at Evans, who didn't have much of an expression one way or another. She acknowledged Jefferson with a slight nod you would have missed if you blink. Jefferson commented, "Wow, that's all I get? A cheap phony-ass nod? Not knowing I risked my life . . ." Jefferson stopped and said, "Not a problem."

She looked at Hollingsworth and Bobby Lee and then back at Evans. "Okay, ready to come home?" Evans looked at her; he didn't say a word or make a gesture of any kind. She said, "They missed you. You have accomplished your goal. You promised you would eventually come back. They did you wrong. Those that did are all gone. Come back." She looked at him and noticed he was hurt; she said, "How bad is it?"

She looked at him; he slightly smiled. She looked around at everyone as if to say she couldn't trust his judgment. Evans said, "Not bad." She looked at Shawn, who just slowly shook his head. Tears began to well up in the woman's eyes; a lump formed in her throat.

Shawn said, "I have set up a specialist we're taking him to. He's lost a lot of blood."

The woman said, "That won't be necessary, Mr. Cook. We will take it from here."

Jefferson said, "Like hell you are! Not so fast, lady. You hot rod yourself in your nice, fancy car and think once you speak, we bow. You can kiss my—"

Shawn jumped in and said, "Jay."

Jefferson, looking angry, apologized. "Nah, Shawn. Not cool, lady. I don't care who you are. We are not releasing him until we know he's safe. Plus who gives you the authority to come up in here and ask us to—"

The woman reached into her jacket. Shawn pulled out his revolver. "Nice and easy."

The woman smiled and said, "Not a problem." She pulled out some papers and handed them to Jefferson; she said, "Please give it to your boss."

Jefferson said, "Do I look like a messenger or an errand boy?"

The woman, looking serious, said, "I'm not sure if you know how to read."

Jefferson looked at her. "Yo, lady, keep insulting me, Why don't you read the directions on how to take that dead-ass weave out of your hair? It's time!"

The woman said again, "He'll be safe."

Shawn looked at the papers and back up at the woman, back at the papers, and then at Evans. He nodded his head and said, "My partner is right. I don't care what your documents are saying. We're not releasing him until we know for sure he'll be safe." Shawn still had his hand on his revolver.

Jefferson was saying to himself but loud enough for the others close to him to hear, "Say hi to my little friend." Shawn told Jefferson to stay there near them.

The woman said, "Look!"

Evans interrupted, saying, "Hey, guys, thanks. It's all good. I'm safe. She's good. I'm safe. She'll get the medical help I need."

Shawn looked at him and asked, "Are you sure?

Evans said with a nod, "Yeah, she's cool, but thanks for the backup."

Shawn asked Evans to give him a second. "Complex."

Complex said, "Shawn, my readings show sincerity with good intentions—unless she found a way to get past my radar, which I seriously doubt."

Shawn said to her, "I trust your judgment."

Evans was taking off his headset. Shawn lightly touched his hand and said, "Keep it. Keep it on channel 7. We may need you again. You never know."

Evans looked down and around; his eyes focused on Serenity. He gave her a weak smile; she smiled and decided to come out of the car, She walked up to him and hugged him. "You take care, the best kidnapper in the world."

Evans weakly smiled with a soft laugh. "Thank you." Serenity went back to the car.

Evans looked at Jefferson, who gestured with a fist pump to his chest. Evans nodded and did the same thing; he was very weak.

The woman said, "We need to go."

Evans limped to the woman's car; he waved and got in. The woman made a 180 and zoomed out.

Jefferson walked up to Shawn and asked, "Wall Street, who was the woman? Those documents?"

Shawn said, "CIA."

Jefferson said, "Get the hell out of here!"

Shawn said, "It's true. I had Complex look up Evans. It shows at one time he did work for the government. Plus Tanya told me her and Evans used to be partners. She was the scientist, and he was her bodyguard."

Shawn looked at Hollingsworth and said, "Your turn. Would you prefer to be handed over to the authorities?"

Hollingsworth smiled. "Definitely the authorities."

Shawn looked at him and said, "Should Hollingsworth be handed to the authorities?" He looked at Jefferson and Serenity. Then he looked back at Hollingsworth and said, "Survey says . . ." Jefferson made the sound of a buzzer. Shawn looked at Hollingsworth with a hard glare and said, "Survey says hell no!"

He continued, "You see, Hollingsworth, the bottom line is I don't like you, I can't stand you, I despise you . . . I despise you the way I despise your brother. I hate the idea that you were born. I would have never thought I would want someone to go to hell, but with you, I hope you take the express there. You are wicked and evil, Hollingsworth, and deserve to be in a place made for animals like you." Shawn paused; he looked the other way, then back at Hollingsworth and said, "You want to be like your brother? Don't just stop there. Take the good with the bad. You will also die like him, and you will also be with him."

Shawn blew out a breath and told Jefferson to get the two men up. Jefferson helped Hollingsworth and Bobby Lee up. Shawn said to them, "If you two want to live, you will work together. The closer you stay to the vehicle, the less pain. The farther away from the vehicle, the more pain you will feel until the pain becomes unbearable and pop."

Bobby Lee told Hollingsworth to stop his bitching and start concentrating on keeping close to the vehicle; they might have a chance of getting free.

Shawn and Jefferson got in the car. Gordon was programmed to follow. Shawn told Complex to start moving. "Complex, start off slow and then pick it up every two minutes."

Hollingsworth and Bobby Lee had to figure out how they were going to do this; the way they were handcuffed together made it very awkward to walk. They started shoving and pulling each other. Complex started the car and gave it some gas. Hollingsworth was alarmed; he said, "Stop, stop, stop! They're starting, come on." They had no idea what the best way to move was; they were like in the potato sack game where you couldn't walk and had to hop side by side instead.

Bobby Lee yelled at Hollingsworth to keep up. Hollingsworth said he was trying; he was having a hard time coordinating his feet with Bobby Lee's. Bobby Lee cursed him out. Complex picked up the speed slightly. Bobby Lee felt a slight pain shoot through his head. There was nothing he could do about it; both hands were handcuffed. He shook his head and cursed; he said to Hollingsworth, "Ahhh, the pain! Keep up, keep up!"

Hollingsworth yelled back, "I'm trying! I'm trying!"

. Complex increased the speed a little more. Hollingsworth and Bobby Lee started to fall back a little further. Bobby Lee desperately pleaded for Hollingsworth to keep up. "Keep up, dammit, keep up! Aaaaggghhh, the pain!"

Hollingsworth's legs were getting tired; he stumbled but managed to stay on his feet. The pain shot again into Bobby Lee's head; he screamed, "This is all your fault! Damn, aaaggghh!"

Complex stopped. Shawn got out of the car and walked over to Hollingsworth and Bobby Lee; he said, "I'm going to set each of your hands free. I will also provide you with a weapon, two knives, to use as you wish."

Shawn took the restraints off each hand. He looked at them and said with a smile, "Keep up. If you decide to escape, you will place your own doom in your hands. Follow the rules—as you say, Hollingsworth—of the game, and you two may get out of this mess. Godspeed." Shawn got back in the car. Complex took off slowly.

It felt much easier for Hollingsworth and Bobby Lee until Complex got a certain distance, and that's when the pain shot through

Hollingsworth's head. The pain became so severe that Bobby Lee started to hit Hollingsworth. Hollingsworth started hitting back. Complex went farther as the pain increased. Bobby Lee started screaming and yelling for the pain to stop. Hollingsworth told him to shut up. Bobby Lee, his face distorting with anger, punched Hollingsworth. Hollingsworth fell to the ground, pulling Bobby Lee with him. The pain intensified. Bobby Lee grabbed his head, pleading and begging for the pain to stop. Complex slowed the pace but was still a distance away, enough for the pain to continue to slowly increase.

Hollingsworth was getting up when Bobby Lee went into his jacket pocket, took out the knife, and stabbed Hollingsworth in the chest. Hollingsworth screamed in horror as he fell back down. Bobby Lee continued to stab him in the chest and stomach. Hollingsworth screamed in horror, pleading and begging Bobby Lee to stop.

Bobby Lee stopped; he realized he had made a serious mistake. He needed Hollingsworth to move, but now Hollingsworth was severely injured. Bobby Lee cried and pleaded as he tried to drag Hollingsworth, but the man was too awkward to drag and too heavy to carry. Bobby Lee fell to his knees, looking up and screaming as the pain became unbearable.

Shawn told Complex to stop. Bobby Lee looked as an ounce of hope surged through him; perhaps there was some hope. Bobby Lee got up and made another attempt to drag Hollingsworth; unfortunately, it was too late—Hollingsworth was dying. Bobby Lee realized the awful truth and started begging and crying and pleading for Shawn to wait. "Wait, please, wait!"

Shawn instructed Complex to wait. Bobby Lee struggled in dragging Hollingsworth, who was moaning in pain; blood was flowing from the knife wounds. Hollingsworth was still alive; he was going into shock. Bobby Lee looked at the car. "Wait . . . wait . . . please wait . . ." Bobby Lee got an idea; it was brutal and raw, but it was the only way for him to live.

# CHAPTER 212

Bobby Lee took the knife and began to saw off Hollingsworth's wrist. Hollingsworth screamed in agony. He went into cardiac arrest and died. Bobby Lee took Hollingsworth's wrist and snapped it off. Bobby Lee was finally free mentally and physically from this monster Hollingsworth. He got up and ran toward the car.

Shawn said to Complex, "Complex."

That was it. Complex took off, playing the song "Bad" by Michael Jackson. Bobby Lee's hopes were dashed as the pain intensified. Shawn took the remote control and instructed Complex to open up the sunroof. Complex did.

The pain in Bobby Lee's head was so bad that he began to slice bits and chucks in the back of his head, trying to pull out the plug that had been planted inside. He shook his head, yelling and screaming and going into convulsions. He started slapping and punching his head as the pain continued to intensify. Bobby Lee was done as he started laughing like a madman; his eyes were starting to bulge out of their sockets as he continued to laugh the laugh of someone that had lost his sense of reality.

Serenity turned away as Complex kept going. The remote control signaled that the control was out of range as a red light started flashing. Shawn told Serenity to look the other way; she did. Jefferson watched as Shawn pressed the Destruction button. "This is for putting your hands on my wife, you sorry bastard." He pressed the button; a few seconds passed before it registered with the bug in Bobby Lee's head.

Meanwhile, Bobby Lee was still hysterically laughing when he heard the sound of *beep, beep, beep,* and then a long beep. Bobby Lee's face had the look of extreme astonishment and shock as he looked at Shawn and said, "Oh sh . . ."

Jefferson said, "Boom shakalaka."

Then they watched Bobby Lee's head explode like a watermelon. His headless body crashed to the ground.

Shawn held Serenity and shielded her face from that horrific scene. He tossed the remote though the open sunroof. Complex said, "Call coming in from asswipe."

Serenity said, "Who?"

Shawn lightly kissed her on her mouth and said, "Long story, tell you later." He said, "Yes, Commissioner?"

Moore sounded content and satisfied; he said, "Uh, Cook, what's up?" Moore did not give Shawn time to respond when he continued, "Listen, Cook, uh . . . I just wanted to thank you and your team . . ."

Shawn slightly smiled and said, "Hmm, my team, eh?"

The commissioner nodded his head and said, "Yes, your team. I know you had help in this. It doesn't matter as long as the end result is what it is." Moore continued, "That dude Johnson . . ."

Jefferson shook his head and said, "People can never get it right. I could make headlines with the wrong name, the story of my life . . . It's Jefferson, you—"

Moore cut him off, which was a good thing. Moore continued, "Yeah, ah . . . Jeff . . . uh . . ."

Jefferson said in a mocking way, "Come on, you can do it. Come on, try it again. Swallow that pride and try again . . ." He broke it down that even a three-year-old would understand.

Moore was feeling annoyed and said, "Yes, Jefferson . . . Well, your team, Johnson . . ." He laughed and said, "Just kidding."

Jefferson shook his head. "Everybody wants to be a comedian."

The commissioner continued, "That Marcus is a smart kid. I may have a job for him."

Shawn thought to himself, *Marcus isn't going to work for anyone but himself.* Then he said, "Wish you the best with that one."

Moore said, "Huh, what?"

Shawn responded, "Uh, nothing. You were saying?"

Moore continued, "Ah, yes, Gordon and Complex . . . I haven't met them yet. But I look forward to meeting them and giving them this Medal of Honor." Moore said, "Look, guys, thank you. You saved my job as well as opened a door for my political career and, of course, hundreds of good

people. Thanks again. Now, Cook, we're closing in on Hollingsworth."
Jefferson laughed. Moore said, "What happened? Did I miss something?"

Jefferson lightly chuckled. "Ah, yeah, kind of."

The commissioner said, "Okay, can someone let me in on the—"

Jefferson cut him off, saying, "Sure. Uh, you have cleanup in aisle . . .
well, uh . . . just check behind the Bay Plaza Mall, Commissioner." He
lightly chuckled.

Curtis Moore's eyes open wide as he raised his voice, saying, "Cook!"

Complex disconnected the call. She pulled along the side with Gordon
following. Complex said, "Hey, Gordon, I heard that you are the man of
the hour."

Gordon responded, "Well, I try to be. But what hour are you referring
to, Complex?"

Complex's colors flashed; she said, "You've got to admire him."

Jefferson said, "We're working on it. Right, Gordon?"

Gordon responded, "Ah, yes, we are, my dawg. I mean yes, sir." They
all laughed.

Shawn said as the police cars zoomed past them, "Complex, tell me
something. When Evans had the gun out on me, you had a chance to take
him out. Why didn't you?"

Serenity nodded her head and agreed with Shawn, "That is so true,
Complex."

Complex's colors were mixed with gray and sky blue, which meant she
had a logical explanation; she said, "Well, a simple case of deduction and
elimination, but mainly discernment."

Serenity slightly smiled. "What does that mean?"

Complex said, "Okay, as you know, I'm able to discern whether one is
telling the truth or a lie. That depends on the individual's emotions. With
Evans, I did a simple quick assessment of deduction and elimination, and
I came up with my conclusion—the man was deceiving Hollingsworth."

Serenity said, "I see. How foolproof is that system?"

Complex said, "That depends on how good the individual is at lying
and deceiving. My system is not foolproof, but it's better than what is out
there now, no matter how sophisticated they may be. I'm the latest and the
best. TJ, my girl, made sure of that."

Serenity nodded her head; she was impressed. Jefferson got out and
ran over to the driver's side; he looked at Complex's animation and said,
"Baby, you are finer than fine." He came closer.

Complex said, "Jefferson, back off. I mean it. What are you doing? My senses are telling me . . ."

Jefferson said, "I just want to kiss you, that's all."

Complex said, "Jefferson, back off. Back up! Last warning, Jay. Back off. Shawn, Serenity, somebody."

They both were laughing. Jefferson was just a few inches from Complex's animated lips. He said, "Man, you are one fine sophisticated cyber whatever you are."

Complex said, "And you're desperate. Okay, I warned you."

Jefferson placed his mouth on Complex's animated mouth when an electric shot through her; it was enough to send Jefferson flying out of the car, crashing to the ground.

Serenity, with concern, said, "Complex."

Complex said to her, "Don't 'Complex' me! He tried to put his rusty chapped lips on me . . . Nasty! I warned him."

She asked Jefferson if he was okay. Jefferson smiled and said, "Nope, I'm not. I just made myself look like a fool because I'm fascinated by an animated computer that has intelligence."

Shawn helped Jefferson up; he asked Jefferson what he was planning on doing. Jefferson lightly chuckled and said, "Getting plenty of rest. I just want to see the world, Gordon and I. And when I come back, I think I'm going to look for my ex-wife."

Complex said, "You no-good two-timing womanizer whore, cyber womanizer whore!"

Jefferson said with a smile, "Well, if it doesn't work out, I'm sure we could—"

Complex said, "I don't think so. Keep it moving to the left." Jefferson smiled.

Shawn said, "I wish you the best. Keep in touch, bro. You have my number, my address. No excuse. Don't have me come looking for you." Jefferson gave Shawn a brotherly hug.

Complex said, "What, you hug everything you touch?"

Jefferson smiled and said, "Complex, I'm going to miss you." He kissed Serenity on the cheek. She thanked him for everything. He hugged her.

Complex said, "See, there we go, the hugger." She smiled and said, "Jay, you know I like playing with you. You are cool. Be safe, kid. Like Shawn said, if we don't hear from you, we're coming after you."

Jefferson smiled. "No doubt." He blew Complex a kiss; her animation made a face. Jefferson said, "I blew you a kiss."

Complex said, "Ah man, I missed it." She smiled.

Jefferson walked over to Gordon; he was ready to get in when Shawn approached him. "You know you don't have to do this, man. You could come and stay with us. Your room is still there."

Jefferson soberly nodded. "I know. You are my family, man, you and Serenity and Ashley."

Serenity said, "You will always be family." Jefferson wiped his left eye.

Complex said, "Somebody is about to cry."

Jefferson said, "Nah, something is in my eye."

Complex said, "The typical male species."

Jefferson said to Shawn and Serenity, "I won't call you tonight . . . I got a feeling a lot of makeup time is going to happen tonight." They looked at him; he said, "Nothing wrong with a little bump and grind." He laughed as he got into Gordon; he looked at them and told them to take care. Then Jefferson took off.

When he got to the corner, Gordon asked, "Where to, sir?"

Jefferson said, "Hmmm, . . . how about New Orleans? The Mardi Gras is about to start in three days."

Gordon said, "No problem, sir. I could break the speed limit and get there in two."

Jefferson smiled. "Hmmm . . . my man. Nah, let's take our time. There is a lot to see and a lot to be grateful for."

# CHAPTER 213

Shawn had pulled over into another part of the mall parking lot; he and Serenity sat there holding hands. He said, "I'll never let you out of my sight again." He softly caressed her face as he slightly smiled and continued, "When we go out, I'm going to be on you, baby. Wherever you go, I'm coming, even in the bathroom."

Serenity threw her head back and laughed; she knew he was exaggerating, but she also knew there was some truth to what he was saying. He continued, "Never again. I'm going to be so attached to you that folks would think—"

She covered his mouth with her fingers; she looked into his eyes. "Shh . . . I know you will, baby. I love you so much, Mr. Shawn Cook. No one could ever take your place. I want you to know that."

Shawn knew she was referring to Evans. He passionately kissed her as the dam of emotions finally opened up, and the tears flooded down from his eyes. Serenity cried as well; as they kissed hard with such passion, he wanted to take her right there. She pulled away slightly; she said, "I knew you were going to rescue me. The nights I thought I wasn't going to ever see you again, that's when I knew that my warrior was still looking for me." She paused and looked into his face and said, "Listen, I must say, Evans was a gentlemen the entire time. He made sure I was okay, and he respected the idea of what you meant to me."

Shawn nodded his head and said, "I know, he and I had a good discussion, and that is why I brought him with me. I trusted him . . . Well, for a minute there, I thought . . ." Shawn paused, put his head down, and shook it; he looked up, "Whew!"

Serenity slightly smiled with a nod and said, "I know what you mean, babe." She wiped her eyes and said, "I want to see my Ashley. I just want to see my baby."

Shawn said, "Okay, we'll see her later. We need to go home and get cleaned up. I can use a nice hot shower."

Serenity kissed him and said, "Do you have room for me?"

He kissed her back and said, "Always, baby."

Serenity and Complex got into their famous girl-to-cyber talk. Shawn thought it was like old times; the two were closer than sisters. Serenity commented on Complex's new makeover. Complex's animation smiled and said, "Well, thank you! My girl Tanya hooked me up. That's my girl, but you are my homegirl."

Serenity looked confused. "What's the difference?"

Complex responded, "What! C'mon, girl, I know you moved up and out. But I know you still have a little hood in you." Serenity and Complex laughed like teenagers. Complex said, "Let me make this quick, okay? When I say she's my girl, I mean we rock every now and then, and she has the hookup. But when I say you are my home girl, we rock 24/7, 365 days, baby."

Serenity laughed. "Okay, gotcha."

Complex said, "Yeah, baby."

Serenity turned and kissed Shawn, who was smiling; she asked, "What are you smiling about?"

Complex said, "I know he's looking like the Burger King dude." Both girls laughed. Complex pulled into the driveway.

Shawn said, "Just like old times, that's all."

Serenity wiped her eyes with the tissue. Complex's compartment slid open; she said, "Here, take a couple of boxes."

Serenity looked at Complex. "Complex, I don't need that much."

Complex's animation made a face and said, "Mhmm, take the boxes, Serenity. Trust me, you're going to need it."

Serenity looked at Complex with an odd expression; as she stepped out of the car, Complex said to her, "Welcome back home, Mrs. C."

Serenity smiled. "Thank you, Complex."

Shawn came out and stood next to her as he placed his hands in hers. She turned to face him and kissed him deeply with such passion. She slowly pushed away and said, "Hon, the place looks wonderful! How did you keep the place up?" Serenity looked around and pointed at the garden. "Wow, a garden, baby! What are you planting?"

Shawn smiled. "Your favorite."

Serenity put her hand to her mouth. "Really?"

He nodded and said jokingly, "Well, that's what I hope would come out." They hugged each other and laughed. Serenity loved it. She loved the idea that Shawn was on her like peanut butter and jelly. She understood why. Right now, it was okay; but eventually, the bird would have to come out of that that nice, comfortable nest and fly on its own. But right now, she needed this. Serenity needed her man all up in her stuff in more ways than one. She smiled at the thought; tears began to fall from her eyes and down her cheeks.

Complex said, "I told you to take those boxes of Kleenex."

Serenity looked at Complex. "Give me a good reason besides using this one."

Complex said, "Not a problem, I'll give you . . ."

Serenity was walking up the stairs to the house when, all of a sudden, the front door burst open. She was startled as she fell back right to Shawn's arms; he said to her, "Welcome home, baby."

Serenity could not believe the floodgates opening up as Ashley and Snuggles came in, followed by Marcus and Sandra, Frank and his family, Michael and Zoe with their twins, and Shawn's parents and siblings. Serenity's family came out too. Serenity and Shawn's pastor came out. Most of the time, it seemed as if they were competing on who had the better prayer; they were adding all of these fancy and theological words that no one knew. Serenity looked up and thanked the Lord. She looked down and swooped Ashley up in her arms, kissing her all over her face. Ashley loved it, and so did Snuggles as she barked, making sure Serenity didn't hurt her master.

They all gathered around Serenity, so happy to see her. Sandra cried happy tears. "I love you, Sen."

Serenity said, "I love you too, girl."

down. Ashley smiled and jumped up and down on her tippy toes. Snuggles joined in the happy moment. Serenity bent down and handed Ashley her headset. Ashley said, "Mommy, who is this? I don't want another Complex. I want—"

Complex said, "Hi, munchkin! You like my new look, my new makeover baby?"

Ashley's eyes opened wide. "Is that you, Complex?"

Complex responded, "Uh-huh, our secret. Ask your mommy and daddy if you can come out later."

Ashley jumped up and down with excitement. "Mommy, Complex got a makeover. I love it!"

Serenity bent down, kissed Ashley, and said in her ear, "You can play with Complex later. Our secret, okay?"

Ashley bounced with excitement. "Okay, Mommy!"

The music, the food, the celebration, the dancing, the DJ. Serenity felt the love; she now understood what Complex was saying about taking a few boxes of Kleenex.

The party continued in the backyard, Sandra made her way out to Complex. She was watching Shawn the entire time. When he put the headset on the seat of the car and went back to the party, Sandra knew this was her moment to get with Complex. She went straight for what she wanted; she picked them up and put on the headset. She nervously smiled and said, "Ms. Complex, I hope I'm not disturbing you. It's me—"

Complex cut her off. "Yes, Sandra. How are you?"

Sandra smiled. "Much better now. I thought you left me."

Complex said, "Never, baby, never ever. I'm stuck to you, sweetie."

Sandra smiled and blew out an air of relief. She continued, "Complex, I have so much to tell you—my marriage, that sex thing we talked about, I'm good at it, Complex."

Complex said, "You're such a ho."

Sandra said, "Huh?"

Complex responded, "Calm down. It is a good thing to be a ho in your town."

Sandra thought, looking a little perplexed, and said, "Oh, okay, I guess I'm the slut and ho in my town."

Complex said, "Now tell me all about it. Remember, no G or PG stuff. I want to hear the raw stuff."

Sandra laughed. "Okay, well, it started like this . . ."

# CHAPTER 214

Everyone had left. Shawn convinced his parents to take Ashley and Snuggles; that didn't take much convincing, Ashley bribed her parents, saying she'd go with her grandparents if he and Serenity promised to take her out for breakfast for the next two weeks. Shawn lightly chuckled and gave in.

The house was quiet as Shawn entered into the bedroom. Serenity looked at him; he looked at her. He walked over to her and said, "Track 15, romance." The music started playing; someone was playing the saxophone. They kissed each other with passion. Their tongues went into each other's mouths aggressively. Serenity started moaning. Shawn's breathing increased as he grabbed her by her shoulders; he groaned from the sexual pleasure he was feeling. They began to frantically undress each other. Shawn helped Serenity, who was sore because of the fight she had with Bobby Lee. She helped Shawn take off his underwear. She was all the way down to his feet; she stayed there, admiring his black beauty.

It felt as if it was a long time, and indeed it was; he missed her soft body, her sexual tone of voice, just the desire of wanting to please him. She continued to play with his joystick; she put it in her mouth. Shawn's head fell back to enjoy the moment. He couldn't take it; he wanted to explode, but not like this. He pulled her up.

Serenity stood there, looking at him; she had her pointer finger in the corner of her mouth. She said, "Baby, I've been a bad girl. I need to be spanked, baby."

The music continued to play as Serenity danced seductively; as she moved her erotic, voluptuous, sexy body, she looked down at his hard hammer. She smiled; she knew he was ready. Her juices slowly slipped down her legs; the aroma of her kitty cat filled the room. Shawn started to drip from his manhood. She cupped her fist and put it around his thick pole; she went up and down slowly. He made sounds of pleasure as he called her name. Serenity increased the pace as she continued to jerk him off. Looking in his face, she said in her sensual, raspy voice, which was an automatic turn-on for him, "Shawn, I need you, baby. I want you. I want you to take me any way you want, but I need for that to happen now, baby. Take me. Slam me hard, baby. I want to feel you come through me. Make it hurt so bad but feel so good."

Serenity lay down with her legs wide open; her pink panther was purring for him, begging for him to bring his black warrior. Shawn tweaked her nipples; she gasped with surprise as delight came over her face. She said in a low throaty tone, "I missed that. I missed you."

Shawn told her he loved her; he was so sincere and honest as always. He knew every tweaking spot, every G-spot, and every love zone on her body. She knew him as well, very well. His pole was thick and hard; her love cave was drenching wet.

They both wanted it all; how many days had passed—they both wanted to make up for lost time. They both had a lot of making up to do.

The room was filled with the smell of sex, aromas clashing into each other, making a fine blend of sex. The sounds of moaning and groaning and gasping and shrieking filled the room; this was the tongues of sexual language. No interpreter was needed. It was obvious. Shawn was so hard and big; she was wet, so wet. She knew with confidence she could handle him. Out of nowhere, he inserted two large fingers into her love zone; she wasn't expecting that. Serenity cried out from an unexpected pleasure. And the pain, it registered all over her face as she clawed her nails into his back; he flinched and moaned as he pulled her hair, causing her head to jerk back while he continued to assault her kitty cat. Shawn went in and out of her cockpit with his fingers with such precision; he was so good at what he did. He took her deeper with his fingers. Serenity's eyes shot wide open as she cursed, staring at him, trying to figure out what the hell this man was trying to do to her.

She grabbed for the sheet as she tried to take as much as she could before the explosion; she clenched her teeth together, fighting the powerful orgasm that was about to take place. Serenity lay there, shaking her head wildly, calling out his name, "Shawn . . . Shawn . . . I'm coming, baby! Take me . . . make me . . . break me, baby! I'm yours forever, baby. I'm . . . comiiiiing." Wave after wave after wave, she cried out, "Oh no, oh no! No no no no no . . ." Ecstasy and desire took over her; he continued to move his fingers in and out as he stuck his thumb up her ass. She cried out as her breathing came fast and quick. Words were coming out too quick, too fast to understand what Serenity was saying; she was talking gibberish.

Shawn finally got what he wanted—a flood of her juices coming down on his fingers. He took his fingers out of her kitty cat and put them in her mouth for her to taste; he moved his hand up, down, one side, and then the other side. He joined her as he put his tongue in her mouth, also tasting the juices of her fruit. He wanted to make sure she had enough as he pulled up and went down as he sucked on her clit. Serenity started off moaning and groaning. Shawn continued; the moaning and groaning turned into screams of delight and pleasure. She begged him to stop; she couldn't take it anymore.

He pulled away and looked at her. Serenity was flushed with tears in her eyes. She pushed him down on his back; she wanted to ride him. She wanted that bronco inside of her; she wanted to ride him hard. She slowly eased her kitty cat down his pole; she smiled. He let out an exasperated breath; he knew he was in for a rough ride.

Serenity started out going up and down, going deep and deeper; she threw her head back and enjoyed the ride. As she rode him, he began to squeeze her nipples with his thumb and pointer finger. Her nipples became hard and erect, standing at attention. Shawn was beginning to feel overwhelmed as she continued to ride that horse; the movement went from a nice sensual motion to a Tina Turner experience as she started bouncing up and down on his hard manhood. Serenity wasn't done as she slammed his cock hard each time she came down on it. She leaned forward as she raised the bar that was her ass; her kitty cat was fully wide and open as she rode him hard and fast, giving a new name to the meaning of roughrider.

The sounds of sex filled the room. Shawn was about to shoot his love seed in her; he quickly flipped her off him on her knees. He held her tight by her thin waistline; she knew exactly what he wanted. He wanted to come in from the back door. They both were breathing hard as sweat poured down their faces like buckets of water as if they just finished running a race. Serenity spread her legs wide; she laid her head to the side, which caused her ass to lift up; she looked back at him, smiled, and winked as if to say "It's all yours."

Serenity looked down at his pole that could make magic; it was still hard. She said, "Mmm, bring that big boy to me." His manhood was nice and shining from her juices. Shawn stood over her and smacked her ass. She yelped and deliciously moaned; he slapped it again. She flinched a bit and let out a naughty laugh. She threw her head back and said in her throaty voice, "I like that." Serenity looked at him and blew him a kiss; she said, "I'm a bad girl, Poppy."

Shawn smiled as he put his thick manhood in her kitty cat; she gasped as she grabbed the sheets. He started going in and out hard and fast and deep and deeper; he filled her up as Serenity screamed the language of the sexual moment. He moaned and groaned as he gritted his teeth, trying not to come.

They were both drunk—intoxicated from the sex—as he continued to slam hard, and she continued to meet him with each thrust. Serenity looked back at him as she watched him perform his wonder, slamming her. She cried and screamed with each thrust; he moaned, groaned, and yelled out with each sensation, trying to overtake him. She looked at Shawn as he pounded away; he knew what she was going to do. He shook his head. She smiled and blew him a kiss; she made that laugh as the walls of her kitty cat grabbed his manhood and put it in a love hold as she squeezed his hard pole until it gave up what she wanted—his juices, his cum.

Serenity quickly turned on her knees, still facing him, as she took his dripping hard pole and put it in her mouth; she sucked on it, pulling his juices out of him. The maneuver drove Shawn up the wall as he tried to hold on to anything—the bedsheets, her hair—as the juices came out of him with such force. Her suction was amazing, so strong, pulling his juices out of him. He moaned and gritted his teeth as he clenched his mouth, growling and moaning from the impact her sucking had on him. As he ejaculated inside her mouth, Serenity jerked him hard with her hand; the sensation of her sucking on him and squeezing him and the come coming out with such force made him surrender.

Shawn fell on her back, exhausted as he rolled onto the bed. They both were trying to catch their breath; he said, "Wow . . . wow . . . oh my . . . wow. You are a bad girl, baby."

Serenity lightly laughed. "Just for you, baby. Just for you."

They lay there in a tangled web of each other, holding each other; they held each other in such a tight embrace. From a distance, they looked like just one person lying there. Shawn kissed Serenity on her cheek and said, "Baby, that was amazing."

She nodded her head. "A little more, I think I would have crumbled and shattered. Oh my goodness."

He said, "I would never ever let anything happen to you, ever again. My love for you, Serenity, is strong, enduring—and, baby, it's inseparable. I love you so much."

# Epilogue

Serenity was running; she looked behind her as panic set in. He was still coming toward her. She was running out of space. She could hear his footsteps approaching her; her heart was racing. She couldn't run any faster; she was starting to get tired. She knew she could not keep this pace up much longer. She looked behind her; she slipped and fell. She scraped her knees pretty bad. She knew it was over. She looked around to pick up something to fight with; she wasn't going to go down without a fight. The person was still coming.

She screamed for Shawn; she called him. She begged him to come—nothing. Serenity closed her eyes as she heard the click and the clack of the person's shoes; she prayed. She hoped it would be quick and painless. She called Shawn's name again as the tears came down her cheeks. A hand came out of the shadows. Serenity was skeptical whether she should trust the hand when she couldn't see the face. She reached out as the hand grabbed hers and said, "I got you and will never let you go."

Serenity was getting ready to scream when Shawn stepped out of the shadows, pulling her up and toward him. She looked at him and smiled; he said, "We're inseparable, baby."

She smiled and said, "I know we are." She kissed him with such passion.

THE END

COMING IN FEBRUARY 2019, *THE CAT AND THE MOUSE*

Bobby was ready to make the biggest heist ever; it would propel him to become the greatest mouse ever. He would become a hero; he would go down in history next to the other great mice.

His daydream was interrupted when Tommy heard something. Bobby was already singing his victory song. Tommy heard it again. Bobby was still humming his song. Tommy told him to stop. "Wait, stop. Hold up, Bobby." Tommy continued, "Shush, hold it. Hold it, wait a second . . . I thought I . . . heard." He listened carefully.

Bobby smiled. "Wait, wait . . . Yeah, I heard it too. What's that song our neighbors plays? 'We Will Rock You'?"

Tommy shook his head. "Stop, Bobby, I'm serious. I heard something that sounded like . . ." He stopped. He had an inquisitive look on his face that went from curiosity to panic.

, Bobby was smiling and concentrating on the prize that he was about to take when Tommy yelled in panic, "Oh no, it's Jesse!"